IN THE SHADOW OF SHACKLETON GRAY

A Kephart Stone Mystery

W. PAUL DUNN

Printed in the United States of America

First Edition

This book is a work of fiction. Names, characters, places, events, technologies, and organizations are either products of the author's imagination or are used fictitiously. Any resemblance to actual events, locales, or persons, living or dead, is entirely coincidental.

Manuscript Proofread by Jackie Jones (JJProofing.com)
Cover Design by 21st Publishing (21stPublishing.com)
Cover image: © Walter Kopplinger (Shutterstock)

Published By

21stPublishing.com

ISBN: 0615967000
ISBN-13: 978-0615967004 (21st Publishing)

DEDICATION

This book is dedicated to God, who inspired me; and to my loving parents who sent me to find that God lives, and to discover that his mysteries are endless.

ACKNOWLEDGMENTS

My deepest thanks to Jackie Jones (JJProofing.com), who gave me indispensable guidance for writing this novel; and to 21st Publishing (21stPublishing.com), who unfailingly brought closure to its publication.

CHAPTER 1

EVENING Star Lane was bright with May sunshine when I first knocked on Shackleton's street-level door—a door seldom used. My first rap of the brass knocker brought no response, so I waited and listened to a piano being played not far inside the white stone house. The music was so captivating on that fresh morning that I didn't want to break its spell. But the pizza was getting cold. I stepped up, knocked again, and thought I heard a voice say, "Come in," but I couldn't be sure. The music continued. Not wanting to interrupt, I stepped back down the two brick steps and checked the house number: 732. It was then I noticed, half-hidden in ivy between the entry and a window shutter, an artistically carved wooden sign, which read "Harvard S. Gray, Piano Studio."

Well, the piano piece might be a long one, I thought. And the pizza was getting cold. Stepping up and knocking a third time, I distinctly heard a polite voice call, "Please. Come in."

The music had stopped. I opened the door, unaware that I was sailing my ship of life into uncharted waters.

I found him seated at a grand piano.

Some years have since passed. Yet to this day I'm still inclined to add "sir" when addressing Shackleton in the most casual of conversations, if you could call any conversation with him casual. But at this first encounter I was abruptly corrected when I said, "I have your pizza, sir. A small pepperoni with—"

"It is well to be respectful toward any man," he interrupted with a warm smile, "but as for me, I wish no formality of any sort. You may call me Shackleton. Please. And *your* name?"

"Kephart, sir—I mean . . ."

His smile broadened and his brown eyes shown.

"Would that be your last or first? It could be either, you know."

"It's my first. My name is Kephart Stone. People who know me just call me Kep, which I—"

"I shall call you Kephart," he interrupted again. "And a grand name it is. Never undervalue either your assigned esteem or earned favorable regard, Kephart."

Here I was, delivering a nearly cold pizza. Usually I would be dropping off a hodgepodge of cargoes—anything from pharmaceutical supplies to airplane propellers. Never before in my three-week career had I delivered a pizza. Certainly my job gave me no reason to feel of special worth. But just now, in Shackleton's presence, I felt strangely valued. And I didn't find his lofty manner of speaking condescending or offensive. He was just . . . different.

I found my voice. "The studio sign gives the name Harvard Gray, so I'm a bit confused." (I had no doubt that he belonged to the house or vice versa.)

"Ah! But there is the middle initial 'S'—for Shackleton. Harvard Shackleton Gray. I have asked that you use my middle name. Few people are so granted the privilege. Please. Use it."

"Well, all right . . . but I don't see . . ."

"Perhaps there is more to see than meets the eye," he said, and his own eyes seemed to look just past my face. I turned my head to see what might have drawn his attention but saw only a massive bookcase behind a recliner and floor lamp.

"You will want some money," he said.

Shackleton had so distracted and fascinated me that I had nearly forgotten the purpose of my visit. He still sat, half-turned, on the piano bench.

"Please. In the next room there." He waved his hand over the piano toward a door in a paneled wall at the back. "You will find a leather cash box on a workbench. Just fetch what you want."

He then moved agilely to a luxurious leather recliner near the west window.

I hesitated, surprised that he would ask me to take money from safekeeping while he sat comfortably out of my sight. Did he trust all delivery men to grab from his cash box? What if the previous one had stolen from it? How often did he check it? While fumbling in my mind for a tactful way to decline, I heard a faint scratching at the door. It sounded unmistakably like a dog.

"That would be Bogart." Shackleton's elbows were on the recliner armrests as his fingers rubbed his now-closed eyes. I went to the back of the studio and turned the door handle.

A young black-and-white Border collie nosed happily through the door, brushed past my legs, and aimed straight for Shackleton's feet. As it rested its head on his knee, Shackleton gently rubbed the dog's left ear, which drooped as though it had been injured at one time. The other ear stood perkily at attention as Bogart enjoyed his floppy-ear massage. Devoted love was obvious on the parts of both dog and master.

Crossing what was apparently a little-used workshop, I found a tooled-leather box on a bench. The leather was tightly stitched, and a separation between the box and its lid wasn't evident. So I held the box up into the light of a multi-paned window for a closer look.

"Just turn it over and then right it again." Shackleton's voice came from the recliner in the studio. I was astonished. Could he see through walls?

I did as he said and the lid popped open. A hidden spring action brought it up, disclosing impressive stacks of bound twenty-, fifty-, and hundred-dollar bills. A few ones and fives were folded at the side. For my young years it was more cash than I had ever seen in one place. More than I could earn in several months—or maybe a year. I took out three ones and a five and then pressed the lid down. It closed with a metallic click.

As I approached Shackleton, I saw that Bogart's pink tongue dangled over his lower lip in peaceful acceptance of me. I extended my hand with the bills.

"A small pepperoni is six ninety-five, plus tax makes it seven fifty," I said, and reached into my pocket for change. I found two quarters and held them out. Shackleton made no move to accept them.

"Put the money back, Kephart," he said softly.

I searched his face. It was youthful despite a short graying beard at his chin. His countenance bore some traces of tragedy, but I also read what I then perceived to be benevolence mingled with victory over pain. His eyes, half-closed, were upon Bogart's head. Light brown hair curved over his ears. Some gray was evident, particularly at the temples.

A firm mouth beneath a straight nose suggested capability to command, as one acquainted with the rigors of discipline—both of self and of others. No hint of weakness or folly there. His countenance smacked of strength and purpose, and that impressed me most at the time.

Still, there is an enigma or mystery about Shackleton. The longer I know him, the less I know him, strange as that might seem. The few secrets he has shared with me these short years have only prompted more unanswered questions and heightened his mystique.

"I really don't want your tip," I replied. "My time is paid for and it's been my pleasure just to have met you." (I meant it well enough.)

"No. That's not what I mean, Kephart. Put all the *bills* you have taken back into the box."

I was stunned.

"You see," he said—and there was a peculiar edge to his voice—"I am blind. Not that you could notice, perhaps, during your short stay. But I am not blind as to character and intent or disposition. You do yourself an injustice."

I stood speechless. Did he really think I had stolen money from his leather box? Was this an accusation?

"Please. Bring the box and place it opened in my lap."

Woodenly I returned to his work room and brought the box to his chair before opening it. I handed him the eight dollars in bills, pressing them one by one into his palm, not daring to count or to speak lest he detect my anger.

He folded them and placed them in the space alongside the stacks of larger bills, never once looking down at the box in his lap. He truly was blind, I thought—and in more ways than one if he couldn't detect my honesty in speech and action. And what about my *intent*? What could he possibly know about that? Did he have the power to read my mind? After hearing his little speech about valuing my esteem, I felt he'd just now measured me—and judged me as a "reject."

These thoughts and feelings flickered and raced through me like uncontrollable flames. I stood numbly, trying to find words, when I saw his hand pull a fifty-dollar bill from its stack. He was holding it out to me, his face radiant with a smile that would melt an iceberg.

"You do yourself an injustice, Kephart," he repeated. "Never underestimate the value of integrity, especially your own."

I remained speechless—ashamed that *I* was the one who had misinterpreted character and intent. Having misjudged him so quickly, I was struck with a sharp awareness of my own weakness.

My silence was quickly becoming awkward. But before I could open my mouth another realization struck me. I found myself both relieved and thankful that my reactions hadn't been exposed as they might have been if Shackleton had been able to see my face. But, again, I was wrong.

"Be kind to yourself, Kephart Stone." Shackleton's voice was firm, yet gentle. The smile lingered but a trace of pain flickered across his brow. "None of us is without weakness. And what man or woman would not hide it if possible? The worst we can do is to attempt to hide it from ourselves. That, also, is how we do ourselves injustice."

"But I . . . I can't take that much money!" I protested. "It would be a reward for what? There's no way I deserve it. I only see that taking it would do a lot to *cheapen* my so-called integrity." I laughed, mostly out of heart's ease, but my words were sincere.

"Oh, I'm certain you will deserve all this and more from me before this week is out," he said cryptically. And while I was puzzling over this remark, he reached out, found my hand, and pressed the fifty-dollar bill into it.

Before I could further protest or phrase a simple question, Shackleton stood, placed a hand on my shoulder, and directed me to the entry door. I turned and saw, past the closing door, that Bogart had eaten the entire pizza. And the box lid was laid back neatly on the floor. Now, Border collies are smart, but they're not *that* painstaking.

* * *

Once again on the brick steps, I took in the glorious sunshine, inhaled deeply, and tried to make sense of this bizarre encounter. Shackleton was inscrutable. It annoyed me. How could I possibly be worth fifty dollars to him? I really didn't see much chance of seeing him again—ever.

I looked at my watch: 11:40. Coming up was a timed pharmaceutical delivery north of Bellingham. Maybe a quick sandwich was possible. The aroma of that pizza had gotten my stomach rumbling.

Turning left, I pressed back up the steep cobblestone lane to Charleston Street, where I had parked the VW delivery van. It wasn't there. The first question to come into my head was, have I lost the VW or have I lost my mind?

I had suffered a severe concussion five weeks back and was still missing pieces of scalp and memory. Writing returning memories in a journal and logging daily events had become a new practice for me. Although time consuming, it was good therapy. My mental stability and confidence were quickly being reclaimed. But misplacing the VW bus had me spinning.

Two young boys came up on skateboards, cutting close by me.

I held out my arms and yelled, "Did you guys see a yellow VW bus parked here in the past half hour?"

One of them looked back at me as he whizzed past. The other ignored me.

"We don't live here, man," the first one shouted.

Then I found relief in wondering why they weren't in school. It was Friday, I remembered, and *that* meant something. At least part of my brain was still functioning.

"Check with Big Tow," a woman's voice said. The street was no longer filled with the clatter of skateboards. I found that the voice belonged to a woman in hair curlers standing on her front porch with a Pomeranian tucked under one arm. Her other hand gripped a vacuum cleaner hose.

"I'm sorry. I don't think I heard you right," I said, crossing over to her side of the street. "Big toe?"

"Big Tow. T-O-W," she spelled. "It's the name of the wrecker company that towed an old, yellow bus away, if that's what you're looking for." She was friendly enough.

"Well, yes. I am."

"Happens all the time here," she said. "People don't see the 'No Parking' signs, or else they ignore them. The street's narrow and folks have to park in driveways or walk a block or two if there's many visiting at a time. Anyway, I'm not the one who called the tow truck. You can come use my phone if you like."

She nodded her head toward the open door and shuffled inside. The dog started yapping as soon as I stepped onto her porch and didn't stop until I left.

* * *

The shortest way to the Big Tow lot, I learned, was to retrace my steps back down Evening Star Lane to its end, then descend a wooden stairway that zigzagged down a steep slope to Old Fairhaven—a harbor town stretching along the shoreline of Bellingham Bay.

The narrow lane itself sloped downward in a deep fold between wooded hillsides that rose abruptly from the picturesque, but impractical, cobblestones. This alley-like street gave access to a few well-made homes interspersed among the trees, each unlike any other and each with its own unique landscaping. A feature common to all, however, was an old-fashioned gas-lit street lamp.

Shackleton's home was situated on the right at the end of `the lane. It differed strikingly from the others, in that it stood within a few yards of the curb and had no driveway or garage. These, I later discovered, were located at the upper end of the house and were approached from the back by a winding drive that led through a forest covering several acres.

This part of his home fronting Evening Star Lane had its character and appeal. Much had escaped my notice before, due to the distractions of my errand.

The lower story was made of skillfully constructed white stones. It had deep-set paned windows and a recessed front entry. Overhanging this was a private balcony with cedar railings. A second story with French doors extended behind this balcony. Topping this was a third story and, above this, there were attic-rooms with dormers and tall gables. The upper structure was covered with weathered shake siding, and the windows all around had decorative dark-green shutters and trim.

A profusion of colors spread out on each side of the short walkway between the curb and the house. Mixed patches of bright flowers stood in well-appointed beds behind meandering rock boundaries.

Nearest the house, but not obstructing windows, grew a variety of azaleas and rhododendrons together with ornamental shrubs and lilacs. The fragrance of the lilacs triggered memories. I wanted to jot these memories in my journal along with brief notes about this first encounter with Shackleton, so I moved on down to what I now call the "Overlook."

Here I found a surprisingly comfortable bench made of wood and stone. It was positioned just to the side of the point-of-descent above the steep wooden stairway at the end of the lane. I sometimes visited this bench during the ensuing months to write brief personal notes or to muse over Shackleton's perplexing disclosures and try to unravel the puzzle of this man.

Treetops and rooftops fell beneath my gaze down the slope. Farther out, Old Fairhaven's commercial buildings, distinctive shops, cafés, and maritime structures clustered along the bay. A railway skirted the water's edge, linking west coast cities to British Columbia, not far to the north. The Alaska Marine Highway Terminal occupied a point along the shoreline very near the railway station, and there, harbored as it was every Tuesday and Friday, the impressive Alaska ferry was being loaded for its voyage through the Inland Passage.

Looking across the expanse of water, I could clearly see Lummi and Portage Islands as well as high points of the San Juan Islands. I savored all this briefly, regretting the scant time I could afford this scene on such a magnificent day.

I regretted, too, that there would be no sandwich. There still remained, after leaving the steep stairs, a fifteen-minute hike to the far edge of town. Fortunately I had been given good directions. I was happy soon enough to find the bright yellow VW parked just inside the business entry behind a chain-link fence.

I was *not* happy, however, to hear that it would cost sixty dollars to reclaim the "set of wheels," as its owner, Bickford, called it.

"How much?" I exclaimed upon hearing this. (I had never had any previous tow truck experience.)

"Sixty bucks, plus tax." The big man's coveralls bore the name Bart. "That's my minimum."

"You're Bart?" I asked, stalling to swallow and recover from the jolt.

"Yeah."

"Well . . . uh . . . Bart, I'm not the owner and I don't have the sixty, or a credit card for that matter. I'm an employee—a deliveryman. The company I work for is located in Burlington, which is a ways away. And even if I hurry, I'll be late for a timed delivery. So I'm stuck if you can't make an exception under the circumstances. Could you reconsider just this once?"

Bart stood stone still as he eyed me impassively. He repeatedly poked his lower lip out, then sucked it back in. Next his eyes squinted sideways at the VW. Then they slowly came back to me. They went to the bus again, then crept back to me. Just his eyes and lips moved. I waited, following his eyes back and forth.

A long wait.

"What kind of a name is that?" he asked at last.

I followed his eyes back to the intensely yellow bus. Neatly painted in black letters against a splash of orange background on the side of the VW were the words, "Hardly Able Cartage Company." This was an embarrassing misnomer reflecting only the bizarre humor of my zany but benevolent employer.

"Oh. Well, that's a kind of joke. It's not the company's real name. The bus was lent for my use as a new hire. I'm sort of on trial, you might say."

"Yeah. I'd say."

Silence. Bart clamped his eyes shut and wrinkled up his face as if grimacing in pain.

I waited . . . and waited.

"Fifty bucks, including tax. You got fifty?"

"No . . . I . . . well, yes. I do happen to have a fifty-dollar bill. But I haven't earned it yet."

"How long will it take you to earn it—without the bus? How long will it take you to walk to Burlington and come back with the money?"

Bart was not stupid.

"On the other hand, how much do you think your boss would take for the old camper bus?" he added.

"Well, it's got a sink and fresh water supply. It has chrome hubcaps. The engine purrs. It's had a recent brake job and the clutch cable was just replaced. The body's sound, no rust . . ." I wasn't so dumb either.

I could see he wasn't going to budge so I fished out the fifty.

CHAPTER 2

ON a farmstead south of Old Fairhaven and west of Burlington, there is a high hill overlooking Samish Bay. The Whipple family calls it Singing Tree Hill, named after a solitary and unique tree that grows there in a secluded clearing near its top. The tree is both ancient and rare. No one knows much about it or how it came to be there. It's not indigenous to the region. Relatively few people have seen it because the hill is on private land accessible only by foot-trail at the end of Whipple Farm Lane.

The tree sings. It sings not only with its leaves, but with its trunk and with its bare branches. True, the singing is mainly sensed by touch; yet, when all else is perfectly still, it can in fact be heard. And there is a haunting, magical quality about it that emanates throughout the glade. One can't visit the place without being touched by its serenity and peace.

When seeking a haven out of the world's reach, I had been influenced most profoundly there by a pervasive sense of reverence. Indeed, Oat and Selma Whipple's youngest son, Jesse, is buried nearby in a private plot not fifty feet from the tree. He was just a ten-year-old lad when he died, and his father and his older brother, Joel, dug his grave there at his passing. The gravesite, enclosed by a white picket fence, is never without flowers, whether wild, planted, or freshly cut. But the grave, itself, didn't bring a prevailing reverential spirit to Singing Tree Hill. It was the other way around.

I had been drawn to the Singing Tree many times during my convalescent stay with the Whipples. Today I felt compelled again to visit, but not until I had put away some sustaining "filler" from Selma's stove. For me, a day was not a day without supper at the Whipples. Still, I was totally unprepared for the day's events that would follow.

The sun was still shining just above the hill when I arrived home and parked the yellow bus in its customary place under two huge chestnut trees near the back porch. Seeing the farm pickup truck in its shed and finding no car or tractor in the drive, I presumed that Joel was working in the fields and that Oat and Selma were away on errands. Their dog, Smooch, was whining—I should say groaning—inside the porch.

Too fat and old to bother with his past ritual of pushing open the screen door and hobbling down the steps in greeting, Smooch kept mostly to his cushioned bed with the expectation that home-comers pass by him and extend a hand for a slobbery lick. As always, I did so and felt myself duly welcomed. But I hadn't yet acquired a "taste" for his face-washing kisses. Only Joel, and sometimes Oat, allowed that massive tongue to rid his face of a day's worth of sweat and grime.

Selma's note was taped to the kitchen-door window:

Kep dear,

Meatloaf is in foil in the fridge. Eat all you like. Veg fixings are beside it. You'll love the baked squash. Put things on a cookie sheet and stick them in the oven on 250 while you wash up. We be late coming back.

Love, Mom

The Whipples were my new family—three fine people I'd known little more than five weeks. Joel had found me unconscious in a crumpled heap by the roadside near the field he was plowing. I had come coasting downhill too fast on a ten-speed when a branch or stick of wood caught in the front-wheel spokes and flipped me over head first (no helmet.) Joel was sitting high on the tractor, making a turn at the ditch, when he saw the accident. My rescue and recovery had come quickly, but my returning memory had still a ways to go to catch up.

My Colorado driver license puzzled us all. I had no idea how or why I'd come to Washington State. My bicycle was new. It had certainly not covered the required distance. I had no extra clothing, no backpack, and no checkbook. They had found forty-one dollars in my wallet and some keys in my pocket, which I couldn't account for.

Nothing in my wallet gave a clue about my past. Telephoned inquiries to my former Colorado address led to a simple report of "moved out." So I was, at age twenty (according to the driver license), immediately adopted and nurtured by a wonderful family despite my disposition to be independent and my temporary incapacity to provide a full account of my past. Even my present delivery job had come by way of a family acquaintance. I was unconditionally loved and accepted by the exceptional Whipples, and Selma's cooking was "Mom's cooking." My stomach had readily accepted her delicious cuisine, and my heart had welcomed her caring.

I hurriedly followed her instructions, ran to the bathroom, and then bound up the stairs to my room to change clothes. There I found another note—this one from Joel. Pulling it from the door, I read:

Hey Kep.

Some woman called for you. Said you don't know her. Important. Call between 6 and 9 tonight for sure. Says you both know a blind man. 211-8009.

Be cool, Joel

I checked the time: 5:40. (My stomach claimed that it was much later.) I decided to enjoy my meal. And the Singing Tree was waiting.

Arranging everything on the dinette table, I sat and ate alone with my thoughts. Did I really want to get involved with Shackleton? I had become obligated to him, like it or not, but not of my own choosing. He was an enigma. Still, I couldn't help liking him; or was it the aura of mystery about him that fascinated me? He was so different from any other man I had met, within memory. I had felt paradoxically both trusting and doubtful while with him. Certainly I felt no physical threat, but for some reason my *mind* felt uncomfortably "exposed" while in his presence.

The apple cobbler dessert derailed my train of thought, which was leading nowhere anyway.

6:15. Not liking to have unsettling things hang over me, I went to the phone and punched the numbers Joel had written.

"Hello." The voice was both feminine and pleasant.

"I'm returning your call," I said. "My name is Kephart Stone."

"Oh, yes! Thank you so much for calling. Can you give the name of our mutual blind friend? Just for positive identification, of course." She was reserved, but gracious.

I decided the request was for her own protection.

"Would that be Harvard Gray?" I answered.

"That isn't exactly what I wanted to hear. Is there another name perhaps? A middle name?" Her voice was soft, almost apologetic.

"Oh. You mean Shackleton. But that's not his common name, I was told. Anyway, I'll say Shackleton."

"Thank you, Kephart. This may seem a very unusual request, I'm sure, but he asked that we arrange a meeting tonight at my place at Old Fairhaven. Is ten o'clock possible for you? Would a later hour be more convenient?

I couldn't recall any late-night meetings ever being on my

agenda. My former night life had been so limited that the prospect sounded clandestine. But then I remembered that day or night made no difference to Shackleton. The dark was all he knew. Still, the thought of a "tired" Saturday made me ask, "How about nine? I get up early.

There was a delayed response. "I suppose that will do, but you may still be late in returning." And before I could question why, she added, "You will want to write down the address. By the way, my name is Laura Rutledge. The name is on a door to the side of the storefront bearing this address. Just open the door and come up the stairs. My apartment is at the top."

I found an envelope to write on. "Okay. I'm ready to write," I said.

"204 Harris Street. The store is an import shop. I live above it."

"Got it. I know the street. I just—"

"Oh. Kephart? Please come prepared for stormy weather. You may want to bring appropriate outdoor wear. See you at nine."

She hung up. I stood with the phone to my ear, not fully grasping her abruptness. I had questions. There seemed to be no point in calling her back. It would be awkward. So I set the phone down and turned to clear away my supper dishes.

Then the thoughts struck me: How did she know my phone number? It wasn't my personal number. It belonged to the Whipples. How could Shackleton have gotten it for her? I hadn't left so much as a trace of a clue about the identity of my employer. No proof-of-delivery or receipt. No name-bearing company uniform. And the VW wasn't parked where it could be seen, even if he *could* have seen it. Besides, the name Hardly Able Cartage Company was a joke. My employer ran a profitable first-class business. He did have an unusual sense of humor, but that came with his intelligence and served to ease the stresses of his livelihood. The bus was a relic of his start-up days.

I looked out the kitchen window. The sun's rays were slanting at just the right angle. This and early morning were my favorite times of day. The Singing Tree beckoned more appealingly than ever.

As I walked down Whipple Farm Lane, my unanswered questions plagued me. Then other questions arose to loom above all the rest.

Why was it that I had never before delivered a pizza during the three weeks I had been working? Didn't pizza companies deliver their own stuff? This delivery to Shackleton had been a strange departure from what had been typical. A quick phone call just might unburden my mind.

I turned and ran back to the house. Soon enough Bickford's wife's voice was in my ear. "Unbeatable Delivery Service, this is Dozie." (Bickford's business was home-based.)

"Hi, Dozie, this is Kep. No problems, just a question. Maybe you can tell me how it is that I was given an order to pick up and deliver a pizza today. Do we sometimes deliver pizzas?"

"We've never made pizza deliveries, Kep. Who asked you to pick up a pizza?"

My face flushed and I swallowed. I couldn't get a sound from my voice.

"Kep?" I could hear the TV going and young kids playing. "Kep. Are you all right?"

"Yes," I managed to croak. "But, Dozie . . . a number came up on the company pager today. It belonged to Top 'Em All Pizza. It was a valid pick-up going to Old Fairhaven. I delivered it. Collected cash, including tax, for—" I stopped short, remembering the fifty-dollar towing bill.

"Kep? Let me ask Bick. Maybe he knows something about it."

"No. Wait. Oh, well . . ." She had set the phone down and was calling for Bick. The TV was loud in my ear. ". . . the news and sports. Now the weather. Continuing sunny and cool . . ."

Dozie's voice came back on. "He didn't take any pizza order, Kep. Doesn't want to. He says it's not worth it. Sounds strange to me. Maybe someone gave the wrong pager number. That's freaky."

"Yes, but the pizza was waiting and it went to the right place. It was a phoned-in order. The address was written on a register slip. No name. Just the address. I wonder . . . uh . . . never mind, Dozie. I'll get the money to the pizza place tomorrow. Thanks. It's okay. Say 'hi' to Bickford."

We both hung up. I turned again to seek my rendezvous with a tree. Today it seemed a thing closer to sanity than dealing with puzzling people and wacky events. Walking the lane once again—this time more briskly—I determined to put my back to the world and lean it, instead, against a singing tree trunk.

As I neared the end of the lane, I found an old, faded-blue Honda parked in the access to one of Oat's hayfields. Inside the barbed-wire fence, early grasses were waving tall in a gentle evening breeze. It was a peaceful, calming sight. Out of curiosity, I approached the car. There was a piece of coat-hanger wire stuck in the place of a missing radio antenna. No one inside the car. No bumper stickers, but a decal in the rear window pictured a fairy-like woman with wings. Circling the fairy were the words "Fairies do exist." And underneath were the words "So do angels." The seats and floor were uncluttered, except for a small, crumpled fast-food bag. The doors were locked. The tires looked good.

I crossed the lane, skirted around an unmarked wooden gate, and began my climb up Singing Tree Hill along its overgrown path. My breathing became increasingly labored as the first several-hundred yards were unrelenting in steepness. Gradually the pitch eased and treetops yielded to provide a more open view of the cloudless sky.

Birds sang. Foliage changed. Deciduous trees became more

abundant, replacing the dominant firs. Wildflowers were seen more frequently. Eventually my eyes met nothing but open sky, varied grasses, and a profusion of assorted colors. Once again the trail became steep. Then at last the Singing Tree presented itself near the hill's crown. I paused, inhaling deeply, to fully appreciate the wonder of this glorious scene.

Traveling westward around the hillside, I found the tree in full view, top to bottom, just below the summit. I had made it my habit to sit on one of a few large, white rocks scattered below the tree. Here I could rest and ponder. Here I could find a marvelous view of the northern waters of Puget Sound. Here was a retreat without intruders—or so I thought. But as I came near the white rocks, I caught sight of a human form.

Startled, I stood still. I wasn't prepared for this. On all my previous visits I had found no one—just the tree, which seemed almost an intelligent entity itself. I liked to think I could communicate with it.

Disappointed, I eased down into the tall grasses to decide my next move. At length I realized that it would be foolish to turn back without first assessing the true situation. I should at least meet the person and learn whether he or she was an undesirable trespasser. Not that I had any say in the matter, but I felt protective of the Whipples.

I decided to move cautiously and make my presence known without offense. A gentle breeze wafted the scent of salt water uphill from the west, blowing my hair and cooling my face. I was upwind from the figure on the bench-like stone, so any sound of my approach should have been undetected. I moved slowly and steadily.

Soon I learned that my fears were groundless concerning my being heard. She was singing—not the tree, but the young woman on the rock. There could not have been fifteen feet between us when I abruptly stopped—my memory jolted free from its prison by the melody she was humming as she bent over a sketchpad in her lap. I didn't see her smooth her dark hair back over her ear, pencil in hand, so much as I saw my mother standing over our kitchen sink crying as she wiped a sudsy hand down her numb left arm, trying to cope with the first sign of her first stroke.

The memories now flooding my mind overwhelmed me. For the first time since my accident, I was able to recall my former Colorado home and the tragic events that led ultimately to my mother's death and my reasons for leaving all behind.

Overcome, I fell silently to my knees. Several minutes passed before I could regain my composure. All the while I heard the melody that my mother played so often on her violin as I grew from childhood into my teens.

Although we had often lived in remote and rough gold-mining camps or in small mining towns, my parents were cultured and well educated. My father had been a mining engineer; my mother was a registered nurse. And I remembered my half-sister, Millie, who was eight years older than me. Now married, she lived in Denver with her husband and two children. They were all I had left of my former family. Ironically, as I began to reflect again upon the present, I felt more attached to the Whipples. They had truly become *my* family in my new life.

I immediately regretted having obligated myself to a late-night appointment. There was so much to write in my journal, so much to think about, so much to share.

Suddenly I sensed that my space was being shared. I looked up and was embarrassed to find that the stranger was standing before me, her head tilted and her face questioning. Then caution, concern, and sympathy were alternately manifest as she stood silently gazing at me with exquisite dark-green eyes. They shone through long, dark lashes and held me spellbound to the point of self-forgetting.

For the moment my senses could focus only on the stranger. Fine, dark hair curved beneath her upturned chin and framed her face—a face with features that reflected intelligence and refinement. Her lips, softly closed in a slight smile, appeared to be naturally red-tinged. She had a small, pretty nose that I might call "classic Irish," and her complexion was radiant with the glow of health.

She somehow radiated genuine goodness and confidence. There seemed to be nothing artificial about her, either in appearance or character. My first impression was one of manifest honesty. Our meeting was, to me, dreamlike. But I was sharply brought back to a wakeful state when she moved to put her sketch book behind her back. She stepped forward and extended her hand toward me.

I took this to be a gesture of aid more than acceptance, and I couldn't bear the thought of what kind of impression I might have given her as I self-consciously wiped tears from my cheeks with the back of my hand. Humiliated, I struggled to my feet. I had difficulty looking directly at her as she spoke.

"I'm Jillian," she said. "Jillian Brynn-Green. And you must be Kephart. Right?"

Stupefied, I closed my eyes and gave my head a shake in disbelief.

"How . . . how could you possibly know that?" I stammered. Have I met you somewhere? I couldn't have! There's no way I could have forgotten you!

"It's my memory. I've had a memory problem because of an accident. No! It couldn't be that! I know I've never heard your name before—or met you. Never. So how is it that you know my name?"

I turned to look squarely at her, troubled at the insecurity I felt in being unable to relate to any memory of her.

Her lips parted and she smiled amusedly. A beautiful smile.

"I'm sorry," she said. Then her head inclined again as she looked at me with a side glance. "You don't know you're sleeping in my bed?"

I clapped my hand to my head and bent over, choking.

"This is too much!" I exclaimed. Then flopping down in the grass, I rolled to my side, propped my head on my hand, and groaned, "This whole day has been too much! Please explain. Please."

Her laughter was like a fresh breeze after a rain. She lowered herself gracefully into the grass on the other side of the path.

"It's your head," she answered. "The wounds still show. And you're here—where few people ever come unless they know the Whipples."

"So?"

"So haven't they ever mentioned my name? Or told you whose room you were given when you came to stay?"

"Oh. Sure. But they said her name was Angel."

"Oh." She smiled, closed her eyes, and lowered her head.

Then she raised her head and looked down the trail as she explained: "It's a family thing. I've been called that for as long as I can remember—ever since I was adopted by Oat and Selma. My friends call me Jill. But Oat has called me Angel from the day he first brought me home. Only, he spells it 'A-N-J-I-L-L.' Selma picked up on it, and so did Joel. But Jesse always called me 'Sissy.' He was two years old when I became his 'big sister' at three."

She paused, pensively. With a sigh she glanced at me and said, "It was such a sad thing, his death. So unexpected and sudden. We still grieve."

"How did he die?" I asked.

"A ruptured spleen. He fell from a tree he'd climbed. He was discovered too late and bled to death on the way to the hospital. The most serious injuries weren't obvious, since they were internal."

She arose from the grass in the same graceful manner that she had sat down. It was then that I noticed her skirt, which fell just above her knees. And so of course I noticed her legs as well, which the skirt revealed as she shifted her body to get up. Their allure was such that they begged to be touched. With one brief look I felt more than just pleasurably distracted. Did she know? Maybe not. It wouldn't have mattered so much with any other girl. Why now? But for some reason I wondered.

So instead of jeans Jill had chosen to wear a skirt, and I was happy for that. I found her to be more appealing and exciting by accentuating her feminine charms in this way. In my view she showed a non-conformity that I admired. For me, she was a model of uniqueness.

She moved to begin her descent down the hill, anticipating that I might do the same. I had now abandoned any thought of visiting the Singing Tree, so I followed.

"Are you in pain?" she asked as I came close beside her.

"No. At least not physical pain. I just had a totally moving experience when I heard you humming that song. It's hard to explain."

"Was I that good or that *bad* that I brought tears to your eyes?" she teased, trying to keep the conversation light.

"It was 'Danny Boy.' It was the song. I grew up with it. My mother used to sing it, or play it on her violin. At least she did until her stroke . . ."

Jill sensed the distress in my voice.

"Your memories are painful then," she said. "Maybe that's why they've been slow in returning."

"Maybe. But they came rushing back with that tune. Funny how music brings back memories. Smells, too. Some lilacs brought back other memories this morning. I wrote them in my journal as soon as I could. Doing that reinforces them. I've never kept a journal before. Nothing much to write about. All I've done is work, try to keep up in school, and take care of my mother. No time for a social life, that's for sure.

"But words have always fascinated me. There's a magic and power in words. I'm finding that I enjoy writing. And what about you? Are you an artist?"

"Not like you might think. Every child is an artist, so why should that change with age? It's sad to me that so many people stop creating. I guess you might say I haven't slipped away from childhood. At least not yet. But I *have* given up my crayon box," she said, and laughed as she opened out the decorative denim vest she wore over her blouse.

The vest was lined with narrow sheath-like pockets containing an assortment of charcoal sticks and colored pencils.

"I enjoy doing a lot of things," she continued. "When I was still at home, I designed and sewed this vest—with Selma's help, of course."

Then, seeing that she had drawn my attention to more than her hidden pockets, she quickly covered herself and sped up her pace. I kept close behind her as we weaved back and forth down the slope. Light-footed, she seemed to dance over the path. At a point where it widened, she slowed to let me come up alongside her.

When she glanced my way, I said, "I can't help but ask, where do you live now?"

"In Bellingham with three other students. We share a small two-bedroom home. We're all education majors."

"What do you want to teach—art?"

"I want to teach elementary grades. Of course, art will be included. My interests center mostly on humanities and the arts. I love to teach—especially young children. But I enjoy working with the elderly, too. I do volunteer work in a nursing home."

"How can you find time to do that and attend college?" I asked in wonder.

She hesitated. Then shrugging her shoulders, she said, "I guess I have an advantage over most other students. I'm fortunate—or blessed—to have a photographic memory. I can glance at pages of study material and retain everything I see. What slows me down is *writing*."

Her smile was captivating, but I was impressed most by the genuine humility in her voice as she spoke. She seemed to be devoid of pride in any form. I found this to be so with the Whipples as well, and it made my association with them more comfortable and enjoyable.

"You gave your last name when you introduced yourself, and it wasn't Whipple. I'm sorry, but it slipped by me," I said.

"When I was of legal age, I changed it. Neither Oat nor Selma took offense. They understood. I wanted to keep the last names of both of my natural parents, so I used them both—with a hyphen. By a tragic mistake my mother had divorced my father just before he died. She died of a broken heart, I think. It's a sad story that I haven't shared with anyone outside the family. Selma told me what I needed to know when I became old enough to handle it. She is the sweetest woman. And I really do think of her as 'Mom.' It's what I've always called her, of course. There couldn't be a finer family to grow up in."

"I've come to think that myself," I said. "Maybe sometime you'd like to share your story with me—that is if we should chance to meet again. Do you think there could be such a chance? I've been here five weeks without ever seeing you. You must not visit home often. Have I crowded you out?"

We both laughed, but I wanted to hear some words of encouragement for a future meeting. And I felt awkwardly situated in a position where I had no previous experience. My only "date" had been a girl I ate dinner with after we performed in a high school play. The whole cast was there in the restaurant with us.

I realized painfully that I was in the "white spaces" of my

social map. School and work and a tragically helpless mother had occupied all my time and attention. And there were no "Jillians" in the little mining town where I went to high school. I felt that this girl was rare and would be so anywhere in my view—which was limited, I admit. Even so, I presently found myself quite ready to accept the challenge of an untried social experience.

"My last name is Brynn-Green," she said. "The first part is my mother's maiden name. Maybe Selma would care to share the story of my natural parents with you. If she feels good about that, then it's all right with me. Oh! Here's the gate already."

I couldn't believe it. We were at the wooden gate. I looked at my watch. 7:40. I had about thirty-five minutes before I must leave for Old Fairhaven. It was hard to think of fulfilling my commitment to Shackleton. I had erased everything but Jill from my mind—even the perplexing questions that had prompted me to climb Singing Tree Hill.

"Could I drive you to the house?" Jill was beside her old Honda with the driver's door open.

"Sure," I said.

The ride was short, about half a mile. Too soon we were stopped at the farmhouse drive. Neither one of us had spoken, each involved in our own thoughts. The questions I had posed to Jill were still wanting answers, along with so many other questions of the day. I was wondering if she had purposely ignored them and, if so, why. Should I rephrase them? Or would she take my persistence as being offensive and pushy?

Maybe it was inappropriate by her standards for me to ask so soon for a time to meet again. It had been less than thirty minutes since we first met. Having had no dating experience, I felt frustrated and inept. It seemed regrettable to have never dated in my life, but I didn't resent my mother's misfortune or the limitations placed upon me because of it. There had been good and abiding love between us. I still had my whole life before me.

I decided the safest thing to do was to keep silent. As I opened the car door and turned to thank her, Jill broke her silence.

"Kephart . . ?"

"Please call me Kep," I said.

Her confident smile was warm and assuring in answer, but her eyes appeared reflective as she said, "Nothing between people is chance, Kep. I believe there is choice and purpose in everything. Let's see if our separate choices bring us onto the same path again. Okay?"

I nodded. But inwardly I felt somewhat confused about the meaning and implication of her statement. Wasn't each day filled with chance and uncertainty? Couldn't we both choose to meet again? It seemed to me that by not making that choice, any future opportunity was left to chance. And that didn't offer much hope. At that moment I began to feel that nearly everything happening in my life was beyond my control. I was able only to react. It was depressing, but I managed to smile and wave as she drove off.

When I turned to walk down the drive, I noticed that the pickup truck was no longer in the shed. Joel must have gone to town. So, except for Smooch, I was alone.

I climbed the stairs and found my journal. After thirty minutes of scribbling abbreviated notes, I flopped down on the bed. Only now it wasn't *my* bed—it was Jill's bed. I began studying the surrounding furnishings and décor more closely, trying to imagine how things might have been as Jill's life evolved from girlhood to womanhood right here in this room. Any notion I may have come up with would surely be a misconception, I realized, but I enjoyed letting my mind take me there so as to include her in my newly perceived surroundings. She was here again in a spiritual sense, and the room was somehow different.

The window curtains at the side of the bed began to billow

restlessly, distracting me from my reverie. Outside, a sharp gust of wind blew down a tin watering can that Selma kept on a bench near her flowerbed by the back porch. The trees waved their arms frantically, their new leaves urging me to make haste. I had an appointment to keep. My watch said 8:35. If I hurried, I'd still be late, but at that moment I didn't care. Somehow I was filled with apprehension. I would soon learn that my intuitive fears were justified.

CHAPTER 3

RELUCTANTLY I opened the door of the yellow bus. The wind nearly jerked it from my grasp; and before I stepped inside, the ending words of my conversation with Laura Rutledge sprang into mind: ". . . come prepared for stormy weather."

I let the wind shut the door and ran to the back porch to grab a hooded poncho I had bought at Goodwill in rainy April. After giving Smooch a second "good-bye" pat, I managed to embark on my night's errand, but not without having my attention diverted by the rapid changes taking place in the sky. Dark, purple-tinged clouds swelled and rolled forth from the northeast—a direction contrary to the prevailing winds. Occasional flashes of lightning accentuated the threat of an impending downpour.

Well, it's just a great night for surreptitious meetings, I thought while jerking the steering wheel to keep the lightweight VW in its lane as it bounced and weaved northward. Laura Rutledge had forecasted well.

Or was it Shackleton's warning that she had relayed to me? As I dwelt on this question, my mind fell back upon the TV weather forecast I'd heard during my phone call to Dozie. Wasn't the prediction, "continuing sunny and cool"? How could either Laura or Shackleton have given a more accurate forecast than the pros—especially considering the severity of the storm? It was uncanny.

Finding the import shop was a cinch and I parked right in front. Rain had begun to wet the sidewalk enough to reflect the light from a streetlamp. A storefront sign beneath the second-story overhang gave the shop name: Reid & Gray Imports. Two large, attractively-curtained paned windows bore settings of displayed items. These were mostly intricate decorative art pieces and small storage boxes or chests made of wood. Even in the dimmed shop lighting I could see that the featured articles were quite unusual and skillfully crafted.

A recess in the wall led to the store entry to the left of the windows. A sign on the door glass read, Handcrafted Exotic Wood Imports. Within the entryway I found, on the left, the door that led to Laura Rutledge's apartment. A small brass nameplate gave the name: L. Rutledge. Hesitating, I stood staring at the door panel wondering why I should feel so anxious. I'd dealt with many "unknowns" in the past, but for some reason this one unsettled me greatly. The wind-driven raindrops now spattering on the walk outside the covered entry intensified my feelings.

My watch said 9:13. Following Laura's instructions, I opened the door, climbed a steep stairway, and stopped before the only door at the top landing. This time I didn't hesitate. I pressed the doorbell. No sound came, but I heard footsteps, and then the click of a deadbolt. Laura opened the door wide, without caution, and stepped back in a gesture of courteous invitation.

She was nearly my height, slender, blondish, and dressed in neatly creased beige slacks. Her countenance and manner were gracious, but her attractive brown eyes intimated a suppressed sadness that belied her smile. I guessed her age to be about thirty. She held out her right hand for a shake, and then closed the door behind me as she spoke.

"I know you must be mystified by all this, Kephart, but your being here speaks well for you, and I'm sure that ultimately you will not regret having come. May I take your raincoat?"

I had pulled the wet poncho off during my climb up the stairs.

Handing it to her, I asked, "Is Shackleton here yet?" (I saw no sign of another visitor in the small room.)

"I'm sorry if you misunderstood. I know our conversation was short. But this appointment was made for the purpose of exchanging questions and answers preliminary to your receiving an assignment. I'm acting under Harv's . . . Shackleton's direction. As I am his secretary and confidante, I hope you will not find yourself uncomfortable being here without him. He trusts me to handle his affairs. I can only hope you will trust me as well."

"Miss Rutledge, I don't feel distrustful of you in the least, but I'm full of unanswered questions that make me a bit uneasy. One thing I'm wondering is why this meeting is scheduled so late. I could only guess that Shackleton had piano lessons or appointments that crowded his evening."

She waved her hand toward a floral-patterned sofa.

"Please sit down, Kephart."

Her hair was attractively gathered in a loose tie behind her head, and she smoothed some fallen strands back into place with both hands as she seated herself in a recliner opposite me.

As I took the offered seat, she said, "I think you will easily understand the reason for the late hour when you learn of the assignment. And please don't be formal with me, Kephart. You can call me Laura. I prefer it." Her manner was congenial and I felt at ease with her.

Her hands moved from the back of her neck, around her throat, and down the front of her blouse as she adjusted and centered an unusual necklace of alternating wood and silver ornaments. Striking as they were against her mint-green blouse, simple elegance was obvious in her dress and in her style. She was not showy, but she had class. I noticed, too, that she wore a ring on the little finger of her right hand. This and the necklace comprised the only jewelry she wore, except for dangling earrings that, in miniature, matched the wood-and-silver necklace.

"Thank you, Laura," I said. "And I prefer 'Kep' over Kephart. Maybe by being informal we can bring things to an earlier close tonight. I'm more than curious about being given an 'assignment' as you call it. I owe Shackleton fifty dollars' worth of service, but not because I *chose* to be his hire.

"The money was forced on me, you might say. I do have a job that gets me by for the present, until I can focus on some goals and restructure my life. I'm just recovering from an accident and a personal loss. It will take a little time to repay Shackleton the money now because I've had to use it to bail out my employer's delivery van. But it's a sure thing that I'm obligated now. The sooner I can pay off the debt, the better I'll feel. What can you tell me about the work I'm being asked to do?"

She remained thoughtful and silent for a minute, and then she said, "What I can tell you is that there is a warehouse not far from here that contains a box of significant value. It belongs to Shackleton, but he is unable to get it for himself under the present arrangements. Paul Reid, who manages the shop under this apartment, is in charge of the warehouse goods. He is in partnership with Harv . . . I'm sorry . . . Shackleton. When Shackleton lost his sight nearly three years ago, he—"

"Then he hasn't been blind for very long, really!" I exclaimed.

"No. But that is not his greatest tragedy—losing his sight. He lost . . . maybe I shouldn't tell you more just now."

Laura straightened her back, then briefly closed her eyes and sighed.

"As I was about to say, he turned everything of the import business over to Paul and Marga Reid. They also oversee another larger store in Seattle. This one is the original, and it benefits from Canadian trade, since it is near the border.

"After his loss of sight, Shackleton became a silent partner, preferring to dedicate his time, talents, and resources to the alleviation of suffering—or better yet, to the prevention of tragedy if possible. He redirects lives in ways that I can't explain just now.

"As to his piano studio, he has just two students left and they are nearly his equal in proficiency. His personal time spent at the piano, which I believe is vital, amounts to only what is necessary for balance and healing. He has many gifts, Kep. There could come a day when you will see and appreciate them. He is quite well-off financially, as you may come to find out. But he has little regard for wealth except as it might serve his humanitarian interests."

"This is all interesting, Laura," I said, "but I'm still having trouble seeing why or where I come into the picture, being a perfect stranger. Why all the time set aside for explanations? What's so complicated about the job I'm to do? How does this relate?"

She paused and sighed.

"There are aspects that aren't yet obvious to you, Kep. That's the reason for arranging this time with you—to explain things and prepare you with what is needed to accomplish your task. Please be patient while I continue."

She smiled, but I sensed that she was a bit nervous about my pressing her with questions. Still, she remained poised and congenial. I smiled back and nodded.

"Paul Reid has a keen mind for business. Shackleton was the adventurer and explorer—the one who sought out the tangible assets, the sources of supply. He often traveled the world and his expertise was critical to the success of the business.

"There was a symbiosis between the two men that was broken with the loss of Shackleton's sight. Paul has not done so well since. I personally believe he resents Shackleton's legal entitlements financially. He has become possessive of all that the warehouse holds and regards these goods as his own. So you can see that Shackleton is presented with a potential risk in obtaining any item that is rightfully his.

"Shackleton owns both the warehouse and this building. He keeps his seaplane in the lower part of the warehouse, which is partly situated over the water. He keeps one of his cars in the structure as well. You must understand, Kep, that Shackleton doesn't want to engage in any contention or conflict over matters of ownership. He has personally removed himself and kept his distance, relying on his accountants and attorneys to protect his interests. His mind is bent on more excellent pursuits and nobler causes.

"There is another thing I want you to know, because you impress me as being one who can keep confidences. Shackleton is complex and unknowable—much more so since he has become blind. He holds many secrets that relate directly to his misfortune. I tell you this for good reason because, depending on what takes place tonight and in the days to come, you may find that he has further need of your assistance.

"Now, with all that said you must feel that I have overlooked your questions or digressed to the point of forgetting them." She smiled, and then sighed again as if relieved.

It was obvious that Laura held a personal interest in Shackleton that wasn't purely business. She seemed to be relieving herself of a burden as she spoke. For some reason I couldn't help but feel sympathetic toward her unspoken concerns. There was an underlying sadness that couldn't be masked by her words or her dignity. She impressed me as being a pretty flower about to wilt for lack of water. My presence and attentive listening seemed to revive her spirit.

"It's not too great a leap for me to see that I'm to fetch a box from a warehouse on a stormy night," I said with as much nonchalance as I could muster, but my palms were getting sweaty and my list of questions was getting longer by the minute.

"Would you like a cup of tea?" she asked abruptly. "Do you like herbal teas? I have several kinds, but ginger tea sounds good to me tonight. Please have some with me. It will perk you up." Her face brightened as she spoke.

"I'm willing to give it a try," I said, not wanting to disappoint her. "Thank you."

"You'll excuse me. I won't be long."

She got up and went to the kitchen. I could hear the rattle of dishware and the sounds of a teakettle being filled. I got up and found my way to her.

"May I use your bathroom?" I asked.

"Of course. Go down the short hallway off the living room. You'll have to go through my bedroom to get to it. It's somewhat inconvenient for visitors, but it's fine for my personal use. Sorry."

I smiled and gave her a nod. Returning to the living room, I became aware of the exceptional quality of her chosen décor and furnishings. She had created an attractive interior environment for herself in spite of occupying quarters over a merchant's store situated opposite maritime activities and a railway station. Her view of the bay might be a compensating factor when the days and nights afforded one. But on a night like this nothing could be more desirable than being inside this comfy, attractive shelter. I considered the prospect of going out into the wild, wet world extremely unappealing at this hour.

When I passed back through her bedroom, I noticed an enlarged, framed photo standing on her dresser. Strangely, I was immediately drawn to it. A close look at the photograph stopped my breath. It showed a younger Shackleton standing behind two young women with his arms draped over their shoulders. The three were smiling. They appeared to be happily enjoying themselves, not just saying "cheese."

Studying their faces, I discovered that one of the girls was Laura. The other closely resembled her, but she had darker hair. They could easily have been sisters. My curiosity was piqued and I couldn't let it go. I had just turned away and was heading down the hallway when I discovered Laura entering the living room. She had come to invite me to her table. Just in time, I thought.

"The tea will soon be ready," she said, "and I have some snack foods set out. Crackers, cheese, donuts—whatever you might find appealing. If you would care for a sandwich, I'll be glad to fix you one. I'm mostly wanting tea, myself, but you must be hungry."

"Not really," I said. "I'm just eager to get my job over with. Not that I don't enjoy your hospitality, or your company. I'm just a little tense about being a 'thief in the night.'"

She sat at the table and invited me to use a chair at right angles to her. I could tell she had something on her mind, but she responded with, "Would you join me in saying grace?"

I was accustomed to bowing my head at mealtimes with the Whipples so I nodded my assent.

After giving thanks, she raised her head and looked directly at me. "We have more things yet to discuss, Kep. Please accept my apology and be patient with me. I have my assignment, too. There are things you need to know and preparations to make."

She looked at her watch and sighed. "And the timing is a factor."

"Why?" I asked. "Is there a guard or security system?"

"No, but it's best that you enter the building after eleven. Please don't ask me why, Kep. I can't tell you why. You'll just have to accept it as a condition of your mission." She seemed apologetic again.

"I don't see why taking a package from a warehouse should call for so much secrecy, or why it has to be done in the dark and late at night—unless it's connected with something unlawful or dishonest," I protested. "I don't have a good feeling about it. I've had to deal with lots of real physical dangers in my life, and I'm not afraid to take some chances, but there are lines my conscience won't let me cross. In the short time I spent with Shackleton, he made a point of my not undervaluing my integrity. I guess I'm in the dark when it comes to seeing how this sort of thing can help it. It sounds suspicious to me."

"Kep," she sighed. "What you carry out tonight will affect someone's future. Please believe me. Shackleton doesn't meddle indiscriminately in people's lives. And he may be daring, but he's never unscrupulous. I can see this is going to take a great deal of trust on your part—trust in him, in me, and in yourself."

"Laura, I hardly know either you or Shackleton. I *do* know myself. I just don't want to regret my having made a wrong choice."

These last words took my mind to Jill's parting remarks about "choice and purpose in everything." I looked away from Laura as I mulled over Jill's words, irritated by the situation in which I found myself and by the indecisiveness I felt.

The teakettle began to sing on Laura's stove. She slowly got up and went to the kitchen. When she returned she carried a brightly decorated teapot and some paper napkins.

As she set them down she said, "Sometimes it's helpful to distract your mind for a while when you're confronted with a weighty decision. There's something I'd like you to look at. I'll be right back."

I hadn't moved a muscle before she came carrying a small laminated wooden box like those I'd seen in the shop windows downstairs. She placed it beside me on the table and began filling our teacups with hot water.

"You've probably seen this type of puzzle box before, but this one is a little different from most. Do you want to try opening it?"

I had always liked the challenges of various kinds of puzzles, but I wasn't much in a mood for one at the moment. Still, I could see that she had a point, so I picked it up and began to examine it. She appeared to be thankful that I showed some interest, and she smiled encouragement as I turned it over, listening to something rattling inside.

"I've never seen anything like this," I said. "Is the box supposed to rattle or is the sound coming from what's inside it?"

"It could be both," she said, "but this one is supposed to rattle, even if it contained nothing."

"Then I'll guess it has something to do with the unlocking," I said. "But I can't tell where the separation is between the box and its lid. Does it have a lid or is there a drawer that comes out?"

"There *is* a lid. The separation is about a fourth of the way down the box, but it's supposed to be undetectable."

The top corners were rounded to indicate which end was up. I held the box to my ear and tilted it slowly back and forth. No sound came. So I turned it upside down and did the same. There came the sound of something rolling. After several tries I found that it came to a rest in the center when the box was held level. I kept it in the position of rest and looked at Laura for a clue.

"There'll be a piece of either the dark or light wood that will slide through the adjacent laminated strips," she said, and her expression was one of confidence in my being able to succeed at the task. She began steeping the tea in my cup.

Soon, by testing the different pieces of wood, I discovered the one that moved. Once I had it pressed to its limit, I found a succession of pieces on the sides that moved in the same manner, only in various directions. At the last, when there was nothing left but to right the box, I was able to slide a dark piece on top that released the lid, which pivoted away from the bottom. I was impressed by the ingenuity of it as well as the craftsmanship.

"I don't doubt your honesty, Kep, but it's hard to believe that you've never opened a puzzle box before."

Laura leaned her head on her right hand and closed her eyes. I began to wonder if she was all right as she started moving her head slowly back and forth, her eyelids fluttering. Presently she straightened up and smiled at me. She seemed more relieved than impressed by my having opened the box. At that moment I became aware of a deep concern on her part for my accomplishing the task—more than I thought it should merit.

She held her gaze on me, smiling warmly and appreciatively. I saw then how naturally beautiful she was—and how poised, with no conscience effort on her part. I sensed, too, a depth to her that wasn't readily apparent. I knew she held secrets and sorrows of her own that she was unready to share at that time.

"Our tea is just a shade above warm," she said as she took a sip from her cup. "Shall I heat it in the microwave?"

I found mine to be just right. "Mine's fine," I said. "I'm ready to snack and sip."

Curious, I tipped the puzzle box to look at its interior. There was what appeared to be a red satin cloth in the bottom. I looked over at Laura and found her eyes anticipating my question.

"Take it out," she said.

Pulling out the cloth, I discovered that it was a bag with a drawstring. I untied it and opened the bag. There was a ring inside. It felt much lighter than I would have supposed, since it appeared to be made of a heavy metal. As I examined it more closely I could see that it wasn't produced from a common precious metal—maybe an alloy. It was beautiful in its simplicity.

"Put it on," Laura said, seeming to hold her breath.

It wouldn't fit my right ring finger, but it snuggly fit my little one. As I worked it onto my finger, I noticed that there was an outer ring that rotated within a channeled groove of the inner one. Because the surfaces were flush, it wasn't obvious that there were two parts.

"Another one of Shackleton's imports?" I asked as I began to remove it.

"Just leave it on, Kep. No, it's not an import as you might

think. But it is something extremely rare. And it's a gift to you from Shackleton. He wants you to consider working for him as an assistant. I can't tell you anything more than this. I know you will view this as another obligation, but you shouldn't. To do so would be to misjudge his intention. He doesn't expect anything from you in return. But he does believe you are the man he needs to fulfill a role in accomplishing his purposes. And please, Kep, don't view this ring as a bribe. Whether you accept or decline the job offer, it's yours to keep."

I was amazed, and then troubled by this development. It was easy to see that my opening the box with the ring was planned prior to my visit and that I had been tested in some way. I guessed I had passed the test but I wasn't so sure that it made me happy, much less comfortable.

"What can this test prove of me, other than to show that I can do what any precocious ten-year-old could do—some child with a talent for solving spatial puzzles? What can it qualify me for in terms of meeting adult challenges, especially humanitarian ones? I really don't get it, Laura. And because I like you, I don't want to disappoint you. Can't you just tell me what kinds of things Shackleton might expect of me? How can I think about a job that has no description? It seems like the more I look for answers in connection with Shackleton, the more questions I get instead."

I reached for a cracker, and then cheese. (My sudden appetite was probably stress related.)

Laura clasped her fingers loosely together and put her thumbs to her lips. Her eyes smiled at me as she said, "Kep, when you do what you do tonight, you will prepare yourself for receiving answers, and they will come from Shackleton himself—if you are successful."

CHAPTER 4

I could see that Laura wasn't able to go beyond the limits imposed upon her for giving out information. Everything seemed to pivot on my doing the warehouse job—successfully.

During my teens I had helped support my mother by doing some things prohibited by law. But that was because of my age. The laws dealt with safety standards for youths. I had worked underground with my uncle, mining for gold and other precious metals before he was killed. I had worked at hazardous construction jobs in and around mines and on the precipitous roads leading to them. My hands were frequently on pneumatic machinery and dynamite.

It was my "thing" then to prove my manhood by showing that I could do a man's job at fourteen. I took some pride in showing my peers that I was the man of my house—the guy who could take care of his invalid mom and still finish school. I had no time for sports or girlfriends. I had achieved a level of "manhood" that made me spurn such things. (At least that was the juvenile rationale that had kept me going then.)

So I had no fears connected with going into a dark place to extract some treasure—as I imagined would be expected of me this night. But I did have qualms about the secretiveness of the assignment, and I had a gut feeling that there was more to it than Laura could reveal—no matter how much she might wish she could spill things to me.

Right now I was curious about some newly formed questions. Maybe she would be able to answer a couple.

"Laura, I couldn't help noticing a framed picture on your dresser as I passed by—the one of Shackleton with you and some other young woman. He obviously had his sight then. You each look quite happy. I'm curious. Do you feel like telling me what the occasion was and who the other woman is? Is she your sister?"

"My cousin," she said. There was a catch in her breath as she spoke. "I don't mind telling you what I can, but I don't want to weary you with family history."

She looked at her watch. I knew I had about an hour to kill. But then there really was no time limit, and the wind-driven rain was still pelting against the windows. I kept silent and waited, hoping to find more to distract my mind.

"I'll have to explain first that Rose and I were practically raised together. We were like sisters. We were born eight months apart and our mothers were identical twins. They had married in a double wedding ceremony. Our fathers were good friends as well as business partners. Their firm, Rutledge and Faix, is headquartered in Oregon. They manufacture dental and surgical instruments.

"On the day that picture was taken, our families had taken our motorboat to an island in the center of Donut Lake for a day of picnicking and relaxation. Because our families were closely tied, we shared a lot of recreational activities, especially boating.

"Although Rose and I were in our early twenties, we sometimes behaved like kids. Rose had found a package of bubble gum in her purse, so she decided to share it with me. It was a breezy day and eventually a gum bubble got into the ends of Rose's hair. We *both* wound up having our hair trimmed because what one of us did, the other often did. It was a 'sister' thing between us. My aunt did the cutting, and she decided to save some of our hair clippings in marked sandwich bags to put in her scrapbook, along with the day's photos.

"As she was finishing up, we were startled by a seaplane dropping down from the sky to land on the lake. It was especially alarming because there were no other people around and it was so suddenly noisy. The plane drew right up to the island, and out hopped this man onto one of the plane's floats. He was carrying a large dog.

"He splashed to shore through the water and put his dog down near some timber so it could relieve itself. Then he came over and introduced himself as Harvard Gray and spent an hour sharing stories and eating with us.

"Rose and I were so taken by him that we could speak of little else for months to follow. He was the most fascinating and attractive man either of us had known. And such a spectacular entry into our lives! He definitely showed a genuine interest in all of us, but we could tell that he particularly liked us girls because . . . well, girls know. "Anyway, before he left he had my mother take that picture. Then he did an unusual thing. He took some strands of our hair from the bags and put them between separate pages of a notebook he carried in his pocket. After making some cheery comments, he took up his dog, waved good-bye, and flew off into the blue.

"We thought we'd never see him again. He had only said that he was based in northwest Washington and that he traveled all around the world looking for things to buy for his import shop.

"Then, months later, Rose and I each received identical copies of a letter from him. How he got our addresses, we couldn't imagine, but we were thrilled that he should write. He wrote that because his life was so taken up with extensive business travel, he was compelled to fit time for romance into his schedule like everything else. After meeting the two of us and our parents, he realized that he had been neglectful of himself in this respect, but more than that he knew that he had discovered treasures not to be overlooked. His greatest difficulty had been to choose which one of us he would approach first.

"The letter explained that he had spent considerable time arriving at a decision. Our locks of hair—of all things—had settled the issue! To my utter disappointment and Rose's extreme joy, he picked Rose—should she be willing and not involved in another relationship. I think I read the letter so many times that I had it memorized and stained with tears.

"Needless to say, he wound up marrying Rose. In order to prevent any rivalry between Rose and me while he was courting her—and to hide my hurt— I moved to Albuquerque, where I took a job in one of our company's distribution centers. Rose and I kept in touch, but I didn't make any effort to see her until she became pregnant, and that was over three years ago."

"Then Shackleton has a wife?" I exclaimed. "And a child? I wouldn't have guessed it. He didn't impress me as being a family man. He seemed more to be a mysterious loner who loved the company of his dog, just as you described him at first."

Laura lowered her head to cover her eyes and forehead with her palms. Strong emotion was evident in her silence. She managed to keep her composure, but her eyes were wet as she brought her head up to glance at me before continuing.

"I don't really know that he has a wife—or a child, Kep," she said. Then she got up from the table and went into the kitchen, where she kept a box of Kleenex. "Would you like some more tea?" she asked.

Hearing the teakettle slide onto the stove burner again, I said, "Yes, please. It's good stuff on a night like this."

Actually I was having a hard time holding back on the obvious question. It wasn't a good time to press it, so I waited for her to come and sit with me again. During the previous five minutes I'd felt a bit uncomfortable as Laura let me peek behind the curtains of her heart—inadvertently or not, it didn't matter. But my perceptions were still to undergo quite a change.

She didn't come back to the table until the teakettle had stopped whistling its tune again. Then she brought fresh tea and a plate of assorted cookies. Sighing, she smoothed back her loose hair and sat down to continue with her story. Only now, she looked at me less often and her eyes seemed to focus on things invisible to me.

"I forgot to mention that Shackleton's father was killed just after it became known that Rose was expecting. His father, Chandler Gray, had been an airline pilot and had recently retired. Finding that his father was becoming bored and restless, Shackleton invited him to go with him on a buying trip to Central and South America. They flew by commercial airlines and then rented local transportation as needed. Often they rented a small plane and flew privately.

"During the third week in February, after some successful buying, they decided to try a little exploring. Chandler had named Shackleton after that famous explorer because he admired certain attributes in him, particularly his tenacity and determination in the face of extreme odds. I guess it was Chandler's desire to challenge himself in things untried that prompted him to explore parts of a vast jungle called the Oriente. Of course, they were exploring by plane.

"When they were flying over the Ucayali River in Peru, a torrential rainstorm forced them down. They were both seriously injured. Harv . . . Shackleton suffered a serious loss of blood. He managed to use his belt to fasten himself to the partly submerged wreckage in such a way that he could keep his head above water, but then he repeatedly lost consciousness. Each time he awoke he could hear his father answer his calls, but at the last there was silence. Chandler couldn't swim.

"Two things saved Shackleton. They had given a general flight plan when they left Lima, and the rented plane's emergency locator signal was activated when it crashed into the river. He was spotted from the air by a mail plane and taken to Atalaya, where he received medical attention. It was late in March before he made it back home.

"Rose vowed that she would never let him go again without

her, which resulted in a far greater tragedy than she could possibly have imagined. One trip to Thailand in her fourth month of pregnancy proved to be a happy occasion—more like a vacation for them. But three months later . . ."

Laura quickly turned her head away. She shielded the side of her face with her hand as she sobbed. I couldn't think of anything to say, so I sat silently in discomfort while she dealt with her emotions. A full minute passed before she could resume her tale.

"Kep, this is hard for me, but it's something I need to share . . . at least I feel you should know what I'm wanting to tell you. I don't think that by telling you I'd betray Shackleton's trust. Someone besides myself should know. But then you'll have to understand that Shackleton will inevitably know that you know a secret that torments him . . . and me. And once you know it, you'll have to be respectful of my wish that you disclose it to no one. I beg you. Still, if you'd rather *not* know, I'll withhold it from you."

Her eyes were searching mine intently. I could tell these last words coming from Laura weren't premeditated or planned to be included as part of my test. But I was slow to answer. I wasn't the least bit comfortable with the thought of taking on someone's tormenting secret. (Whether this points out a distinctive difference between males and females, or if it was my own antipathy at the time, I don't know. I've changed a lot since then.) At that time I felt like I had been riding a roller coaster all day. Why hold hands with a gorilla?

Then as I mulled it over, I could see that it would be foolish to involve myself any further with Shackleton without learning all that I could about him. It would be difficult to assist someone who held secrets, dark or otherwise, if those secrets were even remotely related to his quest. Not to know them would leave me somewhat defenseless or, at the least, unguarded.

Laura had been patient with my contemplation.

"Okay," I said at last. "Count me in. I give you my word not to tell a soul about his secret until he releases me from the promise."

I had become tense. But Laura's entire body seemed to relax in relief. She smiled and briefly closed her eyes, then continued.

"That year, in late July, Rose went with Shackleton to Brazil, where he wanted to add to some buying connections he had already established. His personal financial worth had more than tripled by then because his father had designated him sole beneficiary on his life insurance policy with a face amount running in the millions. He had no siblings, and his mother, Elizabeth, had died in England many years earlier.

"So why he should want to go to Brazil then, I can't guess, except for two possible reasons. One could be that he wanted to remain at home with Rose after the baby was born. The other, which fit in with the first, could be that he wanted to build up the inventory of imported goods for Paul and Marga while he was still free to do so. He would respect Rose's wishes by not taking trips without her, especially after she had their child.

"Shackleton does not have a grain of greed in him. The increased import potential would have meant little to him personally. Traveling gratified his need to explore and to meet and surmount challenges. He was well named; although, I do prefer his first name because it's more familiar. He didn't ask to be called by his middle name until after the events in Brazil, and then it was limited to being a sort of code name to be used discriminately among a chosen few. But there I go—rambling again . . ."

"Wait—I'm sorry, Laura. This story is all very fascinating to me, and I definitely want you to go on, but . . . well, I see red flags go up when I hear you talk about 'Shackleton' being a code name. It makes me feel like—now that I'm *privileged* to call him by that name—I'm to be a member of some secret organization that I know nothing about. I feel uncomfortable with the missing particulars. Shouldn't I be entitled to know more about what I'm getting into? Doesn't that seem only fair—to be informed about the nature and mission of the organization? I was under the impression that I might be a personal assistant to Shackleton, not part of a team."

"Oh, Kep. I'm so sorry. I'm probably not handling this right by giving you too much personal information without purpose. I guess I'm being a bit selfish in the matter by telling things that have burdened me for so long. But you asked to learn more about that photograph, and it just got me going.

"I can assure you that you are correct in your understanding of what Shackleton wants of you. He's not considering anyone other than you, Kep. He grants the use of his middle name only to his household staff, and to me, of course. And he does so for good reason, as you may learn in time. He has extended the privilege to you for good reason as well, but he's the only one who can tell you why.

"As to an existing organized group or team, there is none that you could define as such under Shackleton's command. He is intensely independent, and the few of us who virtually orbit around him do so at whatever distance he impresses upon us as fitting his mood or his availability or his desire to involve us. But because he is a kind man, he's easy to read—and easy to serve."

"Thanks, Laura. I feel better knowing that. So . . . please go on with your sharing."

She put her fingers to her temples, closed her eyes, and nodded slowly before continuing. It was apparent that what she was about to tell me was painful to recall.

"One night, in Rio de Janeiro, he left Rose in their hotel room while he went to another hotel to negotiate with an agent and sign a business contract. He didn't want Rose subjected to the talk and interaction that went with such a meeting. In her pregnant condition at that time, she tired easily. She needed quiet and rest.

"Shortly after ten o'clock he returned to find her gone. When he could find no trace of her, he got the hotel staff to join in his search. Then the police. Taxi companies and their drivers were questioned. Shackleton is good at stirring up action and getting cooperation from authorities if he has good cause to do so. He has certain characteristics typical of a commander. But by three a.m. their usual investigative patterns had produced nothing. All possible resources and explanations were becoming exhausted.

"Shackleton wasn't about to slacken his own search efforts. He moved in an ever-widening spiral outward from the hotel, questioning everyone he could. Rio de Janeiro is like New York City, in that it never sleeps. There is activity around the clock. But all his tireless attempts to gain some clue were futile. At about five in the morning he went back to the hotel room to think the whole thing through in seclusion.

"I have to tell you at this point, Kep, that he has a remarkable gift of clairvoyance. His ability goes beyond what is typical for those who experience paranormal events. And now that he is blind, his powers have intensified and expanded to a point that scares me at times. I knew nothing about this ability until I came to assist him after Rose disappeared.

"It isn't unusual for clairvoyants to be unable to apply their gift in cases where loved ones are concerned. However, he later described to me how, in a meditative state, he could see Rose lying on the hotel rooftop. He actually experienced his *being* there. She was naked, but alive.

"He discovered a way to the roof without seeking assistance. Although it covered a vast area of varying levels and obstacles, he surely found her just as he had envisioned. When he knelt down beside her, he was horrified at what he saw."

Laura choked up. I wasn't sure she would continue, but her resilience surprised me, especially when I learned the cause of her acute distress.

"Rose's breasts had been surgically removed. Her abdomen was flat. Their child had been taken, together with her womb, apparently. And the surgeries had been bloodless. The surgical lines were visible, but there were no sutures and no bloodstains. Strangely, some healing had already taken place.

"Shackleton fainted from shock. When he regained consciousness, he felt for her pulse and found none. He tried artificial respiration to no avail. At last, when he could gather his strength and senses, he notified the police. When he led them to the place on the roof, Rose's body wasn't there. An extensive search ensued, but her disappearance was complete and final.

"Shackleton lapsed into a state of delirium requiring some medical assistance. He began to doubt his sanity. He even began to question the entire experience. After a couple of days of supervised rest, counseling, and observation, his faculties returned to normal.

"He went through days of interrogation. The governmental authorities in Brazil don't scoff at this sort of thing. People are encouraged to report bizarre experiences or events, particularly unusual sightings or abductions. His story was believed, especially in view of his grief and personal credentials. No lie detector tests were ordered, but they wanted a full account of all the details connected with the incident and an explanation of his reasons for being there.

"They questioned everyone from the hotel staff to the nearby street vendors. They looked for consistency in every aspect of his story. And they were quite patient and willing to record every relevant statement. What is remarkable to me is that there was no ridicule or attempt to disprove his credibility. He was believed, and he was allowed to return to the United States with his dignity intact."

Laura had been resting her elbows on the table as she talked. Her hands had been restless or gesturing, and she fidgeted with her teaspoon at times, but she had kept her poise all the while. Her back was straight and her chin up for the most part, even during those emotional moments when she relived Shackleton's gruesome and distressing experiences. Now her hands were relatively quiet as she consciously twisted her ring.

For my part, I sat dead still, thoroughly fascinated as I absorbed every word. I was hearing an account, at the last, that touched on things fantastic and unbelievable. And yet I believed what Laura said. It rang true. There was no fabrication to detect. It was as though it was her own sincere testimony, and she rendered it convincingly. Yet it was Shackleton's story as he had related it to her. Still, what could have possibly motivated him to devise such a convincing tale? What purpose could it serve? Hadn't he lost everything precious to him? And where had it left him?

I was just going to ask Laura how it came to be that he was blind when she stood up and said, "Please excuse me, Kep. Please eat something, and I'll be back to tell you more."

She went into her bedroom and I heard her close the door. From inside my shirt I took out the small notebook I used for taking abbreviated notes that I would later transfer to my journal. Eight or ten minutes of scribbling brought Laura back. She looked refreshed and more alert.

Smiling as she passed by me, she went to a window and spread apart the venetian blind slats. "This is more like a winter storm," she said. "It isn't at all like May."

I saw that she had a small brown envelope in her hand as she sat again at the table.

"I see that you're taking notes," she commented. "Shackleton would like that."

"It's a habit with me now," I said.

"Kep, it's nearing ten thirty. I may be able to tell you a little more about Shackleton—to answer certain questions if you want to take up some time. Maybe you would care to write a few things down. That would be fine with me."

"I'm willing to learn all I can, Laura. Shackleton is my primary concern right now, like it or not. I'd be pleased to know more about you too, though. It seems you both have untold burdens, and I'm willing to hear whatever you want to share."

As I spoke these last words, I became aware of the change in the way Laura and I had come to relate to each other in just a little over an hour. It wasn't so surprising, considering the way she had opened up to me. But I wondered.

CHAPTER 5

LAURA folded her arms across her breasts and hugged herself as if she were cold.

"You're easy to talk to, Kep, and I have difficulty refraining from telling you too much—more perhaps than you need to hear."

"Could you tell me how Shackleton became blind?" I asked. "Or is that a secret too?"

"I can tell you *when* it happened, but I can't even guess *how*. It's a strange thing. "He waited until he got back to the Northwest before he broke the news of Rose's disappearance. He especially didn't want to tell my aunt and uncle over the phone, so he met with our parents in Oregon. He withheld details concerning her mutilation and the taking of their unborn child. He told them only that she had been abducted and that, because there had been no attempt to obtain ransom, and in view of her being relatively unknown, the authorities had given her up for dead. Such things, he said, were not uncommon there. Events involving missing persons of all ages were all-too-frequent, and, although taken seriously, investigative efforts seldom resulted in happy endings. Of course, it was the hardest thing any of us had ever had to bear.

"Actually, I was notified by my mother and I immediately flew home from Albuquerque. By the time I arrived Shackleton had already come back here to Washington State. We held a memorial service for Rose in Oregon, mostly to bring us to some sense of closure to an apparently hopeless and tragic event. But Shackleton was convinced somehow that she was still alive—somewhere—and so he didn't attend.

"When I came here with my mother and aunt to go through Rose's things, we found him despondent and broken in spirit. It was heartbreaking to see him in such a pathetic state, especially because he's naturally filled with boundless energy and zeal. But who could have expected otherwise? He dearly loved Rose and they had wanted a child so much. Her pregnancy had been long awaited. Everything he'd cared for and hoped for had been snatched from him. He was truly desolate. And then there remained the probability that Rose would never again be able to bear a child, should she turn up alive.

"Her inexplicable mutilation is still a nightmare to me, as I'm sure it is to Shackleton. And that is the secret part we have to bear alone. The full details can't be disclosed to anyone else. For some reason I feel secure in sharing this with you, Kep. There must be a good reason for your knowing these things, other than to help me bear the load. I suppose there will come a time when our loved ones can accept and deal with the truth of the matter, but it isn't now.

"When my mother and aunt were preparing to return to Oregon, I was privately approached by Harv . . . Shackleton. He put his arms around me and held me close and wept. It was the first and only time that he ever demonstrated affection and compassion for me personally, and I can't tell you how much I cherish that moment."

Tears welled up in Laura's eyes and she spoke in a whisper. There was a sob with the intake of her breath, but she went on, seemingly unable to stop the flow of words.

"He told me how very sorry he was and asked if I would please come to Old Fairhaven to assist him. Of course I agreed, even though I was well aware of the emotional risk I was taking. Just to be a part of his life meant something to me. It still does.

But my pain is inexpressible when I think of my own ability to bear children and the futility of the situation in which I find myself. Yet I must live with the consequences of my choice—for now, at least."

During the evening, I had tried to avoid looking at Laura as she shared her very personal feelings. By keeping my eyes mostly on my notebook, I hoped to hide my discomfort. Hard-rock miners and road construction crews don't share feelings in this manner, and my mother had never openly shared her relationship with my father. So I wasn't accustomed to this kind of exposure of personal feelings from anyone, especially a woman. But then I was thinking I might have to get used to it if I were to ever become involved in "humanitarian matters," as I imagined them to be at the time. This very thought made me realize that I was seriously entertaining the prospect of being an assistant to Shackleton—and that was a bit disturbing.

I yanked my attention back to Laura as she resumed her tale.

"One day he took a ferry to the islands and disappeared. I guess you don't know about his houseman and chauffeur—Bones. His real name is Benjamin Judd, but he prefers to be called Bones. Shackleton rescued him from a severe beating several years ago. After bringing him home and restoring his health, he appointed him manager of all things domestic. Bones and his wife, Phoebe, live upstairs in their own wing of the house. They are more vital than ever now.

"Anyway, on this particular morning Shackleton asked Bones to pack a small travel bag for him and drive him to the ferry terminal at Anacortes. Bones actually saw him board the vessel bound for the San Juan Islands. He went aboard as a foot passenger, carrying his single piece of luggage. He didn't tell Bones where he was staying or when to expect him back. This was unusual. Shackleton often drove himself. He liked his independence. On the rare occasions when he had Bones drive him someplace, or even when he and Rose had been driven together, Bones was asked to either wait or return at a specific time. But this time he put his hand on Bones's shoulder as he left the car and said that he would be calling him and not to worry.

"We have unlisted phones, but Bones knows my number. On the fourth day after Shackleton's departure, Bones called to tell me what had happened. He was getting worried. Actually I was wondering myself why I hadn't received any calls or requests from Shackleton. His strangely altered daily routines and work patterns had been troubling to both Bones and Phoebe, although understandable. In some ways he had become a recluse in his own home. But being concerned about him made them more noticing of his unpredictable behaviors, and this last episode had rung an alarm for them.

"So Bones filled me in and asked what I thought he should do, if anything. I told him to wait another day and I would offer suggestions. Truthfully, I had no idea about what action to take, and I was becoming very uneasy as I thought about Rose's own disappearance. Then I was thinking that if one of us reported him missing, he would most likely turn up only to be annoyed at our believing him incapable and yet even more irritated that we had attracted the attention of the police. He abhors being the object of attention in any manner.

"On the fifth day I was quite distressed and, finding no peace and little with which to occupy myself, I told Bones and Phoebe that I was going away to consult my family about the matter. I asked them to keep as busy as possible doing whatever useful thing they could find to do and to be patient until my return.

"The thought of having both Shackleton and myself away was especially disquieting to Phoebe, since she had adored Rose and was crushed on learning that she had vanished without trace or explanation. Of course, with Shackleton's prolonged absence, their devotion to him brought great anxiety to both Bones and Phoebe. It was Bones who later gave Shackleton his dog Bogart as a companion, and he has proven to be the best gift possible. Before I left I gave Bones my parents' phone number in case he'd have anything to report. This provided some comfort for all of us.

"I then took the train to Portland, where my mother met me. From there we drove to our home near McMinnville, where I spent three days jumping every time the phone rang. I tried to distract my mind with family conversations. But much of our talk was about everything from strategies for reporting Shackleton missing to ways I might conduct my own search for him. I finally decided that I would personally begin my own search by questioning Washington State Ferry employees as I took a tour through the San Juan Islands with his photograph. This really didn't seem so desperate an idea at the time, but it now seems foolish on reflection.

"On the twelfth day, when I returned, I found Bones and Phoebe beside themselves with worry. They were at the point of not being able to eat properly. I asked Phoebe to prepare a simple meal for the three of us and promised to spend the evening with them—and the night if necessary—keeping busy at watching TV or playing board games until we couldn't stay awake any longer. I said that we should not discuss Shackleton or even mention his name and that I planned to begin my own personal search in the morning. If that led nowhere, then I would notify the police. But they knew as well as you and I know, Kep, that beginning a search so late after a person has disappeared leaves little to go on and little hope for success, even for skilled authorities.

"It was a very stormy night such as this one. We had been playing Scrabble when suddenly the lights went out. There had been no lightning or thunder. Without warning we were in total darkness. Strangely, a bluish-white light came through the blinds *after* the blackout. Then the light became orange, then brilliantly white. After that the house lights came on again. We could hear the rain striking the skylight in the Judds' kitchen, but that was all the sound there was.

"Shortly after that Shackleton came stumbling and feeling his way up the stairs. It must have been about eleven thirty. At first we were overjoyed, but then we became dismayed on discovering that he obviously couldn't see. He was groping about so unsteadily that he almost appeared to be drunk, although we knew he never touched alcohol.

"Shackleton was surprised to find all three of us there as he felt for our hands and heard our voices. He looked wonderfully restored and healthy. In spite of his inability to see, he was smiling at us, and his eyes shone as though he *could* see. I wondered at this, but I naturally felt great anguish over his loss of sight. When we asked then what had happened, he merely shook his head and held his hand out, palm down, signifying that he couldn't talk about it. And he still won't talk about it, no matter how we approach him with the subject. He simply shakes his head without a word and smiles to put us off. I wonder about his blindness constantly. It brings me great sorrow to see him so. And yet he doesn't seem to be in the least distressed over it. He just accepts it.

"There are several things about his reappearance that have come to puzzle me since then. I was too excited at the time to fully realize the bizarre aspects of his return that night, but there are certain details that may be worth your noting, should you care to write them, Kep . . ."

Laura paused. My eyes had been intent upon hers as she spoke, but now she regarded me curiously. I suddenly realized that my hands had been still, that I was no longer scribbling fragments of words on paper.

"Oh. Sure," I said. "I'm sorry, Laura, but I really am being attentive, in case you've wondered."

"Oh, I think you're a marvelously attentive listener, Kep. I'm sure that this trait of yours, together with your easy receptive manner, will influence people to open up and share things they're unlikely to disclose to others. It's been so with me tonight—obviously. I'm sure Shackleton has a need for these qualities in his assistant."

Her smile came relaxed and easy, and it felt good to sit there and hear her flattering words at that late hour in spite of everything else. Regardless, I truly was absorbed.

"Four things stand out as being unusual at that time, Kep. The first is that Shackleton was absolutely dry when he came to us. His hands and clothing weren't the least bit damp when I touched him. His hair and face appeared to be perfectly dry. He had no rainwear or umbrella. But the rain was pouring down that night, just as it is now!

"The second is that he came up from the lower house, not through the main entrance as he would have done had he come home by cab. The main entrance is located at the upper level where the wings split off, separating the Judds' quarters from the rest of the house. It provides access to both wings. Shackleton's driveway and garage are located at the upper level, approached by a private road that passes through dense woods. This road is only accessible through a gated entry off Charleston Street. As you must know, there's no space for cabs to turn around in the lane below. They're always directed to the gated entry. He didn't take a cab. I'm certain of that."

Laura fell silent. I looked up at her. She was waiting for a response, but I was intent on trying to quash some unsettling thoughts. I deliberately stepped off her path.

"That upper approach sounds neat, Laura. But, you know, I really like Evening Star Lane. I don't see that it matters that it's so narrow. And Shackleton's home appeals to me, especially because it's situated at the end of the lane, where it affords a great view of everything to the west, including the bay. There's a lot to like about it."

"One thing you may not know about the house, Kep, is that it has four levels. The lowest—the studio level—has a hidden entry on the west side. It's hidden from the lane by a high, gated board fence, and you can't see it from the west because of thickly planted shrubbery. It opens onto a very small enclosed courtyard. The entry door has a latch that can only be opened with a key.

"No one except Shackleton and me—not even the Judds—has access to that part of the lowest level just behind the studio and workshop. It's kept locked at every point inside and out. I'm an exception to the exclusion because . . . well, I can't say why.

"There are two routes from there to the upper levels. One is a closed-off stairway and the other is a hidden elevator. As I've given it much thought, I feel certain that Shackleton used that hidden entry, although doing so doesn't explain how he avoided getting wet.

"Bones says he found Shackleton's main key ring in the small luggage piece that he emptied out later. The key to the hidden entry was never kept on that ring. Shackleton always keeps this special key separate—usually in his pocket.

"Which brings me to the third puzzling thing. Phoebe told me that none of Shackleton's clothing appeared to have been worn, or refolded as it might have been after a laundering. Everything was just as Bones had packed it."

"And the fourth?" I asked, glancing at my watch (10:56).

"I'm going to have to let you go, I know. But, for your notes, the fourth outstanding thing about his reappearance is what occurred over the days that followed. He became aloof and kept much more to himself. He seemed to be intensely absorbed with something—something obsessive. He remained friendly to us, maybe more so. And he retained his former good humor. But then his habits and routines changed. They became totally unpredictable. I'm sure this wasn't all a result of his blindness.

"Then no matter how we pressed him, he refused to see an ophthalmologist. Even to this day he still hasn't seen one. Along with that, Bones and I urged him to get a trained guide dog, but he refused. It was for that reason that Bones later decided to find a companion puppy that Shackleton couldn't refuse, and he went to a lot of trouble looking for just the right dog. Bogart has been a tremendous blessing, one that exceeds any gift of therapy we could have imagined. He seems to have an uncanny sense of what Shackleton wants and where he intends to go. So he has shown himself to be a natural guide dog. And as a result of his accepting some dependence on Bogart, Shackleton has improved in many ways.

"What is most difficult about the new man is his being so secretive. Not only does he refuse to explain the cause of his blindness, but he disappears at odd times and is gone for hours. On those occasions he doesn't tell anyone where he's going or when he intends to come back. And at those times he doesn't take Bogart along, which is most perplexing because we can't imagine how he possibly gets about. He simply vanishes. Oddly, Bogart doesn't seem to mind when that happens. But other times, such as when Bones drives Shackleton somewhere on a special errand without him, Bogart tucks his tail down and sulks on his bed.

"Shackleton seems to be in the best of health now, and he has great enthusiasm for his private quests—the ones in which he involves me. I do have to say that he has disclosed some secret things to me that I can't share with you at this time. But maybe that won't always be the case. Maybe he'll share them with you even sooner than he did with me. Still, I don't suppose that will ever happen if you fail your mission tonight. But I feel certain you won't, Kep."

Laura smiled at me warmly. During the past hour and forty-five minutes, she had shared much about Shackleton—and about herself. It seemed that she had dismantled the exterior reserve that she had presented to me at first. I felt she was easy to be with and much easier to "read." I had enjoyed being with her and listening to her.

We both knew the time had come. I heaved a sigh, got up from the table, and put my notebook inside my shirt.

"Thanks, Laura. Is there anything else you'd like to share with me—like where I'm to go and what I'm to look for and how I'm to get inside and . . ?"

She laughed for the first time that night. Then she held out the little brown envelope for me, which I took.

"Keys," she said. "One for the office door upstairs and one for a filing cabinet. The cabinet you'll want is the last one on the far right as you face several just like it behind a large desk. There's a skylight over it . . . which reminds me—on a night like this you'll need a flashlight."

She went to a kitchen counter drawer and pulled out a small pocket-size light. After testing it, she handed it to me.

"Don't let any light show through the windows. The box you want is at the very back of the bottom drawer behind some file folders. It's the only box there. Please don't try to open it. Your assignment is to bring it to me as soon as possible without being seen. It's not possible for me to get it myself, but I can't tell you why. Again, you'll just have to trust me, Kep.

"There's an outside stairway alongside the warehouse building that leads up to the office door. When you get inside, immediately relock the deadbolt by hand. After you have the box, close that drawer, then open the top drawer and put the keys inside it at the front of the files. Shut the top drawer and push the lock button to secure the cabinet. There are other keys."

"What about fingerprints?" I asked. "Don't professional thieves wear gloves?"

She folded her arms and shook her head, smiling. Then she led me through her kitchen backdoor to an enclosed upstairs porch. Here she rummaged around inside a utility closet and pulled out a pair of rubber cleaning gloves.

Dangling them in front of me, she said, "Are you sure you aren't experienced at this sort of thing?"

Then her voice took on a serious tone as she said, "There is one thing about this assignment that I can't stress strongly enough, Kep. And I need your solemn word that you won't fail on this point."

"Laura, I think you know by now that I'm fully committed to doing what Shackleton wants done per your instructions. You have my word. And that's because I feel that I can trust you. After listening to all you've shared and confided in me tonight, I find that an easy thing to do—to trust you. It's probably because I don't want to disappoint you that I've come to be so willing to do what is being asked of me. I really don't know what to think of Shackleton yet. But I'm about to find out what I can, and I'll be glad when this debt is settled."

"Kep, the critical thing for you to remember, and what you are to pledge to, is that under *no* circumstances—tonight or in the future—are you ever to connect Shackleton with what you do for him. His name must never be revealed, no matter what happens. There is an exception, which is that you may associate his name with your mission if and when he specifically grants you permission to do so."

I nodded my agreement and said, "Will you be waiting up for me? If I suspect that I've been seen, I may have to delay or reroute my return."

"I'll be waiting, Kep. The warehouse is below Tenth Street. Just drive up Harris to Tenth, then go left to the nine-hundred block and look for a gravel lane heading down toward the bay. There is no number or mailbox to go by, but there's no other lane. You'll have to cross the railroad tracks after a couple of bends. It's the only building at the end of the road and it's quite large.

"Since you'll be locking the office entry door from the inside, you will take another way out. Go to the back of the office and you'll find two doors. One leads into a restroom, and the other opens onto an inside stairway that descends to the lower warehouse area. At the bottom of the stairs you'll find two more doors. One leads to the main storage area toward the front of the building, and the other gives access to the rear, where Shackleton keeps his seaplane. Both areas have exit doors that can be opened only from the inside of the building. Whichever one you take will get you back out, and no alarm will ring. Just be sure the exit door is securely shut when you leave."

"Got it," I said.

She handed me my poncho and we went to her front door, where she turned to face me. "Any questions?" she asked.

"Plenty," I said. "But I don't dare ask them. It's like swatting hornets: kill one, and forty come to the funeral."

She smiled, opened the door, and held out her hand. This time she put her other hand on top of mine as we shook. Her eyes spoke her confidence in me. As I turned to leave, I noticed a picture of Christ on the wall beside the door. He was pictured with his head covered, looking away. To the side there were some words about making a choice, which I didn't take time to read.

I smiled back at Laura as she closed the door behind me. Pulling my poncho over my head and clutching the gloves and flashlight, I went down the stairs wondering what her life would have been like if Shackleton had not chosen to land his plane on the lake that day, or if he had chosen Laura to be his bride instead of Rose, or if Laura had not chosen to be his assistant, or . . .Well, "what-ifs" could go on forever. But there was one thing that had become clear to me. Individual choices make ripples that affect other people's lives and options. And here I was, doing something that I would never have chosen to do twelve hours earlier. I wondered how other people's lives might be changed or influenced by what I was about to do. I could in no way guess what the consequences would be, let alone anticipate the immediate outcome of my actions. I only knew that I felt apprehensive and couldn't define a reason. It seemed almost an assumption on the parts of both Shackleton and Laura that I would become Shackleton's assistant, whatever that entailed. I was beginning to have doubts again about my having any control of my life.

Was I just reacting to other people's choices? I could still choose to drive the bus home and forget the whole thing. In fact, it was tempting once I got outdoors into the damp and dark. But my mind wouldn't let go of Laura's words or her eyes as I parted. And I couldn't take back my commitment. Somewhere during the evening I had made an irretrievable big choice by making a series of small ones. Whether it would be a good or a bad one remained to be seen. The little ones all seemed to be okay at the time. So why was I so anxious?

CHAPTER 6

THE bus was still there, waiting. No choice. The wind had died down for the moment, and the rain had become a steady drizzle. As I pulled away from the curb, I noticed that the windshield wipers weren't very effective. The headlights weren't doing all that great a job either, but I laid the blame on the atmosphere, not the bus—just to be fair. Actually, I had never needed to drive the old bus in the dark during a rainstorm before this night. We had been mostly daylight companions during the three weeks I'd been making deliveries.

Finding the nine-hundred block in the misty rain and darkness called for my getting out and pointing Laura's little flashlight at house numbers a couple of times. Then, since I could find no other people out and about on similar errands at that hour, I crossed over into the oncoming-traffic lane to see where the graveled access road took off toward the bay on my left. Once I got onto that road, the headlights seemed brighter due to the light-colored gravel.

Everything about the drive was just as Laura had described it, and not long after I crossed the train tracks, the big warehouse thrust itself at me through the fog-like drizzle. I decided to hide the bus behind a tall, dense growth of firs, where it couldn't be spotted from someone's upper-story window. After all, it was painted bright yellow to attract attention.

The wind came back and the rain began again with greater

force just as I turned off the headlights. So I sat in total darkness listening to the heavy pelting on the VW roof. I waited for it to ease up. It didn't. There was no longer the faintest glow of light from the street above, and if there were any security lights around the building, they were either turned off or burned out.

The flashlight proved to be vital. I used it to locate the stairs at the right side of the building. Then I used it to find the keyhole of the office door at the top landing. I hadn't forgotten what Laura had said about not letting the light be seen, but if I couldn't see the stairway in front of me without the flashlight, how could anyone see its light from the street two blocks away and above me? Or so I thought.

On entering the office, I did as Laura had directed and reset the deadbolt. A single large desk bearing filing baskets, a phone, and a computer monitor stood within ten feet of me. Everything about it looked tidy. Behind the desk, against a partition, I counted six four-drawer filing cabinets, some with catalogs and folders stacked on top. At the far right, the cabinet I wanted had nothing piled on it, but there was a big skylight over it where the roof sloped down toward the side wall. The office space was filled with the noise of rain spattering hard against the skylight glass.

Moving quickly, I passed around the desk, inserted the small cabinet key into the lock button, twisted it, and yanked the top drawer slightly open. When I dropped to the floor to open the bottom drawer, I noticed that the flashlight was starting to grow dim. Sticking it between my teeth, I used both hands on the box at the back. It wasn't a metal box and it wasn't heavy, but it spanned the width of the drawer, which made it awkward to grasp. When I got a fingertip grip, I lifted the box out over the few folders and stood up to place it on top of the cabinet. As I did so, the flashlight dropped from my teeth and went out.

Luckily, it fell onto some file folders in the opened bottom drawer, and I was able to find it by feel. But when I slapped it against my palm, it would only put forth an orange glow. To spare what little power was left for finding my way out, I turned it off, shoved it into my pocket under my poncho, and felt my way through the rest of my task. Closing the bottom drawer with a foot, I opened the top drawer and placed the ring of two keys in the space ahead of its folders by touch.

Working blind as I was, my mind flitted to Shackleton, and I experienced a momentary sympathy for him, along with a feeling of gratitude for my own sight. A flash of memory took me back to a time when I was working alone in a drift of my uncle's gold mine and my carbide lamp went out. I hadn't panicked then, and I kept my cool during these moments. But I couldn't shake an intense foreboding of some impending trauma, together with a sense of some nearby extraordinary presence.

Troubled that I couldn't account for such weird feelings, I felt compelled to leave at once. (Not that I was driven by panic—just urgency.) Then, just as I pressed the cabinet lock button and reached for the box, my private little world became literally "alien."

An extremely bright light filled the skylight. At first it was an electric blue-white, and then it transformed into a deep orange. No sound came at first, but soon I could detect an undulant, humming frequency that rose and fell above the sound of the rain. Then the rain stopped striking the skylight as though it had been shut off.

Suddenly a greenish beam of laser-like light shot down through the skylight. Actually, it looked as though it *slid* down. I was lifted up off the floor by it—suspended and paralyzed inches in the air. Although my mind fully comprehended all that was taking place, I was powerless to speak or to move. I felt no pain or fear, just complete detachment and immobility. The beam held me levitated in a vertical position.

Next, I was aware of two human-like forms approaching me from out of the room's darkness. Strangely enough (in my particular case), they somehow emanated good feeling rather than intent to do harm. I felt nothing as one of them inserted a small instrument deep inside my nostril and extracted a tiny spherical object from a point between my eyes. (More about this later.) This was deposited into a bright container held by the other person. I have to say "person" because they both seemed definitely human in appearance and form.

They wore shiny uniform-like garments unlike anything I'd ever seen. Except for metallic-appearing headbands, their heads and hands were uncovered. Each of their faces looked at once both old *and* young. Still, their features were pleasant, reflecting intelligence and wisdom, and their hair fell nearly to their shoulders. I couldn't distinguish gender, but I sensed that one was male and the other was female. Their mannerisms and movements differed noticeably.

The paralyzing beam had no effect on either of them as they worked on me. One of them reached for my right hand and placed it against my head while the other held out something like a slender rod and briefly waved it over me. They did nothing to my left hand. Next, they withdrew a couple of steps out of the beam, smiled, and gestured good-bye. Not a word had been spoken.

As they disappeared into the surrounding darkness, the greenish beam seemed to be sucked up through the skylight, and I fell to the floor in a stupor. I have no idea how long I lay there until my senses returned, but I can vividly remember each detail of the event. (No notes needed!) At first I was in a state of alternating shock and denial as I struggled to accept the experience as being real. I have since gone through a change in my *perception* of reality.

Although my mind and memory were sharp enough, my body felt depleted of energy. A lengthy time passed before I could move my arms and legs. My head hurt. I fell several times as I worked my way to the back of the office in search of the door to the inside stairway.

The flashlight was strangely brighter now, and I held it with my left hand while I clutched the box under my poncho with my right arm. When I at last reached the two doors at the bottom of the stairs, I chose to go into the seaplane hangar. Here I was surprised to find that Shackleton's plane was held suspended in slings from a traveling crane on the ceiling, much like those used to pull boats up into dry dock. My light couldn't reveal much, but I found the twin-engine plane to be a beauty, one that I could readily identify with Shackleton—the younger Shackleton that Laura had described earlier in the evening.

Again holding the flashlight with my teeth, I looked at my watch. It was dead.

The exit door was easy to find. Before opening it, I pulled the box up under my poncho and prepared for the rain I could now hear pouring down outdoors. It was then that I discovered that I had left Laura's gloves somewhere upstairs. I couldn't remember taking them off. Maybe the aliens had removed them while I was immobilized. This was mighty unsettling. What to do? Numbed by the realization, I was torn between my options. It was quite some time before I chose to go back for them. I just couldn't bear the thought of implicating Laura in my actions.

Luckily the flashlight held up. But I considered it my greater good fortune to have the ability to climb the stairs in my weakened state. I still held the box close beneath my poncho as I searched for the gloves. To my great relief I found them on the office floor next to the wall under the skylight.

Giving the file cabinet a last look, I discovered that the top file drawer was not fully closed. Using a glove, I pressed it until it clicked shut. It was then I realized that I had opened the doors between the office area and the hangar with my bare hands. I had left my fingerprints after all! What an inept thief.

I had a saving thought, and that was to go to the restroom, put soap and water on a glove, and wipe the doorknobs clean on my way out. I stuffed one of the gloves in my pocket underneath the poncho and entered the little room by pushing the door open with my elbow. Since there was no window, I closed the door and turned on the light, using my elbow again. As I wet and soaped the glove with my free hand, the tactic struck me as being both ridiculous and necessary, but concentrating on this act kept my mind focused and diverted from defeating thoughts.

Glancing in the mirror, I saw that there was quite a lot of dried blood on my upper lip and chin. I stopped myself from rinsing it off by thinking ahead about the possibility of leaving other telltale evidence behind. Blood was as bad as fingerprints.

Wiping doorknobs as I went, I retraced my way back down into the hangar. When I reached the exit door, I rechecked to see that I had everything: gloves, flashlight, box—and a remaining trace of my wits.

Hoisting the box up higher under my poncho, I bumped the exit latch-bar with my back and practically fell outdoors. The only sound was that of water dripping from the eaves, trees, and foliage. I gave the door a final closing bump and sloshed my way through the dark toward the bus while breathing deeply of the damp, salty air. I began to feel some of my strength return. What a day this had been! Needless to say, being Shackleton's assistant didn't hold much appeal for me just then.

Thankful for the little pocket light, I turned it on and pointed it straight down as much as possible. When I got near the bus, I was startled by a bright beam of light thrown on me. Only this time it stabbed out at me from a sheriff's patrol car parked right behind the bus.

A voice from behind the light loudly commanded me to stop and put my hands over my head. I nearly collapsed in fright. As I raised my hands, the box slid out from under my poncho, struck my knee as I tried to slow it, and flipped upside down in the mud.

Two law-enforcement officers, a uniformed deputy and a detective, approached me. I was handcuffed. The detective did a splendid job of reciting the Miranda rule for me and asked the deputy to pick up the box. When I was asked what it contained, I said I didn't know. When I was asked what I was doing there, I was tempted to respond with "I don't know" but thought better of it.

"I came to get this box for a friend," I said.

"At two thirty in the morning?" the detective said. "What is the name of your friend?"

"Did you just say I could remain silent?" I asked. "I guess I'll have to remain silent on that one." (I couldn't believe it was two thirty.)

"You can do that and still nod an answer to my next question, if you will. Is that your vehicle?" He flashed his light on the very yellow bus.

I nodded yes—then quickly shook my head no.

"Move over next to the patrol car, please," the detective said curtly.

Just as I took my first steps around the box, the deputy reached down, picked it up, and turned it over to wipe the mud from its lid. As he turned it right-side up, the lid popped open and I was flabbergasted to see that it was the same leather box that Shackleton used to keep his cash in custody. Either that or it was one just like it. All that time I had been lugging it around in the dark, I had been too involved to become curious, and I had kept it covered with my poncho.

I could now see in the deputy's light that it was stuffed with banded bills. This time the detective put his hand on my arm and led me briskly to the patrol car.

Numbed with confusion, I could see only one thing clearly. That leather cash box had marked both the beginning and the ending of my first day in Shackleton's world, and I had serious doubts about wanting to stay in it.

CHAPTER 7

DETECTIVE Graham Walker was, I could tell, not a man to treat with any degree of disrespect. He wore neatly pressed pants (despite having sat buckled up in a patrol car on a soggy night), and he meticulously folded his suit coat and raingear over the backs of two chairs before arranging himself slowly and with deliberation in a chair opposite me. A blue-and-gray tie was secured squarely in the center of his white shirt. From a pocket situated behind dressy (but conservative) suspenders, he drew forth a pen and laid it on the table between us. Reaching inside his suit coat, he pulled out a much-used note pad and placed it beside the pen. Then he aimed his penetrating brown eyes directly at mine and waited. We were alone.

Somehow I managed to withstand his expectant gaze, mostly because it held no hint of an attempt to intimidate. But then, I had already spent some hours trying to disentangle myself from mixed emotions ranging from astonishment and puzzlement to outrage and dejection. These had been intertwined and sprinkled with feelings of frustration, betrayal, resentment, and self-pity (unfortunately). At the last I had arrived at a state of stoical resolve, having determined to uphold my pledge and sustain my personal integrity despite all odds. I had clearly made a choice.

Maintaining a semblance of dignity was not so easy, considering that I sat in wrinkled clothes and was disheveled, mud-spattered, and bloody faced—in abject contrast to Detective Walker.

"You will preclude a great deal of trouble for yourself by cooperating," he began. "You can start by giving your correct address. We have your name, Mr. Stone." He picked up his pen and opened his notebook.

"I'm not sure I want to tell you. I stay with new friends. I respect them, but they don't know much about me. I know they would be really disappointed if they learned that I've been arrested. They wouldn't understand the reason, and I have to say that you wouldn't understand it either if I could explain it—which I can't. I really don't understand it myself."

"The reason you're here, Mr. Stone, is that you're being held on suspicion of larceny. That is a serious charge for which you will be held accountable, should the offended parties so choose. It is not beyond our skill to ascertain the names of the owners of the warehouse you were seen leaving. By all appearances, particularly under the circumstances surrounding your trespass and attempted departure with many thousands of dollars, we have sufficient reason to obtain all the facts needed for prosecution if necessary. Your identity was obtained from your driver license. Do you still reside in Colorado?"

"No sir." (I was hoping that humility and deference toward an authority might prove helpful. Things were looking worse by the minute.)

"You're driving a vehicle registered in Washington State. It is registered under the name of Bickford Tidwash, who resides in Burlington. Is this the friend whose name you declined to reveal in connection with your stated purpose for being at the warehouse?"

"No sir. He's my . . ."

I stopped short, realizing that I couldn't bear to let either Bick or Dozie know of my activities or involvements of the previous night. When I was told earlier that I could make a phone call, I had run into this dilemma. I couldn't call Shackleton. I had pledged not to connect myself with him. Laura's unlisted phone number was on a note I'd left at the Whipples'. And even though I had permission to enjoy personal use of the VW bus, I couldn't see Bick accepting my night's errand as being one of "personal enjoyment."

"The vehicle has been impounded awaiting owner notification, Mr. Stone. Mr. Tidwash may prove to be more informative than you. I'm certain that he will. I hope you can see that we will learn all that is necessary with or without your cooperation. I must remind you again that you will save yourself much trouble by cooperating. This means answering questions truthfully. Hedging or stalling will gain you nothing. By giving direct answers that may serve to explain your position, you may avoid a police record, at best, should you be innocent of any wrongdoing. Quite frankly, considering the evidence and circumstances surrounding you at the moment, I believe you will need an attorney."

I slumped back in the chair and turned up my palms on the table. It was a black moment. I couldn't think of anything to say that might help. Anything I could think to say would ultimately lead to my association with Shackleton while leaving me disgraced in the eyes of my friends. The only way to keep my friends out of it would be to point a finger directly at Shackleton—or to Laura, which at that moment I felt would be worse. I must admit, though, that deep down I was aware of some very unsettling suspicions regarding my purposely being made a victim of the alien experience.

Regardless, on the surface my view was that I had failed Laura and had failed my mission. And it seemed inevitable that all would be known eventually. Still, I had made a choice and had resolved to keep it. Knowing that I wasn't just reacting to other people's choices felt good. Silence felt good.

Detective Walker sat motionless, eyes fixed upon me, reading the resolve on my face. After satisfying himself that I wasn't going to open my mouth, he calmly stood up, returned his notebook and pen to their appointed places, and gathered up his clothing. As he approached the locked interrogation-room door, a deputy came to let him out. Before leaving, he turned to face me.

"Should you decide to talk, or if you need to use a restroom, you may signal to the station deputy, who will take a message or accompany you down the hall," he said. "In any case, you may be spending a considerable amount of time in this room. As you may have observed, the officers and deputies have been quite busy with processing other individuals arrested ahead of you this morning. I suggest that you use this time to carefully reflect on the gravity of the consequences of your behavior and insistence to remain silent."

I was alone. Through the door glass, I could see a wall clock. It read 5:43. Since entering the county sheriff's building, I had spent more than two and a half hours in the interrogation room, most of the time waiting alone. The cuffs had been removed, and I had placed the contents of my pockets in a large envelope, which the station deputy took away after getting my confirmation signature.

Apparently there had been several youths caught in drug trafficking. I hadn't been able to hear much of what went on except during the brief times the door had been opened. It was enough. And I really didn't need any more time to think about the "gravity" of my situation. At this point I was too tired to think clearly about anything, especially the events of the past eighteen hours.

Folding my arms on the table, I rested my head on them and closed my eyes. In a twilight state of exhaustion, my mind flitted over fragments of memories, especially those recently recaptured. I saw my mother's eyes. They had spoken to me at the last, telling me she would be leaving soon.

On the very day she died, her eyes had implored that I not go to work, that I remain at home with her. But I had been unwilling or unready to accept the message I read there. After giving her an encouraging hug and a kiss, I went to work, only to be informed soon after that she had passed on. One of the few women who could briefly look to her needs in my absence had found her dead when she came to bathe her. My choosing to ignore her last appeal had magnified my sorrow.

But in happy contrast, memories took me again to those countless times when her eyes spoke her delight as I read to her from magazines and books I had brought home to elevate her spirit. The magic of words had transported her from the imprisonment of paralysis to realms of boundless freedom, where she had experienced adventure, romance, mystery, and humor, as well as unlimited pursuits of knowledge and wisdom.

And there had always been those certain scriptures that she treasured—the faith-promoting, hope-filled, and comforting verses that would carry her through the oncoming shadows of nightfall. But for me, unfortunately, the contemplation of these had fostered many seemingly unanswerable questions, and so I had set them aside in favor of pragmatism (which wasn't serving me so well in my present dilemma).

There was also the memory of my high school graduation ceremony, at which I was given, prematurely and unearned, a signed diploma in spite of my having missed many end-of-year school days due to illness resulting from little sleep. A benevolent school board, considering my place in a class of thirteen graduates and believing in my demonstrated determination to complete the required course work, had arranged for me to receive the diploma on a condition. The condition was that I undertake post-graduation sessions with certain dedicated teachers who would assign and evaluate my missed work over a period of two weeks. This was done partly out of kindness and consideration toward my mother in view of her poor condition, and to preclude her being disappointed at graduation time, since I had kept my deficiencies secret from her.

Her eyes had shone with parental pride as she sat in her wheelchair that graduation evening. Of course, I fulfilled the requirements and earned the diploma as expected. I was also granted a scholarship, which I was unable to take advantage of, since it meant moving away. But the integrity that I had earned then meant more to me than the papers representing my achievement.

Now, in my confinement and facing the bleak prospects before me, I felt that my shameful aspect was too much to accept. Deserved or not, I must live with the consequences of my recent choices. But were they really made with wrongful intent? On reflection I couldn't see where I had messed up. I felt bewildered and bitter. And bitterness led to questions. Where was my mother's God in all this? What had been so wrong about my trying to honorably fulfill an obligation thrust upon me that I should find myself arrested and brought to this shameful condition? What meaning could be taken from good intentions rewarded with suffering and degradation?

These questions then led me into a defeating mental rut that I had fallen into many times before. If there was a god—a benevolent and loving god—why had he caused my good mother to suffer widowhood and multiple strokes and an untimely death? Or, at the least, why had he allowed it? She didn't deserve any of it.

Presently, a host of insidious questions began to surface as I rested my head—questions that I had suppressed because of their immensity in relation to my capacity to deal with them. Where did these alien beings come from? If Adam was the first man, as Genesis states, what could their relationship possibly be to the people of Earth? I felt certain that the alien beings imposing their will upon me were human species, not weird extraterrestrial creatures. And what could they possibly have been doing with me? What purpose could I serve? Was I some peculiar specimen being examined, recorded, and tracked? If I was on a lower scale of development with respect to them, where was this incident supposed to lead me?

But the most perplexing and troubling questions centered on my belief that Shackleton had contrived the staging of the warehouse event. He surely must have had a hand in it. The timing and setting had to have been pre-arranged. I felt certain of this. It seemed so obvious. Why else would I have been detained until after 11:00 o'clock?

This led me to a prime question: How could he be linked in any manner with alien beings? Other questions brought both pain and confusion: How much did Laura know of the magnitude of this event? Did she really know what I was getting into? If so, had she been false with me?

But now I was thinking again, and I wasn't in any condition to think. And I couldn't imagine anything but disappointment in either my mother's eyes or in the eyes of my new friends and "family" members. To steer my mind onto a less depressing track, I began contemplating the luxury of retreating into some comfortable warm bed, as unlikely as that could be. (Jail cots didn't conform to what I had in mind.)

Suddenly my head was brought up by the sounds of a door being unlocked and opened. Detective Walker came toward me with the large brown envelope that held my wallet and personal items.

"Well, Mr. Stone, it is my privilege to inform you that you have been exonerated," he said as he tossed the envelope on the table. "Not only has the owner of the warehouse verified your honesty, but he has gone to the trouble of sending a car for you, since retrieval of your employer's vehicle will be delayed a few hours."

I swayed as I stood gripping the edge of the table for support. Words failed me. My eyes blurred and my tongue stuck to my palate.

"If you will follow me, there is one matter of formality necessary for your release. Your signature is required to confirm receipt of your personal belongings and to exempt the sheriff's department from any liability in connection with your being held here under suspicion of having committed a crime. You may, of course, seek legal counsel and contest your detention, but that would delay your release. Is it your wish to contest your having been detained?"

"No sir," I managed to croak.

The clock said 6:07. As we passed by it, I spotted a drinking fountain underneath. "May I stop for a drink of water?" I asked.

"Certainly. There is coffee on a stand on the other side of the deputy's desk. You might find a donut left, which you're welcome to take if you wish." (At that moment I hungered only for freedom.)

I read in Detective Walker's eyes a distinct look of approval as I raised my head from the drinking fountain. This puzzled me, considering the formal reserve in his manner during our previous time together.

After emptying and checking the contents of the envelope, I signed the release form and turned toward the entry door. As I did so, Detective Walker pointed to a short hallway.

"You'll find a restroom, second door on the right, if you should want to clean up," he said.

He held his hand out toward me in a friendly gesture. I took his hand and we shook. He was a respectable and likeable man doing his job as it should be done, and I felt no offense or resentment. There should be more cops like him, I thought.

The guy staring back at me in the mirror looked awful. I hardly recognized myself. Tossing my stuff on the floor, I doused my head and washed my hands and face. Being cleaner helped, but it would take some food and a good sleep to make me feel presentable. I dreaded, again, having to meet up with Shackleton. I didn't feel ready for him, and I wanted time beforehand to write down a long list of questions to ask him. But that didn't seem possible. I felt as though I were going to meet a dragon without sword or armor.

As I came up the steps from the low building entry to street level, I was approached by a thin, diminutive African American. About five and a half feet in height, he was neatly dressed and wore, with dignity, an English-style woolen cap. He smiled broadly as he neared me and extended his hand in greeting. As he came closer, I could see that his face was covered with many scars and the top of his left ear was missing. This could be none other than Bones, I thought.

"Mr. Kephart?" he asked.

I nodded and shook his hand. Although he appeared to be frail, his bony fingers gripped with surprising strength.

"I'm Bones . . ."

"Yes, I thought—"

". . . Bones Judd, Mr. Kephart. Mr. Shackleton sent me to . . . to . . . fetch you to his place." He pointed and turned back up the street, hobbling as he went.

I learned later that his recurrent pauses in speech were thought to be the result of brain damage. They now seemed to be emotionally induced, particularly in the presence of strangers. The problem occurred less often in conversations with his wife.

"I had . . . had . . . to park away around the corner, but it ain't far to go. Oh my! Oh my, but that was . . . a . . . a terrible storm last night! I could-a-thought I was a 'gator a waitin' for ol' Noah to . . . come rescue me from out the bayou, with all that water dumpin' down! I couldn't sleep none at all. My Blossom, she couldn't sleep either, so we sat . . . sat watchin' TV a good while, but there . . . wasn't no news 'bout that weird nor'easter. It's a real strange thing they didn't get no . . . no rain right south of here, too, Mr. Kephart. Real strange."

"This doesn't happen here in May often?" I asked.

"Oh no! No. Not since ever . . . ever I've . . . I've been here, Mr. Kephart. Leastways not no . . . no storm so fast an' pow'rful."

"Bones, why don't you just call me Kep? That's what my

friends call me, if it's okay with you."

"Sure, Mr. Kep. That's real good. Good that you let . . . let me."

Around the corner of the building, a solitary, dark-maroon sedan was parked curbside. Its polished, showroom-like aspect was garish in the gray morning mist. Bones limped ahead of me, eager to usher me into the car's luxurious interior and close its doors against the unhappy environs I was leaving. He was, to me, immediately likeable. It was hard to imagine how men would become so incited to violence toward him that they would inflict such brutal wounds—those evinced by his less visible impairments, much less by his obvious scars. I wondered, too, how it was that Shackleton had managed to rescue him from what must have been a life-threatening situation.

Bones was a cautious driver, and he tended to go much slower than the speed limit. But eventually we were turning off Charleston Street and facing an electrically controlled iron gate at the entrance to Shackleton's wooded acreage. Bones pressed some buttons on a post-mounted call box outside his car window, and the heavy black gate swung back to admit us.

A paved drive wound through dense stands of evergreens interspersed with various low shrubs. Ferns grew along the margins of the drive. Alders, maples, and dogwoods appeared intermittently. The route was totally secluded, and it took longer than I expected before we came around the last bend to find the cleared, beautifully landscaped grounds that spread before the main upper structure of Shackleton's home. All this was a pleasant surprise to me. Only professional landscapers and gardeners could have produced the welcoming scene.

There was nothing elaborate about the house at this level. An attractive, simply constructed cedar railing stretched across a wide porch in front of the entry. This railing supported decorative flower boxes containing assorted colorful blooms—a welcome sight in the early dawn. A single adornment to the home was a heavy wooden entry door with a full-length oval of etched glass.

Simplicity and good taste would best describe the place overall.

On the west side a detached three-car garage was connected to the house by a breezeway. When Bones came to a stop in front of the garage, the home entry door opened and an attractive middle-aged Black woman stepped out onto the porch smiling a welcome for us. She wore a colorful cooking apron and waved a large pancake turner at us as we got out of the car.

"I started breakfast fixin's just as soon as I saw the gate light come on," she called out in a melodious voice. "It won't take long now, so you can just wash up and sit down."

Although Phoebe's hair was graying, she had a youthful enthusiasm and liveliness about her. She was fully more than twice the weight of Bones. However, I would best describe her body as having a "perfect plumpness," which enhanced her winsome character.

"Oh, Mr. Kep, this here woman is my Blossom," Bones said apologetically. "Now . . . now she's done beat . . . me to introducin' you, but she's a mighty good woman, 'spite of . . . of all she forgets."

As I passed through the open doorway, Phoebe took my poncho from my arm and the big brown envelope from my hand (it still contained Laura's flashlight and gloves), and then she gently steered me in the direction of their bathroom with her hand on my back.

"These things will be waitin' for you in the guest room," she said, shaking the envelope and poncho. "You just make yourself at home, Mr. Kephart Stone. Bones will take you to the table when you're done here. Do you like eggs scrambled? How do you like 'em cooked?"

"Oh, scrambled dry is fine, Phoebe."

"Well then, do you like pancakes or hash browns most? Bones likes his hash browns, but I've done fixed some batter for pancakes, too, so's you can have both if you want."

"Thanks, Phoebe. I'll try both. Will Shackleton be eating with us?"

"Oh, he's already done had his breakfast, Mr. Kephart. He most always eats in his study room now that Miss Rose is gone, God rest her soul. Oh, how I do miss her so! She was the sweetest lady ever I could have been help for, but she's gone now. Gone, I guess, for good now. An' the little child that was a comin' . . . he's . . ."

Phoebe pulled the poncho up to hide her face and turned away. I didn't know what to say as she stepped slowly down the hallway, her shoulders shaking as she went.

I was going to ask when Shackleton might be seeing me, but it didn't seem at all important just then.

In the back of my mind, I now realized that there had been a close relationship between Shackleton's wife and the Judds. It was almost as though Bones and Phoebe had comprised part of the family—or family to be. They apparently weren't regarded as "hired help" to be kept at a distance, emotionally speaking. And so I suspected that Shackleton himself would have had to be an extension of that relationship, sharing in personal vicissitudes all around. I imagined, though, that he would have restricted himself in his own personal disclosures, considering his secretive nature.

The formidable aspect of his character seemed, in this light, to be less a reality than something I had conjured up while dwelling on all those unanswered questions pertaining to yesterday's protracted events and disturbing experiences. Still, the extraterrestrials and his link to them had me deeply troubled and stumped.

As I again washed my face and hands, this time less hurriedly, I looked in the mirror for any traces of blood and was suddenly struck with the thought of my failed assignment. The box! What had become of the box? Bones hadn't mentioned it, and it had not been in the car. Walker had not said anything about it when

I left him. Because of my fatigue, and in my eagerness to escape my unhappy situation, I had completely forgotten about it. Here I was, about to be fed in Shackleton's home, with the prospect before me of accounting for my performance, and I had nothing to show for my efforts. I had both succeeded and failed.

Surely, though, Detective Walker must have discussed the circumstances of my detention with someone. And at that hour of the morning, it would have been unlikely that Walker could access county records to learn who owned the warehouse. The discussion would have been the result of an inquiry, or he wouldn't have told me that I had been exonerated for having made an honest statement. So a call must have come from Shackleton, or possibly Laura, when I didn't return within a reasonable time—or so went the reasoning of my tired brain.

As I left the bathroom, I found Bones waiting patiently in the hallway. On our way to the breakfast table, I decided not to mention the box to him. It was unlikely that he knew anything about it, much less the reason for my having to be picked up at the county sheriff's building so early in the morning. He could have guessed at any number of reasons, but judging from his gray hair and polite decorum, I supposed he knew how to be discreet and refrain from gratifying his curiosity.

Phoebe was in full control of her emotions when we reached their dinette, and I intuitively felt that she had learned well over the years how to mask many disappointments and hide many sorrows, despite her cheerful mien.

Sausages, eggs, pancakes, and potatoes were laid out on platters, together with bottles of three kinds of syrup, a butter tray, and a pitcher of orange juice. Each place setting included—besides cups, saucers, and silverware—a blue-and-white checkered cloth napkin and two drinking glasses, one empty and one filled with water.

"Mr. Shackleton likes best to have hot chocolate 'stead of coffee, Mr. Kephart, so I hope you don't mind, 'cause I've got a whole pot full of it here," Phoebe said as she came forth with the steaming container. I had thought I would be too tired to eat much of anything, but now, seating myself alongside Bones and inhaling the mixed aromas, I found my stomach to be wide awake.

"Now, Blossom, Mr. Kep says he likes to be Mr. Kep 'stead of Mr. Kephart . . . so you should know," Bones informed her gently. "An' we can fix coffee if . . . if he'd like that." He gave Phoebe a loving smile as he spoke, but his eyes came quickly back to the business of loading his plate. It was a pleasure to witness the complementary unity of the couple.

"Cocoa sounds just great, Phoebe," I said, "and I don't suppose anything could keep me from falling off into a deep sleep once I get around all this food. I'm going to thank you both now, before my eyelids drop.

"Oh, Mr. Kep, you'll be findin' a place . . . upstairs for to sleep as long as you like," Bones said. "Now, Mr. Shackleton says I should tell . . . tell you not to worry none. He's got his things to do, but you can ask . . . ask . . . your questions later, he says. Those were the words he said, Mr. Kep."

"Thanks, Bones," I replied.

I was wondering what to expect next, and I hadn't dared to hope for a chance to make up my list of questions. But now it seemed possible that I might after all. While we ate and talked, my mind jumped on to questions of how and where I could reconnect with the VW bus, and how I would explain my overnight absence to Oat and Selma, and how I was to get money to the pizza place, among other things. But the longer I ate, the less I cared much about anything except finding a place to lie down.

Phoebe saved me.

"Mr. Kephart—Mr. Kep, you're lookin' to drop your head on your plate," she said. "Bones can show you the way to that guest room so's you can rest up."

"Sure, I'll do that, Mr. Kep. You come with me now if . . . if you'd like." Bones slid his chair back and stood up.

He led me to the entryway at the start of their wing and then up carpeted stairs and down a broad hall, where we turned to face the first door we came to on the right. Before opening the door, Bones pointed down the hall.

"There's a bathroom with a tub . . . an' . . . an' shower at the end there, Mr. Kep, but . . . you've got a toilet an' sink in this room, too." He opened the door and showed me inside the bedroom. "There's all . . . all you need here, leastways till you're done restin', I'm thinkin', Mr. Kep, but you say if . . . if it ain't so."

He limped across the room to a doorway leading into a half bath beyond the bed and pushed the door open for me to see inside. "You just get comfortable now an' . . . an' no . . . nobody's goin' to bother you."

"Bones, I appreciate the kindness and hospitality you and Phoebe have shown me. Just let me know when I can do something in return, if that's possible, will you?"

He smiled his broad, crooked smile and said, "Sure, Mr. Kep. That's good you said that . . . to me. Real good."

When he had closed the door, I went to the window and looked out over Old Fairhaven and the bay extending beyond. The sun was climbing the sky now, highlighting patches of mist with a golden hue. From this height I could see Shackleton's warehouse in the distance at the water's edge. It appeared to be just a typical waterfront building, having no ominous aspect. Nothing about it spoke of the wild storm or of my disturbing experiences. The now-departed black night seemed more like a bad dream and less like a true event in my life.

Everything about the new day seemed normal as well. But inside of me a troubling cloud lowered itself and cast a dark shadow. I felt again as though I were not in control of my life, that in some sinister way I was being "set up" and prepared for—

for what? Maybe it was just my imagination—my tired brain producing distorted pictures and forming false perceptions as a result of emotional trauma.

Maybe.

CHAPTER 8

THE little finger of my right hand woke me up. Shackleton's "gift" ring was causing a fiery itch. As I reached with my left hand to pull it off, I was startled by the sound of Laura's voice. Wondering at the sound, I quickly rose up in bed to look around, only to become bewildered by my strange new surroundings. The tingling itch had stopped, and I was about to remove the ring when the voice came again.

"Leave the ring on, Kep." It was definitely Laura speaking. My head swiveled as my eyes searched the room.

"Where—where are you?" I exclaimed, frustrated at not seeing her.

Bright sunlight filled the guest room, shining through the open shades of the west window. Clearly, she was not in the room. Now she laughed somewhat girlishly (which was uncharacteristic of Laura). She seemed amused at my puzzlement and confusion. Her laughter was right in my ears, or so it sounded.

"My voice is in your head, Kep. We're communicating by brain wave impulses. You don't need to use your voice. It's your ring that makes it happen. It's called a 'stellar ring.' You may not have noticed it last night, but I have one too. It doesn't look like yours, but it allows your thoughts to come into my head just like mine are coming into yours."

My senses reeled as I tried to grasp the reality and significance of Laura's words—or thoughts. I was astonished, to say the least. Suddenly I felt that my privacy had been violated. Mentally, I felt openly exposed. To add to my discomfort, I became keenly aware that I was wearing only my shorts and socks, and I wasn't sure if she could *see* me as well.

"What else can the rings do?" I asked anxiously (and vocally). "Can you *see* me, too? I guess not, since I can't see you." (All the same, I instinctively pulled up the sheet and blanket as I spoke.)

"No, Kep. Our rings only send and receive our worded thoughts. They are capable of transmitting images, and more, but for now they are kept limited to word sounds and tones. I think you're still using your voice. Are you?"

"Yes. Yes, I guess I am," I said aloud.

"It will take some practice, but try to just think your words to me, Kep."

"Okay. I'm thinking. Do I have to think hard? Can you hear me?" (I thought these words to her rather strenuously.)

"Oh, you're coming through perfectly clear. You don't need to force your thoughts at me, Kep. Keeping your ring near your head helps the transfer both ways, though."

"Well, Laura, if the rings send only words, how come I can hear you when you laugh?"

"The rings transmit audible voice sounds as well as worded thoughts," she said. (Or should I say "she thought"?) "The technology can distinguish between all kinds of brain wave patterns and frequencies in the sender and then direct them to specific places in the receiver's brain. I guess every living being has its own body-energy frequency. We're all unique. We can each be identified by our distinctive vibrations."

"This is fantastic, Laura. It's incredible. But I don't think I like it at all. It takes away my privacy. I want to keep my thoughts just to myself. Why can't we just use a phone if we need to talk? Besides, I failed miserably last night, and I can't see how I could possibly qualify as Shackleton's assistant—doing whatever."

Thoughts—images—came into my mind of the bizarre alien episode of the night, and I resented the aliens' control over me, benign or not. I felt vulnerable and defenseless then. Now, as my thoughts were being transmitted, I felt much the same way.

I hate being stripped of my personal freedom and volition, I thought to myself, and these thoughts were immediately transferred to Laura, even though I hadn't intended that she receive them.

"I share your feelings, Kep—not about failing to deliver the box to me, but about privacy and freedom to choose and to act for yourself. But you can shut your thoughts out of my head quite simply. Just twist the outer part of the ring until you feel it click into a slight notch. When you do that, it will be like hanging up a phone.

"If you twist it farther, you will feel the fiery tingling for about five seconds. During that time you can think out my first name. It's like a code word. This will signal my ring and alert me that it has become active. If you don't think out my name during the five seconds, the ring becomes quiescent again. It always finds a new rest point. There's nothing for you to remember."

As Laura was describing these procedures, I became aware of a mounting distrust—not of her, but of a technology that might fail or be abused. I sensed that nothing ever devised by man was fail-proof or goof-proof. How could I really know that I wasn't being spied on? (I didn't express these feelings in words.)

"You will always know when I'm trying to reach you," Laura continued. "The ring does its thing to your finger. If you don't slide the outer part, we'll be connected in five seconds. But then if you don't want to communicate with me, you just twist the ring a notch, even when you first feel it tingle. That cancels the call. I can't listen to your thoughts without your knowing it or without your permission. The same goes for any attempt from Shackleton."

I still didn't find Laura's words assuring, despite my liking for her and some remaining gut-level trust in her personally. And my day was already getting loaded with new questions before I'd even slid out of bed.

"I have so many questions, I don't know where to begin, Laura. You're talking as if I'm already included with you as being Shackleton's qualified assistant. Am I? What if I don't want to be? Are Bones and Phoebe privy to all of this? How much do they know? And two big questions are, Did you know what I was getting into last night at the warehouse—about the experience I was going to have? And did . . ."

She was laughing again.

"I'm sorry, Kep. I'm not laughing at you. I'm just reacting to your frustration, and I really am sympathetic about your being put in this position of knowing so little about what you deserve to know. With your permission, I will see how many of your questions I can anticipate and try to answer them without your having to ask. Okay?"

"Okay." (I used my voice on that one.)

"Yes, I knew that you would be arrested as you left the warehouse with the box. Shackleton will discuss this and many other things with you later, probably today. How much he will be willing to tell you then, I can't say. I can tell you that I was waiting as I said. But at the time, I couldn't explain that I'd be waiting for confirmation that you had succeeded in getting the box. Your arrest and conduct during questioning were the most critical parts of Shackleton's test. I felt terrible about having to lead you into all that, Kep, but I felt strongly that you would prove to be all that Shackleton believed of you.

"And you did succeed on every point. I have the box. It's your box, Kep. The money in it is yours, too—for undergoing all you did to qualify yourself. If you choose not to be an assistant to Shackleton, you're free to go. The money and the ring are yours to keep. The ring will be deactivated. But you don't have to decide now. I'm sure you'll feel better about whatever decision you make if you first give Shackleton a chance to give you answers that I can't provide and to explain other important things as well. According to Detective Walker, you never once let out any information that would connect you with Shackleton. You kept your vow and proved your integrity all around. So I must say that—"

"Wait a minute, Laura," I interrupted aloud. Then, thinking out my words, I said, "Is Detective Walker one of Shackleton's assistants? Does he have one of these rings, too?"

"He assists Shackleton in many ways, Kep, but not like you might think. He's not an assistant as you or I might be. He feels forever indebted to Shackleton—although he's not, really.

"Shackleton provided critical information leading to the location of Graham's daughter. She was kidnapped four years ago, when she was about six years old. Because of Harv's . . . Shackleton's clairvoyance, she was found in time and under favorable circumstances to be rescued.

"Ever since then, Graham Walker has alerted Shackleton to unpublicized things like missing people or persons placed in threatening circumstances—the kinds of things that usually interest Shackleton. He often supplies helpful information not readily made available to private investigators or to the media. That's because he knows he can trust Shackleton to be discreet and effective while working within the law. He knows, too, that Shackleton doesn't seek public notice and that he doesn't perform for personal gain. No, Graham doesn't have a ring. You and I, besides Shackleton, are the only ones that I know of . . . except . . . well, I think Shackleton will have to explain more about that. There's a lot I'm not—"

"Is Shackleton's ring the thing that enables him to see and know the things he does?" (Aloud again.)

"No, Kep. His paranormal power is a gift. It's like other gifts that people are born with, or develop. You'd have to describe it as something more spiritual, not physical. It isn't dependent on known physical or elemental laws as we understand them. Some people would try to argue with that, but no one has proved otherwise. Besides, Shackleton demonstrated this power, this gift, long before he was blind—or before he had a ring, which he didn't have before his own lengthy disappearance. But since then, his abilities have intensified. It's like . . . I can't explain it, Kep."

"All right, Laura," I said aloud. Then I thought, "If we're the only ones other than Shackleton to have these rings, who developed the technology? How are the rings controlled? Or who controls them? If they depend on our individual frequencies, can't we be tracked or manipulated in some way? And how did they—whoever—get our body-energy vibrations, as you describe them? Are you sure we're not—"

She was laughing again.

"Oh, Kep! I could never think of all the questions you come up with. I think you're going to have to save a lot of them for Shackleton. He did explain to me that my personal energy identification came from the lock of my hair that he took and saved—you know, the trimmings he took when he met Rose and me at the lake."

I didn't dare think the words that were on the edge of being formed in my head. I could only imagine pictures of my experience with the aliens. But then I involuntarily let the words tumble out in a hoarse, audible whisper.

"Laura, do you . . . have you ever dealt with . . . have you had any experiences with extraterrestrial beings—personally, I mean?"

Laura was silent for a time before answering.

"I'm sure Shackleton has, or does. But if you have questions about that, where I'm concerned, you'll have to ask him. I guess I'm not so surprised that you have associated the rings with other-world beings. But no—I'm sorry about that . . . I just can't tell you anything more unless Shackleton asks me to, and then he'd have to tell me what to say. Maybe that will change when, or if, you accept his offer to work with him. I hope you do, Kep. It would be hard to find anyone else who could so readily match his restrictive qualifications. And I'm sure he would probably disclose many more things to you than he does to me because . . . because of what happened to Rose, partly."

"When will he see me? I don't know if he's here in his home or out. Your call woke me up, and I don't have a clue about anything. Not even what time it is. I guess you answered my questions about Bones and Phoebe, Laura. They're wonderful people. I can see what their place is in Shackleton's world. Is there anything you can tell me about what's next in my day—in what's left of it?"

"It's three twenty, Kep. I'll get in touch with Shackleton and call you back on the ring. Give me about twenty minutes . . . oh! Do you remember what I said about how you reach me?"

"Twist the ring, get the buzzing itch, then think your first name?"

"Exactly, Kep. Your ring will be functional unless you ask that it not be anymore. And Shackleton's code is just his name, his middle name. It seems so simple and child-like, considering all that the rings can do. I don't suppose there are to be any other names for us to know. Your code word is 'Kephart,' as if you couldn't guess."

"Well I certainly won't be calling myself—at least not today, Laura. Thanks."

Suddenly Laura was no longer in my head. (I suppose you could say she "buzzed off.")

Now I was left alone with my thoughts, and this brought me an exhilarating sense of freedom. I had never before thought of what a precious thing privacy is in this way, or just how much I lived in my mind, or what a privilege it is to enjoy the private workings of my mind without someone's intrusion—whether legally or by stealth. It was scary to contemplate the loss of such a freedom.

After visiting the bathroom porcelain and hurriedly washing up, I dressed and went downstairs to find Bones. No luck. It was the same with my search for Phoebe, so I made my way outdoors for a look around.

The maroon Lincoln sedan wasn't in sight, but I ventured out just in time to see a tow truck pulling the VW bus into view farther down the drive. It was Big Tow. Bart was at the wheel. Happy day.

After Bart rolled around past the garage and circled to a point where he could unhitch and deposit the bus, the Judds drove up in the big sedan. Evidently, they had gone to meet him at the iron gate. Phoebe got out of the car first, being the more agile of the two. But then she let Bones precede her to the entry, where I stood watching the procession.

"Oh, Mr. Kep!" Phoebe called out happily. "I've done fixed your lunch and packed it so's you can go if you need to. Mr. Shackleton won't be seein' you 'til this evenin', I guess. He had my Bones drive him to Miss Laura's place while you were a sleepin'."

Her voice would have easily reached Bart's ears, since his truck was standing just to my left.

"Now Blossom . . . Blossom, you just let Mr. Kep learn . . . learn for his own self when Mr. Shackleton wants to be . . . be . . . seein' him," Bones admonished her in his quiet, humble way. "Miss Laura will be callin' to say. And, Mr. Kep, you . . . you . . . your lunch . . . you just eat it now if you like. My Blossom can put it right on the table if you . . . you like. That would be real good for you . . . real good, if you're hungry now."

"Well, now that you mention it, I guess I could eat a bite, Bones. Thanks for offering. And thanks, Phoebe, for thinking of me as you do. Maybe I should make a quick phone call, though, before I eat. And I'll have to take a minute here with the tow truck driver before I come inside. He'll be wanting some money, I think."

"Oh, Mr. Kep, I done gave him his money accordin' to Mr. Shackleton's say," Bones said softly as Phoebe went into the house.

"Really, Bones? Well, I suppose that puts me back into debt with him," I said, mostly to myself.

So I had been spared another embarrassment in having to deal with Bart, I thought. I was relieved on the one hand and distressed on the other. I had no money. With a questioning look, Bones nodded at me politely as he moved on into the house.

The bus had just been lowered onto the cement drive. I got the notion to walk around to the back of the truck and inspect it. Bart was pulling his towing gear free and pitching his taillight extension wires onto the back of his rig with obvious vehemence. Wondering why the angry mood, I walked up close and caught his eyes with mine.

"Hello," I said.

He blinked his eyes and grimaced, then puckered his mouth and blew out his breath forcefully. Just his head moved as he stood statue-like beside his truck, blinking first at me and then at the bus, the house, the landscaped grounds, the Lincoln sedan, the house, and then back at me again. Heaving a sigh that lifted his coveralls a couple of inches above his shoes, he swiveled his head in a full half circle, eyes blinking, lips squeezing . . . in, then out, in, then out.

Between blinks, his eyes fell repeatedly on the house, the glaring yellow bus, the maroon sedan—and me. Suddenly he threw his head back, blinked at the sky, flung up his hands, and rasped in a low, hoarse voice, "He doesn't have sixty bucks. He doesn't have a credit card. You got fifty? I ask. No, but yes, he says. But he hasn't earned it yet, he says. Your lunch is waiting, she says. I fixed it while you were sleeping, she says."

Bart looked at his watch, squinched up his face like a prune, and gave me a final scowl of deprecation before hoisting himself into the cab of his truck. I found my own lips puckering in and out as I tried to think of something to say to him in parting—something smart or funny. Then, just as he lifted up his clipboard and reached for a pen in his coveralls, my little finger itched and buzzed.

"Hello," I repeated—this time absently responding to Laura's voice while my eyes were directly on Bart.

He turned his head and stared hard at me, eyebrows up, lips out.

"Hello, Laura," I said aloud again, my eyes still on Bart. "What a time to buzz me."

Bart tossed his clipboard, crammed his truck into gear, revved his engine, and sped around the circling driveway strewing whatever was loose and free to fall overboard. As I watched him disappear into the woods, I could only hope that the gate would open automatically—and in time.

CHAPTER 9

I guess you could say the money box found *me.* When I first spotted it on the passenger seat of the VW bus, I shook my head in disbelief. I discovered it after I had eaten the lunch Phoebe had prepared for me. She had taken the lunch from its bag and laid it out on her dinette table—graced again with a blue-and-white checkered napkin and fresh flowers. I don't think my meal would have been such a pleasant experience, had I discovered the box *before* going back into the house. The sight of it unsettled me.

Now, as I drove south toward Burlington, my eyes and thoughts were repeatedly drawn to it there on the seat beside me. Curious, I had stopped earlier to privately peek inside it just after I exited through Shackleton's restricted-access gate. (Yes, the gate did open automatically.) A hurried count of the banded bills gave me a staggering figure of $35,000.

How the box could have been placed in the VW was a total mystery to me. I had locked the bus at the warehouse, and its only key was in my pocket—retrieved from the brown envelope at the sheriff's station. Laura had said that *she* had the box. It was inconceivable that she would have involved Bart to gain access to the locked bus. I felt sure it had been towed rear-end up from the time it was taken away for impounding. No one could have driven it. And since the key had been in my pocket until the time it was taken from me by the station deputy, I could only guess that owner identification had been learned by a computer check of the license-plate number. No need for a deputy to use a key to look for registration inside the vehicle.

Puzzled as I was, these thoughts distressed me because I really wanted to focus on my persisting mental stack of questions for Shackleton. Laura had given me eight o'clock as the appointed time to meet with him at his studio.

I was specifically asked to park somewhere below the stairs leading up to the Overlook, someplace where the bus would be inconspicuous. How could Shackleton possibly know how ludicrous this sounded when no words could adequately describe its vivid yellow paint job? Still, I fully understood the reason for the request, and I knew I had to allow extra time to find a suitable parking place.

Laura had cautioned, "Always make certain that you approach and leave Shackleton's studio without drawing attention. Do your best not to appear to be associated with him in any way except, perhaps, as a piano student."

I guessed the present time to be about five o'clock. Both my watch and my pager were dead. I hadn't been able to reach Bickford or Dozie from the Judds' place. Their company 800 line had been busy on two tries, and I didn't know their private number. It was Saturday, and they usually took weekends off to spend time as a family. Even so, I wanted to check in with them and drop off my week's gas receipts and proof-of-delivery sheets.

Then, too, I had a partial explanation to offer about the unusual pizza delivery. When I called the pizza company to assure them that payment was coming, I learned that the bill had been prepaid. After my call, Bones told me, as I ate lunch and voiced my perplexity, that *he* had paid for the pizza the night before I got it! He had the cashier write down the address, the time for pick-up, and my pager number—all according to "Mr. Shackleton's say." The delivery information and bill amount had been handwritten and attached to the pizza box, as instructed by Bones. I didn't think to question anything about it at the time, partly because the note included instructions:

Go down Evening Star Lane on foot.
The area has limited parking.

I hadn't connected the "limited parking" with Charleston Street as well. But how did Shackleton get my pager number? That really had me stumped.

Suddenly I found the bus turning onto Valley Drive, much like a horse finds its way home without its rider's guiding hand. I had become so engrossed in thought that my driving was detached and automatic.

The driveway to the Tidwash home led on past the house and into a large parking area in back, where Bick's delivery vehicles were kept. A small warehouse and loading dock extended along the back of the parking apron. Adjoining this was a shop for servicing trucks and vans. Besides the VW bus, Bick owned a large truck with a lift gate plus three commercial vans, all of which he serviced himself as much as possible. He was skilled in many things and had enjoyed considerable success in the eight years he had been in business for himself.

Bick and Dozie were expecting their third child in a couple of months, and despite the demands and challenges of creating and managing a family-operated business, they had kept parenting their top priority. I admired and respected them. Their kind offer of employment had served to rescue me from depression at a critical time—just two weeks after my accident, when getting a job seemed hopeless.

Just as I stepped out of the bus, a shiny new van pulled up behind me in the parking area. The doors flew open and two very excited small boys came running up to me. Each was exclaiming, "We got a new van, Kep!" "Come see our new van!" Bick was right at their heels. Although he didn't come running as his sons did, his face had a boyish grin that spoke his delight.

"Hey, Chappy! Good news, eh? Just when I finds myself in need of another van and driver, God delivers. Our prayers are answered, they are." (He always credited God and his wife for his successes, great or small.)

Boisterous and happy, his boys began chasing and circling each other around me while grabbing at my pants.

"Whoa, whoa there, lads! You know better than to be havin' a shindy about Kep's legs. Do your whoopin' and scrappin' 'round the tree over there."

Despite their characteristic roughhousing, Bick's sons were quite good about obeying his soft-spoken commands, even at those times when play crossed over the line into disorderly conduct. However, Selma had mentioned that they were more docile when they were in Dozie's care alone. They somehow understood that she would not tolerate any unruly behavior.

Bick was exceptionally tall and angular. I nearly always saw him with a smile on his face. He had an awkward, eccentric appearance that was deceptive, particularly because of his unusual straw-like hair, which stuck out in all directions. Then, too, there was his unconventional preference for loose baggy clothes. And he usually wore shirts in dominant colors of bright orange or yellow. His shirttail had a habit of creeping out, and his pants looked as though they would fall down any minute. But he was neat and orderly in all other aspects of his life and possessions.

"And what brings you to pleasure us with your good spirit on a sunny Saturday, Chappy? You ought to be learnin' to play a little bit, or you'll soon be too much wearin' a long, stony face like those clock-chained slaves of the corporate blokes. They're out of sync with nature, they are. Work's a good thing, but too much is a poison, it is. Kills your spirit, it does, Chappy. But mostly it's greed at the top that does the killin'. That, and the drudgin' for next to nothin' with no thanks, lad. Come to think of it, I've not been givin' you too much to do, have I, Chappy? But now I'm just remindin' myself that—"

"Are you going to get him that other key, Bick?" Dozie broke in as she approached us. "What does he think of the prospect of having his own transportation?"

She smiled at me as she said this, and then her eyes went to Bick's face as she saw the bewilderment on mine.

"You didn't tell him?" she asked.

"Just about to, I are, I are," Bick said sheepishly, twisting his mouth to the side of his face. "But Kep would enjoy hearin' it best from you, Luvvy. I'll go snatch the key from the shop."

When he was out of hearing range, Dozie said softly, "Sometimes he just gets blinded by his own brilliance, Kep. I guess that's where I come in—for steerage.

"You probably don't know it, but my maiden name was Sapp. I always had trouble with it growing up. And Tidwash is no improvement. But like I told my parents when Bick proposed to me, 'If I didn't marry a Tidwash, I'd be a Sapp.' And I love him still, despite his oddity, or even maybe because of it."

Dozie played vital roles, not only in their business but also as a devoted wife, mother, and homemaker. My hat was off to her. And as we laughed together, I realized that by choosing to marry Bick, she had in some ways made my current employment possible.

"You were going to explain something about another key?" I asked, inwardly amused that Dozie herself had problems with staying on course. "By the way, my pager is dead. I think it just needs a new battery."

"Well, I think Bick is going to give you a cell phone to use, Kep. It will be a better choice if you're going to be on-call and less available."

"Less available?"

"Oh, I guess I'm handling this backwards. I should start by telling you that the woman who bought the bus said that it was to be given to you for needed transportation. She said it would enable you to perform your proposed duties as a special assistant and that there would be no objection to your continuing employment with us on-call as time permitted. You seem to have hit it off pretty well, Kep!

"And she did say, too, that there was no question about your being chosen for the job but that *you* were the one still considering the employment offer, not them. An envious position to be in, I'd say! She confided that this was a rare opportunity for the right man and that it required exceptional qualifications, but she couldn't say anything more about it, since it was confidential."

My eyes began to blink just like Bart's.

"We think this will fit in beautifully with our situation here, Kep, since we really can't afford to hire a new person except as part-time. It's hard to find someone responsible who is willing to be available on an 'as needed' basis. Of course we're happy for you, but if you want to stay on full-time here, we'll work around any problems we might have in order to keep you. You're more like family than a team member, Kep."

Then, while I stood dumbly staring at her—struggling to accept the impact of the message behind her words—she added, "Of course, we just assumed that you would be jumping at such an opportunity, especially when we learned that the bus was to be thrown in, and we thought that you would find it hard to bring it up . . . to us . . ."

She paused, searching my face.

"You act like this is unexpected news, Kep. Did I spoil a surprise? Is something wrong?"

"No . . . no, Dozie . . . it's just that . . . no, you haven't spoiled anything. Nothing's wrong, really. And I guess I shouldn't be surprised myself. Not surprised at all. But I have an interview—you could say—coming up tonight, and I won't be able to say what I've decided until I'm past that."

Bick lankily strode up with a troubled expression.

"That other spare key must have got bored and tired of just hangin' there on its nail, Luvvy. It's wandered off on some adventure. But there's still the one you gave the lady. She'll give Kep that one I'm sure, I are, I are."

He looked at me and shook his head. "It's hard givin' up the old bus, Chappy. But it couldn't be goin' to a better keeper. And I'll be seein' it often enough, won't I, lad? You let me do the oil changes and all, and together we'll keep her hummin'!"

Dozie touched my arm. "You know, Kep, that woman gave us twice what we would have asked if we were to try selling the bus ourselves. And we hadn't even intended to let it go. But it was nearly the exact amount we needed to make a down payment on this new van that Bick's been eyeing for some time now. So when she came by this morning and made the offer, that clinched it for us. It's a blessing out of the blue!

"The good-old yellow camper van is yours to keep, no matter what, according to her. Just think—you can cook in it and sleep in it and call it 'home' when you want to, Kep! And if you need work, there's plenty of it here for you. Don't be afraid to ask."

I couldn't help smiling at Dozie's enthusiasm, especially when she wiggled her shoulders and hips in a little dance of happiness. In her pregnant condition, her "tummy" put on a comical show of its own. Holding Bick's hand as she stood and leaned close to him, she came to little more than half his height. She had an obvious warmth and radiance about her, and she was quite pretty in her motherly way.

Outwardly I showed my own sincere happiness for their good fortune. But at the same time, I fought to suppress my negative reaction to what I viewed as Shackleton's audacity. I would have more than questions to voice tonight, I thought.

"Before I forget, I want to give you my week's POD sheets and my receipts for gas," I said, turning back toward the bus.

"Oh! Kep, would you take some slices of pizza with you?" Dozie asked. "We always buy more than we can eat, and the kids don't usually touch it as a leftover."

She called to her oldest boy. "Rollie, go to the new van and bring Kep the take-home box with the pizza. Please get a tight grip on it and carry it right-side up. That's great! Thank you."

I handed Dozie my paperwork and said, "Pizza does sound good just now. I just hope I won't be disappointing Selma if I don't eat *her* supper. She always saves something for me when I'm late. Maybe I should give her a call—if I could use your phone. It's not a long-distance call from here."

"Say, Chappy, that reminds me," Bick broke in. "I've got a cell phone with your name on it. All my drivers are gettin' cell phones now. Trade me back your old pager now, workin' or not. You'll like the cell phone, Chappy. A whole lot better, it is. And you can use it anytime, anywhere. Delivery work or not—it won't matter, lad. You can call it a gift from old Bick. I'm happy with that thought, I am."

As he turned toward the house, I tried to protest but Dozie stopped me.

"Let him give, Kep. Take it. It's his thanks to you for your friendship and reliable help. Besides, he feels he owes you something, indirectly, for making the new van a possibility.

"And you just reminded me that Selma called here this morning before that young woman came. She said they got home late last night and found you still out, which was unusual. But what worried her was that you weren't there for breakfast, which was unthinkable. I couldn't explain it, but I told her that one of the late-returning drivers had mentioned there was an unusually heavy rainstorm along Bellingham Bay. I told her that the storm probably delayed you and that you had called here earlier in the evening and seemed to be okay. I tried to ease her mind by suggesting that you might have had trouble and decided to stay the night to finish up your work. Just think—if you'd had a cell phone, you could have called her! Long-distance would have been no problem."

"Thanks, Dozie. You're right. I did stay in town, and it was partly because of the storm that I was detained.

"Please do me a favor? Give the Whipples a call and tell them I'm fine and that I was just here. Tell them I have more errands to keep me out late and that I'll gladly eat any leftovers when I get home, no matter what time it is. That should keep Selma at peace for the evening. Saturday nights, they usually go visiting, so it would be best if you call before they get away. If you can't get them at home, you might try Arnie Klinkenhoefer's place. Thanks again for everything, Dozie."

Bick came striding up just as I climbed into the VW. His eyes squinted and his face wrinkled into a smile.

"I say, you're not about to leave without me givin' you your pretty present, are you, Chappy?"

He stuck his hand out with the box that held the new cell phone.

"It's been activated and all. Instructions inside. Easy readin' for you, lad. Take care now. And keep up the mileage log on the old bus so we can look to her needs. She'll sing a long time yet if we keep her happy."

I smiled my thanks, handed over the dead pager, and shook his hand. It was hard to find words to express my gratitude, but I knew he felt it just the same.

"I'll be in touch," I said as I held up the cell phone box and gave it a shake. My thumb up said good-bye.

After turning the bus around, I waved at Dozie and the boys and squeezed past the new van in the driveway. Three weeks ago, Bick and Dozie had helped to set my ship of life on a new course. But now I drove away feeling that Shackleton was at the helm.

CHAPTER 10

I pointed the bus west toward Whipple Farm Lane, but I had no intention of stopping at the old farmhouse if I could slip past unnoticed. My appointment with Shackleton was less than two and a half hours away. No time for getting involved in conversations. I wanted to write down questions and be prepared in every way to make the most of my meeting time.

There was also my neglected journal. Even by entering sketchy "trigger" notes, I wouldn't be able to catch up on recent events in anything less than thirty minutes. And I couldn't think of a better place where I might isolate myself from distractions than Singing Tree Hill. I felt drawn to it more than ever before. The very thought of being there alone in the late afternoon sunshine was comforting.

I had absorbed a lot of stressful and fantastic experiences in the past twenty-four hours—everything from the unexpected to the unbelievable. So I felt a compelling need to escape into seclusion and "lick my wounds." Obviously, I had a lot to sort out in my mind, along with drawing up a list of questions for Shackleton. As I drove, I began my sorting.

A problem arose. I found myself dwelling more often on Jill. Thoughts of her were a pleasant contrast to contemplating a job change that seemed both imposed and inevitable. To be in any way associated with Shackleton was a troubling and formidable thought for me at the moment. I couldn't imagine doing anything for him that didn't involve challenge and stress. His uncanny power to see and learn hidden things was rather daunting, especially when he used it to manipulate or control others' lives. I really didn't feel equipped to deal with this on a daily basis. And the mystery of the man invited endless questions.

I opened the box of pizza as I drove. Oddly, at this moment in time for me, the pizza box held more appeal than the money box because it brought satisfaction without enslaving obligation. (Yes, I know you find this unbelievable.) And I did think it laughable that putting my fingers on cheese and tomato paste felt preferable to putting them on $35,000 in U.S. currency.

Although most people might objectively view my situation as auspicious, I held a strong aversion to being obliged to Shackleton. I viewed his so-called "gifts" as inducements that hinted of bribery. Servitude had no place in my desirable future. I cherished freedom in every sense of the word. The pizza had been a true gift, one that had no strings attached (except, maybe, for the strings of melted cheese) and it appeased an immediate and healthy appetite.

I had grown up in a simple world with simple tastes, and the most recent years of my life had been fraught with material impoverishment. I had learned to be personally content with little. I admit I had felt increasing frustration, in that I was unable to provide adequately for my invalid mother—to sufficiently offset her disability income. Even so, caring about *someone* had come to mean more to me than caring about *things*.

Now I was without anyone of close personal attachment. I wondered at this, now that Jill kept wandering into my thoughts. At first sight she aroused natural desires—feelings not new to me, but stronger than any I'd known before. Still, there was more.

As I forced my mind to face the new prospects before me, I caught myself envisioning the look in Jill's eyes. When I was very young and dealing with hard-choice situations, I would picture my mother's eyes. Her caring look had strong influence. Why should I care now what Jill thought? I found it strange that I should be influenced by her non-existent expectations of me.

I had spent less than thirty minutes with her, in which time she evidently had gained a profound influence on my regarded acts. And this had apparently come about without any conscious effort or expression on her part.

Somehow her values had transferred to me. She personified her standards and values in a way I found to be extremely attracting. I had no memory of being acquainted with any other female like her—one who so effortlessly emanated such desirable spiritual qualities.

But now as I mulled it over, I saw that I hadn't so much cared about this aspect of womanhood before. I hadn't even thought about it. Why now? And wasn't every adult human a reflection of his or her own guiding principles, to whatever degree they embraced them? Weren't the unprincipled ones obvious? No matter, Jill was distinctly exceptional. I presently regarded her as a treasure among women. She radiated her own inexpressible light.

* * *

Once more I discovered the bus turning of its own accord onto a familiar road. Wanting to keep the dust and noise at a minimum, I eased up on the gas, shifted down, and slowed to a creep before passing by the entryway to Oat and Selma's place. For the first time ever while driving down Whipple Farm Lane, I was relieved to see no car in the farmhouse drive. As I had suspected, Oat and Selma were spending the evening with their neighboring friends.

I was thankful that no explanation or apology would have to be made for my having missed suppertime with them. And yet, this had become a meaningful "family" time of day for me. I had already learned to look forward to it. This evening I struggled a bit with its loss. Just now I felt a bit sad that my ship of life had no sure place of moorage.

Except for a single "wow" in Whipple Farm Lane, it was a straight shot to the lane's dead end and the trailhead at the bottom of Singing Tree Hill. But there was this little jog in the road around a point where a small creek flowed down and crossed through a culvert. As I steered around some trees at this forested point, I saw Jill's faded-blue Honda parked on the right. It was tilted at an angle with its wheels off the shoulder of the lane. Yesterday it had been parked in an access to a field farther down on the left. Concerned, I stopped and ran over to see if she might have had trouble—maybe a flat. I found everything to be in order. The wheels were in a shallow ditch. She could easily drive out of it. The tires were up. The doors were locked.

Across the road there was an old gray mailbox with the name "Potts" painted on its side. The faded white letters were barely distinguishable. A narrow, rutted easement led away from the mailbox and wound across Oat's hilly fields. Selma had told me that this was where a rather poor and reclusive older couple lived. They raised chickens and pigs, among other things, in their attempt to be self-sustaining. Their several children were now grown and gone. They had their own power generator and a telephone that was frequently disconnected. She spoke kindly of them, calling them "friends of occasion."

I had given little attention to this point on my travels back and forth along the lane. But I wondered now whether Jill might have gone on foot down this narrow, uninviting track, since there was still a long stretch to go to the wooden gate at the trailhead. Surely she had known the Potts family since childhood. Still, there was a chance that she could be up on the Hill. I couldn't take time to investigate the rutted road, but I was definitely going up to the Singing Tree. Even so, the positioning of her car puzzled me.

I drove on down to the lane's end and parked the bus. Before locking up, I hid the money box inside a small cabinet under the camper sink. Then I jogged up the trail at a lively pace, fully aware that my speed was prompted by something more than the prospect of visiting the Tree. All fatigue and depressive thoughts had left me. Hope, no matter how dimly it flickers, kindles wondrous energy.

When at last I reached the high point of the trail where the Tree and the white rocks beneath it were visible, I saw no sign of Jill. Breathless and sweaty, my heart pounding in my chest, I slowed to a stumbling walk and made my way to a favorite flat stone—the one that Jill had previously chosen. As I bent over and placed my hands on it to ease myself down, I noticed a colored drawing pencil in the tall grass. Picking it up, I turned and sat facing the bay westward to let the cooling breeze refresh me. While my heartbeat slowed, I studied the pencil, and since it was obviously Jill's, I studied my reaction to finding it. Not good—I was smitten for sure. I could think of nothing but Jill.

Forcing my mind onto my task took more strength of will than it should have demanded of me. Each thought required deliberation, and every act was a conscious effort. I was repeatedly fending off thoughts of Jill, and this robbed me of the ability to focus effectively on the job at hand, especially under the pressure of having so little time in which to remember and record events.

Questions slid out of my head. All that I had stored up to fling at Shackleton seemed to melt and vaporize like an accumulated arsenal of snowballs in a chinook wind. What had once been so vitally important to me now seemed insignificant. My priorities had shifted, but I couldn't even assess them. I soon found myself in an acute state of frustration and exasperation.

Time was slipping away, and I had no idea what the actual time might be. I finally decided to scrap my exercise in writing and head down to the farmhouse. If I had enough time, I could take a hot bath. I certainly needed to change my clothes and become more presentable, whether Shackleton could see me or not. What mattered was that I needed to feel better about myself than I did at the present. Maybe I could do something to reshape my physical image, if not redefine my goals and priorities. I was in a sorry state. And I was in a rare grumpy mood.

I put my notebook back inside my shirt, slipped my pencil into my shirt pocket, and pulled out the colored pencil. I wasn't sure what to do with it. Should I leave it or take it? I decided to leave it on the stone slab, in case Jill should get back to it before I saw her again.

When I laid it on the inclined flat surface, a strange thing happened. It rolled *uphill* and fell into the grass. Not wanting to believe what I saw, I picked it up and laid it on the stone in line with the slope. It stayed put. I then turned it ninety degrees and set it down. It rolled uphill again, and I caught it before it fell. After repeating this several times, I decided to test my own mechanical pencil with its pocket clip. This too rolled up the incline with enough momentum to overcome the hindrance of its clip. Amazed and distracted by this phenomenon, I lost awareness of everything else.

Moving to the Tree, I felt its trunk. Strong vibrations were clearly evident to the touch. Turning my back to the gentle prevailing breeze, I cupped my ears with both hands and faced the Tree. There was no mistake—it was singing. This was my first personal experience of actually hearing it sing. I had felt vibrations at other times, but I had never before *heard* the Tree sing. It was a magical thing—both mentally and physically exhilarating. I could only conclude that this was one of those rare geological places where the Earth's gravitational field flowed in a unique vortex pattern.

But, just maybe, could it be that the Tree was itself the cause of what happened? Who could tell for sure? There was, as I have said, a reverential or sacred quality to this location—one that could be felt in a non-physical way. Trees were living things. Like other living things, did they have spirits, too? There was much to ponder here . . . if only I had the time to linger.

Reluctantly, I turned my back to the Tree and took to the trail. It seemed to flow beneath my feet. I felt totally detached from the Earth and its immediate hold on me. My mind floated in a sphere of its own, unfettered and free, focused on a horizon of its own making. But all these sensations were short-lived.

Whipple Farm Lane was empty. Jill's car was gone. The driveway and adjoining yard at the old farmhouse were empty as well. I was alone, and Smooch was snoring. He stirred and licked my hand as I pressed it against his wet nose. The farmhouse itself seemed morose. No notes.

I took down a drinking glass from the kitchen cupboard and filled it with water. Having come from a well, it was refreshingly cold, and I gulped it down. I filled the glass again, gulped, and set it down. The clock on the stove showed 6:52. I checked the grandfather clock in the living room: 6:49. Close enough. Time for a bath . . . and a shave.

Taking the stairs two steps at a time, I went to my (Jill's?) closet and found a clean pressed shirt and a pair of wrinkled pants. No need to press blue jeans, so I grabbed a pair from a clean-clothes basket in the corner of the room. As I turned to the dresser drawer for clean underwear, I caught sight of a large sheet of heavy paper on the bed. Finding it blank, I turned it over. It was a page torn from a sketchpad, and the drawing on it was an unmistakable portrait of *me.* I stood holding it, studying it, until my hand began to shake.

It was an excellent rendering, reflecting remarkable talent. Since no one had taken any recent photographs of me, I knew it was a product of Jill's photographic memory. The portrayed expression on my face was one of self-assurance and confidence. But I certainly couldn't recall any moment in which I had exhibited such characteristics during my brief time with her. In fact, I could remember only being rather unsure of myself in relation to her. And when we first met, I had been struggling to regain my composure after receiving a flood of returning memories.

But this portrayal suddenly took on significant meaning for me. It reflected a perception of me that Jill held, accurate or not—one that I wanted to match in truth. My face showed a certain kind of faith that I wanted to attain in some way. There wasn't a trace of doubt in my eyes, and my lips held a determined smile that said I knew where I was headed. If this was the Kephart Stone that Jill believed of me, it was who I really wanted to be.

I hadn't ever given any thought to that before. Giving of myself had been a good thing—nothing to change there. But who was I now, really? Some internal self identity was missing, and I sensed that it was tied to some purpose in living.

What would it take? I wondered. How long would it take? It couldn't happen in a day or a week, but I could begin the process of transformation *now*.

I thought on this while the bath water ran and while I studied my face in the mirror as I shaved. It wouldn't do to imitate a face depicted in a drawing—that I knew. And it would take more than trying to emulate Jill's perception of me—that could change. Above all, I didn't want to be continually striving to measure up to someone's expectations in an effort to win or retain a conditional kind of love.

I knew there was an answer somewhere—somewhere in time. But time was so unrelenting in its demands. I felt impatient. Yet I resolved now to begin living as though my believed future was a certainty. Wasn't that a close definition of faith? The immediate problem was to decide what I truly desired, since the path I must take to achieve it would shape my true self. My intended self and future would be inescapably linked, each fashioned by the journey.

I could not have supposed, nor remotely suspected, that Shackleton would offer the needed map.

CHAPTER 11

AS I parked the bus in Old Fairhaven, the sun was just setting. Above the bay the western sky shone in glorious pink and gold. A college student working in a twenty-four-hour convenience store had assured me that the alley behind the store was an "okay place" to park. He parked there himself. But he couldn't promise immunity from theft or vandalism. Fine. What worried me was a phone call to Big Tow.

I paused at the Overlook and took in the sunset while waiting for my breathing to slow down. The wooden stairs were steep, and I had acquired a habit of climbing all steps two at a time. It kept me in shape. Besides, the exertion helped me dispel the negative feelings I was still harboring toward Shackleton.

As I approached Shackleton's studio, I found the door open and Bogart sitting on the threshold waiting with bright eyes and a wagging tail. He waited as I closed the door behind me. Then, as he led me through the studio past the extensive bookcase wall, he looked back a couple of times to see that I was following. I had no doubt that he was smiling his approval. We passed around this wall into a cozy, comfortably furnished den.

On my right, the backside of the same wall was also covered top to bottom with shelves of books. Two winged, leather armchairs were positioned at angles to each other on either side of a low, beautifully tiled service table. These high-backed chairs faced an attractive stone fireplace built into the wall before them, and because the backs of these tall chairs were directed toward me, I didn't at first see Shackleton seated in the one at my right.

My noiseless entry was detected. Whether alerted by Bogart's return or some unique sense of his own, Shackleton arose, faced me, and held out his hand. Smiling warmly, he silently waited for me to approach. He found and shook my own extended hand after placing his left one on my shoulder, and with a wave invited me to sit in the other chair.

Some glowing coals and white ashes of the wood fire indicated that it had been burning for quite some time. Flames still flickered brightly behind the screen, lending an inviting and peaceful ambiance to the den. The soft hissing and popping of the fire made thoughts of opening a conversation seem rather inappropriate. I felt inclined to maintain silence, which seemed not at all awkward but more comfortable.

Shackleton's low voice blended in with the prevailing quietude. "Perhaps that bright little container on the table will answer most of your questions, Kephart. Please. Open it." His smile remained as he faced the firelight.

I hesitated. Those questions that seemed most paramount had submerged to a lower level of my consciousness, while the trifling ones floated to the surface. I grasped one of these before reaching for the circular shiny box resting on the table between us. It seemed that with Shackleton, there was always a box of some sort to deal with.

"Why is it that you sent me to get money for a pizza that had already been paid for?" I asked. I felt rather foolish once the words left my mouth.

Smiling more broadly, Shackleton nodded and spoke to the fire. "If I remember correctly, I said, 'You will want some money,' then asked you to take what you wanted. You construed this to mean money for the pizza. Then I asked you to return the bills to the box, after which I gave you something as a gift to reward your integrity. It was purely a test to confirm your honesty, Kephart. In truth, I need not have tested it at all."

He turned toward me and said gently, "You really do need to regard yourself more highly, Kephart, though not with pride. However, I confess that I had set you up, for which I owe you an apology."

He chuckled softly and pointed in the direction of the shiny round container on the service table. "The little item in that box should answer your next question. Prove me on this. Please."

My hand was already on it. "But how did you get my work pager number?" I asked as I twisted off the lid.

Then I stared in amazement at what was surely the tiny metallic sphere that the aliens had extracted from my forehead. It was nested in a cushioned pocket of protective material. I was speechless.

"You may take it out, Kephart," Shackleton said, hearing only my silence.

"But what . . .?"

"What is it? It is everything you have thought, said, and done since you were five years old, Kephart. It is a comprehensive, all-inclusive record of the better part of your life. It is also, at the very least, a tracking and locator device."

"But I don't remem . . . how . . . when did . . .?"

"If you think you had questions before, Kephart, you will be dizzy with them tonight—unless, of course, you will permit me to supply answers in a somewhat logical order *before* you attempt to utter those anticipated questions randomly. I believe I can put your mind at rest on most matters of concern."

He felt for an electronic device on the arm of his chair.

"But before I begin, what say we start the evening with refreshments and understandings? I have rung for Bones. Before he comes down, I want to convey to you my sympathy for all that you have been put through. It is regrettable, but I'm sure you will see that it was necessary. I'm certain, too, that you will appreciate my position, as well as my offer, before the close of our meeting.

"In truth, Kephart, I cannot act effectively without your assistance, so I must appeal to you to be patient in listening to what I have to say. Time, unfortunately, presses me to engage you in a potentially dangerous assignment—one that requires immediate action. Of course, you are free to act in accordance with your conscience and disposition once I have fully described the situation as it is now unfolding.

"I am prepared to provide some of the answers you seek, Kephart, but please understand that I am bound to keep some secrets that I may never be able to divulge. I have my own integrity to look after."

As he laughed silently to himself, Bones appeared from behind our chairs and placed a loaded tray on the tiled table. On it was a steaming teapot of hot water, together with empty mugs surrounded by a variety of snacks, including meats, cheeses, crackers, pastries, and fresh-cut veggies with dips. Packets of herbal teas and cocoa filled one bowl. Another offered packaged sugar and honey. Phoebe had also provided teaspoons and napkins (blue-checkered, of course).

Leaning close to me, Bones smiled and said softly, "It's sure good . . . good to see you here, Mr. Kep . . . real good."

Turning toward Shackleton, he said more audibly, "Mr. Kep's done got his self all spiffied up like as . . . as he was to be a . . . dinin' out. But I do . . . believe he likes eatin' my Blossom's . . . cookin' best." His shoulders shook as he laughed in his high-pitched hearty way. Then he obligingly inquired, "What is it you'd like in . . . in your cup, Mr. Shackleton? There's cocoa and herb tea."

"Cocoa is fine, Bones. Thank you." Shackleton smiled warmly and held his eyes on him as though he might actually see him.

As Bones shook an envelope of powdered cocoa mix into Shackleton's mug, he looked to me. But before he could ask about my own preference, I said, "Oh, I'll decide after I've snacked a little. Thanks anyway, Bones."

He nodded and, after pouring hot water into Shackleton's mug, quietly limped away without another word.

"One question I'd like to ask concerns Bones," I said to Shackleton. "I doubt you'll think that I might ask it. Maybe you can't answer, but I'm curious. Laura said that you rescued him from a beating. Could you tell me about it?"

"Yes. He was working at a gas station where I had stopped. To be discreet, I will withhold even the name of the state where the incident occurred. I heard him screaming, so I left my car to investigate. His employer was kicking him and beating him with a heavy torque wrench. They were at the bottom of a grease pit, and Bones was down on the floor. He was incapable of defending himself from the vicious onslaught—certainly no match against the powerful and enraged man.

"At the time, they were the only ones at the station. I managed to quell the assault using a fire extinguisher, after which I called for aid.

"It seems that money was missing from the till. Later it was confirmed that the employer's own son had stolen the money for drugs.

"Bones fortunately recovered, but not without incurring permanent physical damage. It is possible that he suffers other irreversible losses as well."

Shackleton slid around in his chair and turned his face toward me.

"Kephart, this brings up a point. I beg that you permit my indulgence, for you will soon see that I am not digressing from our purpose in meeting here.

"Imagine that this world is a stage where everyone acts out his or her own part. Accordingly, let's presume that we are to write our own script and create our own performance as we go along. Each of us is to prove who we really are in the scheme of things. That is what the performance is all about: to demonstrate our eventual true inclinations and dispositions, whether predominantly good or evil, as well as to apply and share our acquired talents or capabilities.

"We must also assume that everyone knows what constitutes evil at the start, which we will equate with that which works counter to certain irrefutable and universal laws of ultimate happiness. *Good* shall be defined as that which works in compliance with these laws, and we can safely say that no one actor is entirely devoid of goodness.

"That understood, let us suppose that one who is more fully disposed to do evil must find or create opportunity to manifest this by perpetrating an act upon one who is inclined to do good.

"Now the question is: If a performer sees an instance of an evil act being perpetrated—or knows of one *about* to be carried out—is his or her intervention to be considered an act of interference, one that works counter to the scheme of proving who and what we are?"

I quickly responded by saying, "No, at least I don't *feel* it would be so."

"And why, Kephart?"

"Well, I'd say the person interrupting or preventing the evil act is proving goodness."

Quite so. But let's add another dimension to the scheme. Let's say that the stage is also a place of schooling and that each acting participant is to demonstrate learned traits that correspond with his or her own development. One cannot progress without having been subject to learning experiences. And what if a particular learning experience was to have involved one's being a *victim* of evil in order to learn, say, forgiveness? How in this instance would you regard the intervention?"

"I guess you'd have to say that good acts don't bring up reasons for forgiving. But isn't it okay to consider that the acts of others can be misinterpreted? Can't some of them be good or bad only as we interpret them to be?

"I remember that I was always falling asleep in class after my mother had a stroke. One day I fell asleep during a history exam. A girl was sitting next to me who knew about my mother's condition and my work schedule, and she decided to save me by passing test answers across to my desk. I guess you could say she had good intentions, even though she was being dishonest.

"As the teacher came close by, the girl nudged me awake with her foot, thinking I could hide the papers in time. But, being groggy and confused, I just picked up the cheat sheets and stared at them until it was too late. I was caught and accused, even though my own test paper had unfilled blanks for the answers the girl supplied. So what was I to think?

"The girl and the teacher had both failed me. Neither one had done the right thing in my view, but maybe they each *thought* they had—maybe their intentions were good. I guess it's all in how you choose to look at each situation."

"Splendid, Kephart! And how is one to accurately assess another's intentions? Regardless, whether intentions are correctly understood or not, your own behavioral choice is all that really matters—for your sake."

"Well, that makes sense to me," I said. "Skipping past the judging could sometimes keep me from just reacting to other people. And I suppose that would give me more control of my life. It might make it easier to practice being what I want to be or to become—which is something I was thinking about before I came here. Funny it should come up."

I was both absorbed and inwardly impatient during this portion of our meeting, but I sensed that Shackleton was enjoying my company, and I suspected that discussions of this sort were an infrequent occurrence for him. He sipped his cocoa and felt for a donut before continuing.

"Now we come to the point of your understanding my situation, and then we shall get on with your questions. There are many times, Kephart, when I have an opportunity to intervene or to prevent—or to do both. I'm aware that Miss Rutledge . . . Laura has informed you about my so-called paranormal ability. At times it can be a vexation, but I have determined to use it in a beneficial way. There is an indescribable agony associated with seeing the evolving certainty of a tragic event while being powerless to prevent its occurrence—even though it may be preventable. This is especially so because I can see in one sense but not in another.

"I must also confide in you that I am under surveillance, and in more ways than one. Oh, don't misunderstand me, Kephart. I am not in trouble with any law-enforcement agency, but I am being watched, and I must be circumspect in all that I undertake to do.

"There is no explanation that I can safely offer you at this time, but it is quite possible that you will be able to arrive at a satisfactory one, something near the truth, as you work with me. I know—I am stating a presumption of your acceptance, and that rankles you. But when I look at your past road traveled, it is an easy thing for me to see your road ahead."

"Then you can see something that I can't," I said, "even though I know what's behind me too. It's strange that that should come up as well. I was thinking about this very thing earlier this evening—about my future. But I'm really puzzled about how you could know my past as you do by using that tiny ball. Can you use it to tell my future?"

"No, Kephart. And I have no desire to use any device for prognosticating. Even the most sophisticated computerized systems fail. What is to be understood here is that I am speaking of your journey within. A person's past choices and behaviors are indicators of future acts. They demonstrate values. True, when values change, both choices and people change. But a trend becomes apparent over time.

"What one looks for, he will find. If we look for trouble, we shall surely find it. If we truly look for hope, we shall find it. The same goes for happiness. But few, Kephart, have the courage to look for truth. The search has its price. And it requires honesty in purpose, together with genuine humility.

"If I hand you the truth, you may neither recognize it nor value it. You may not even be ready to deal with it. You must pay the price of acquiring it. This applies as well to my supplying you with all the answers to your questions.

"Please. Accept what I offer this evening. I am confident that you will be capable of putting the puzzle together over time.

"Now, to prepare you for answers to your questions regarding the tiny sphere, you must first answer some questions yourself. Are you willing to do so?"

"Yes, sir—if I can."

Shackleton clasped his hands together on top of his head, closed his unseeing eyes, and smiled approvingly.

"Are you familiar with all the myriad life forms in the seas?"

"Hardly," I said. "I've read that new ones are always being discovered."

"Can you interpret the languages of whales, dolphins, land mammals, and various birds? You do acknowledge that they have their own communications, do you not?"

"No. And yes."

"Can you personally produce honey or manufacture a silk web having twice the tensile strength of steel?"

"No. And no."

"Then, do you agree that there are certain abilities and skills that humans are incapable of acquiring, and that perhaps this is a desirable thing? In other words, is it not possible that each thing created has its place and its purpose, as well as its limitations?"

"Yes. I can see that."

"Are you aware that there are certain birds that can sew leaves and others that can devise their own tools?"

"I guess I hadn't learned that. No."

"Your answers, Kephart, lead me to infer that you have more to learn than you can possibly learn in many lifetimes. Is that so?"

"Definitely." (He was obviously enjoying himself by now.)

"Do you believe that there is ultimately an end to all learning and creating in this life as we presently experience it?"

"I'm inclined to answer no on that one."

"No. But bear in mind that if we restrict our concept of life to beginnings and endings, we may not answer the same.

"Can you appreciate the meaning of 'reverence' as it was used by Dr. Albert Schweitzer in his phrase 'Reverence for Life'? Let's take this to include all life."

"I like to think so, especially when I think of a certain tree that's deserving of that attitude," I said on reflection.

"Can you accept even the suggestion that the universe is replete with an infinite number of life forms having widely varying social structures, intelligences, and purposes?"

"I can accept that, yes. But I think it's more a matter of believing, which I'm willing to do."

"Kephart, you have distinguished yourself, in my estimation, as one having an open and questioning mind, as well as a believing heart. And the latter is the more important trait. 'Unbelievers' deny themselves the power of truth. Never forget that. And, of course, to stop learning is to stop living, so never cease to question. Please.

"Now, I believe that you are prepared to accept a truth—one that has thus far escaped the conclusions of certain scientists and intellectuals. Maybe I should qualify that statement by saying that no findings have been publicly disseminated, should they exist. However, I am convinced that if there is any one thing that confounds the discovery of truths about our universe, it is man's egocentric misperception of himself. You might say that we would do well to contemplate Einstein's offering when he said, in effect, that our very perception of physical reality is an illusion, 'albeit a mighty persistent one.'

"Kephart, I can attest that societies of human beings exist throughout the universe. We are not alone. Except for expected differences in racial characteristics and features, they are just like you and Bones . . . and Jillian. Yes, I know of her as well, Kephart."

"How could you possib . . ."

"It may comfort you to learn that your personal dossier contains nothing but blank pages since that tiny globe was extracted from your head. The time of your ordeal in the warehouse was the time of your liberation. It was also the time of activating your stellar ring, which we will discuss later on. You might say that I have intervened in your behalf as well as my own."

"But . . . how did you know that this thing was inside my head? And how were you able to learn what it recorded?" I asked in absolute perplexity.

"You do believe me when I say that there are other humans besides those endemic to this planet?"

"I guess I'll have to, yes. But it seems to refute the story of Adam and Eve, doesn't it?"

"Not at all, Kephart. But we'll reserve that topic for another day. What you must understand just now is that there are *non-*human life forms visiting this Earth as well, and they have been doing so for times out of mind, with differing motives and purposes. Incidentally, if any had ever intended to control or destroy us, it could have been a possible achievement for some in any era. Needless to say, some of these beings, regardless of their technological superiority, have put us in a test tube of sorts—recognizing their own limitations.

"This does not give us cause to say that they are evil, for these creatures are bound by no moral law. Would you label as 'evil' a bear that kills a child? And what do we truly know about intelligence? Are we not extremely limited in our concepts and measurements of it? Consider again the honey bee—and there are many fascinating facts concerning the mathematical aspects of their communicative 'dances' that may astound you. They exhibit just one of infinite kinds of intelligences, which we cannot measure comparatively.

"Kephart, the attainment of an advanced technology does not necessarily denote superiority in every other aspect of a life-form identified with such achievements. The same holds true for its society. Mankind is most critically endangered by a persisting tendency to deify or idolize that which is undeserving of a supernal status. This undoubtedly stems from man's innate desire to worship.

"Now—I want you to know that this little ball was inserted deeply into your forehead through your nostril when you were five years old by non-humans. You are but one of countless individuals that have been subjected to this procedure over time. Why? I must set aside the answer to that for now, but you are entitled to a later discussion of the matter.

"Evidently, in the Bitterroot Mountains of Idaho, your father left you playing alone for a period of time one day while he prospected for minerals. The first records of your life reflect your father's dismay upon finding you prostrate in the sagebrush with blood running from your nose while in this specific region of the United States. You viewed him setting down a prospector's pick, along with ore sample bags, as he knelt to question you. Of course, you then had no personal memory of the insertion procedure because it had been blocked from your awareness during the incident.

"Perhaps under hypnosis you might recall sighting, eight years later, what some call a 'mother ship' with some small, disc-shaped craft issuing from it while you were prospecting with your father in the San Juan Mountains of Colorado. Not long after that, your father was killed in a rock avalanche. As you know, his death occurred when you were thirteen. What you do not know is that his untimely death relates to this particular sighting incident.

"That too will have to wait for a future discussion, since there is much to get through here tonight. And, again, an urgent matter awaits your involvement, should you agree to undertake it on assignment. There is a mystery to be solved, and I am convinced that you are the only unfettered man who can do the job in the little time we have."

At this point I was so absorbed in Shackleton's narrative of my early-life events that I failed to respond to this last comment. And newly formed questions were billowing up like cumulus clouds in my head. Suddenly a couple of answers rained on me and yanked me back to the present.

"To answer your first question, I was told about the object in your head by a Dr. Voss, a friend of mine who had previous experience with these things while working as a radiologist in Germany. It seems that two children, one in Switzerland and the other in Belgium, had been x-rayed for head injuries on separate occasions. Upon examining each of their skull images, Dr. Voss had discovered what appeared to be a tiny ball in the very same location as that for yours. Surprisingly, no follow-ups were initiated by the physicians involved.

"The x-rays of your own recent head injury had so disturbed your radiologist that he took them to consult with Dr. Voss in Seattle, where he now serves on a university medical staff. Apparently, your x-rays also presented unusual aspects besides the ball and its location. Having had knowledge of my involvement with investigations of disappearances, Dr. Voss shared this information with me out of concern for you, because the two European children had each subsequently vanished and were never found.

"Your second question can be answered only by telling you that, since my wife's disappearance, I have been privileged to have an exclusive association with a society of humans that I call the 'Abiding Ones.' This is not their own appellation, of course, but I have titled them so for two reasons. The first is that they collectively abide by, or submit to, advanced spiritual laws—laws of selflessness that, when obeyed, serve to qualify them for intergalactic assignments and performances that far surpass our own space exploration endeavors, especially where motives apply. The second is because of their periodic living, or *abiding*, among Earth-bound humans from time to time.

"These particular human aliens—and various societies of such—have lived briefly among us periodically over the centuries. The purposes of their visits may be inconceivable to a great many of us. Certainly they are no threat to us. In truth they are, due to their compliance with certain cosmic laws, disinclined to interfere with our progression or regression in any way, leaving us to our own destruction if necessary.

"As you know, Kephart, where a natural physical law is concerned, our making a wrong choice is destined to result in an undesirable consequence—regardless of our ignorance of that law. If we violate physical laws, mercy has no place. Spiritual laws are another matter involving accountability. We are personally accountable to the degree that we understand them. The Abiding Ones have unsurpassed understanding in this regard, which leaves them little room for error. But let's just be content with knowing that they are neither saviors nor angels.

"At the risk of annoying you, Kephart, I must interject a religion-based remark. I do so because it serves to make a critical point regarding man's erroneous deification of unworthy objects or creatures. And should you serve, among other things, as chronicler of certain mysteries that occupy our attention, I would hope that you will convey certain truths to your readers as I have personally come to appreciate them. That is not to say that your records should be in the least burdensome, or that they should attempt to convince others on any point. Neither should they invite confutation or contention. Such things rob truths of their perceivable verity.

"The point I want to make is derived from the King James Version of the Holy Bible. If you will kindly fetch my own from the eye-level shelf of books on the wall, far left end, I will have you read a simple verse. After I have made my point, we will move on to a discussion of your personal attributes as they may relate to the types of tasks I have in mind for you, as well as our current mystery. And, of course, your stellar ring deserves some remarks, Kephart."

Thinking that I could safely get away with it, I crammed my mouth full with half a maple bar (I had been busy taking notes) and proceeded slowly, trying to give my mouth time to deal with it. Thankful for the chance to move and stretch, I went to the wall of shelved books, where I spotted the Bible in the exact place Shackleton described. It had never entered my mind that Shackleton might be religious. He didn't impress me as being a church-going man. But then, I was barely acquainted with him. His commanding countenance and demeanor were, I later discovered, misleading. He is in fact a truly humble, sensitive man, but that is all I will say for now. To this day I'm not sure about his having any religious affiliations. But, again, to this day I still can't say that I really know him.

He had swallowed the last of his cocoa and was returning his cup to the tray as I approached.

"Perhaps you will want some tea to wash down your pastry, Kephart," he said, laughing with his body more than with his voice. "Oh, I quite understand. I have not given you a moment's relief from note taking. But I have a ready solution to that problem, if you will permit me to offer it after we have dealt with the verse and other topics for discussion.

"Please. Turn to the first chapter of Genesis and read verse twenty-seven."

I found the verse rather quickly, having read biblical verses to my mother almost daily.

"So God created man in his own image, in the image of God created he him; male and female created he them," I read aloud.

"Just assuming this to be true, Kephart, would not the converse be true—that God is in the image of man?"

"That's how I would see it, yes," I said, wondering where this was leading.

"I can only offer at this time that no being lacking the identical physical characteristics of man fulfills the depiction rendered. And those who accept anything other than this description are in danger of a great deception—regardless of any impressive peculiar intelligence, social structure, or technological trappings presented by the would-be god."

"I can see that you believe in a god," I said, "but I struggle with what this god allows, if he exists."

"No, Kephart," he replied softly. 'No. I do not believe in 'a god.' I *know* that God is. And that is all that I can attest to as matters stand with us at this time."

His smile radiated profound warmth and expressed an embracing acceptance of me despite my contrary view. At this moment his face also reflected a quiet conviction—a certainty of confident faith that I had seen in Jill's penciled portrait of me. When studying her portrayal, I had seen an emanation that I had wished truly existed for me. Just now, I was impressed to find Shackleton's own face manifesting this condition.

"Now, let us discuss your personal attributes as I see them, and then your stellar ring, and then . . . well, as I said, there is a mystery to be solved—a disappearance—and perhaps a death to be prevented.

CHAPTER 12

I poured myself hot water, dipped a bag of ginger tea in it, and studied Shackleton's face. He had turned again toward the fire, which now barely flickered with diminishing flames. Bogart was stretched out on his side near the fireplace, contentedly absorbing the heat. In the dimly lit room, a ruddy glow from the coals reflected off the hearthstone. The shadows mixing and contrasting with colors of yellow and deep red matched my mood as I considered where I was being led. Feelings of anxiety, doubt, and dread interplayed with desire, hope, and optimism as my mind touched on the various aspects of joining up with Shackleton.

I wasn't ready to respond to his obvious presumption that I would be his chronicler and face-to-face delver into mysteries, among other things. I had little experience in writing and none at all in untangling the unhappy affairs of men. But it did seem that Shackleton was intent on conducting happy outcomes and in preventing tragic consequences, particularly for those who would be victims of secret selfish or desperate acts.

To participate in redirecting people's lives for good had its appeal. Linking my life up with extraterrestrials, no matter how remotely or indirectly, was scary. But then, for more than fifteen years, hadn't I already been "linked" to less desirable beings than the Abiding Ones? Apparently so. And was I to be content with being a delivery man? Didn't I have latent abilities to be developed? Was this opportunity knocking? Such was the pattern of my thoughts when Shackleton deflected them back on course.

"I would best describe you as a rather pristine young man, Kephart. By that I mean that you are thus far uncorrupted, partly because of your having dedicated yourself to supporting and sustaining your invalid mother while at the same time completing your schooling. Indeed, you have given little time to anything else. By some, you could be given the dubious label of 'unreal,' to apply a term both modern and prevalent.

"But contrary to worldly notion, there are great numbers of young people whose values align with yours. I just don't have time or opportunity to sort out and prove others as I have done with you. That little ball has been an indispensable boon for me, as it has permitted me to access your biographical record with unfailing accuracy. Every person is of some worth, Kephart, but few prove themselves worthy. For my purposes, I must say that you have done so.

"Kephart, where I am concerned, your demonstrated values and principles of conduct qualify you to receive great monetary rewards, and I intend to pay you handsomely. That aside, I am well aware that you will not accept any offer of employment by reason of income only, no matter how enticing. I will therefore appeal to you by way of your intrinsic values.

"As my assistant, you will have ample opportunities to learn and to develop talents. You will enjoy a high degree of autonomy. Your communication skills will be enhanced—both oral and written. You may expand minds, soften hearts, and make people more discerning and receptive of certain truths about themselves, the world, and the universe. Your proactive influence for good could reach far beyond the range of any other thing of which you might avail yourself, primarily through your writing. But on that subject I must place a condition, one that I am sure you will not object to."

"But my writing experience amounts to nothing, really," I said. "Mostly it's been restricted to keeping a journal, and little of that."

"Writing is essentially *thinking*, Kephart, and you have shown yourself to be very active at that performance, especially when it comes to questioning and analyzing. Then, too, you must not overlook all the hours spent reading to your mother from a wide variety of materials and authors. This has been an education in itself. You have thus associated with some of the best of minds, for you have drawn upon some classics. You have thereby had many mentors. And don't forget that one learns to write by writing. Just think of it, Kephart—as my assistant, you will be paid for *learning*."

His countenance showed eager and confident anticipation as he spoke these last words. At that moment I realized that Shackleton never allowed a negative or defeating thought to enter his mind. Apparently nothing was to hinder or obstruct his achieving a worthwhile or defensible objective.

Maybe this is what it took to be successful. What I had construed earlier to be "rude impertinence" on his part, I might have to re-interpret more correctly as "bold determination." The thought crossed my mind that Harvard Shackleton Gray was certainly unique and indefinable in any case.

"I was about to stipulate a condition bearing upon your writing," he continued. "And that is that you never record vulgar slang or offensive language, even though you will find it unavoidably profuse in your daily encounters. Such language can do nothing to enhance your written product, and it would certainly detract from your purpose in relating events as you devote yourself to improving minds and motives while at the same time engaging in acts of prevention or intervention. Reform must supplant realism at the expense of popular appeal. I feel certain that readership shall not suffer for want of vulgarity. Your words will find their way into the hands of those ready to receive them, and that is all that really matters, Kephart.

"As I said, I doubt that you will have any trouble complying with this constraint, particularly because you have personally dealt with overcoming your own habitual use of profanity, since its use was so prevalent among your peers and co-workers, though not within your family. Do you recall that particular time of your life to which I refer?"

I shook my head in amazement as I realized the depth, range, and detail of recorded events derived from that tiny implanted ball.

"You must be thinking about the summer when the sheriff's son and I couldn't get through five minutes of labor at the Turkey Foot mine without peppering our sweat with cusswords. It got so bad that we agreed to clean up our language by putting 'bad-word nickels' in coffee cans. The one with the least nickels in his can won all the other's nickels at the end of the shift. It worked. That summer, we both became keenly aware of our words, and I have kept a subconscious awareness ever since."

"Indeed, your very thoughts bear this out, Kephart."

"But I can't help asking how you could possibly have reviewed so much of my life as it's recorded on that ball. It must have taken months of listening—or whatever—to assimilate all that you apparently know."

Shackleton nodded, I presumed, in agreement. But after some thoughtful silence on his part, he corrected my false impression by disclosing a remarkable feature of the alien technology involved.

"Actually, the assimilation took only minutes at a time, over the days that I engaged in it, Kephart. By means that I can't explain at present, all of your sensed lifetime experiences and thoughts spanning the recorded period were 'downloaded' into my brain while the ball was still implanted near yours. I underwent several transfer sessions, all of them brief. The last was on Friday evening."

I sat speechless, contemplating all that his words suggested.

"It's a rather overwhelming process, one that I don't desire to be subjected to if it can be avoided, Kephart. But in your case, it has had its rewards."

A look of pain briefly passed over his face as he reflected on his experiences. Bogart suddenly got up from the hearth to lick Shackleton's hand and settle at his feet. There was something uncanny about the mutual communication displayed by the two, and I marveled at it.

Shackleton turned toward me with an appreciative smile, but I felt undeserving of it, mostly because of my own uncomplimentary thoughts and critical feelings regarding him over the past trying hours.

Again, he seemed to read my very thoughts on this when he said, "What you radiate is what you truly are, not what you pretend to be. And what you are is the result of your thoughts and choices. I have selected you with good reason, Kephart. I understand your aversion to my seeming insistence. You are entitled to your human reaction. I want you to understand that I would surely suffer more for attempting to rob you of your freedom to choose than I would for your choosing to not serve with me. Please understand, too, that I have your best personal interests at heart."

"You seem to know me better than I know myself. I find that a bit scary," I said. "And if you have stored so much of my life in your 'memory bank,' how do you keep yourself and your own memories separated out? Don't you find this confusing?"

"Oh, there is a cure for that," he said with amusement. "And I will have your recorded life and thought expunged from my memory, now that the record has served its usefulness for me."

He didn't elaborate on this, but I felt much more comfortable knowing that it would be so.

He went on. "Even though certain alien technologies extend beyond much of our own present scientific understanding, the continuing processes of development are endless. Of course, this is also true of earthly human advancements. There is no state of perfection in any case. Any goal of perfection is thus elusive.

"It is the same with the spiritual evolution of the Abiding Ones. For them the journey has become the joy, not the sought-for destination. They fully comprehend this law of happiness. They live it.

"Earth man, collectively speaking, struggles with this. Our happiness seems always to be dependent upon the attainment of something or other, and so real happiness remains forever beyond our grasp until we learn, individually, how to find our unconditional peace and contentment. The key is in giving, but we can't give of our emptiness, so we had best consider the 'what' and the 'where' of our filling.

"But now I'm digressing into philosophical realms somewhat outside our purpose for meeting tonight. I must add, however, that so long as we remain intent upon self-serving conquests, we will never develop or evolve to the point of being sustainable in the realms of what we presently perceive as space. For man, there is a worthiness and responsibility associated with the acquisition of certain technologies, the disregard of which will result in self destruction, as I'm sure you know, Kephart."

We both fell silent as we became momentarily absorbed with our individual thoughts. White ashes and dying embers were all that remained of the once-cheering fire. I scanned the den for a clock but saw none. This sharpened my awareness of Shackleton's sightless world, and I admit I was touched with poignancy regarding his need for assistance in carrying out his self-appointed humanitarian callings.

Once again, he apparently tuned in on my thoughts or feelings when he broke the silence.

"There is a woman, Kephart, who needs immediate help. According to Detective Walker, her husband has vanished and is presumed dead, possibly drowned. But a quick reconnaissance of the site of his disappearance has left me with an insistent impression that he is alive, or at least he was at the time Bones drove me through the area on Thursday afternoon. And I strongly sense this to be so now.

"In this case, however, there is confusion for me that I don't often experience. When we drove past a certain house not far from the man's abandoned truck, I sensed death as well. The truck was found out of sight along a road that runs beside the Skagit River dike a few miles south of Mount Vernon. It was parked over the dike itself near the water's edge on a narrow accessible beach. Its doors were locked.

"The fisherman who found and reported the vehicle claims that he touched nothing. He stated only that he was suspicious of what he called 'drag marks' and what appeared to be blood on a large stone beside the river. He had spent the day in the area since early dawn and had seen no one. The truck was there when he first arrived, and it appeared to have been parked during the night. The headlights were left on and were growing dim.

"The incident is under investigation by the Skagit County Sheriff, but as I understand it, the search for clues has been discontinued in the immediate area. Search dogs picked up the man's scent, but this was confined to the region between the truck and the river bank. The missing man's wife claims that he was never a sport fisherman, which deepens the mystery."

"Can't the Abiding Ones provide you with help?" I asked.

"As I said earlier, they do not interfere in our affairs, particularly in a physical, open way. However, they may at times *influence* events in undetectable ways, should there be significant justification for doing so. Such acts may be defensible as when, for example, Earth humans discover extraterrestrial artifacts, or remnants of such, that would give us technological clues prematurely, with respect to our spiritual evolution. Our heedless involvements with these findings—attempting such means as, say, 'back-engineering'—may jeopardize not only our own civilization, but they may threaten galactic societies remotely in ways we do not fully understand. We truly have no concept of the reach of our earthly thoughts and acts, Kephart.

"The Abiding Ones must certainly conform to their constraining laws. They are bound to witness only, for the most part, and to allow Earth men their agency. Why? Because they comply with irrevocable and universal laws that proscribe intrusion into the unfolding events leading to the fulfillment of Earth's purpose and ultimate destiny."

"Then why have they involved themselves in removing this fantastic ball from my head, or in providing you with the ring technology?" I asked. "I'm guessing the rings are derived from their technology."

"Yes. Excellent questions, Kephart! I can only answer by saying that they may *at times* protect certain individuals from both human and non-human beings who have violated the law, either knowingly or unknowingly, as it pertains to this planet. It is not their primary mission to do so, however. They are, for the most part, attempting to fulfill their various galactic missions without intrusion. In any case, the Abiding Ones typically do not engage in concerted efforts to combat evil on a grand scale.

"But then there are the 'Fallen Ones,' who deliberately transgress the 'hands off' law in greater measure. These beings must be unavoidably dealt with at times. They have sinister aspects that pose a greater threat to Earth humans, although not in ways that you might imagine. It is because of my own personal experience with these Fallen Ones that I have come to enjoy the unique privilege of associating with the Abiding Ones.

"The stellar rings, with their remarkable capabilities, were offered only upon the condition of my binding myself to certain rules. Unspeakably harsh penalties would be invoked, should I fail to uphold my obligation. But these very same penalties apply to the Abiding Ones as well.

"Incidentally, Kephart, your ring is a gift from *them*, not me. However, I am accountable for it just the same. Whether or not you choose to have your ring deactivated, you must forever regard it as a rare and precious thing—something that could be eagerly sought after by an assortment of characters having all sorts of undesirable motives."

He held his right hand out toward me, exhibiting his own stellar ring, which was quite unlike mine. Each was visibly unique in design.

"There are but three of these rings presently on the fingers of Earth humans, Kephart. So you might now more fully appreciate the heights and depths of honor and responsibility placed upon you by the bestowal of your own ring. Another thing you should know is that in the event of either your death or the removal of the ring from your finger, the ring becomes instantly dormant. It will be subsequently deactivated as well. Its inherent properties would remain, but reverse-engineering it as a device would be an impossible task.

"There are countless such rings worn by the Abiding Ones throughout the galaxies. They are considered a commonplace device, such as the telephone is to us. However, when programmed to the maximum capacity of their design, they have extensive capabilities. These include transference of images as well as other physical senses. Your ring is limited to verbal-aural transmission and reception, which is sufficient for our interactive needs. Needless to say, having been assured that your absolute privacy of mind is safeguarded, you will undoubtedly regard it as a marvel.

"I'm sure you will soon have occasion to value it increasingly—particularly because it can serve to provide an immediate recording of all worded thoughts, conversations, and verbalized descriptions of events as they transpire. This should greatly relieve you of the distractive burden of taking hand-written notes when your attention should be directed elsewhere. It will definitely provide infallible accuracy and afford you future convenient times for editing and transcribing.

"And now, Kephart, if you are to join with me in my humanitarian quests, I must explicitly hold you to a mandate. You have admirably demonstrated your willingness to adhere to such a charge already. But I must ask you to again pledge that you will not in any way identify yourself with me as you conduct your investigations, and that you will refrain from openly associating yourself with me except as I permit or direct you to do so.

"Under no circumstances are you to use a telephone of any sort to speak directly with either Laura or myself. Your ring is far superior, and it is undetectable. Should either of us find it necessary to ignore or cut off your call, the ring can also enable you to record messages for later retrieval. Laura will be available to explain the simple procedures of operation tonight. That depends, of course, on your acceptance of my offer of employment and on your pledging yourself to secrecy as I have asked."

In the dim glow of the fireplace I could see Shackleton's head drop as he brought his fingertips up to stroke his forehead. He seemed suddenly fatigued and depleted of energy. This was a sharp contrast to his previously buoyant disposition. Bogart stood and placed his chin on Shackleton's knee. Both man and dog remained silent.

CHAPTER 13

TO give myself time to consider all that Shackleton had presented, I decided to stall with an off-the-wall deflective question.

"Can our weather be controlled or manipulated by aliens?" I asked. "I'm thinking of that unpredicted storm Friday night. It seemed to be planned, as if to hide the event of my liberation—and my *initiation*, if I can add one of my own terms to describe your agenda for the night."

Shackleton dropped his hands to his lap, lifted his head and exploded in a hearty laugh.

"Great galloping gastropods!" he exclaimed. "You do have a devious way about you, Kephart!"

"May I turn on a light?" I asked. "It might help prepare me for the en*light*enment you're about to offer."

He laughed again and said, "Thank you, Kephart, for your injection of much-needed humor. Yes. Turn on all the lights you can find. Please."

I stood, stretched, reached for a slice of cheddar cheese, and then wrapped it in a slice of pastrami before heading toward a couple of lamp switches. (I firmly believe eating reduces stress.)

As I returned to the service table, I grabbed a slice of turkey and held it out to Bogart, who gingerly lifted it from my fingers. His eyes fully expressed his gratitude.

"Would you care for a snack yourself, sir?" I asked, lifting the tray toward Shackleton.

He felt around and asked, "Is there a maple bar left?"

I handed him the single remaining one and searched his face. His eyes shone with warmth and anticipation. (I don't mean with regard to the pastry.) His remark was uncanny.

"Kephart, before I answer your question about controlling the weather, I want to direct your attention to the exquisite communicative properties of eyes—not just human eyes, but those of other mammals as well."

I was startled by this abrupt divergence because my mind had been intently focused on Bogart's expressive eyes in the previous moment.

"You may well recall your mother's eyes," he said, "and how effectively she communicated with them, especially after losing her capacity for speech. There are many avenues of communication, body language being one. But never fail to first apply your acquired skill for reading eyes. It may serve you best in your dealings with humans—and animals, should the need arise."

"I'll take that to heart, sir," I said, and as I spoke, I became aware of my inward conclusive acceptance of joining with Shackleton. (Of course, he had already detected this earlier.) I quietly wondered at this realization while he continued.

"Yes. Weather can be easily and dramatically controlled by aliens when it serves their purpose. But not as Earth humans attempt to control it. They employ a language of sorts that defies description.

"All I can say is that what we perceive to be matter is just manifest energy. All matter has intelligence, Kephart. Intelligence abounds in our very atmosphere.

"You might say that programmed energies behave and interact in specific patterns, which are made evident to our senses. But then, aren't our physical senses just programmed energies reporting manifest forces and information? And they report this to what? A spirit entity becomes undeniable when you think about it, Kephart.

"Now, some people may find it hard to accept that all matter has intelligence. So, to 'enlighten' yourself, you just might find it interesting to contemplate two short verses of scripture bearing on this subject, particularly since your last name is Stone. Please. Look up Joshua twenty-four, verses twenty-six and twenty-seven."

His silence expressed his insistence, so I reached for his King James Version of the Bible and read the verses to myself. I wasn't sure about the implied association at first, but prompted by Shackleton's lingering smile, I read and pondered the words a second time.

"And Joshua wrote these words in the book of the law of God, and took a great stone, and set it up there under an oak, that was by the sanctuary of the Lord.

"And Joshua said unto all the people, Behold, this stone shall be a witness unto us; for it hath heard all the words of the Lord which he spake unto us: it shall be therefore a witness unto you, lest ye deny your God."

"You may find it hard to accept, Kephart—and it may astound you to learn this—but that little sphere taken from your head can't begin to compare with the very cells of your body for keeping your personal record. The problem lies in retrieval of explicit cell-stored data. Although it is verifiable that the stored intelligence exists, its meaningful, comprehensive extraction presents a challenge, even to advanced alien branches of applied science.

"There is a recent incident in your life worthy of mention here. Do you recall at the time of your accident that you witnessed Joel Whipple bending over you? Although you were unconscious, you observed him as he knelt beside your body to check your vital signs. Your observation was from outside and above your body, yet it was recorded by the sphere just the same! What does this out-of-body experience tell you?"

Wondering, I silently shook my head. (I admit I was stumped.)

"Think, Kephart! Think! It can only mean that the body is a replication of the spirit. Out-of-body observations clearly indicate that we are spirit entities being subjected to mortal-sense experiences as we perceive them to be.

"Obviously, upon your spirit's return, your body's cells incorporated your spirit's experience as if you had not been absent. Your sensory systems transferred all this to your brain and the little sphere for recording. This is something for you to dwell upon and contemplate when you are bored or cannot sleep," he said with a smile, perceiving my perplexity.

"You've made me see that what I've learned to this point in my life is next to nothing—just a drop in the ocean compared to all there is to soak up," I said. "It's very humbling. But at the same time, it's exciting to realize that life has so much to offer if I wonder at it. I've enjoyed listening to all you've said, but I'll need a lot more time to mentally digest it."

Shackleton's face brightened. "Take all the time you need, Kephart. Fortunately, it's true: The more we learn, the less we find we truly know," he said.

Then, briskly rubbing his palms together, he laughed and added,"I will take those last words of yours to confirm that you have accepted my offer and that you look forward to our *future* meetings and discussions!"

He quickly arose from his chair and felt his way around the low table to stand before me. His face was beaming as he extended both hands toward me, and I confess that I didn't hesitate to engage in a handshake of affirmation. Strangely, I found it a relief to commit myself to serving him.

Bogart, with his tongue hanging loosely over his lower lip, came up alongside Shackleton. His eyes were shining and intently directed toward me. Knowing it wasn't because he was eager to show me the way out, I bent down to snatch a few pieces of meat and cheese from the food tray and, spreading them out on my hand, I offered them to him. He delicately plucked them piece by piece from my outstretched palm, using his tongue and teeth with precision. His dignified performance impressed me. It exceeded that of some humans. I would not have been surprised to see him wipe his muzzle with one of Phoebe's blue-and-white checkered napkins.

"You will want a dog, Kephart," Shackleton said.

"Well, I'd really like to have one, but I'm afraid it wouldn't work out just now. I couldn't expect the Whipples to look after one during my times away. Besides, they have their beloved old Smooch to care for yet."

"Of course, Kephart. What I mean to say is that you will want to find a dog with a good nose to assist you tomorrow. Your first assignment will briefly require the use of a search dog. That will be the task of the morning—to locate a reliable hound.

"I regret that you must begin on a Sunday, but we are dealing with an urgent matter, and timing is critical. Finding such a dog on short notice and on a Sunday may be a challenge, but I'm confident that you will succeed."

"I'll get an early start. The Whipple family's country lifestyle always sees to that," I said, stretching as I eased my way toward the studio.

Shackleton smiled, nodded, and walked beside me.

"Now, you must see Laura," he said. "She will be expecting you. There are some items and instructions awaiting you at her home. You should not be detained there for very long."

He held up his right hand, extended his little finger, and wiggled it at me.

"Stay in touch, Kephart. Three-way conversations are also possible. Laura will show you the procedure."

Bogart had led us to the front door. He was definitely smiling at me. A warm, friendly smile.

Shackleton turned to face me squarely and said, "You may want to carry a clipboard with a few papers when going about investigative activities that could arouse curiosity. I'm sure you can see, as a courier, that doing so would tend to dispel inquisitiveness—if your pretense is not associated with officialdom. At times, your delivery van might add to your deception of being on a valid errand as well."

"Carrying papers is almost second nature to me now," I said. "And the VW is my only means of getting around. Sorry—I meant to thank you for that earlier, Shackleton."

"Oh, yes . . ." he smiled and raised his eyebrows as he spoke. "You may want to compare your notes with mine."

He held up his stellar ring finger again.

"I have here recorded all that is significant of our conversations tonight. Laura should be quite willing to assist you in retrieving my record at your convenience."

It seemed that my note-taking during the evening had been in vain. But then, I felt better for having my own tangible copy to rely on at this point.

"I guess you know that I will do just that—compare notes," I said laughing. "I suppose I've come to rely too much on my fingers. I'm not ready to depend on 'foreign technology' just yet."

"Kephart . . ." Shackleton began, then paused. "Kephart, there will be times of danger ahead for you. I can make no guarantee for your safety. You will have to rely on your wits and your instinct."

"I shouldn't have any trouble with that," I said and smiled as I thought of some very recent experiences in a certain warehouse.

"But in most of my past dealings with danger, I've known in advance what to look for and what to expect. I can see that this might not be possible anymore.

"Just now, though, I can't help wondering about such things as where I'm to take the dog—when I get one—and what I'm to use for a scent. Maybe an address would help too . . . or even a map or sketch of the area I'm to search. Not having any idea of what road I'm to travel puts quite a strain on my limited intuitive powers."

Shackleton closed his eyes and silently chuckled.

"Ah! Of course. The *outward* journey. Thank you for drawing my attention to what is an apparent oversight. Looking for a road to travel, eh, Kephart? I'm reminded of what I believe is a Zen quote—rather insightful: 'Walker, there is no road. The road is made by walking.'

"You have taken your first step along your new journey within by accepting my offer tonight. I am confident of your inner direction. Laura will provide all the information you need for taking *outward* steps. Welcome to my exclusive world of mystery, challenge, and wonder, Kephart."

His lips tightened as he found my right hand and gripped it firmly.

"I hope I won't disappoint you, Shackleton," I said. "You seem to hold expectations of me that may be above my reach, but you know I'll do my best to measure up."

Shackleton replied only with an affirmative nod.

Bogart tilted his head to one side as if to ask why I should doubt myself. He liked me, and that was all that mattered as far as he was concerned.

With a wave to Bogart, I turned away and stepped down the two short brick steps that had brought me to that door leading into Shackleton's mysterious world just thirty-six hours earlier. I had been totally unprepared for what was to follow. What would the next day and night and day bring? The thought was scary.

As I walked down Evening Star Lane toward the Overlook, I could faintly hear the grand piano come to life again.

CHAPTER 14

I awoke to the sounds of a piano. They came more clearly than those that reached my ears as I walked away from Shackleton's studio the previous night. Sunlight streamed through my curtains to illuminate a patch of wallpaper printed with patterns of floppy-eared bunnies nestled in gray-green grass amid a variety of brightly colored flowers. This had been Jill's pick of décor at some point in her youth, I supposed. But then, maybe Selma had chosen it for her. The paper was obviously old and flaking. The restful patterns had become a familiar part of my present surroundings.

What wasn't familiar was the piano music. I had passed by Selma's old Ivers and Pond upright almost daily without giving it a second glance. Never before had I heard her play it. Now the music was a pleasant introduction to my Sunday morning. I stretched out, put my hands behind my head, and basked in the early morning's offerings.

After a few minutes of welcome tranquility, my brain switched on to a different wavelength, and I rolled over to look at the bedside clock: 7:40. I could afford to lounge twenty more minutes. But when my head dropped back onto my pillow, I began recalling the events and conversations of Saturday night. I still felt good about having made a commitment to Shackleton, but I now sensed the urgency of following through on my first assignment. Timing was critical, as he had said. Laura had confirmed this when I initiated a ring talk with her right after leaving Shackleton. (I couldn't resist giving the ring a try.)

Not long after our thought exchange had ended, I found her front door open in expectation of my arrival. Holding a plastic bag in one hand and an envelope in the other, she had met me with tears on her cheeks. She was wearing an orchid-colored satin robe, and her hair hung full-length about her shoulders. Unable to detect the cause of her emotions, I stood silently in her doorway, waiting for her to be the first to speak.

Suddenly she dropped the bag to the floor and stepped forward to give me a hug. Surprised, I didn't resist but just let the hug linger as I felt her trembling. Abruptly she stepped back to smile and wipe away tears with her free hand.

"You can't possibly know how thankful I am for your choosing to work with Shackleton, Kep," she said. "I'll do everything I can to help you succeed. You've given me relief and freedom I can't explain—or ever repay you for."

I then gave her a smile and a nod, not knowing how else to respond.

"Please don't overlook the value of the stellar ring, Kep," she said. "Use it as often as you feel a need to communicate. I'm just a thought away. Shackleton prefers that you ask questions of me first, or that you relay information to me for transfer to him. But if your situation calls for immediate advice from him, don't hesitate to contact him directly."

She then handed me the envelope.

"I've written down the cue words for you to think out for every function of the ring. The procedures are so simple. You'll have them memorized in no time. All the instructions are here, including how to record and address specific notes you want to retrieve. I've also put in a map and other information to bring you up to date."

She reached down to pick up the bag she'd dropped.

"These things don't need to be returned," she commented.

"I'm surprised because there is a little notepad in here that the missing man's wife, Letha, pitched in with his unlaundered socks and things. I found that it contained some notes that are rather revealing. Maybe she didn't bother to look at all the little book contained.

"Letha turned out to be quite different from what I'd expected, considering the mysterious aspects of her husband's disappearance and this sudden loss in her life. They didn't have any children, so you'd think her loss would be more deeply felt. I mean, she seemed stoical or unmoved by the circumstances.

"When I asked for some of her husband's personal things to use with a track dog, she handed me this bag—already prepared. Graham Walker told me that the deputy had found her reluctant at first to give him the scent items he got. That was on Thursday. I picked up this bag at her home Friday afternoon—no problem. Maybe you'll have a chance to meet her, Kep. I'd be interested in your impression of her."

I smiled and shrugged my shoulders. "I guess we'll just have to see where my road takes me," I said. (Obviously, Shackleton's parting comments still lingered in my mind then.)

"What time is it, Laura? My watch didn't survive Friday night in the warehouse."

With an understanding smile, she stepped back to look at her pendulum wall clock. "It's eleven thirty-six, Kep. I know you'll need to catch up on some sleep, so I won't keep you any longer."

I then thanked her and turned to go. As I did so, I noticed again the picture of Christ on the wall to the left of her doorway. This time I took in the message that was decoratively inscribed beside it. It read, "If, in the end, you have not chosen Jesus Christ, it will not matter what you have chosen." No authorship was credited.

Laura had watched as I descended the stairs. Her eyes were brighter then, her expression softer. It seemed then that the "wilted flower" had been somehow watered and refreshed. I didn't think I could take any credit for that personally, and I had wondered at my feeling thankful that she found solace and strength in her personal faith—lonely and unfulfilled as she was.

I'd thought, too, about her cousin Rose and the inexpressible grief that must still cloud Shackleton's inner world. I recalled his words of conviction that "God is" and tried to imagine what experiences might have made him feel so certain of this. He too must have to rely heavily on his faith to cope with his losses. Was this faith just something that he generated and developed within himself to keep his sanity? Was it planted in his youth? Was it the result of some epiphany? Or did he know secrets that gave him total confidence based on experiences he was unable to share?

Afterward, as I drove home, I had reflected on what I felt was the unfairness of life as I viewed Laura and Shackleton kept apart by tragic circumstances. They seemed a pretty good match to me, if only . . . well, if only.

My mind skipped back to Friday night, when Laura related the questions she had about Shackleton's mysterious condition: his new behaviors after his return from the San Juan Islands, his unexplained loss of sight, and his strange habit of disappearing without a word—and without Bogart. I remembered her saying that he was totally dry on entering the house when he should have been exposed to a drenching rain, if only briefly. I could see now that she had tried to prepare me for what she must have deduced: He was brought home by aliens. The thought of this still disturbed me, despite all I had since learned and come to accept of Shackleton's world.

If Laura had questions about his blindness and changes in habits, she still knew more than I did. What was hidden in the lower part of the house that they both shared exclusive access to? Then, again, why was he so secretive—even with her? Would I ever find answers to these questions?

Laura's brief handwritten instructions from Shackleton now lay on top of the envelope, which I had placed on the stand beside my bed. I had read them, and I had flipped through some pages of the missing man's notebook before going to sleep. Laura had also given me the extra key to the VW bus.

I picked it up and turned it over between my fingers while my mind turned over what I anticipated to be the day's events. But as things turned out, the anticipated didn't happen, except for finding a dog. And even that task proved to be unimaginable in the way it evolved. Still, getting the dog was to be an unforgettable experience—the most pleasant of the day.

I slid out of bed, pulled on my jeans, slipped into my shirt, and headed barefoot for the bathroom downstairs. Impressed by Selma's skill at the piano and ready with a compliment, I poked my head through the archway leading into the living room at the foot of the stairs.

Selma was not at the piano. It was Jillian.

Incapable of any other reaction, I stood watching her with my mouth open. The piano became suddenly silent. As was typical of her, Jill tilted her head to one side and regarded me with an expression of quiet expectancy and amusement. Her green eyes sparkled.

Once again I forgot myself and my disheveled appearance. My eyes fell on Jill's dark hair, where it curved at her chin and touched her loosely folded pale-blue collar. Resting her hands in her lap, she swiveled on the piano stool to face me. A trail of silver buttons led my eyes down the front of her embroidered beige skirt to meet enticing legs in dark nylons. She wore blue dress shoes with two-inch-high heels. They looked new.

I managed to overcome my fascination sufficiently to utter a profound observation.

"You're not dressed for Singing Tree Hill," I said after clearing my throat.

"Oh? Well, Kephart Stone, I can't quite decide what *you're* dressed for. Digging clams? Catching tadpoles in a ditch?" She laughed softly as she swiveled lightly back and forth on the piano stool.

Her playful manner invited my participation, but I was caught off guard. I turned to finish buttoning my shirt and then tucked it into my jeans.

"So far you haven't ever caught me at my best, have you, Jill? I wonder why that is," I said jokingly. (But I meant it.)

"Am I supposed to think your best is something else?" Jill teased as she inclined her head farther toward her shoulder.

I tightened my lips into a smile while trying to think of a sharp comeback when Selma appeared, wiping her hands on a dish towel. Her fine gray hair was neatly combed and tied back. Some stray wisps fell against her ears and clung to her cheeks. Perplexity clouded her gentle, soft features.

"Anjill, dear, why did you stop so sud . . . oh! Kep! What a pleasant surprise to see you down early . . . or at all, for that matter! What ever has been keepin' you away so? Oh, but I'm forgettin'! Kep, this is the angel you be hearin' about all this time. And Anjill, this is—"

"I know, Mom," Jill broke in. She smiled at Selma and then glanced at me. "We've already met. Last Friday."

"Friday? But how . . .? Oh, dear. I guess I be losin' it lately."

Selma's lively brown eyes swept from Jill to me and then back.

"We just happened to find each other on Singing Tree Hill, Selma," I said. "You and Oat were away that afternoon. You'd left me a note—and a great leftover supper. Remember?"

I snapped my thumb and finger.

"Which reminds me! I've got my memory back—all of it now! It happened when I met Jill. She was humming a song and . . . never mind for now, Selma. Maybe Jill can fill you in. Right now I've got to get moving. I need to find a dog—for my new job."

"New job?"

"I was sort of led into a different job over the weekend. I think it will be a good thing. I'm still working for Bick and Dozie part-time. Bick gave me a cell phone to use for when they need me—if I can work a delivery into my new schedule. I might be pretty busy. And I can't count on a definite schedule either, come to think of it. I'll be always on-call, working mostly on my own for whatever hours it takes to complete an assignment. Right now I'm . . ."

I suddenly became unsure at this point as to how much I should tell anyone about my present activities, so I tried to divert to a description of my job title. It came off clumsy.

"I'm an assistant P.I., working on a case that's . . . well . . . secret."

"You mean you're becomin' a private investigator?" Selma said in a disquieted tone.

"Oh, not like you might think, Selma," I said.

Then, hoping to reassure her, I added, "I'm not to be involved in divorce cases or the kinds of things you'd usually associate with private investigations. It's more like prevention and intervention—activities that might keep unhappy things from happening or that help bring about happy endings if possible. I guess you could say that 'P.I.' stands for 'preventive intervener,' where I'm concerned."

Lame as this explanation was, I hoped it might both appease her and preclude her typical protective admonitions. Fortunately, any further conversation was prevented just then as Oat came up behind me and put his hand on my shoulder.

"Finally got hungry enough to come home, Kep? Sooner or later we're all led by our stomachs, especially when we go on adventures. It's hard to say what brings us home, hearts or stomachs. I'll say stomachs. Too bad, son, but Joel and I ate everything up. No more breakfast left. You might check

Smooch's bowl."

Oat gripped my shoulder with his big, powerful hand and laughed his hearty, outdoorsy laugh. I turned to face him. His steel-rimmed glasses couldn't hide exceptionally kind eyes or disguise a fatherly mien.

Sturdily built and ruddy complected, he presented a striking image. Although his closely cropped hair was often hidden under a Great Northern Railroad engineer's cap (a cherished gift of bygone days), this morning it bore evidence of hair oil and a brushing. His white mustache and goatee, always neatly trimmed, contrasted favorably with the dark-blue suit he wore.

Still, those eyes were his dominant feature as they regarded me. I admired the man, and now his easy smile brought out in me a playful spirit—something that I didn't often feel or care to exhibit toward others.

"Just point to a chore, and I'll do it for a scrap of food, Oat. Just point. (Food *was* actually on my mind for some reason.)

Oat grinned, pointed toward the open kitchen doorway, and said, "There's a stovetop out there with cookware on it that needs to be cleaned up. Use your mouth to do the job."

Just then, Joel came up behind Oat, wiping his hands on a dirty rag. "It's on," he said to Oat. "I think it'll get us through the day. Guess I'd best change back into my Sunday duds." He looked past his father and grinned at me.

"Hey, Kep. Good to see you. Must be hungry, huh?" (I couldn't believe it. Two hits in a row.)

"I'm beginning to feel so," I answered, twisting my mouth and blinking.

Joel had a sharp sense of humor, but his countenance usually reflected youthful wisdom and thoughtful contemplation. Always active, he was a strong young man of twenty-eight who worked unceasingly to help his aging parents support themselves on this fourth-generation tract of homesteaded land. One day he would inherit the choice farmstead. He would certainly deserve it.

He was quite good looking: tall, with dark hair and dark-brown eyes. His deeply tanned face was always clean-shaven, even when his chores and labors demanded long hours and an early rising. I knew he had a girlfriend, but I had never met her, and I wondered how he ever found time for her.

My personal debt to Joel couldn't be measured. At the time of my accident, his quick action had doubtless saved my life. As with his father, I regarded him with great respect.

Selma spoke up in my behalf.

"Well now, Joel. Changin' a flat tire has most surely put you in need of a second breakfast. So if he's willin', maybe Kep'll share a wee bit of his that I've saved back in case. But you better be movin', 'cause we be leavin' in twenty minutes." She winked at me and untied her apron.

Joel grinned at his mother and shot a glance toward Jill.

"Guess we won't need a ride from you after all, Sis," he said. "Are you going to church with *us* today?"

Jill's face reflected patient affection as she replied, "I have my Primary class, remember?"

Joel pursed his lips, gave a slight nod, and smiled warmly at his sister. "Miss being with you, Sis. Seems like we're never together anymore."

"I miss you too," Jill said and quickly left the piano stool to cross the room and give him a hug around his neck.

For me, it felt good to witness this open expression of love. It reminded me of a close family bond that I had once known but could no longer experience. I thought it a privilege to be included and treated as one of the Whipple family.

Oat put his arm across my shoulders, excused himself, and headed for the back porch to check on Smooch's supply of food and water.

Joel moved toward the bathroom to wash up, so I changed course and followed Selma into the kitchen. Her short, stumpy legs caused her to walk with a slight rocking motion that gave her the appearance of being in pain, but I couldn't know if she suffered or not. She never complained about anything, no matter what the days or years inflicted upon her.

Through the open kitchen doorway, my eyes met Jill's as she seated herself at the dining room table. She rested her chin in her hand, smiled, and said nothing as I heaped my plate with scrambled eggs, sausage, and biscuits. Then I caught her still watching me, obviously studying me, as I reached for the honey jar and pulled silverware from a counter drawer. Beginning to feel self-conscious, I approached her carrying all I had gathered up.

My mind was intent upon finding something to say, something that wouldn't make me sound foolish or invite Selma's notice, when at the table's edge I bumped the back of a chair and dropped the silverware and honey. The silverware clattered to the floor, but I managed to flip the honey jar sideways onto the table. While trying to set the jar upright, I nearly dumped my loaded plate of sausage, eggs, and biscuits.

Jill put her hand over her mouth and turned her head away, unable to keep from laughing.

As I bent down to pick up the flatware, Selma said, "Kep, dear, you needn't eat from the floor. You won't be offendin' Anjill none to sit up at the table with her. She had her breakfast early on."

Her face was wrinkled with humor as she brought me a clean set of silver.

"I'm so happy to hear you've got your memory back, dear. I be wishin' to have you tell me all about those missin' pieces of your life. Maybe at suppertime. Please do be here. We be havin' spaghetti and meatballs with garlic toast 'cause it's quick and easy.

It keeps if you be late, but let's hope you won't be.

"Oh! I'm losin' it! You said you be wantin' a dog. Whatever for?"

"I need a dog for tracking a scent," I said. "And don't worry, Selma. I won't be searching for a dangerous criminal."

She looked over at Jill and said, "What about Bessie Mae? Would one of hers do, do you think?"

Jill nodded her head in the affirmative. "Let's see if she still has Pokey," she said. "Do you suppose her phone is still working?"

"Oh, honey, do try to call her yourself now, if you will. I'm goin' to spruce up a bit. We be leavin' soon."

She gave me and then Jill a parting hug and left us to ourselves.

As I lifted a forkful of lukewarm scrambled eggs to my mouth, Jill said, "Your food could probably use some heating up. I can do that for you if you'd like."

I was happy that she chose to sit with me. Her quiet acceptance of me in spite of my clumsiness and untidy appearance began to put me more at ease in her presence.

"Well . . . sure. Thanks," I said.

As I watched her move to take my plate, I was struck again by the gracefulness of her feminine form—beauty made all the more attractive by her choice of clothes. It was now my turn to study *her,* and I did so until it became a bit too obvious.

There was a magnetism between us. It seemed that we were both aware of it. Something told me that neither of us had dealt with an attraction quite like this before, but then, I could only account for myself.

"What brought you here this morning?" I asked tentatively. "I mean, if you have a class to attend . . . wait a minute. I don't get it. What kind of college class would you take on a Sunday?"

"I don't *take* a class, Kep. I teach a group of Primary kids at church. It's what I do every Sunday. And I play the piano while they sing. I was going over some prelude music when you came downstairs."

"It sounded great. I was going to compliment Selma, but then I was surprised to find it was you at the piano. Which brings me back to my question. Why did you come all the way from Bellingham this morning? It sounded to me like you didn't need to come here just to practice. Well, maybe you came to visit your family, but considering the short time you could all be together, your long drive didn't offer much. I would have slept in late."

Her eyes stayed on her task as she answered with an evocative tone in her voice. "Not all my choices are practical. I'm not perfect."

She laughed. "Sometimes I can't account for the way I'm led to do things. Sometimes I don't see any reason or good sense in what I do. But I usually find out why later on. Or at least I come to know myself better because of my choice."

Thankful for the opening, I said, "I've thought a lot about your parting comment last Friday—about choice and purpose in everything. It looks like our separate choices have brought us together again after all. Our paths have joined without our planning. Is that okay with you?"

She didn't answer. Instead, she put the warmed-up food back on my plate and placed it before me. Then she went back into the kitchen and filled two tall glasses with cold water. After setting the water glasses on the table, she sat down opposite me, rested her chin on her interlaced fingers, and stared thoughtfully at the tabletop.

"Sometimes little choices have big consequences, Kep. I really don't think I can answer that. It might not be a good idea for me to stay alone with you here . . . I mean after the family leaves."

She got up and went to a kitchen drawer. After pulling out a phone book, she went to the phone and punched some numbers she'd looked up. She held the phone to her ear long enough to learn that there would be no response—just a recorded announcement.

"The phone's been disconnected again," she said.

Just then there were "good-byes" coming from the back door, soon followed by the sounds of car doors being slammed shut. Jill looked at the kitchen clock. It was eight twenty-five. She seemed to be struggling with indecision.

"I'm sure I'll find a dog some way on my own," I said. "And if you're worried about being alone with me, I can be gone in no time. When do you teach your class?"

"Church starts at one o'clock," she said. "Kep, it isn't that I don't trust you. And no one is telling me how to live my life. I just . . ."

"Jill, I guess I have a confession to make. I hope you won't take this in the wrong way, but . . . well, it sounds stupid, but I've never been alone with a girl ever . . . you know? I guess I'll have to take that back. I was alone with you on Singing Tree Hill. But that's it. It seems like my whole life has been work, school, and my invalid mother. I've never had a social life and I've never really missed one. Not before now.

"So I wish you could feel safe with me. I respect you. You might say that in my mind, there's a fence around you. You'll be the one to build a gate—and you'll be the one to open it, not me."

Placing her hands behind her, she leaned back against the kitchen countertop. She raised her chin and licked her lips and smiled. Then, closing her eyes, she sighed heavily.

When she opened her eyes again, she said, "You seem so experienced, Kep. And you look strong, but I don't feel vulnerable in your presence—not as if I might think you'd take advantage of me. Maybe you've explained why just now. All the same, there's something about you—us together. Maybe it's me that I don't trust. But I've always kept myself out of harm's way, if you know what I mean."

She tilted her head slightly and studied my face in an appealing way.

In that moment I sensed a unifying bond between us, one that transcended natural physical attraction. Not that the magnetism wasn't there—it was there, definitely. We both felt it. But we mutually seemed to connect with a stronger kind of link, one that I didn't recognize and couldn't define.

I nodded and said, "I can see that. I mean . . . well, I think what I want to say can best be expressed the way I heard a man put it last night. He said that we radiate what we truly are, not what we pretend to be. To me . . . well, I like what you radiate. Can we let it go at that?"

She smiled at me, closed her eyes again, and nodded twice sharply.

Opening her eyes, she moved away from the countertop and said, "I can take you to meet Bessie Mae. Her place is just down the lane. She has several dogs, but one of them *lives* by her nose. Her name is Pokey. It's short for Pokeyhuntus. Bessie has her own unique sense of humor.

"I suppose it won't do any good for me to try to prepare you to meet her and her husband Wilbur. You'll just have to arrive at your own appreciation of each of them. They're good people. Just . . . unusual."

"Great!" I said. "Just let me finish this last biscuit, and I'll whip through my morning wash-up.

"Oh! Would you do me a favor? There's a key to the VW bus on the stand beside my bed—*your* bed. I've got a leather box in the cupboard under the camper sink. Could you bring it in and put it on the table while I get ready? There's some money in it that I'll need. Do you have any idea how much the dog will cost—to rent, I mean?"

"Probably nothing, if you don't *insist* on Bessie Mae taking something," Jill said. "But it would be nice if you'd give her whatever you can afford. They aren't very well off."

"I'm sure that won't be a problem, Jill. How does a hundred dollars sound? I have an expense account."

Jill leaned her head over to one side and looked at me with raised eyebrows.

"More?" I asked.

"Are you sure your new job is legal?" she asked. "A hundred dollars is more than enough—*much* more than enough."

"Okay. I can afford to be generous with poor people. I'll be generous."

Laura had told me during our Saturday-night ring conversation that the thirty-five thousand dollars in the cash box was to cover my first three months' salary, plus a five-thousand-dollar "initiatory bonus." Shackleton would then pay me every three months in advance. I was to keep receipts so I could be reimbursed for any expenses I might incur. Now, when discussing expenses with Jill, I was struck with a full appreciation of Shackleton's staggering offer. My mind could barely grasp it. But I was also struck with the weight of my importance to Shackleton—and the responsibility attached to it.

As Jill came back through the kitchen doorway, she audibly sighed as if relieved. Then she paused, smiled her beautiful smile at me, and lightly touched my shoulder as she passed by to go upstairs for the key.

I was dealing with feelings I'd never had before. I was rich—in ways I had never known. But Jill was the treasure I most desired. I realized that little else mattered to me now. As I spooned honey onto my last piece of biscuit, I noticed that my hand was shaking.

Life was amazing. Truly.

CHAPTER 15

A quarter mile down Whipple Farm Lane, Jill had me steer the VW bus onto the rutted road leading eastward out over the fields from the gray mailbox marked "Potts." She explained that this was an easement over Oat's section of land that permitted legal access to the Pottses' five-acre parcel at the back. Many years in the past, Oat had quitclaimed it to them. Their acreage abutted the railway on the east and was situated behind two low hills that obstructed views from the west and north.

After what seemed a lengthy time of dipping and bouncing over the crude road, we came in sight of a dilapidated old barn and a low, humble house sheathed with stained wood siding and warped batten-boards. Its mossy roof sagged a bit.

The house stood at the center of everything. It was surrounded by leaning fences, garden plots, raised vegetable beds, and various sheds—some for housing animals. Spread out haphazardly near the house, huge broken crocks of flowers took defiant stands against overwhelming growths of besieging weeds.

The whole farm looked both tired and productive, both neglected and nurtured. There was order. There was disorder. Carcasses of rusting farm machinery appeared to be abandoned wherever the machines had expired. Ruptured wooden halfbarrels overflowed with bright flowers—some trailing and some upright. A few of these were scattered among piles of old boards and discarded junk. An ancient wringer-type washing machine occupied its final resting place on the front porch, festooned with loops of a kinked and split garden hose.

The "aroma" of pigs pervaded the air as we approached. Dogs came at us, barking while chickens fled. Jill looked over at me and laughed.

"You see? Bessie Mae's endearing farm prepares you better than I could have with words," she said.

I had wondered why Jill associated the farm mostly with Bessie Mae, rather than attach it to her husband as well. It didn't take long to see why. As we drove up, Wilbur came out of the house behind Bessie Mae and stood on the porch. He waited with his hands in the pockets of his tattered overalls while Bessie strode eagerly toward us, her buxom form rocking with each step. Her eyes were nearly hidden in the folds of her eyelids and the deep smile wrinkles at her temples. Her broad, cheery smile revealed missing teeth.

Wilbur's face was long and his eyelids drooped. His entire body drooped. His mouth was a narrow straight line. A Great Northern Railroad cap seemed to have perched itself atop the pinnacle of his tall, sloping head. I got the impression that the cap had arrived there on its own, because Wilbur's slight, skimpy body seemed incapable of producing the strength to lift it there. The cap was identical to Oat's, so it aroused my curiosity.

Comparing Wilbur and Bessie Mae, I got the impression that their outward physical appearances were reflections of their characteristic motives and thoughts—their strengths and weaknesses, victories and defeats. The farm itself was a mirror of their paradoxical combination. Its substance expressed their individual spirits together.

We got out of the bus and were immediately surrounded by a canine chorus. Bessie Mae drew near.

When she recognized Jill, she joyfully thrust out her arms in welcome and exclaimed, "Oh, Anjill! Dear, sweet child! Heaven's not forgot me after all!

"It's been soooo long, Anjill! My, but have you ever grown into a beautiful thing! You always was a beautiful child, but now . . . oh, my! I scarce can believe what time does. Well, it sure ain't done to me what it's done to you. Why ain't you ever come to see me, child? Oh, never mind now. I'm just so happy you're here! So happy!" Her voice quavered and cracked with her last words.

"I was here with Mom not too long ago," Jill said tenderly. "Remember? We brought you an Easter basket with the chocolates you like so well. But I suppose it has been quite a while ago, Bessie. At least it has been for you. You don't get many visitors. I'm sorry. We'll just have to come see you more often."

Bessie Mae shook her head up and down vigorously as tears welled up in her eyes and began flowing down her wrinkled red cheeks. I could see then that what I had thought were "smile wrinkles" were, in fact, "cry wrinkles" as well.

Her coarse gray hair, apparently scissored from various angles, looked as though birds had nested in it and suddenly taken off in fright. A torn straw hat, decorated and tied with a sun-faded yellow ribbon, clung to the back of her neck. She wore a simple floral-patterned dress that ballooned out from her body, exposing stockings with holes. Her shoes, well worn and splitting, looked to have been once upon a time more appropriate for city streets than country soil.

A hundred dollars isn't nearly enough, I thought as I watched Bessie Mae's hands reach out to embrace Jill's cheeks. They were clean hands. Wrinkled and calloused, but clean.

Most of the dogs were quieting down, but one particularly lively one kept jumping up at Jill with wild enthusiasm and obvious affection. Each time it sprang at her, Jill caught its paws, trying to protect her good Sunday clothes from being clawed and torn. She had been successful until Bessie Mae touched her cheeks. Then one of the silver buttons was unavoidably torn loose from her skirt about ten inches above her knees. Jill ignored this as she clasped Bessie's hands in her own. I reached down to pick up the button.

As I raised myself up, Jill said, "Bessie Mae, this is Kep Stone. He's one of our family now, and my friend. He needs a search dog for his work. Do you still have Pokey?"

Bessie Mae briskly waved her hand to one side and said, "Oh, I'll always have that dog! She's so slow, if she started dyin' today, it'd take her three years to go."

She turned to me and held out both hands to take mine. They were warm but trembling.

"It's *Kip*?" she asked as her eyes searched mine. It was then I noticed that her left eye appeared to be flawed. It may have been sightless.

"Kep," I corrected. "It rhymes with 'step,' Bessie Mae. It's short for Kephart. I'd like it if you called me Kep, but you can call me anything you'd like to."

She looked at Jill and asked, "Can I call him 'Honey'?"

Then she looked back at me, put her head down, covered her mouth, and laughed in embarrassment.

Jill and I couldn't help laughing with her.

"If she's so slow, what does it take to get Pokey to move at tracking?" I asked.

"Oh, just give her a scent and you can't hardly hold her. It's the only time she comes alive. She ain't really dead as she 'pears to be. I s'pose she's like me that way."

Once again Bessie Mae dropped her head down, only this time she covered her eyes. Jill and I exchanged discreet smiles.

"Can she pick up a scent that's maybe five days old, especially one that's mixed in with others?" I asked, having had no experience with dogs that selectively sniff out things.

Bessie Mae's face returned to its expression of mingled sadness and humor as she raised her head again. I got the impression that she struggled constantly to keep her spirit buoyed up with humor, and I felt a pang of compassion for her.

Her eyes smiled as she said, "Well, I know she can smell out a set of false teeth in a barrel of wet garbage. Now don't ask me how I know!"

Laughing once more, she put her hand over her mouth, and I realized that her missing teeth were actually missing pieces of her dentures. Jill and I joined with her in laughter as the three of us looked at each other while sharing this candid moment. It seemed as though Bessie Mae had just thrown wide all her window drapes to sun her inner house.

Suddenly Bessie turned and gestured for us to follow her. When we came to the porch steps, Wilbur's hand leaped to the bill of his railroad cap to jerk it up and down a quarter inch. The corners of his mouth went up and down that same distance, while his eyes briefly brightened in greeting. His eyes were mainly on Jill, though. I guessed that there was a spark of life in Wilbur yet. One can never tell.

Instead of climbing the board steps to the porch, Bessie Mae led us along a narrow path to a huge lilac bush at one corner of the house. Its profuse blossoms exuded a sweet fragrance. Stretched out underneath its abundant branches, Pokey lay oblivious to our approach. Her sonorous snoring reminded me of Smooch. It seemed a shame to wake her.

Bessie Mae bent down and lifted an enormous ear flap up from the dirt.

"Bath!" she yelled. "Bath!"

Pokey lifted one eyelid, then the other. Her expression was piteous. Rolling to one side, she put a paw over her nose. Clearly a mixed breed of basset hound and beagle, she set her short legs in motion. They drove her in a circular pattern farther under the bush and out of reach. She looked exceptionally large and heavy for her breed.

Bessie Mae stood up and said, "She don't get a bath 'cept when she's messed with a skunk. Then I puts in lots of vinegar. Oh, she hates it, she does. So when I says 'bath,' she takes notice of the waked-up world. Now she'll do most anything to please me so's to get out of it. I know it's a mean trick, but I rewards her well later on."

Turning to me, Bessie Mae put three fingers to her cheek and said, "Say, Kep, I do believe Pokey's collar and leash got put in the old washer on the porch. While you takes a look, I'll go fetch a couple or so pork chops for rewards."

Her face wrinkled into a warm smile for me.

Next, she looked at Jill and said, "Now Anjill, child, Pokey's sure to stay put here with you till we comes back, so why don't you just pick yourself some purty lilacs whilst you wait?"

I gave Bessie Mae a smile and a nod, waved a hand at Jill, and retraced my tracks back to the front porch. Wilbur was gone. The dogs were nowhere in sight and, except for an occasional cluck from a chicken, peace prevailed.

Rummaging through the contents of the old washing machine was an adventure. Besides the dog collar and leash, I found, among other things, a toothbrush, a deck of well-worn playing cards bound with a rubber band, a jar of Vicks VapoRub, several hair curlers, three paper plates, an unopened box of cough drops, a can of sardines, a spatula, a pair of broken suspenders, and two mouse traps—one clutching a dead mouse. Using the spatula, I buried the mouse at one side of the porch.

When I returned to the lilac bush, I found Jill bent over Pokey, who now lay at her feet. Jill held a bunch of lilacs to her shoulder with one hand while her other hand alternately stroked Pokey's long, soft ear flaps. The dog's unbelievably sad-like eyes gazed dreamily up at her in ecstasy.

Seconds later Bessie Mae came up from the opposite direction. She was carrying a small white package and a pickle jar filled with water.

"Here's the cooked chops," she said, handing me the white parcel. "They's left over from last night. Sometimes we hungers more for greens than pigs. Just maybe you ought to keep these chops purty much hid from Pokey till she's earned 'em, Kep. She won't quit slobberin' if they's close by."

Turning to Jill, she said, "Anjill, honey, you just poke them purty posies in this here jar of water. They'll keep a good while longer for sure."

As Jill stood to take the bottle, I noticed that she had unbuttoned the lower part of her skirt below the missing button. But my attention was quickly yanked back to Bessie Mae as she clapped her palms across each other in a gesture of sudden recollection.

"Phooey!" she exclaimed. "I done forgot Pokey's water pan. I'll go fetch it quick." She started off, then stopped and turned to me.

"Oh, say, Kep. Do you have somethin' to keep water in for her? A jug maybe? I ain't . . ."

"Sure, Bessie Mae," I interrupted. "That yellow bus is like a camper. It has a sink and a supply of water. We'll be okay. Pokey's pan is all we'll need."

"Good! I'll be right back."

As Bessie Mae hurried off, Jill and I exchanged smiles. I reached in my pocket for her silver button.

"I've got your button, Jill," I said, holding it out to her.

"Could you just keep it for now, Kep?" she asked. "I've got my hands full with these flowers, and my purse is in your van. Selma has needles and thread. I can sew it back on later."

"Sure," I said, and after returning the button to my pocket, I knelt to fasten Pokey's collar around her neck. She didn't cooperate much but lay on her side eyeing me with a sad, submissive expression.

As I knelt there beside Jill, I couldn't resist glancing at her attractive legs. Her dark nylons only accentuated their allure, and I couldn't help wondering if she could possibly know just how much the exposure of her thighs tantalized me. With each glance I realized more fully the meaning of "temptation." I could see that if her skirt was fully buttoned, it might have been a bit too snug for her to kneel down and pet Pokey. Maybe she would have lost more buttons. How would I know? Still I wondered.

Jill had conveyed earlier that she was not without feelings of weakness and that she had always avoided situations which might lead to her yielding to enticement. I believed this of her because when we first met, she radiated an unusual innocence and purity. This was a rare kind of beauty that had attracted me to her. At this moment I was certainly being tested to confirm which kind of attraction I valued most. It was a value-choice thing again.

I heard myself asking her a question.

"Jill . . . would you like to come with me while Pokey does her nosey thing? It shouldn't take more than a couple of hours. I could get you back in plenty of time to start your trip back north. Besides, Pokey seems to take to you. I could use your help."

I was surprised when she didn't hesitate to answer.

"I'd like that, Kep. I'd like to help you. But I've got to leave for Bellingham by noon at the latest. Are you taking Pokey far?"

"The area that I'm to check out is just a few miles south of here. It borders the Skagit River, and it's not as far as Conway. Maybe we'd even be able to have a lunch together afterward."

She nodded and smiled a yes at me.

Because her manner was so naturally at ease, I was impressed with a sense of her confidence and trust in me. I wanted to be deserving and protective of that trust. With Jill I really knew what I valued, but at the same time, I was now becoming aware of just how much my natural tendencies made me vulnerable. I could see that *strength* was to have a new kind of meaning for me.

Wearing a joyful countenance, Bessie Mae came up excitedly and quite out of breath. She was clutching a checkered brown-and-red recipe box to her breast. Pokey's water pan dangled from between her thumb and forefinger.

"Oh, sweet Anjill," she exclaimed, "I just wants to share my diary box with you! An' Kep—you too, please! Maybe you could catch some time to read my pome cards whilst you goes travelin' about today. There's never anybody reads 'em 'cept Penny, an' she's been gone so long I can't no more see her face in my mind. An' like today, no company stays long . . . if ever I gets company, which I seldom does. So's I can't share. Anyways, these ain't really recipes 'cept for dealin' with life as I do. They's diary pomes. I loves to make up rhymes. Some's for when I laugh. Some's for when I cry. Just you pick through some, an' it will be like you stayed with me a while. You can bring 'em back with Pokey."

Her need for human contact touched me. I held out my hand for the treasure, but she let Pokey's water pan fall as she pressed the little checkered box against my chest.

Holding it close, I said, "I can promise you that we'll be reading some of your rhymes, Bessie Mae. So you can know for sure that you'll be with us today. It really is too bad that you don't get visited more often. I guess you know how hard life can push, but there's really no need to let it push us away from friends. I'm sure I can speak for Jill too when I say that I won't overlook you. It's been a treat to spend this little time with you."

Again, she shook her head up and down with intense feeling. Then my eyes caught Jill wiping away tears as she bent down to pick up the dropped water pan.

"Well, Bessie Mae, another thing you can count on today is that Pokey will want us to bring her back home to you," I said. "So we should see you again later. Is there anything you need that you'd like to have us bring back with her?"

She shook her head. "No . . . thanks. All I need's right here," she said, holding her hand to her heart.

CHAPTER 16

AT the time of our parting, Bessie Mae had been too tearful to be persuasive with Pokey. After hooking up Pokey to her leash, I had no success in leading her to the bus. She might have been awake, but she was also willful. However, Jill had no problem with her. With Jill's hand on her leash, I believe she would have gripped a bar of soap with her teeth and walked right into the ocean for a bath.

I was fortunate to have had Jill along, if only because she loved animals and they loved her. But I counted it far beyond good fortune to be able to share this time with her.

Now as we traveled south on my errand, I felt that we belonged together—that this was as it should be. It seemed so right, our being together. It made me feel complete. Today I felt comfortable with life, more so than I had ever felt before.

For a mile or so Jill had been busy with her own thoughts. Now she reached down beside her seat and picked up the brown-and-red recipe box. She had seen me press two fifty-dollar bills into Bessie Mae's hands at the last minute, but she didn't know that I had snatched four more fifties from my cash box while she was giving Bessie Mae a good-bye hug. I had folded these and inserted them in front of the cards in the recipe box.

As Jill began fingering through the cards, she abruptly stopped and turned to face me. She didn't speak, but her face said again, "Are you sure your job is legal?"

I answered her unspoken question.

"I know what you're thinking, Jill. It's okay. I guess I should tell you that I'm working for a wealthy man whose personal quest involves such things as finding missing persons and preventing wrongful acts if possible. He tries to give people a chance to redirect their lives. It's a worthy cause, but he wants to remain anonymous, and I must protect his identity.

"I've pledged to keep some secrets. It goes with the job. That's the hard part. I don't like being secretive. But he's a secretive man—and for good reasons, as far as I can see. I just can't disclose his name or openly associate with him. So that puts me in a tough position. You and anyone else I'm close to will just have to trust me. You'll have to believe me when I say that I'm employed in honest work, even though I may be gone at odd hours or fail to explain my whereabouts satisfactorily."

"Is it dangerous work?" Jill asked.

"I suppose I'll find that out soon enough," I said. "Hard-rock mining was dangerous work for me at times, but who's to say what isn't dangerous anymore? Just being in a public school classroom has brought death to some. People have to make a living, and there's really no such thing as safety or security in this world that I can see. When it comes to a choice between security and freedom, I'll take freedom any day.

"Best of all, Jill, part of my job will be to document everything that happens. I'll be doing a lot of writing—something I've thought I'd enjoy doing. I guess I'll find out about that, too."

Jill nodded in reply.

"Anyway, back to the donation: I've never been an extravagant guy. Even though I'll be paid more money than I could have ever imagined, I don't see myself changing. I can be generous and not be foolish. My employer—I'll call him 'Mr. G'—would have been even more generous with Bessie Mae, I'm sure, if he could have seen what I saw. And he won't ever question my judgment about how I use my expense account. He trusts me. I'm not 'losin' it,' as Selma says."

Jill smiled, gave her head a shake, and returned her attention to the recipe box. Fingering through the cards, she pulled one up and read it to herself. She laughed, then fell silent and reflective.

"Aren't you going to share it?" I asked.

She read:

There ain't much I can say—
The cow dried up today.
She got so dry
The wind came by
And blowed her clean away.

At first I laughed, but then I noticed that even though Jill's smile lingered, she held her thoughtful expression.

"What is it?" I asked. "Is there more?"

"No . . . it's just that there's more to the limerick than humor. I know that one time Bessie Mae and Wilbur did have a milk cow. The cow *did* dry up. Then she got sick and died. They depended on her a lot, but they didn't have money to replace her. She provided some income as well as food while their kids were still at home."

"They had kids?" I asked. "How many?"

"Three. A son and two daughters. She mentioned Penny. Penny's been gone over five years now. She married a long-haul trucker and lives in Tennessee. Then there was Johnny. He joined the Army. Neither of them finished school."

"What about the other daughter?"

"Her name is Gracie. She's confined in an institution for the mentally disabled. It's so sad. She's the reason Wilbur is the way he is. It isn't the other way around as one might assume.

"Gracie is the youngest. When she was very small, she became totally deaf. They say it was due to a virus infection, but if it was, it eventually got to her brain and she became incapable of responding to people.

"It broke Wilbur's heart. Then he became deaf, too. It may have been a sympathetic emotional reaction. I've read of such things happening. The tragic thing about it is that he just withdrew into himself. There was a complete personality change. At one time he played the banjo and was very popular at country grange dances."

Unable to say a word, I just drove and stared at the road as I recalled my unkind thoughts toward Wilbur—my hasty judgments. I could see that I needed to do a self overhaul. I felt terrible.

Then I thought of Bessie Mae. No wonder she was so heartrending lonely. She was evidently married to a man who could no longer relate, and her children were out of reach in different ways. I was right about one thing: Bessie Mae and Wilbur were each reflections of their individual victories and defeats.

The next thing my mind jumped to was my often-asked bitter question: Why would a kind, loving god allow such things to happen? But before I could dwell on the seemingly unanswerable, Jill pulled up another card and read:

It just don't make no sense,
What Big Brass calls defense.
They sells foes guns,
Then back they runs
And builds a bigger fence!

Jill explained, "I think Bessie Mae had a hard time dealing with Johnny's wanting to get away to join the Army. I'm sure she's patriotic. She could probably see only her need for his help in their impoverished circumstances, and she couldn't justify the Army's need over her own."

I studied Jill's face as she paused in thought. Seeing the gentle, uncritical sensitivity in her expression endeared her to me all the more.

Presently, she smoothed some strands of hair back behind her ear and continued.

"I think she was a good, loving mother. But Selma said she always took too much on herself that should have been delegated—especially for training her children. Selma told me that in some ways Wilbur was more like a child himself, even when he was at his best. Bessie did delegate chores to him, and he did whatever she asked. He loved her. I'm sure he still does. But now he can't hear her, and he lives mostly in his own inner world."

A heavy sigh escaped Jill as she reached for another rhyme. This time the message brought some comfort:

When winter blasts its breeze
My bottom's sure to freeze.
But then at night
I feels all right,
'Cause Hubby's got hot knees.

Our laughter brought a lighter mood, so Jill shut her eyes and lifted out another card.

I hates to be so poor.
I wanders through the store.
I shops, compares,
Goes home an' wears
The same things as before.

Too sad, I thought. Then an idea came to me.

"Jill, do you think there are enough rhymes in this collection to make a book, something that would bring Bessie Mae a step up out of poverty?"

"Maybe you've got something," she said. "Let's keep reading all we can in the time we have."

She was laughing before she finished reading the next limerick to me, so she started over and read it twice:

All day I frown and pout.
My mood turns Pa about.
Tonight for sure
I finds the cure—
My bra's been inside out!

Jill didn't offer any comment on that one.

Unfortunately, she didn't get to share any more because I saw that we were approaching a landmark called out on Laura's map.

"Sorry, Jill," I said. "We've reached a point where I'll have to pay closer attention to where I'm going. Would you reach back on the floor behind us and get that brown envelope? There's a map inside it. Maybe you should look at it with me, and then you can be my navigator. I'll look for a place to pull over."

"Just how long do you think my arms are, Kep?" she said, laughing as she unbuckled her seat belt.

It hadn't registered with me that she would have to leave her seat and climb over Pokey to get to the envelope. And Pokey could just as well have been a sack of potatoes for all the notice we got of her presence.

"Buckle up, Jill. I'm not thinking clearly. I guess I've always driven this bus alone before. Having you along changes the way my mind works."

A meaningful glance conveyed her reception of my intended message well enough. Just then I spotted a convenience store in time to steer into its parking lot. I stopped at the side of the building. Hopping out of the bus, I walked around to Jill's door and opened it.

"Maybe Pokey needs to take on water, or else contribute to the foliage nutrients," I said. "I'll take care of her needs if you'll just encourage her to get back into the bus afterward."

Jill slid around and scooted herself down from the seat in her typical graceful manner. She didn't succeed in keeping the front of her skirt closed up, although she tried. I took this to show that her modesty was still intact. This time I didn't try to guess about reasons for her skirt being unbuttoned. Besides, why should I care? She was what she was, and I couldn't be happier for that. I enjoyed all I could see she was—every aspect of her.

"I'm going in the store for a minute, Kep," she said. "There must be a restroom inside. I won't keep you long."

Pokey wouldn't budge. No amount of tugging at her leash would dislodge her.

I reached over her and pumped water into her drinking pan. After setting it down in front of her nose, I lifted both ears, pinched them together, and shouted, "Bath!"

Even in her comatose state she must have sensed how ridiculous this sounded. Maybe a *bird* could take a bath in that water pan, but that was it. Kephart Stone wasn't about to bamboozle a basset-beagle. I took her persisting repose to be evidence of her disdain for me.

Jill came up to my side just as I finished my study of the marked-up area map.

"That was pretty fast work, Kep," she said. "I see you got her out and in and back to sleep already. And you gave her a drink too! My! I'm impressed! You'll make a wonderful daddy someday."

"Thank you! And I can see that you won't keep a man waiting while you primp."

"Actually, I didn't touch my comb," she said.

"Actually, neither did I this morning. I didn't want to impress you with my good looks. You'll never see me at my best, remember?"

We laughed together, but we both knew that our verbal interplay held deeper meaning. Although it could be said that we hardly knew each other, given the little time we had spent together, I felt at that moment that we had known each other always—maybe in a previous time dimension. I couldn't help wondering if Jill felt the same. And there was another thing I had wondered about.

"Jill, is there . . . do you have someone you're dating or seeing on a regular basis? I mean . . . well . . . when is your birthday?"

She turned her head away and covered her mouth with her hand to stifle an audible laugh. Next came the inclined head and the look of engaged attention sparkling with amusement.

"What does my birthday have to do with anything?" she asked, giving way to laughter.

"Well, I'm guessing you're about my age. And I don't have to guess that guys have been attracted to you—probably lots of guys. So I'm wondering how you could possibly have turned them all away by now. You don't impress me as being someone who enjoys breaking hearts, but I can guess there's a trail of broken hearts behind you just the same."

She closed her eyes and shook her head and smiled. Then she gazed directly into my eyes and said, "Kep, there are some things you need to understand, but I don't want to explain them all to you just now. Let's just take a day at a time. When the time is right, I'll give some reasons.

"I'll be twenty-two in July. I suppose I can tell you that. And no—I don't have anyone I'm spending time with right now.

Two of the reasons I can give you are the ones you've given me: school and work. My third one is something like yours, too. It has to do with being devoted to something—or someone. You had your mother. I have my religious faith. I've never found someone of my own faith that I've wanted to spend much time with—someone I've been attracted to. And that's important to me too."

"That explains things well enough for me," I said. "And I don't want to know anything else right now—except for maybe one more thing I hadn't thought about until you mentioned it just now. Where *do* you work?"

"I do handwriting analysis. Graphology. It's something I got interested in when I was working part-time in the university library. I'm self-employed in a way, but I have a few clients who make that possible because they call on me often enough."

"Isn't that something like palm reading?" I asked.

Jill smiled her patient smile and shook her head.

"No, Kep. Graphology is a scientific art, like a lot of professions. People with degrees in psychology who have qualified themselves as expert graphologists are called on in certain kinds of court cases. Some are employed by the government, especially in law enforcement. It's surprising how accurately handwriting can describe critical personality traits. It's a common practice to use handwriting analyses to prove identities and disclose forgeries.

"Mostly what I do is work up personality profiles for employers and employment agencies filling responsible positions. But I've done work for legal firms—and even for people who want to know more about the person they plan to marry!"

"It must take a lot of time. Does it pay well?"

"Actually, I spend less time for my income than I used to when I worked part-time at a minimum wage. This work is something I can fit in around class schedules and study times.

But that's because I've got the procedures pretty much mastered now. It used to take a lot of time when I first started."

She glanced at her watch.

"Speaking of time," she said.

"Right. What time is it, Jill?"

"Ten fifteen. Do you have much farther to go?"

"Five miles. Maybe less."

I closed the sliding van door and moved to open the passenger door for Jill. As she stepped up to her seat, I noticed that her skirt was buttoned again. The empty button space was evidently pinned shut as well.

Then when she reached for her door handle, I saw that she had a ring on the little finger of her right hand. I didn't remember seeing it when she was going through the cards in the recipe box. I felt sure she wasn't wearing it then. My curiosity nudged me to ask about it, but then I thought better of it.

As I pulled out of the parking lot, I had a different question come to mind.

"Jill, speaking of personality profiles and marriages, what do you suppose keeps people like Wilbur and Bessie Mae together, especially when they've changed a lot or had reasons to grow apart?"

"I think that they each must still have something to give that the other needs, and that list of needs could change over time. Most people want to be needed. Maybe some just need to share. But when only one does all the giving and the other doesn't contribute, I suppose the marriage could be doomed. My belief is that the key is unselfishness—both ways."

"My hat's off to Bessie Mae," I said.

"Yes. But we don't really know what all of Bessie Mae's needs are, Kep. We have our eyes open to some, but we have no idea what Wilbur provides for her. Maybe the hardest thing for her is not being able to communicate. Communication is a key, too. We each have our own perceptions and misperceptions. I would think that being able to communicate different needs accurately and honestly is what keeps marriages alive, too. "But some people don't know how to listen. As I understand it from Selma, it's that part of communicating that might have saved my own parents' marriage, and maybe my mother's early death."

Jill closed her eyes and then looked away at the passing scene. I felt her sorrow in her silence.

"It's good you brought up communicating, Jill. I failed to both tell and ask you something. I'm embarrassed that I haven't mentioned this before now, but you reminded me of it when you spoke about perceptions."

She looked my way and raised her eyebrows in silent curiosity.

"I forgot to thank you for the drawing—the portrait you did of me. It's obviously a product of your exceptional memory. Thanks. I'm impressed, really. I do wonder about that expression you put in my eyes, though. I don't know how you did it, but it conveys a favorable perception of me that I don't see. I guess what matters about it is that I want to *have* what you seem to see in me. Does that make sense?"

She nodded slightly and then said, "What do you think I see that you don't?"

"Confidence. Conviction. Faith, maybe."

"There are lots of things to put your faith in, Kep. What kind of faith are you missing? I think you show a lot of faith in *yourself*, in your willingness to try something entirely new, for instance."

"Sure. But I've proved myself to *myself* in several ways. I don't have much faith in most other people, though. Just a few. You're definitely on my list."

"Oh? Why should I be? I haven't proved myself to you, have I?"

"No. But as I said earlier, you radiate some things I like—one of them is something that says I haven't any reason to doubt you or your honesty."

"Oh . . . well, Kephart Stone, I don't have anything to doubt in you either. I feel I can trust you. And I feel that you're honest, too. And those are two very important traits that I value, especially when I consider . . . never mind."

She turned her face away and covered her mouth again.

"Jill, you said you *feel* these things. The same thing goes for me. I wonder why that is—or what it is."

"I'm sure I know why, Kep, but it goes along with some things you need to understand that I don't have time to explain today. It's not the right time."

"Okay. I'll just have to *trust you* on that," I said, and we laughed together again.

CHAPTER 17

SOON my eyes caught sight of a street-name sign that Laura had marked for a right turn. As I made the turn, my thoughts turned again to my immediate task. Today, having Jill included in my activities made me aware of just how much I had been alone when making deliveries. I had never realized just how alone I had been before. This got me to thinking of including Jill in some of my work activities. Whether I could ever have her help me with future assignments was an open question, but it was worth exploring.

"My employer trusts me to secrecy, Jill," I said. "But I guess it comes with discretion. I can't tell you anything that would lead to his identity or to the identities of others who work with him. I suppose it's all right to share some things with you about my present assignment, though.

"Still, I'll ask you first whether you'd mind my sharing, because it does place a burden of secrecy on you, too. I have my reasons for asking. They center on what you just told me a while ago, about your doing graphology. So I'm asking: Do you mind?"

Her response wasn't what I might have expected.

"I don't ever want to cover up or to lie, but I can keep confidences. That comes with doing my analyses. I have to protect private information. Will I ever be put in a position of being questioned about anything?" she asked.

"I guess it all depends on what an assignment involves," I said. "Let's just say that I'll do all I can to protect you from being vulnerable on that point. Does that sound okay?"

She thought about it and then nodded.

"It's okay, Kep, but I don't see how I'll be having much time to spend with you like this. Today is not a usual kind of day. For one thing, it's Sunday. I try to honor Sunday according to my faith and commitments. Maybe someday you'll understand that part of me. I don't expect that you will right now.

"So far, things are good between us. I'd really like to keep it that way. I don't want to compromise my standards, and I don't think you would want me to either, if I'm not mistaken."

She looked at me intently, but it was a look expectant of agreement.

"Right, Jill. I'm just for you being true to yourself and for our being honest with each other. I know it's something we both want to practice and hang on to.

"For today, I think your helping me will meet with Mr. G's approval. Just so you know, I'm certain that he would like for me *not* to have to work on Sundays. He said so in his own way. But when it comes to life-or-death situations, my readings of the New Testament tell me that it's okay to give aid or save lives on the Sabbath. Am I right?"

Her face brightened as she tilted her head and faced me. She studied my eyes.

"Yes, Kep. In more ways than one," she answered.

I had secretly hoped that I could get her to rationalize being with me on a Sunday if an activity involved saving a life or finding a missing child—something her religious beliefs would condone. But I knew I couldn't push it. Her eyes said things more perfectly than words could ever say them. I thought I could never get enough of what I read in them. And I knew I would have a terrible time living with myself if I should ever disappoint her.

We came to a "T" junction. I made a left onto the dike road that skirted the extensive Skagit River embankment. We were getting close.

"There's a little notebook in that plastic bag behind us that contains some revealing notes written by a missing man," I said. "If you were to study the handwriting, could you get some insights about that man's true character—maybe about his being depressed or troubled or angry?"

"Do you mean in the little time we have today?" Jill asked.

"Well, yes."

"There aren't any shortcuts to accurately analyzing handwriting, Kep," she said. "It's easy to slip up, especially if you try to base judgments on just a few components such as slant, speed, baseline, and letter formations, for example. There are lots of things to consider—to measure and interpret. If there aren't enough elements or samplings, I could get a limited, distorted picture. Just the same, I'd be willing to try, for what it would be worth to you. A hurried analysis could throw you off, though. Do you still want me to look at the writing anyway?"

"Could you just give it a quick once-over to see if there's anything that stands out?" I asked.

"I can do that," she said.

"Great. I guess the main thing going today is to learn what I can from Pokey's nose, but maybe you could look through the notebook while I'm doing that. You might come up with something valuable to offer.

"My mission today, according to instructions, is to find out if this missing man's scent can be found in more than one place along the river. I'm especially interested in an area around a certain house. The man could have met with foul play. He could have committed suicide. He may have drowned accidentally, or faked his abduction. He's been missing several days now. The county sheriff's deputies have found nothing to go on. Not that they haven't tried, but no dead body has turned up, and no valuable clues have surfaced. Right now they are concentrating on the man's personal life.

"One thing you'll need to understand is that I'm working secretly and independently of any law-enforcement agency. So if I were to discover anything of value to an ongoing investigation, I would be given a way to communicate that information through discreet channels. Mr. G has connections. He would never withhold any vital findings."

"And what if I should discover something in this man's handwriting that would be of value?" Jill asked. "Or possibly someone else's writing? Isn't there a chance you could stumble onto a clue while I'm with you that I can't avoid knowing about? I don't see how you can keep me from being implicated if you have me along with you, Kep."

"I can see you have a point, Jill. It's good that you brought it up. But for today, there's no need for me to tell anyone about anything you might glean from a cursory look at this man's notes. All that can come of it is that you might help prepare me for whatever I'll be confronting in the next twenty-four hours. Right now I'm just going on a hunch, but I feel a need for your input. Sometimes I've been able to sense danger in advance. It's happened recently. For some reason I feel a little uneasy right now. I can't tell you why."

For the first time since we'd met, I saw an anxious look on Jill's face. It troubled me to see it, especially since my words had put it there. The look somehow clashed with her natural spirit.

"If there's a chance I can help you avoid a dangerous encounter, I'll do that Kep," she said. "I'm really not afraid for myself. I just don't ever want to be the cause of your appearing to have broken a pledge of secrecy. That could happen if I got questioned and had to admit knowledge of something that you couldn't prevent my knowing about."

At that moment I would have given her a hug, but it wasn't an option. All I could do was reach over with my hand and touch hers. She responded by giving my hand a squeeze. I had a hard time letting it go. When I finally did, Jill grasped my little finger and studied the stellar ring.

"Kep, I've been meaning to ask you about your ring. I noticed it earlier this morning. It's strangely beautiful. You haven't worn it before. My memory is pretty reliable . . . if you'll recall."

She was smiling now, and she gave me a quick, significant glance before letting go of my finger.

"Right . . . uh . . . well, it's new, Jill. It's something I got from Mr. G for agreeing to be his assistant. In a way it signifies my being a member of his staff. And it reminds me of my commitment and pledge—not that I need to be reminded. Right now it reminds me of how much I hate being secretive because there's so much I'd like to share with you that I can't."

As I said this, I became aware of how easy it would be for an awkward situation to develop if I should get a call on the stellar ring, which could happen at any time. Trying to account for anything resulting from this might prove to be a definite challenge as well—all the more so because I disliked hiding anything from Jill. And I still hadn't mastered giving an unvoiced answer to ring calls. I decided to preclude any cause for wonder on Jill's part—anything that might produce some doubt about my honesty, or my sanity.

"One thing more I have to tell you," I said. "I have to go by certain procedures. Like, if I meet up with situation A, then I'm bound to do X. (In my mind situation A would be a ring call.) Because of that, I may have to change my course unexplainably. Can you understand how that might put questions in your mind about my behavior? Do you think you can keep on trusting me if I should do something that doesn't make sense to you? Something I can't explain?"

Jill's expression was one of serious contemplation. She remained silent for some time. Then I was relieved at last to see her tilt her head, give me her knowing look, and smile.

"Didn't you say something about how we radiate what we truly are? If you don't radiate something weird, Kep, I can live with unexplained actions. Does that say enough to satisfy you?"

I clenched my fist and gave it an upward jerk of agreement.

It was such a frustration not to be able to give her a hug, if she would permit me to, which I felt that she would just then. But I had another side-tracked question waiting, and this was my chance to ask it.

"Okay, Jill. You asked about *my* new ring. What about yours? I don't remember ever seeing you wear it before, not even at Bessie Mae's place when you were petting Pokey. It's your turn."

She became quiet and thoughtful before she spoke.

"Well . . . I'll explain this much about it for now, Kep. My ring isn't new, but it's like yours in a way. It reminds me of a commitment that I made a long time ago—one that I've tended to forget recently. I'm finding out just how human I am—how easily I can be led down a path I wouldn't think to choose.

"I've had this ring safety-pinned inside my purse so I wouldn't lose it, but it doesn't do me much good out of sight. I used the pin to close up my skirt for now, until I could sew the button back on. So now my reminder ring is back on my finger. Maybe it's good that we both have rings—for our own reasons."

Jill didn't look at me as she spoke. Instead, she calmly twisted her ring around her little finger, apparently contemplating its meaning or message. I sensed that she, too, was weighing values as she studied it.

"I think most all rings are reminders," I said. "Not just of commitments or vows, but of special occasions too. I suppose most have sentimental value, even if they're for show. But I'm guessing that your ring has religious significance. Am I right?"

"Yes. It does. But it's simply a reminder, as I explained."

"My mind isn't closed when it comes to religion," I said. "And I know your faith is important to you, but I have a problem with the terrible things that happen to good people—the suffering that seems so unjustifiable. Most of the time it gets in the way of my believing that there is a god, at least one who really loves us."

Jill gazed thoughtfully out her window. She was silent and her hands rested quietly in her lap for some time before she spoke.

"Would you prefer to be Pinocchio before or after he became a real boy?" she asked in an engaging tone of voice.

"Pinocchio?" Her question seemed so far off the mark that it threw me.

"You do know the story, don't you?"

"Well, sure . . . but . . ."

"If you're talking about the horrible things that people do to each other, you should remember Pinocchio, Kep. Was he happy being a puppet—having all those strings attached?"

"Of course not, Jill. He was happiest when he was free."

"Free to . .?"

"To live his life the way he wanted to live it."

"To choose for himself?"

"Yes."

"Well, Kephart Stone, what's so hard about seeing the obvious answer? Do you think you should be the one to decide who should have strings and who shouldn't? We're all free of strings. God isn't a puppeteer. He gives us all freedom to be and to act however we want to. He gives us 'happiness laws,' but he doesn't force us to live them."

At that moment my mind somehow made a connection with Shackleton's statement on the previous night. Something about our being performers on a stage—each of us creating and acting out our own parts. But Jill's offering didn't quite satisfy me.

"Okay. But what about Gracie? You said yourself that her plight was sad. And as a result, look at the tragic figure that Wilbur is today . . . and how all of this has affected Bessie Mae. I can't see where other people's choices played any part in this, Jill. How are we to account for it?"

She smiled and patiently studied my face before answering.

"I think you're ready for the 'big picture,' Kep. If you can catch the vision of it, a lot of questions and doubts will fall away. I believe there is purpose and meaning in everything that happens in this world—every experience. Even the events we see as being cruel or ugly happen for reasons that can make sense if we have the big picture. We may not always understand the reasons right away, but in time we do, or will.

"I suppose it's like finding places for the pieces to fit in a jigsaw puzzle. It's a lot harder to put things together when you don't have the picture to go by. But having that overall vision helps us endure the challenges until we understand what purpose each piece has to play.

"I can't explain much in the time we have now, Kep, but I'll give you a question to think about. No . . . make that two questions. And don't try to give answers yet. I'm just trying to prepare you for what can follow if or when you want it.

"First question: If something doesn't have an ending, can it have a beginning?

"Second question: How many seeds are there in an apple?"

My face must have shown my inability to relate the questions to the subject, which shows where my mind took me when I didn't need to go there. I guess you could account for this by another difference between men and women—the way their minds work. Anyway, Jill interpreted my puzzled expression as I supposed a woman naturally would, so she offered a clue.

"Okay. I know you've got a lot on your mind, Kep, so I'll give you a hint. I think these words are the lyrics from a song: 'Nothing comes from nothing. Nothing ever could.'"

I pinched my lips together and stared ahead at the road.

"Thanks," I said. "What if I don't come up with the answers you want? Is there still any hope for me, do you think?"

"I don't think I'll give up on you that easily," she said. "In that case, though, I suppose I'll still hold on to the puzzle piece that you are. There just may be a place where you could fit in . . . sometime. Right now it's just a piece at—"

"Sorry, Jill," I cut in. "See that barn on the left just ahead? I'll need to begin my search just past that point, but along the riverside behind the dike on the right. Don't let go of your thoughts. We can talk more on the way back."

"I think I'll listen first while you do the—what's wrong, Kep?"

I hit the brakes pretty hard and then put the bus in reverse and started backing up along the empty road behind us.

"That house we just passed. It's the only place I can see against the dike along this side of the river, and so this stretch of the road is one I need to turn Pokey loose on. I've got a hunch I should check out this section first."

I made a U-turn and parked on a wide stretch of shoulder opposite a long entry drive to the house. The location was unusual because the house was set back where the river and dike looped away from the highway. All the other homes were situated on large farmsteads extending along the opposite side of the road.

A row of old poplar trees ran along a fence line on the south, or left, side of the property. The long access drive closely paralleled these trees. Behind the high-gabled old house, a mix of tall firs and huge cottonwoods grew from the foot of the dike embankment to the back of the property. From the highway the place appeared to be lifeless.

"This seems an unlikely place to catch a scent because the house is upstream from the point where the truck was found. I'm told the deputies' dogs didn't pick up any scent along this part of the highway during their Thursday-morning search. It just might be a waste of our time, but some senseless hunches have paid off for me in the past. What time do you have now?"

"It's ten thirty-five, Kep. How long do you think you'll need?"

"I'm guessing at thirty-five minutes—once we get Pokey up and moving. That should get us back to your car before noon. Let's see if a pork chop will get some action going."

I went to the back of the bus, where I had stowed the package of reward chops in the engine compartment. They had warmed up a bit. In contrast, a chill breeze was stirring and clouds were quickly gathering. There was a hint of rain in the atmosphere.

Jill had opened the sliding door and was stroking Pokey's incredible ears as I came around with the pork chops. I handed a chop to her and said, "If Pokey won't respond to this, I don't know what it will take to wake her up. I guess I could pour the pan of water over her head."

Jill wrinkled up her face at me.

"I'm going to remember that, Kep," she said. "And if ever there should be another sleepy morning when you would like to have your breakfast warmed up, I just might douse *your* head with a glassful of water instead."

"In that case, please give Pokey your offering with kindness," I said. "Try rubbing her warm breakfast gently over her nose, and don't forget that it was my less-than-best self that suggested it."

Oddly enough, it worked. Maybe our laughter contributed to the success of it. Pokey was probably not accustomed to much laughter in her world. Her eyes popped open and her legs stiffened. Soon she was on her feet and leaning out of the van toward the pork chop.

Jill held it just beyond Pokey's nose as an enticement to draw her out and to the ground at her feet. At the same time, I grabbed the leash near her collar, making ready to restrain her from jumping up at Jill in case she should be overcome with eager excitement. As it turned out she was somewhat eager, but not excited. I was beginning to have my doubts about her.

"Let's wait with her breakfast until we've got her across the road," I said. "There are some things I'll need to take from the bus before I get her started."

I handed Jill the leash and took the brown envelope and plastic bag from the back seat. Among the missing man's scent items, I found six surgical-type rubber gloves and a pocket flashlight. (Laura had remembered!) I stuffed the gloves into my jeans pocket and took the man's small notebook from the envelope, where I had inserted it along with Laura's handwritten notes.

I gave the notebook to Jill with a smile and said, "For whatever you can learn from this that seems reliable . . . thanks."

I was about to take Pokey's leash from her hand when I remembered what Shackleton had said about being obvious. I could "obviously" be taking a dog for a walk. But Jill would be alone in the bus for a while, so I grabbed my clipboard and some old proof-of-delivery sheets from under my seat and showed them to her.

"I'll leave these between the front seats. If anyone should stop or come up to the van, hold the clipboard up and pretend that you're checking it over. Just be your sweet self, and nobody will think to question you. Keep the doors locked, Jill. And honk the horn if you need me."

After taking the leash and pork chop from Jill, I felt uneasy about leaving her. But before I could change my plan, I found her climbing confidently into the bus and smiling at me. So I dismissed my fears and moved ahead of Pokey.

Holding out the pork chop and tugging at her leash, I managed to get her across the road. Then I pulled an unlaundered sock from the plastic sack and held it to her nose. (Yes, I know. It wasn't fair to get her started before giving her breakfast, but I wanted to see if she might put work ahead of pleasure, just in case.) Her reaction shocked me.

She sprang into a frenzy of action. Her nose went to the ground, and her legs became stubby springs flying about in all directions. It looked as though she was trying to get all four feet off the ground at once. Her rear end bobbed around like a balloon on a string in a stiff wind. I could hardly hold her back as she surged toward the mailbox post.

Here she planted her muzzle into the weeds surrounding it and did a clockwise pivotal maneuver that defies description. Then she strained to go down the long entry drive leading from the mailbox to the house. The impetus of this was like a red flag to me, but she tugged me ten feet before I could stop her. No way, Pokey . . . no way, I thought as I dug my heels into the gravel.

Jill had witnessed the commotion and was soon at my side gripping first Pokey's leash, then her collar, all the while laughing at my frustrated attempts to deal with this newly awakened vitality.

Prying the pork chop from between the leash and my grasping fingers, Jill tried to bait Pokey with it. But Pokey was evidently determined to accept it only as her *earned* reward. After we struggled with her for a while, we managed to get her back to the shoulder of the road using the sock as a lure.

"Well, now we know," I said. "And this is a real puzzler to me. I'm going to check the highway both ways from the mailbox, Jill. In the meantime, whatever you can learn from this man's handwriting will be a great help to me—more help than your controlling Pokey. There's a bad feeling here, and I want to get you away as soon as possible."

Jill's face clouded again with anxiety.

"Let me just help you along this side of the road, Kep. Please. It could speed things up some if you would."

The breeze was becoming gusty and a rainstorm was imminent. Seeing this, and reading Jill's eyes, I couldn't help but consent.

"Okay, Jill. You're probably right. Let's cover the property frontage first. The sooner we can get Pokey out of sight of the house, the better I'll feel."

Using the sock again, we lured Pokey along the front property line away from the mailbox post. Then we returned back along the opposite shoulder to the bus, where she strained at her leash in an attempt to cross the road to the mailbox. She had obviously shown no interest in the sides of the road just traversed.

After locking up the bus, we headed in a southerly direction from the post toward a point along the highway nearest the site of the abandoned truck. Again, Pokey found nothing of interest and repeatedly struggled to return to the mailbox.

"Well, it seems certain that the man's scent is restricted to the drive between the mailbox and the house, Jill. I'd say he's still alive—or was for a while after leaving his truck for the river. If the deputies checked for scent along this stretch of road, as I'm told they did, and unless the dogs missed the mailbox post, which seems unlikely, I can see only two ways he could have got to the house. Either he went up the river against its current, or he got a ride from someone. But either possibility brings up a lot of questions, especially since the incident was so thoroughly investigated and locally publicized."

Jill's eyes were bright with interest.

"But how can you learn if the man is still alive unless you actually see him, Kep?"

"I'm sure I'll have to find a way to see him—or some sign of his being alive. It's what I've got to figure out, Jill. I know there are some revealing statements in his notebook, some things that might provide a starting point for me if I can buy enough time. But I'm guessing you would probably not spend much time yourself on *what* he wrote. Am I right?"

"I have to be objective, Kep. So I look only at the physical product to make my judgments. Besides, for your sake, I don't want to learn things I'm not supposed to know about—despite my being a woman."

Her humor said so much. It reflected intelligence that I admired in her. My eyes must have said so as I smiled my appreciation her way. Then, as she returned a smile, the first drops of rain began to fall.

"I'm walking back to the bus with you, Jill. Then, while I take Pokey over along the riverbank, you can go through that notebook. I can't see that it should take us very long to cover an eighth of a mile, even if it does involve going along the river side of the dike."

Pokey showed her approval of our decision to return to the mailbox by doing all she could to drag us there. But this time she yielded somewhat to our control.

After unlocking the VW bus, I handed the key to Jill and said, "Just remember to honk the horn if you need me. Please don't try to come after us, even if we push beyond the expected time. You'll just get wet. I've got my poncho here."

Taking my poncho from the back seat, I pulled it over my head while Jill held Pokey and watched me. She seemed amused to see me wearing it . . . or was she smiling because she thought I looked comical in it?

"Do you always wear it with the hood in front?" she asked, this time laughing at me.

I rolled my eyes toward the cloudy sky and shook my head.

"This is something *near* your best, I'm sure," she said. Then, covering her mouth, she turned her head away until I could swivel and squirm myself into place inside the poncho.

"Okay, Jill. Have your laugh. But I'm really not as helpless as you might think. And there just might be a time when you'll be glad for a little help from *me* . . . some day when you can't quite reach a place where your back needs scratching, for instance.

She shrugged her shoulders and wrinkled up her nose. Although she laughed with her eyes, I read a trace of feminine challenge in them.

Lifting her chin and smiling, she said, "I know this is pretty bad, Kep, but I can't help giving you the obvious response to that: Should I be *itching* for that day?"

Then laughing, she handed Pokey's leash to me and climbed into the bus with her usual poise—and without my help.

CHAPTER 18

LEAVING Jill alone was harder the second time. Maybe it was because the raindrops had begun pelting down and the thought of sitting with her in the shelter of the VW bus held more appeal than the prospect of being jerked by Pokey along the riverbank in the rain. But more likely, it was because I was having trouble dismissing a premonition of what was to come.

Once I got Pokey started along the fence line south of the property, she must have sensed that we were paralleling the trail of scent she had picked up. Her nose was always aimed toward the drive running along the line of poplar trees on the other side of the fence as we pressed beside it toward the dike.

Through the trees and undergrowth I could see that a gated chain-link fence extended from the house to the front corner of a detached garage at the end of the drive. The garage doors had no windows and were closed. A single small window faced the south, and as we came up alongside it, I found it impossible to see inside because of the dark interior and the gloom of the storm.

As we neared a wire fence extending along the back of the property, Pokey put her tail down and showed signs of distress. There wasn't anything I could see to account for her behavior, but she shied away from the large enclosure of yard behind the dark house. About a hundred feet farther on we reached the earthen dike. Pokey clambered up the dike embankment, and we came to a fence running alongside a maintenance road built along the dike's ridge. Because the fence was built to prohibit only vehicles, we had no problem getting through it and onto the crude dirt road.

Once there, I again gave Pokey the scent and she put her nose to the ground, darting in various directions to no avail. I then led her down the dirt slope toward the riverside, where she literally sprang into action. Here, where a beach spread out between the dike and the water's edge, she pulled me through undergrowth, around small trees, and over rocks. I struggled to keep my balance as she yanked me along, but her enthusiasm was both entertaining and encouraging.

We were now covering the riverside northward. This could have been the only approach to the house other than by car. Pokey had not detected a scent as we crossed the beach between the dike and the river, so this seemed the best choice of direction.

I was wondering whether the rain would have reduced the strength of any remaining three-day-old scent. I soon learned it hadn't. At least the scent had not diminished beyond Pokey's ability to detect it. She yelped and leaped when she first sniffed it. Then she went through her comical spinning and springing, first to the river's edge and then away from the water. She began a circular dance until she found and traced the man's track back up over the dike and down its slope toward the wire fence at the back of the somber house.

Suddenly she tucked her tail down, stopped dead still, and began a mournful howling. She wouldn't budge. This was frustrating because I wanted to get up close to investigate the back of the house and garage without attracting attention. Pokey's howling was like a siren of alarm.

The only direction I could get her to take was south and away from the fenced backyard. I managed to get her around the property corner and tie her leash to a tree behind some dense brush where I could conceal and quiet her. After a while she became distracted from whatever had caused her to howl.

Evidently she thought she had earned her breakfast at last, because she took an offered pork chop and gnawed at it with total attention and relish

Feeling it safe to leave her for the time, I crouched low and crept to the back of the yard, where I could gain a vantage point and stay partly hidden in the greenery. Two dark forms provoked my curiosity. They were lying about fifteen feet apart in the yard between the garage and the house. I couldn't be sure at this point, but they appeared to be dead animals. At times the gusty wind wafted a stench my way, so I sensed that some dreadful situation lay before me. My green poncho lent camouflage as I crawled under the wire fence behind the garage to get a closer look.

Keeping low and moving from tree to tree, I reached the back wall of the garage. Then I hugged the wall as I made my way to the corner to scan the backyard. Here I saw that the dark forms were in fact bloated dead dogs, probably Rottweilers. They had obviously been dead for several days.

I studied the side and back windows of the house for lights or movement, but there was no sign of life. No sound came above the wind and rain.

A small enclosed back porch drew my attention. Four wooden steps led up to its door. Some overturned feeding or watering pans lay beside these. Heavily curtained, the door window sent an unwritten message of "keep out." I could imagine that in some past era the house had been a respectable, fashionable place, but nothing about it now seemed inviting or conducive to good health and happy living. It exuded a dreary, foreboding spirit.

Now I became uncertain about how far I should probe in the little time I had left before I must return Jill to her car. A trail of scent had been confirmed. The man had been here. He had walked between the river and the mailbox. He might still be here, for all I knew.

My instructions for the day were to learn whether evidence of his presence could be discovered anyplace besides the site of his abandoned truck. Shackleton wanted me to give extra attention to this particular region because he had been confused here by an impression of death—even though he intuitively felt that the missing man was still alive. That was on Thursday, more than two days ago. Although I had accomplished this day's assignment, I felt an urgency to press on. I knew there was a lot more to learn here if I could continue probing. That was out of the question, of course, but maybe I could come back later.

I decided to check in with Laura and fill her in on the events of the morning. A report was due anyway. She responded to her ring signal immediately.

"Hi, Laura. Good news. I found a dog with a remarkable nose, and she picked up the missing man's scent less than an eighth of a mile from where he left his truck. Ruling out other possibilities, he came by river to this house that Shackleton questioned. I'm in the backyard behind a detached garage even as I speak—or think, I should say. I've spotted two dead Rottweilers in the yard. There's no sign of life that I can detect yet. I'm sure there's more to learn here if I could stay, but I'm up against a problem."

"What is it, Kep? Do you need help?"

"No. I've had wonderful help, but that's my problem. Are you aware of Jillian? Has Shackleton told you about her?"

"Yes. I know that she's the Whipples' daughter. What about her?"

"She located the dog for me this morning. It's saved a lot of time for me, and she can get this dog to do things I can't. So she's here with me . . . well, not here, but in the VW out in front of this place. I'm going to have to take her and the dog back now. I don't need the dog anymore, at least not—"

"You say she's in front of the house, Kep? Is your van parked right in front of the house?"

"Yes,"

"Oh, Kep. I'm not so sure that's safe for either one of you. And she's alone? You should probably get her away as soon as you can, Kep. You can—"

"Laura?"

"Yes."

"Sorry. I just spotted another dead dog at the back of the house under a section of picket fence. The fence is resting on top of the dog's body. I don't see how this . . . it couldn't have fallen on the dog . . . and the fence couldn't be that heavy. It's . . ."

"Kep. Just leave now. You'll have to return later."

"That's just what I was thinking, but—"

Just then I heard the VW horn. Jill was honking it repeatedly. My heart stopped and my breath caught in my throat.

"Laura? Jill is honking the horn. I'm leaving. Talk to you later."

I twisted the ring and ran to the place I had found in the back fence where I could squeeze under it. When I came to the spot where I had tied Pokey, I saw the end of her leather leash dangling from the tree. It was flopping loosely in the wind. Pokey was gone.

Racing back along the fence toward the highway, I wildly grasped at the hope that I would find her with Jill. Maybe her showing up at the bus was the cause of Jill's sounding a signal of distress. But my hope was quickly extinguished. The bus was nowhere in sight.

My heart pounded as I sped to the center of the road. The wind-driven rain spattered against my face as I spun from north to south, my eyes squinting for a sign of the bus. Nothing. Only empty highway in either direction.

Recalling Laura's last words of concern, I felt an

overwhelming sense of emptiness myself—then dismay, then outright alarm as I struggled to accept the reality of this situation. I knew it simply would not be like Jill to leave without giving me a chance to respond to her sounding the horn. Very few minutes had passed, and I had run the distance with good speed.

And what about Pokey? How could Jill have gotten her into the bus and driven off so fast? It had taken the two of us to coax her up and aboard. Pokey was heavy—and wet. I doubted Jill would try to lift her in her good Sunday clothes.

I hunched over and put my back to the wind as I searched the shoulder of the road for paw prints. There was more gravel than mud, but I did spot some gouge marks in the gravel that indicated force and struggle. The next thing to grab my attention sent chills down my spine. At the shoulder's far edge lay one of Jill's blue high heels. It had been torn from her shoe. My hand shook as I picked it up and studied it before hurriedly scanning the roadside for other tell-tale signs of unwanted events.

Behind, where the gravelly shoulder narrowed, I came across tire tracks. Some spinning of a wheel was evident in a muddied section near the pavement, but its trace was much wider than the tires of the bus and definitely fresh. I felt certain that another vehicle had come up behind Jill while she waited in the parked bus.

My suspicion was confirmed when I discovered two distinctly different tire tread prints on the shoulder farther south. Here, the VW tread marks were still visible where they had arced onto the shoulder when I made the U-turn. A wider tread had afterward crossed over the turning tracks of the bus.

Then I became more deeply puzzled and anxious when I discovered a third set of tread marks still farther south. These made a shallow curve, first off and then onto the pavement, maybe signifying that a vehicle had been slowed and turned aside for someone to give attention to the scene ahead. All sorts of possible explanations crowded my head as I sought for something plausible to quell my mounting fears. I could think of nothing that made sense that would comfort me. For the first time since my bike accident, I felt literally sick at my stomach. My head began to reel in anxiety and confusion, but I refused to yield or to lose control.

Still clutching Jill's broken shoe heel, I moved northward along the highway, hoping to discover other clues about what might have taken place. Then, feeling a sense of urgency to get off the road and out of sight as soon as possible, I broke into a jog as my eyes swept the highway from side to side. A gust of wind caused something white to flutter quite a distance ahead on the left. I ran toward it, certain that I hadn't seen it there when Jill and I had led Pokey along that stretch of the opposite shoulder. It looked like a thing out of place—not natural. When I came within ten feet of it, I recognized my clipboard with white papers flopping in the wind. And on top, clamped together with the papers, was the missing man's notebook! I nearly fell over as I knelt to pick it up.

Now my mind plunged helplessly into a maelstrom of questions. The location of the clipboard didn't fit into any picture of my quickly formed scenarios. I closed the wet pages, stuffed the clipboard and notebook under my poncho, and made one last fruitless inspection of the highway before running back to the southern fence line.

Unable to cope with the overwhelming evidence of Jill's endangerment and totally thrown off my previous course of action, I stumbled toward the cottonwoods stretching along the riverside over and behind the levee. All I could think to do was to hide out and try to come up with some sensible report for Laura or Shackleton to act on—something that didn't make me out to be a fool. I needed time to gather my wits and to think, but there was no time to waste. My having had Jill along had unexpectedly complicated the whole search affair. And I dared not consider what the cost might be to all concerned.

CHAPTER 19

As I came in view of Pokey's remnant of leash on the tree, I felt both a pang of loss and a keen disappointment in myself. I had failed at being the temporary steward of Bessie Mae's beloved tracking dog. Despite her joking comments, I knew Bessie Mae truly cared for Pokey. And wasn't Bessie Mae lonely enough already? She didn't need another loss. Whatever had happened to Pokey, I couldn't guess. I didn't know for certain whether Jill could have gotten her into the VW. Searching for Jill would offer no assurance of finding Pokey. The unknowns and perplexities became a living nightmare for me, and my mind strove to shut out all that was real.

When I went to the tree to remove Pokey's dilapidated leather leash, I discovered that it had been chewed apart. Pokey must have freed *herself*, and there was no telling how long before the sounding of the horn she had set herself free. She had been distressed over the scent of the bloated dead dogs, I felt sure of that. My hope rose when I considered that she would most likely have returned to the bus. But then my hope fell when I remembered the repeating sounds of the horn and saw again in my mind the new tire tread marks. The troubling pictures that arose harbored dreadful feelings.

The pictures became uglier the longer I dwelt on them. I eventually recalled Jill's words about a "big picture" and wished that she had been able to explain what she meant. If every unhappy life event, no matter how horrendous, heartbreaking, or ugly, contributed to an ultimately good purpose as she believed, I felt more than ready for her big picture. I was becoming suddenly aware of just how much human life fed on flickering hope.

Taking the fragment of leash and my tokens of dismay—the piece of broken heel and the clipboard with the notebook—I ran up over the dike toward the riverside with its fringe of cottonwoods and dense undergrowth. Wet and cold and drained of energy, I sat in the rain among the bushes under the wind-tossed leaves of the trees. I cared not so much about my physical discomfort as I did about my being consumed with the agony of the unknown. Jill's whereabouts and personal safety were the things that presently mattered to me most.

I briefly entertained the notion of hitching a ride and abandoning both my quest and my commitment. But it didn't take long for me to see the possible consequences and futility of doing so. I had no doubt that if I were to quit, I'd lose more than my self-respect and Shackleton's trust. Surely any continuing relationship I might hope to have with Jill would be impossible without my personal integrity being intact. Regardless, I still felt bound to my word.

Thinking was getting me nowhere. I knew I had to act. It was imperative that I let Shackleton know of these latest events. I was in no position to do anything but report the facts and receive instructions. Reluctantly, I reached for the ring. But before I could give it a twist, my finger felt its fiery signal of activation. I waited out the seconds. Laura's voice came to me.

"Kep? Is this a time when you can communicate? I've become quite anxious for you. What's happening?"

"All I can say is you were right, Laura. It wasn't a good idea to leave the van parked in front of this place. It's gone. So is Jill, and so is the search dog. I can't account for any of it.

"There are signs that other vehicles came up behind Jill while she waited for me. The dog chewed itself free of its tether, and it hasn't shown up. I only hope that Jill has her. But if that's the case, I'm worried about what could have happened to them both.

"It looks like I've really messed up already, Laura. There must be more to this than a man's disappearance, though. I have a feeling other people are involved.

"Jill left a broken heel behind, which tells me she first ran into trouble outside the van. Then she tossed my clipboard with the missing man's notebook farther up the road, which says she had time to think of more than her personal safety. We were on good terms. She knew I needed that notebook. She wouldn't have left out of impatience. It's not in her character."

"Did you see any other people or cars on the road before you left the van, Kep?"

"No. Nothing. We spent twenty minutes along the highway with the dog's nose to the ground. No traffic—at least while we were doing the search. The same goes for the time I spent checking out the roadway since my last ring call to you. It's strange that all this activity has taken place while I've been out of sight. Maybe I'm being watched, but I don't see how."

"Are you away from the road now? Where are you, Kep?"

"I'm over the dike ridge, hidden in the trees. I'd see anyone else before they'd see me. There's a narrow beach between me and the river.

"Laura, something has to be done for Jill. I know she's in a situation that calls for help. There's no time to waste. Shackleton must have ideas and access to resources I can't guess at. Should I call him in on this?"

"He's been involved in a new development, Kep. He hasn't responded to any of my calls in the past two hours, which is unusual. You're going to need help yourself, since you don't have transportation. I'll keep trying to alert Shackleton. Signal for me if anything new comes up. Please stay out of sight. I'll learn what is to be done and relay it to you."

"Okay. But I can't just sit around, Laura. I've got to keep occupied and learn what I can here while I'm waiting. Don't worry, I can look out for myself—and no one's going to see me."

I stuffed the little notebook and Jill's heel inside my shirt and stashed the clipboard under a bush. The only way I could get rid of my distress and agitation was to keep moving. And I had to make my movements count for some useful purpose.

Of course, my time would best be spent investigating the old house and its grounds. I crouched low and moved back up over the dike. This I did a few yards at a stretch while keeping a constant watch for *other* watchers. It crossed my mind that if Pokey and I were to reconnect, she would be the one to find *me*. So I kept an eye out for her as well, just in case I might spot her nosing along my recent tracks.

Repeating my first tactical approach to the rear garage wall, I made my way to the corner nearest the house and again tried to detect movement or light or sound within. Nothing. I sensed only wind, rain, and fluttering leaves above and around me.

Rounding the corner, I came in full view of the house windows that faced the garage. The house itself seemed lifeless. But an ominous spirit came from it, and I could only look at its exterior shell with apprehension. I then spotted a side entry door to the garage. Its window had no cover, so I shielded my eyes with my hands to peer inside.

A fairly modern four-door sedan had been backed inside facing toward its access doors. The garage side-door was unlocked, so I slipped inside and gave my eyes time to adjust to the dim light. Except for the dark-blue car and two short stacks of cardboard boxes, the garage was empty. No tools or equipment of any sort. Nothing stored. The interior walls were bare. So the garage, too, seemed lifeless.

The car was covered with a fine, light dust, which gave evidence that it had not been driven for quite some time. Curious, I tried the handle on the driver's door. It was unlocked.

As the door opened, the interior lights disclosed empty seats, front and rear. But there was something unusual about the driver's seat that caught my attention. It was positioned very close to the steering wheel, while the passenger seat stood more typically back from the dash. I inferred from this that the last driver was rather small in stature—perhaps a female. But there was no way to be certain.

I then opened the back door to see if there were any articles out of sight under the forward bucket seats. While lowering my head for a look, I put my hand on the rear seat and was surprised to find that the cloth fabric was wet. It wasn't just damp; it had been recently soaked. Then I felt the carpeting and found it wet as well. A check of the front seats and carpet proved them to be dry.

Not having anything better to do, and obviously putting off my proposed venture nearer to the dark house, I yielded to curiosity and opened the car's glove compartment. It contained absolutely nothing. This had to mark a departure from what I thought was a most typical behavior on the part of car owners. Weren't glove boxes supposed to be stuffed with all kinds of human trappings? Didn't they house disclosures of the activities of the vehicle's owner? How about a vehicle registration certificate? Not to find *that*, at the least, was a disappointment.

I closed the front passenger door and moved to the short stacks of cardboard boxes against the south wall. They proved to be empty liquor cartons. The interior dividing partitions had been removed and were nowhere in sight. I guessed that the cartons had served to transport personal belongings or household goods, possibly during a recent move. They were still dry and smelled like new cardboard.

At this point in time I realized that I was trespassing, but how else was I to learn anything significant? (Yes, I was rationalizing.) I became tense as I reflected on my recent arrest. I was well aware that Shackleton was in no position to rescue me, should I invite the attention of local law enforcers. There would be no

Graham Walker playing a beneficent role. This was no "test" as before. I was strictly accountable for my own actions. Maybe this was why Shackleton had warned me that I would have to rely on my wits and instinct. If caught, I would be bound to answer in a way that would not serve my best interests.

These thoughts led me to realize that I presently had no *self*-interest per se. My interests now centered on Jill and my quest. I was not self-absorbed. There was purpose and direction to my life. No matter that my efforts and prospects seemed dismal just now; I was already taking steps along my inner road. Admittedly, they were tentative steps, but I really didn't care, except for the way they might affect Jill.

There she was—in my thoughts again. What about her own commitment for the day? She was to have left the Whipple farm at noon. What time was it? I wondered.

My mind must have recorded an earlier observation that hadn't deserved a top level of awareness, but now it suddenly surfaced. It had been submerged until the need for it arose. I opened the front car door and again scanned the dash board. A glowing clock at the side of the instrument panel gave the time: 11:32.

Wherever Jill was at this moment, I doubted it was where she had intended to be—or wanted to be. Again these thoughts brought a sort of fear-induced paralysis that tended to shut me down and thwart my mission. I forced my thoughts and attention onto the very dismal house. I couldn't put it off any longer. I must deal with what it had to offer.

Looking through the garage door window, I could see that the rain had stopped. There were no rain drops spattering on the stepping stones leading from that door to the back porch steps. The leaves and branches of a nearby cottonwood were still restless but less agitated.

Reluctantly my eyes went to the dark, bloated bodies of the dogs lying on the lawn near the house. They were several yards away and about fifteen feet apart. The third dog lay at the back of the house, around its corner and out of sight from where I stood. What could have caused all three to die? I strongly felt that they had been kept as protectors, not pets.

It took deliberate force of will for me to open the door and move out of concealment into the open. There was no way to tell if I was being observed from within the darkened house, especially because the second-story dormer windows were set farther back into the steeply pitched roof. Anyone watching from inside could easily remain hidden by staying back out of my restricted field of vision.

Deciding it best to move in a relaxed, natural fashion, I walked first to the back porch steps to check the large, overturned feeding and watering pans. Strangely, I found several cups of once-dry dog food underneath two of the pans. Most of the food lay under the pans, but some of it was scattered, as though each pan had been flipped over onto the ground where it had been placed. The lightweight metal pans could easily have been shoved aside by a powerful Rottweiler wanting to eat. Obviously the dogs had not starved to death. I suspected they had been poisoned.

I lifted one dog's head from the deep, wet grass to check for hidden throat wounds. There were no visible bite marks or lacerations. Gripping its legs, I rolled it over to look for bullet holes or torn flesh. No marks of violence were evident, so I concluded that it had been poisoned. The deteriorating condition of the body, together with its stench, made me feel disinclined to probe any further.

A close look at the second dog reinforced my belief that the dogs' deaths could not have resulted from any cause other than poisoning. I seriously doubted that the owner of the dogs would have poisoned them in any case. Could their pans of food have been flipped over *after* the poisoning, possibly as an act of disdain?

Moving around to the back of the house, I approached the

puzzling scene of the third dog's demise. The body was lying under an eight-foot section of wooden picket fence. I saw that a neglected garden plot at the back of the yard was enclosed by similar lengths of picket fence. Due to rotting posts, most of these were leaning over. Some had already fallen to the ground. Apparently the fence piece covering the dog was one that had been moved from the garden location, because there was a gap in the plot enclosure. The removed section had been carried about ten yards. Why drag it that far to cover a dead dog? And certainly the fence was not heavy enough to restrain even an ailing dog of this breed.

I studied the back wall of the house. There were three windows on the ground level and two more upstairs. Above these, a small attic vent was positioned at the apex of the high, peaked gable.

As I stood staring at the windows, I noticed that all of them had closed drapes or blinds, except one. That window was right over the piece of fence lying on the dead dog. It didn't take long to see that this fence section could have been placed to lean against the wall beneath that window. The house had a high foundation, and this particular window stood higher off the ground than the other two. I supposed that it might be a bathroom window. Should I dare use the fence as a ladder to find out?

I now felt certain that there could have been no reason for the section to have been lugged there except to serve as a ladder. So, one thought leading to another, I arrived at a decision. I would not track a suspected intruder into the house—even though by entering the garage uninvited, I had to recognize *myself* as being an intruder.

Although there hadn't been any sign of life inside as yet, I felt unsure of what I should do or say if I *should* meet up with an occupant—no matter whether he or she was an intruder or a tenant. And someone's resulting phone call to report my illegal entry would put a halt to any further investigating (snooping?), and possibly to my "career" as well.

The intruder might well be the missing man. But how far should I go with pursuing positive identification? What else could I learn without actually seeing him? Even so, I wasn't given any physical description to go by.

Maybe his little notebook would offer something of a character description. I had only briefly skipped through it the previous night before going to sleep. Studying it might divert my mind from the frustrations and worries of the moment . . . if I could just keep focused on it.

The best place to keep out of sight would be inside the car, and I could study there in comfort. On my way back to the garage, I kept close to the house by heading first around the corner toward the closed-off back porch. Just as I neared the back steps, I made a startling discovery: The house telephone wire was ripped loose from its service box on the side wall. It had been yanked out with great force, judging from the appearance of the multiple wire ends. How could I have missed this before?

My attentiveness to observation needed a lot of practice, obviously. I looked closely at the hanging wire. It was wet with drops of water, so I guessed it had been pulled loose *before* the rainstorm. No need then to be concerned about a 911 call to the police if I got caught nosing around. But I did have a thought or two about the temperament and strength of the person I'd be dealing with, should I be confronted by him. Poisoned dogs, overturned feeding pans, and a ripped-out phone wire were not signs of a placid disposition.

By this time I was feeling less inclined to study and more disposed to snoop. I made my way around the back wall again to see what the north side of the house looked like. Here I found a chain-link fence with a gate, an arrangement similar to the one between the house and the garage on the opposite side. It appeared to be a new one, recently installed, spanning the distance between the house wall and an old fence running along the north property line.

Beyond the new fence, a large covered porch extended in an "L" shape around to the house front. There it faced a graveled parking area bordered by perennial shrubs. I opened the gate and quietly stepped up onto the porch. Feeling more bold than cautious, I peered through each of three large uncovered windows as I eased my way along toward the front.

I saw only an unfurnished living room having several unopened boxes stacked against an empty built-in bookcase. That was all. Everything I'd seen about the garage and house so far indicated a recent move—one without furniture. But now the extensive lack of attention to livability gave me an uneasy feeling. I suppose I derived this in part from the unused dusty car, which indicated that life and living were overdue. Something wasn't right. Apart from the lack of furniture and a curtailed move-in, darkness and emptiness emphasized the dreary, unwholesome aspect of the place. Along with that, it emanated an ominous spirit. Even though the wind gusts were subsiding around me, I could detect no sound inside.

As I moved around the "L" of the porch, I found four more uncovered windows to look through, two on each side of a brown weathered front door. The window at the left of the entrance provided a view of a partly enclosed stairway and a small dining area. These could be seen through a wide archway farther back. A card table and two folding chairs held stacks of various household articles amid small boxes and plastic bags. The far left window disclosed an empty room with another window facing the garage.

By now I had placed myself fully in view of anyone traveling the highway not fifty yards distant. Not very smart. I had told Laura no one would see me, but now I was letting my impatience and curiosity carry me away from good sense. Even so, it did cross my mind that I might learn something by inspecting the roadside mailbox. Was it illegal to just *open* someone's mailbox? (At this time I really didn't know.)

Resuming caution once again, I retraced my way back around the porch, through the gate, and along the back wall of the house. Suddenly I was jolted to a stop by undeniable sounds of human life. Two distinct sneezes, one after the other, reached my ears as I passed under the bathroom window. I froze dead still, trying to decide whether to move on or to stay stuck in my tracks. When a third sneeze came, I could tell it didn't come from the window over my head. It came from higher up. But there were no open windows on that wall—the bathroom window included.

My eyes swept upward to the louvered attic vent. That had to be it! But why? A whole empty house to sneeze in, and he's in the attic? (Or she.) Well, there could be all sorts of answers to that question, but I wasn't going to stay there and guess at the one that made the most sense.

After a hasty retreat to the garage, I crawled into the car and sat in the front passenger seat with the door closed. This time I didn't feel so confident about not being discovered. I sat there for nearly an hour in an awful state of indecisiveness. Why no ring call?

I had pretty much made up my mind to head back over the dike to my former place of seclusion when I heard a car horn blowing. It sounded as though the car was moving slowly along the highway out front. What could that be about? There were no houses across the road either way for quite a distance, and I had not seen a vehicle pass since I arrived. Could someone be honking at Pokey? Or was that a signal? Would the guy in the house soon be leaving to meet someone? Should I keep watch through the window to see if he'd leave the house? It didn't seem likely that he would come to the car. Or would he?

I squinted at the clock on the dash: 12:40. Why no ring call yet?

Suppressing my mounting impatience took some effort, but I chose to stay in the car and wait out the time until Laura called with news or instructions. There wasn't anything she could do with *my* news, except to become more anxious.

After a short time, I got to thinking. I didn't like my choice. Fear was my adversary. Why should I let it win? Why should I let fear imprison me inside this car while I waited for words from Shackleton? Since I was in no mood to go through the man's notebook and arrive at a character assessment (probably an inaccurate one), I decided to get a look at the man (whomever) before he got a look at me. I needed to get some action going—impulsive or not.

I left the car, went around it, and stood back from the garage door window to stare across at the house. If the guy were to come out, would he leave the house by one of its doors? Probably so. Would he crawl back out the bathroom window? Probably not. I decided to make that my way in.

Setting caution aside, I opened the door and headed straight for the back of the house. I lifted the fence from the dog's body and angled it against the wall under the window. It leaned to the side a bit but felt sturdy as it took my weight for the climb up.

Finding the window unlocked was a relief, but opening it was a troublesome job. The window was built to open upward. The lower half resisted my fingertip pressure as I tried to slide it up through the framework. Eventually I was able to work it up to a position where I could use both hands. It made noisy protests that added to my tension. And, yes, I had become tense because it had finally registered somewhere in my depths that I was making a very serious illegal entry. Foolishly, I chose to ignore the promptings of my conscience. And adding to my stress was a dominating sense of the possibility of an unwanted confrontation.

I dared myself to continue. (Shackleton would later have something to say about this undesirable aspect of my character.) I was right. It was a bathroom window. And judging from the trapped odor that swept out at me, I wondered why it wasn't left open. But I'd soon find out that keeping it open wouldn't have helped. I was about to make a horrendous discovery—one that would change the entire course of my assignment.

CHAPTER 20

THE bathroom was small, with the window positioned between the tub and toilet. A short counter with a washbowl stood between the toilet and a half-opened door. Various shaving and toiletry articles were strewn over the little countertop—all men's items. Bottles and tubes were left uncapped. Everything was in disarray. Clothes and towels were draped over the side of the bathtub and scattered over the floor.

Stepping over and around things, I went to the door and opened it wide enough to look into a short hallway. It led from the dining area to a closed door on my left. A nauseating stench pervaded the place. Silence ruled.

The closed door immediately became a compelling attraction for me. As I crept toward it, my poncho made unwanted noises, and the sounds reminded me of another time (was it just two nights ago?) when my stealthy acts involved the use of rubber gloves. I scolded myself for blatantly disregarding precautionary measures and made a mental note to wipe the bathroom window and sill before leaving. And don't forget the doorknob, I thought. (I didn't think of the fence at the time . . . or the garage door . . . or all the places where I'd touched the car.)

Thankful once more for Laura's contributions, I carefully lifted up my poncho and felt around for the gloves inside the back of my shirt. It was a hassle trying to locate them among the things I was packing there. I nearly had my shirt off before I remembered I'd stuffed them in my jeans pocket. (Stress is no friend to memory.)

Gloves on at last, I gripped the doorknob and pressed my ear against the door's peeling paint. Again, I could say that silence ruled, but it would be more apt to state that a miasma dominated over all. Even before I turned the doorknob, it struck me. And when I began to slowly press the door open, I became sickened by it.

A dead man clad only in wrinkled and soiled pants lay partly over a bare mattress on the floor. As I approached him I saw that his left eye had been gouged from its socket. An ugly sight, it grabbed my attention right off. His face was grotesquely contorted in death. Strangely, there was no evidence of blood on the twisted face or on his upper torso. This was spooky because it made my mind flash back to Laura's worded picture of Rose as she was found by Shackleton on the hotel rooftop in Rio.

But this man's condition didn't quite jibe with Laura's depiction of the aliens' bloodless surgery. These wounds presented evidence of physical trauma, not surgery. And there was no apparent healing.

A sharply bent metal spoon on the floor near the corpse might explain the means of removal—the instrument used. I bent close to examine it. (No, I didn't touch it.) A dark substance clung to the edges—possibly a fleshy residue. It certainly bore no resemblance to decaying food. But how could a spoon have been used to extract an eyeball without causing blood flow? Could it have been gouged out *after* the man died? And, if so . . . why?

Taking an eye from a living man would be a tough job involving a violent struggle. It would take two or more people to do it, I felt sure. My mind was screaming over and over, *why?* Why gouge out a man's eye? That single question about his eye disturbed me more than any other concerning his death.

There really was no sign of a struggle here, only evidence of slovenly, disorderly living. The room, a small bedroom, was a chaotic disaster. The bathroom was nothing compared to this. I saw tossed soiled clothes, pitched books, scattered note papers, compact discs, and toppling stacks of file folders spread about over the floor. There were intriguing articles of scientific equipment shoved or heaped against a wall, some of them electronic, including what appeared to be an unusual kind of microscope.

A closed laptop computer was placed on a card table. The laptop was plugged into an electrical outlet. A tiny yellow light blinked between two steady green ones at its front. Except for the mattress, the card table provided the only surface above floor level. A disconnected printer stood on the floor underneath it. A folding chair leaned against the wall at one side. There was no other furniture.

Strewn about were smelly sardine cans and empty soup or chili cans. There were juice bottles, beer cans, discarded cereal and cracker boxes, brown apple cores, shriveled orange peels, candy wrappers—you name it—remnants of anything consumable that didn't require cooking. Scattered among these things were tossed metal utensils, dirty plastic ware, and used paper cups and plates. Everything spoke of indolence—or possibly an extremely obsessive involvement in some activity. It might be, too, that the scene reflected a severe state of depression. My impression was that all this mess developed over prolonged days of occupancy. It certainly wasn't the result of an intrusive search. Obviously the dead man had prepared for a lengthy time in this solitary room. I couldn't imagine what would bring him to spend his final days as he had in this forlorn place.

But how did he die? Who was he? He looked too old to be the person I was tracking. And it seemed easier to associate him with the house than with an abandoned truck down the river. Whoever was in the attic definitely knew this dead man was here. How could he not? The whole house reeked. It also seemed a likely possibility that whoever was in the attic was accountable in some way for this death. Why else would it not have been reported to the police by now? A phone call wasn't the only means of reporting it. Several days had passed. The body was in a deteriorating condition not much different from those of the dogs outside.

So now I was thinking that if the person in the attic was the missing husband I was sent to track, he might have faked his own death and didn't dare let his presence here be known. But then, why his trail of scent to the mailbox as detected by Pokey? Why take the chance of being spotted? And who else was involved? I suspected there must be someone, or others, because of Jill's sudden departure from the scene, for one thing. I felt sure she'd been forced to leave by people associated with someone in the house.

The deceased wasn't a small man, which made me doubt that he was the one who had backed the car into the garage. If he wasn't the car's owner, who was? Had there been another occupant? Was there another body to be discovered?

Clearly the dead man had been eating—maybe not cooked food, but he had been satisfying an appetite. It then didn't seem possible that he had died of any health disorder. The missing eye, the disconnected phone, and the poisoned dogs all had something to say. So if he had been murdered, how? And why would anyone want his eye? I couldn't let go of that question.

If the sneezer upstairs wasn't the missing man, why would he stick around? Could he be a deranged killer? Maybe he wasn't the missing guy after all, and maybe my own life was now in jeopardy.

Too many questions! And no sure answers. Anyway, I was having trouble thinking clearly in the nauseous atmosphere. I could easily come up with a dozen more questions, but the big one now was, what do I do? I definitely had to relay these findings to Shackleton.

I was just thinking of looking at everything in the room

significant to memorize and later transcribe when I remembered that I could immediately record it all on the stellar ring. Obviously when Laura had lauded the ring's potential, it didn't impress me enough. Now I couldn't praise it enough. Again, just as I reached with my left hand to peel down the glove and activate the ring, it did its thing to my little finger. (Could it be that the ring triggered telepathy? This was uncanny.)

At that instant I distinctly heard a toilet flush upstairs. Now I could hear the waste pipe gurgling in the wall beside me. (They don't usually put toilets in attics.) I was making a speedy departure when Laura first spoke inside my head.

"I have something important for you, Kep. Can you talk?"

Passing into the short hallway, I could only answer with, "Sorry Laura. Bad timing. I'm just leaving the house. In a rush. There's a dead man here. Talk when I can."

As I focused on making a quick and quiet exit, I neglected to twist the ring. Laura was still tuned in on my thoughts as I retraced my route while thinking to myself. "Close the bedroom door. Pull that glove back up. Rub the sill. Rub the window. Close it. Drop the fence across the dog. Stay cool."

As I ran through the backyard, the sound of her voice startled me.

"Kep! What's going on? Are you in danger? Did you go inside the house? Talk to me."

"I'm okay. I found a dead man in the house. His left eye's been gouged out. But he can't be our missing man. Too old, I think. There's someone alive upstairs in the house, though. Could be the man we're looking for. Maybe not. He hasn't shown himself. But I don't know what our man looks like. Can you describe him? How old?"

I had now come to the back fence and was dropping down to squeeze under it.

"He's in his early thirties, Kep. A big man. Over six feet.

Sandy curly hair. Sorry. I didn't think you'd need to know that yet. You've already done what Shackleton wanted you to do today."

"Well, whoever's in there is moving around. He was in the attic—or someone was. Now he's moved down to the second floor. It's a creepy place. I'll tell you more after I decide where I'm going to hide out."

"Kep, there's something you need to know. You were right about others being involved in this disappearance. Shackleton has learned about a possible new link that could prove your mission to be quite dangerous. Be extremely watchful and cautious. Please don't go near the house unless you hear otherwise. Above all, avoid being seen. Shackleton will have more to say in the matter, but for now you'd best keep hidden. Call me when you feel it's safe."

"Okay, Laura. I'll ring you later."

I crouched low as I headed back along the south fence line toward the highway. The foliage was dense enough to prevent my being seen from the house. I'd made up my mind. I wasn't going back over the dike to the river. I wanted more answers. My curiosity demanded action.

I could still learn more. I could still see if the mystery man was leaving the house now. (I had the advantage of the undergrowth to spy through unseen.) I could see if Pokey was anywhere along the road. Maybe that horn *was* warning her out of the way. I had to know.

The closer I got to the highway, the slower I crept. Every few feet, I would look back through the bushes toward the house. No one had left it. No cars were passing or parked along the roadway ahead. If a car should approach, I would hear it coming. In that case, my plan was to drop full length in the green and depend on my poncho for camouflage.

A breeze swept through the leaves of the undergrowth along the fence line. When I got within thirty feet of the road, I spotted something bright resting on top of a post in the foliage near the shoulder. This was something new. It definitely wasn't there when I had run back toward the levee. Surprise and wonder overcame me. Restraining my movement and staying my pace became impossible. I crouched and ran.

The object I pulled off the fence post was an orange-and-blue box. It was the cell phone box Bick had given me! I was stunned.

It had to have been delivered by Jill, I thought. There was no other person who knew I'd left it on the back floor of the VW. I'd never taken the phone out of the box, or the box out of the bus. Now, at this moment, I felt relief beyond measure as I considered the freedom Jill must have obtained in order to risk making the phone available for me. And the act itself said something of both her character and her feelings for me.

But then . . . it wasn't a VW horn that I'd heard a while back. So if Jill was the one who had sounded the horn, she wasn't driving the van. She must have been driving her own car . . . or maybe she was riding with someone else—but who? She wouldn't have involved anyone else in this—not family, not friend. She was too smart to do that. Then, if she was a captive, would someone else have taken the phone and set it on the post to draw and entrap me? Was this rational thinking? Regardless, I hurriedly glanced around as I thought this.

Then, too, it was quite possible that I was making a mistake in associating the sounding horn with the placement of the phone. In any case, it could be that Jill wasn't free after all. I really didn't know anything. My elation now flopped to deflation. I realized I was being a fool to let emotions drive me in this way, but I excused myself in part because I'd not eaten in quite a while. I'd been deprived of my customary stress relief: food. And I didn't see any prospect of nibbling in the hours I envisioned ahead.

There was no sign of Pokey. If she were still nearby, she surely would have come to me by now, unless she was injured—or dead. Figuratively, every "hope candle" I lit just sputtered and went out. And I had run out of things to do to deflect anxiety or depression. Staring at the house through the bushes got boring in a hurry. The man I had pegged as the "intruder" was evidently not going to show, at least not in the daylight. Although I knew it was time to get back in touch with Laura, I wasn't mentally ready for that just yet. I had to stay out of sight, but I was becoming impatient with hiding. Doing nothing wasn't a part of my constitution either. The only place I had left to hide was in the bushes along the river, and once there, I'd be doing essentially nothing. Or would I? Maybe I could study the notebook. It might have something yet to offer, if I could just put my mind to it.

I tried to grab at some positive thoughts as I edged back along the fence. At least it wasn't raining now. That was a "plus." What else did I have going for me? I had the cell phone. My understanding was that Shackleton and Laura were the only ones I couldn't call with it. Bick said it was activated. But who could I call? And what would I gain? I couldn't report anything about my activities. And if I should attempt to learn something about Jill, which would be my only true reason for making a call, questions were sure to be asked.

I now had an increasing awareness of my present reluctance to exchange thoughts with Laura. Why so? Maybe I felt rebellious about having no control, no freedom of movement, no happy vision to reach for. I felt helpless and too restricted at this moment, even if I was serving a good cause. Waiting things out was really tough for me. And I hated the thought of having to be rescued, but there was no escaping the necessity of it.

Whenever I had been troubled in former times, I had sought for peace in nature's solitude. But now there was no such comfort to be found—not since I had experienced the satisfaction of sharing life with someone meaningful. Jill had brought about a significant change in my disposition. Her disappearance was affecting me deeply.

In so many ways, I needed Jill's "big picture" however she

could describe it for me. Coping with uncertainties hadn't been so bad when I was alone. But it was a difficult thing for me to deal with the unknown picture that existed for Jill. If only I could rise to a higher level, to climb to a perspective with an advantage.

My eyes went to the brightening sky. Things didn't look so gloomy up there now. My eyes went to the gently swaying treetops. There were tall fir trees among the deciduous cottonwoods and alders at the back of the house. They were darker trees, but they were comforting in their enduring green. I spotted a very tall fir that seemed both secretive and welcoming. It pleased me to think that for some small creatures, it offered seclusion and shelter. It pleased me, too, to see that it grew quite a distance back from the backyard fence—back and away from the scene of ugly events I'd just left.

Then it flashed into my mind that running away or hiding from a situation wasn't always possible. Some things you can't escape. I was looking at a fir tree living right next to a vile situation. Unlike me, it had no power to choose, but over time it had grown and risen above everything around it. Did Kephart Stone have the power to gain a loftier view? If so, was he willing to make the effort?

As I gazed at the fir, a solitary sparrow fluttered into its upper branches. Go for it, I thought.

When I reached the tall fir, I took off my poncho and spread it out, wet-side-in. Then I unloaded everything onto it that I'd been toting with me: dirty sock, notebook, penlight, gloves, remnant of dog leash, Jill's broken heel, and the cell phone. The only thing that still burdened me was the sight of Jill's blue heel.

My eyes went to the orange-and-blue box. I'd never opened it. My mind had seldom touched on it. Now, believing that I had it back because of Jill, I decided to open it. At least I could occupy my mind with reading the user instructions.

I was in for a shock. The first thing I saw was a folded note.

It was from Jill:

Dear Kep,

I can only hope you will find this, in case it can help. I'm really worried about what has happened to you. Pokey came to the bus with a broken leash so I know something must be wrong. I was having trouble getting her to the bus when two men drove up behind me. They helped me get her into the bus but then ordered me to leave, saying the road was under surveillance and it was their job to see that no one stopped or parked there. They said I had to leave immediately. They didn't give me a chance to explain anything. Maybe that's just as well. These men didn't look like police. They didn't show me any ID or credentials, just insisted that I leave. I killed the engine once as I started out. I beeped the horn when I found out they were going to follow me. It scared me having them so close behind. They stayed right behind me all the way to that store where you and I stopped before. I pulled into the lot and parked, waiting to see if they would turn back. After a few minutes they did, but there was another car behind them that turned back too. It makes me wonder about this job you're doing. How could a missing person bring all this about? I'm going to take this to you in my car now. Maybe if I just make a quick stop and keep moving I won't attract attention. Those men probably won't recognize me in a different car. I don't think they're staying very close to the house. I wonder how you're going to get away from there. I know I can't tell anyone about this. I'm hoping you will be where you can see me when I pass by. I'll go slow and watch for you. I pray for your safety. I miss you.

Jill

I read the note twice. When I read that Jill had made it back to her own car, I closed my eyes, breathed a deep sigh, and threw my head back in thankful relief. Then to realize it was true that she had risked coming back again for me was exhilarating. Her words brought hope and a new perspective. (And I got both without having to climb a tree.) It truly is a marvel what words can do to shape our moods, thoughts, and actions—to shape our very lives, really.

But I was preparing to climb this tree, no matter. It seemed the best solution to my immediate problem of keeping out of sight while keeping an eye on any activities that might be worth reporting. Being higher up might even bring some delusional sense of control.

Although I felt anxious about the chances of Jill's having met up with more questionable characters, I couldn't give in to worrying. Worry couldn't change whatever happened to her after she came back with the phone—nothing could change the past. I had to focus on the present and give it my best shot. By doing so, I might gain some control of my future, because it was being reborn each minute. If there was to be any peace for me, I had to believe that Jill was all right, that she had been guided by her intelligence and personal beliefs.

Now I caught myself believing that Jill's own faith was working for her good. Maybe it was working for my benefit as well. How might I know?

I hadn't given in-depth thought to faith before, but I was beginning to see how important it was and how it was linked with hope. I could now see that my life wasn't going to be much good without either. But when I considered whether relying on faith in myself would do the trick, I had to shut down. Deep down I knew it wouldn't. I needed a faith in something greater than myself. I sensed my limitations, but I didn't want to face them.

This feeling reminded me of the earlier conversation I'd had with Jill when we were discussing her penciled portrait of me. I had realized then that a faith in some higher power was something I lacked. She had asked what kind of faith I thought I was missing, but I wasn't ready to define it for her. Then the subject got sidetracked.

Here I was, thinking of Jill again, reflecting on our time together. It was time for more "act" and less "think."

I twisted my ring.

CHAPTER 21

LAURA responded soon after I thought her name. "Kep! You couldn't have called at a better time! There are some things you need to know for your safety. Are you where it's safe to talk?"

"Yes. I think so. I'm about to climb a tree for a view. I'll need my hands and my head free, so now's the best time."

"I've told Shackleton about the dead man—and about his eye being gouged out as you said. Kep, this news has made everything about this case critical. Are you sure his eye wasn't just missing—that it was actually taken in some violent way?"

"I'm positive, Laura. It looks like a metal spoon was used to do the job. My guess is that it was taken out after the man died. There's no blood on the man's face or upper body. He's wearing just his pants. It's really weird. The whole scene is weird. I'm happy to be out of there."

"Kep, I was about to tell you earlier that Shackleton has been involved since early this morning in what is proving to be another aspect of this disappearance. Your latest news has made the possible link with a man's story a certainty.

"You asked for help for Jillian. I'm sorry. I tried many times to reach Shackleton, but he didn't answer my calls. I can see now why he couldn't, Kep. But he does know about her unexpected and sudden departure, and he's got some action going for her safety. So please be assured that he's doing all he can for her. It may be that—"

"Laura," I interrupted, "I've found a note from Jill. I think she's going to be okay. But please let me know if anything comes up where she's concerned. Thanks."

"You're going to need to get away from there, Kep. But it may not happen until much later today. In the meantime I'm preparing a pack with food and things you'll want. You'll need water, too. I may make the delivery myself, but I'll need to know where and when it's safe to drop it off without drawing attention to either one of us. Did you just say you're about to climb a tree?"

"Right. A very tall fir that's in among other trees clustered between the dike and the yard behind the house. I think I'll be able to climb up to where I can see the highway in both directions—and the river. Maybe I can spot a good place for you to make your drop."

"There are some complications, Kep. The dead man has to be reported to the police very soon. Shackleton is bound to keep his word on that kind of finding. And if there is someone else alive in the house, he'll probably need to be dealt with by the police before the coroner is called. If the man we're looking for is a murderer, he'll have to be brought to justice. Shackleton is working on more than just sequences and timings, but timings will be tricky if we're to keep you out of the picture."

"Right. It would spoil more than my day if I became a blip on the police radar screen. I'll make my climb and let you know what I can learn that may help. The prospect of getting something to eat sounds great, but I'd hate to see you put yourself in jeopardy to bring me your care package. Don't take unnecessary chances. I'll survive. I'm not going to become emaciated if I miss a few meals. Water might be a bigger issue, but I've heard people can do without it for several days. Right now my main challenge is to keep my mind occupied with good stuff. Talk to you soon."

"I'll be waiting for your call. I won't call you, Kep—not while you're climbing."

After nudging the ring a notch, I pulled the rubber gloves from my pocket and tugged them back on. I'd had enough experience climbing trees to know how dirty and pitchy limbs can be, and I hadn't forgotten that all sorts of spiders, ants, and bugs liked to explore as much as I did.

The boughs were still dripping wet, but to climb a tree while wearing a poncho would be a stupid invitation for disaster. So I folded and wrapped it over my assorted trappings, slid everything under cover, and reached for a limb. The gloves helped a lot in securing a grip. The dark-blue shirt I wore was a lucky pick, not because it didn't show smeared-on dirt, but because it didn't show *me*. Wearing a light-colored shirt as I climbed would be like hoisting a flag up a mast.

The higher I climbed, the happier I became with my choice to accept the fir's invitation. I got a view of the highway a good distance each way, and I could see beyond the bending of the dike farther south. There was a gated access to the dike maintenance road just past the river bend. Two or three miles beyond that point, I could see the cluster of buildings that comprised the little town of Conway. Farmlands spread away from the river on both sides.

I could see that the levee road-access could best serve as a drop-off point for Laura . . . or for whoever came with my survival kit. (Bones, maybe?) It would provide a brief park-and-wait spot for a driver, where I could approach from out of sight just over the dike. It didn't appear to be a place that would arouse suspicion—if the wait wasn't a long one.

Getting back down the tree took more time than climbing it. My shirt was damp and I was cold as I peeled off the glove to get to my ring.

Laura didn't answer.

When she didn't come through on my second try, I

remembered her telling me how to access messages. Maybe she'd left a message for me. At first I couldn't recall the exact word order needed to access a message, but eventually I got it right and connected.

"For Kep: Sorry about this. I'm going on a quick shopping trip. When I'm finished, I'll share something Shackleton has prepared for you to hear. If you retrieve this message, I'll know that you called. Expect a call at about two fifteen."

Maybe she'd forgotten I had no way to tell time. But it really didn't matter. I just needed to *kill* time, not track it.

I decided to occupy myself. I opened out the poncho and reached for the phone box. After shoving Jill's note into my pocket, I pulled out the instruction booklet, along with the cell phone. Never having had one to use before, I soon became interested in all it had to offer. When I turned it on, I discovered it gave the date and time. Then it wasn't long before I learned its battery had very little charge left. A car charger was included, but that was of no use to me now. I'd just have to keep the phone turned off to conserve power. I presently had no intention to use it for making calls, but I could use it for telling time if need be. (I would *never* forget the date.)

By the time I'd finished reading about the cell phone, I was feeling hungry, thirsty, and grumpy. Idleness was never a thing I'd looked forward to, while thirst and hunger were things I'd always avoided if possible. I began to imagine what foods Laura might include in her care package but soon found this to be an indulgence in self torment.

I reached for the much-traveled notebook. It looked pathetically worn and used up. It was just a common shirt-pocket notepad fastened together by a spiral wire at its top. Its blue cover was scuffed white in places. The front and back covers gave no owner identification. The book seemed sadly derelict.

Some of the upper pages had been torn out. Notes were

written with pencil at times, but more often with pen. Many were dated. Most were not. I spotted one entry dated October 20. That last-year's date told me the book hadn't been used much in the past. But as I neared the ending pages, I found an increasing number of more recent dates.

Overall, the pages contained mostly jottings of addresses and numbers followed by units of measure. One page showed an address, along with a list of tools. At its bottom was a word printed in large letters: DOGS. Sometimes noted digits were preceded by the capital letter R. On one page, the man had underscored "need tall inside ladder." Most pages showed Bellingham addresses, but there were some that designated outlying towns. No names or phone numbers were written anywhere—just addresses. This puzzled me.

Recurring journal-like jottings at the bottoms of many pages became the only intriguing aspect of the notepad. Among these were such brief phrases as "lousy day," "Frank didn't show," "how wrong can I be," "she's mad again," "no satisfaction," "nothing in this for me," "looks said more than words," "no win," "would you believe it she asked my opinion," and so on.

As I slowly flipped the pages over, I looked for anything irregular about the handwriting. Most all the notations were written using a very small cursive form. I wondered if this was typical of the man's handwriting or if he'd just tried to cram as much as he could in limited space. At the time I regarded this as unusual for a big man, but I didn't know then that size of handwriting had nothing to do with size of person.

I was having trouble seeing how Laura could say these notes were "revealing." But then I saw, as I turned over the very last pages, that there were more fragments of thoughts written on the backs of the sheets. Up to this point, the back sides had not been used.

My interest piqued once I flipped the book over and began reading from the last leaf forward. These notes seemed to be more sequential, written in a progressive pattern leading up to the time the man vanished. Here there were no addresses or numbers, just expressions of thoughts or feelings. No dates were written. My attention was drawn mostly to the following fragmentary passages:

"she doesn't hear me not for two years," "can't take much more," "who's to talk to? unloading on paper writing helps," "she doesn't need those people," "her sick old man never did anything for her," "the changed man is too suspicious to buy," "maybe her plan is my good news," "afraid change won't last hoping it will," "never enough money this could be big," "hate this job chained dogs better off dead," "glad when this is over," "she's got to come through," "maybe chance for new start too alone," "new life sounds good," "this latest makes me want to be with her she's prettier too now," "hope she treats me better than woman I've been with last 2 yrs," "she doesn't know how good this makes me feel," "maybe when we get away from here," "hate water not a good swimmer not my choice," "have to trust her with plans and secrets."

My study of the notepad gave me these overall impressions of the man:

He was dissatisfied with both his work and his relationships. He was lonely and a bit unsocial or withdrawn. He definitely wasn't happy, but he had some hope for a planned change offering a better life—possibly with another woman. Still, he held a negative view of life, and his happiness seemed to be dependent on the performances of others. He seemed unwilling or unable to take control of his own life. Maybe, too, he was a bit cynical. He might have been ineffective at communicating, and as a result, he could have been manipulated or controlled.

I knew I could be way off on my interpretations, but I felt fairly certain that this guy wasn't about to commit suicide. Of course, the absence of dates on the notepad's flip side added challenge to unraveling the man's mystery. A lot could have transpired since the last note was written. But even if his hope for change (with another woman?) had fizzled out, he came across as a man wanting to make an escape from an unhappy situation. It seemed obvious to me that he was seriously attracted to the woman he referred to as being "prettier"—the woman who had to "come through," possibly to fulfill some contrived plan on her part. The intent to simply abandon a wife and take up with another woman was a despicable aspect of character that my conscience censured. But I knew better than to allow myself to pass judgment based solely on my amateurish attempts to define him.

The thing I most wanted to glean from my study was a picture of the man's disposition to be angry—angry enough to do harm or to kill. It wasn't there for me to see. He did say chained dogs would be "better off dead," but that could have been a metaphor. I had no experience at analyzing people in this way. Maybe it wasn't possible to accurately or fairly define a person's disposition from such minimal expressions of thoughts and feelings. According to Jill, handwriting analysis would serve best because it would use an entirely different approach—an objective one based on the tangible product, not on worded content.

When my thoughts went to that missing eyeball and the repulsive scene I witnessed in the small bedroom, I had trouble associating the severity of it with the unhappy man I had just met in the notepad. But then, I knew nothing about him, really. People had been known to suddenly jump outside the realm of normality into a state of insanity. Long-term stresses did trigger strange acts of release. How could I know but that he was a "user"? Drugs altered both brains and behaviors.

And yet I couldn't disregard the convincing evidence of other people being aware of, or involved with, someone in that house. The link may not be with the "attic man" (if he was actually the one I was sent to track), and I tended to think it wasn't with him, because his notes typified him as being one socially detached—pretty much a loner. He wrote of getting away—apparently with the one woman. Everything relating to that house was still a mystery to me. Again, I really didn't know anything for sure. My time with the notebook hadn't offered anything substantial to relate to or to act on.

So far my experiences of the day had left me wary, weary, and wondering. But from what Laura had said, I felt sure there would be some closures coming up in this case, at least for me at this site. The police would soon take the mystery man for questioning, and the coroner would take the one-eyed man's body away. So I held out hope for meeting up with Jill in the next twenty-four hours. I looked forward to a snack, a drink, and a rest.

I was wrong about everything—except getting a snack and a drink.

* * *

Time was beginning to drag again. I dozed off occasionally. I'd been low on "fuel" too long, and my damp shirt added to my discomfort. My chilled body had sent blood to where it was most needed, leaving me with a numbed brain. After a while I turned on the cell phone to check the time: 2:37. Now, groggily wondering why Laura's call was delayed, my senses stirred and my brain yawned to wakefulness. From out of my foggy mind, a thought loomed: Why should Laura bring me a pack of food to snack on when she could just as easily take me away with her?

Couldn't I eat a sack lunch in the car while she drove? Or if Bones came, couldn't he bring along all I'd need to survive until we got to wherever?

It seemed to me that one of two things would happen. One: The police and the coroner would arrive at about the same time to dispose of both the living and the dead. Or two: The police would take away the mystery man *before* the arrival of the coroner and his crew. There would be forensic investigations continuing on in either case, and it would be best (in my view) that I be far from the scene. The sooner I got rescued, the quicker Shackleton could report my findings. Then police work could begin with a better chance of catching the "lost" one—possibly a murderer—before he could get away. There wasn't any way I could see myself apprehending him if he did attempt to sneak off. All I could do would be to sound the alarm, and then I'd surely put myself in jeopardy as I tried to make my own getaway.

I could see no advantage in my hanging around any longer, especially when I'd be susceptible to being found. What could be a better way to "stay out of sight" than to move some miles under me? Hadn't Laura said I'd done everything Shackleton had wanted me to do already? How about a tad more than expected? But then I couldn't overlook the damage I'd done by taking Jill along on my errand. And there was no telling how far-reaching the consequences of that innocent slip-up would be.

Now I began to suffer more from being disgruntled and impatient than from physical discomfort. Again, I chose to get some action going. I reached for my ring.

Laura was slower at answering my call this time.

"Kep, I'm so sorry to keep you waiting. There have been a lot of things going on that I can't tell you about just yet. Mostly they're the result of new information and unanswered questions. I know you're frustrated by unanswered questions, Kep. I'm no different. And right now I'm troubled. But I'm ready to bring you food and water. If there's anything else you need, please tell me so I can come prepared. Maybe you—"

"Laura . . . Laura, I have to interrupt you with a big question that needs answering. I'm having trouble with this plan. Why am I going to meet you to get supplies and not leave this place when you come?"

I kept silent and forced myself to be content with just one question and one answer at a time.

"I've had a reason for hesitating to explain it to you, Kep. It's my reason for not being prompt in calling you when I said I would. Now that you've asked, I'll feel better about telling you. Actually, there's more than one reason.

"Shackleton was going to have me relay to you a recorded consultation with someone, but he's thought better of it since he's done some research. This latest information changes everything about timings, and it definitely limits the strategies he can employ. It gives him a whole new view of this disappearance case.

"There's more that he needs from you. When I told him about your finding the dead man, he was concerned for several reasons. It confirmed a need to search more deeply for clues about possible relationships. The man's missing eye was troubling enough at first, but now someone has come forth with a story that dramatically changes the scope and danger of our involvement. Things aren't so simple.

"What Shackleton gets from you next may critically affect his agenda. And he needs your input to deal wisely with this new development. This latest information hints at great danger for you, Kep. That's what makes it so disturbing. I can ask one question right now that you should be able to answer for him."

"Laura . . . why can't I just supply all the answers with a ring call to him? And why not have Bones make the trip? I'm uneasy about the chance of your being followed in your car as Jill was, according to the note she left me. Maybe a woman is more likely than a man to be tagged like that. She was ordered away by two non-cops who stayed close on her tail for several miles. She came back later in her own car with my cell phone box and a note explaining what happened. She left the box on a post for me to find."

"Sending Bones isn't workable, Kep. He doesn't have a ring, and we need to coordinate on the exact time to meet. That will mostly be determined by you. Can you view the highway and the house from the tree you said you'd climb? Will this work—as a place for you to watch for me to safely drive past?"

"Yes. The best and safest place to park is on the dike road-access at a bend just south of the house. You can get clear off the highway and stop where the access road heads up to a gated entry. I think people use it to get to fishing places. You won't want to go through the gate, though. You can just park off the highway and wait."

"How long do you think it would take for you to get down from the tree and be at the meeting place?"

"I'm guessing fifteen minutes. Give me twenty. But you still haven't answered my big question, Laura. What's wrong with exchanging information with Shackleton directly—using the ring?"

She kept her mind a blank. I waited, wondering at her silence. The silence was becoming uncomfortably prolonged before she said, "Please, Kep. Answer just a few important questions for me. Shackleton is expecting the answers from *me*. When you do that, I'll answer *your* question."

She sounded strangely emotional.

"After that I'm going to have to sign off . . . until our time to meet."

By now I was certain that she was crying. Her thought-out words were distorted, as though she were speaking them tearfully. Maybe I was catching an audible sob or two. I couldn't tell. There was nothing I could think to say to her now, except to invite the questions she had for me.

"What do you want to know, Laura? What are the questions?"

"Did you examine or touch the dead dogs? Did you touch any of the dogs that you told me about?"

"Well, yes. I rolled one over to look for wounds or marks that would account for its death. There weren't any that I could see. I felt certain it was poisoned. Why?"

"Was it stiff? What was its condition?"

"It was a bit bloated, but it wasn't stiff . . . you mean like with rigor mortis?"

"That's exactly what Shackleton needs to know, Kep! Thanks so much."

"Sure, Laura. Anything else?"

"I suppose you could answer the same about the dead man, Kep. Did you touch him?"

(By now I was becoming a bit concerned about what my touching "the dead" had in store for me.)

"No. I didn't. Why? Would I be doomed to a horrible death if I did? Was I contaminated by touching the dog?"

"No, Kep. Nothing like that. I can assure you on that point. But I'm very concerned about something else. I don't want to be the one to have to tell you, but Shackleton's latest gathered facts make it necessary for him to rely on you to do something neither of us wants to ask of you. But . . . you're the only one who can do it."

She sounded both apologetic and emotional when she answered. I remembered it wasn't so untypical of Laura to be one or the other. I waited.

"Kep, the reason you're not coming away with me is that Shackleton needs to have you go back into the house. You'll need to do some investigating and gather important information for him. There's no one else who can do it in the little time we have before the police come. Honestly, there isn't any other time at all. It could be a life-saving act on your part, but not in the way you might suppose—or for whom you might suppose. Everything you learn will be reported to Graham Walker, and he'll screen it and take it from there. But timings are so important."

(No need to tell you how I felt about this choice piece of news.)

I swallowed. I swallowed my thoughts as well. There wasn't

anything I could express to Laura at this moment. Nothing that either she or Shackleton would care to hear . . . or to have me *think*.

"Okay . . ."

My one-word thought surprised me. I couldn't believe I'd heard it in my head. Maybe it was just a word leading into an internal dialogue that got cut short. Now it was too late to retrieve it. That one word had already declared my consent to Laura. I would be embarrassed to try to take it back or to excuse it as a mistake.

"Kep, if it's any relief to you, Shackleton can reasonably assure you that no law-enforcement people will confront you. If there would be any chance of that happening, he would make every effort to see that you were given fair warning. I'm sure you know that you're breaking the law when you trespass, and good motives won't change the consequences. So you're taking risks.

"You know there are others watching the area. Some could cause a problem. I can't give you any help where they're concerned, so you'll want to make certain that you're not seen. And try not to leave traces of your presence, especially in the house. Fingerprints may not be a problem if you've never had prints recorded. Have you?"

"No. Well . . . yes. They took prints of the soles of my tiny little feet when I was born. I don't think it was for any wrongdoing. But I won't take off my shoes and socks to go sneaking around the house. You can count on it."

"Kep, I didn't think I'd ever be called on to put you in a dangerous position such as this. But you probably realize by now that I pray for your safety and success. It's something I do."

"Thanks, Laura. How soon will you be leaving?"

"Very soon. I'll call when I'm near."

That's all she had to say. It was enough.

CHAPTER 22

I calculated that if Laura were to leave in five minutes, she would show up in forty. That would make it about 3:25 on my cell phone. So how was I to spend the next half hour? I didn't want to spend it up in a tree. Tree branches don't make comfortable seats, and to be constantly changing positions gets tiresome pretty fast.

Although I could wait until the last ten minutes to climb to the point where I could watch for Laura to go past, I knew how important it was to keep watch on the house so as to not miss any departures—or arrivals. I anxiously hoped the mystery man hadn't left while I wasn't attentive.

Concerned, I started back up the tree again. As my body climbed, my mind swam amid a flood of disturbing thoughts. One thing that gave me a sinking feeling was the thought that the person in the attic may not have been the one who flushed the toilet on the second floor. Wasn't it possible that there could be another character up there? But then why limit the possibility to two?

Laura's comment about my taking risks as a trespasser pushed some anxiety buttons. Her words were already doing their work at some level. Once again I became sharply aware of the power of words as they influenced acts and feelings. Sure, I'd done some trespassing of my own volition. I knew that I was wrong and that I was breaking the law. It had been my own stupid choice born of curiosity and impatience. But hadn't I just heard Laura say that Shackleton wanted me to go back into that nauseous house? This time it was *Shackleton* giving the word to trespass (at my personal risk) and search for—whatever.

I recalled the time when Laura was explaining the working relationship between Graham Walker and Shackleton. She had said that Walker knew he could trust Shackleton to be discreet and to work within the law. How could my upcoming illegal intrusion be justifiable to either one of them? I found this troubling for several reasons, the main one being that if I were discovered and caught, the axe would fall on me alone. Right after that came the conclusion that this must be a pretty big deal if Shackleton was willing to call for this kind of risk. And if he chose to include himself in risk-taking, how could he effectively defend my act without disclosing his personal involvement in my doings? He must then reveal the very thing that he had me pledge never to reveal—my association with him. The thought blew me away.

As my mind swam on, another thing became obvious: If his involvement did come to light, there would be severe consequences relative to his personal quest and his future. Shackleton's being implicated could lead to his being prosecuted. This would definitely quash opportunities for him to apply his rare talents and resources. Many future victims of misfortune or evil would then be robbed of a chance to be secretly plucked from their weed patch and replanted where they chose to grow.

Still, I wondered how he could know any more than I did about the true identity and disposition of the sneezer hanging out in the attic. And just how far did he believe my own resourcefulness could take me when he warned that I might have to rely on my wits? Heavy as my thoughts were, I still felt the weight of my responsibility to Shackleton and my commitment to him. I had to trust him.

His secretive association with extraterrestrials had always been troubling. My ring was an ever-present reminder of his link with them. I suspected he had many unimaginable far-out resources I couldn't guess at. The positive side of this was that I felt some higher ground to stand on when it came to trusting in what he was capable of knowing and doing. Yet the knowledge and tangible evidence he gave me about non-human aliens in my past, coupled with my personal experience in the warehouse, isolated me. It separated me from others, in the sense that I dared not share that part of me with them. To do so would ensure their standing back in doubtful wondering. I held the notion that a weird tale would clothe the teller with weirdness.

My subconscious mind still wanted to deny the reality of my recent experiences, because they fell outside the sphere of my former reality. But on a wakeful level I knew that extraterrestrials and their technologies were undeniable. And it was hard for me to accept the possibility that human ties might be challenged by the esoteric knowledge Shackleton had given me. I felt it wouldn't matter whether he had transferred a part of some belief system or an indisputable fact—if those I loved couldn't buy it, some cords would unravel. That was human nature—the nature of Earth-bound humans. So it was depressing to think that I must hold back the part of me I couldn't share. This could threaten my chances for building the kind of relationship I wanted with Jill. I could see that secrets wouldn't contribute to a trustful unity.

Disturbing thoughts like these weren't helping me keep myself afloat. My mind and spirit were naturally coalesced. If one sank, so did the other. Once, when I found life to be unbearable, I devised a saving motto: "master the moment." I arrived at it because there was no one but myself to lift me up when I was down. So now I resolved to buoy myself up by focusing totally on my present task—the task of observing.

Unfortunately, in this moment "observing" meant "staring." For the past few minutes, I had been positioned high in the tree with my legs dangling from spindly limbs. I had gained an optimum view of the house and its yard, but my task was totally boring. I was struggling with mastering the moment when a fiery tingle around my right little finger jolted me out of my stupor.

I wasn't expecting a call. It was too soon for Laura. Before my brain could fully register the explanation, Shackleton was up there in the tree with me, his voice in my head. No cozy fireside conversation this time. My breezy treetop was quite a contrast in settings.

"I presume you are not very comfortable at the moment, Kephart—particularly since you have been subjected to so many distressful events. I regret that I was unable to foresee much of this for you, but as I told you before, I hold no prognostic gift, no crystal ball. If I did, there would be little need for your own unique gifts.

"Perhaps you've now climbed that tree Laura just told me about. Not the most comfortable place from which to view the theater of events, but a splendid idea for keeping an eye out just the same."

"Hello, Shackleton. You're so right. I'm pretty high in one sense and low in another. But speaking of 'an eye out,' I'm hoping you can tell me first off why someone would want a dead man's eye. I'm certain it was gouged out after he died. It seems a gruesome thing to do, no matter. It's the most puzzling thing I've run into on this adventure. Well . . . not really. I wouldn't dare unload every perplexity on you right now. But I'm also mystified by someone who not only sneezes in the attic but also prefers to hole-up in the stench of this lifeless house. Maybe the attic vent is his only source of fresh air. I'm guessing he's our missing man, but if I'm wrong, he could be a loony killer. Laura implies you want me to find out which one he is—among other things. I can hardly wait."

Shackleton's chuckle said he recognized my back-handed bid for answers. I was also inviting a listing of things he wanted me to investigate. And I would definitely take anything he had to offer about the scooped-out eyeball.

"We will briefly discuss some things of interest to you, Kephart, but first there is a matter I wish to put forth. I have not been led to comment on this subject because of any particular incident. I bring it up because I want to enlarge understandings and to soften the impact of the stresses you suffer. For your sake, take my next words to serve only as a preventative or ameliorating formula. Please.

"Kephart, I want you to understand that Laura has never expressed the least unhappiness regarding your conversations or dealings with her. She esteems you highly. I believe she regards you with adoration. Therefore, it is important that you know that she has deep concern for your safety—and justly so. However, she cannot disclose the causes of her anxiety. It would be a kindness on your part not to press her too hard for information. She is bound to confidentiality. This places her in the difficult position of being aware of much that she must withhold from you at this time—strictly for your own ultimate good.

"Then, too, she is a woman under much stress, performing many demanding and time-consuming tasks for me. Among these there have been visits with Mrs. Crotty, the missing man's wife. Then there was her previous drive to your present location so as to provide you with directions for getting there. She routinely performs many vital errands that you are unaware of at present. Of course, all will be made known to you in due time.

"That said, we will move on to the information you provided about the condition of the dead dog. You say the body was somewhat bloated but not rigid. Was this a large breed of dog, Kephart?"

"It was a big Rottweiler. There were two others, but I turned just the one over to look for wounds. They all appeared to have been poisoned at about the same time. All of the bodies looked and smelled the same to me."

"How was the weather there this morning?"

"Sunny, cloudy, breezy, and rainy—a mix."

"And the temperature?"

"Cool. About the same as it's been these past few days. Why? Is this important?"

"It may surprise you, Kephart, but yes, it can make quite a difference in my deciding whether or not to send you back into that house."

"I'm sorry, sir. You lost me. I fail to connect this morning's weather report with a repeat tour of the house. Will I enjoy performing a more extensive search now that weather conditions have improved outdoors? It was the atmosphere indoors that made me gag."

Before Shackleton responded in thought, sounds of audible laughter came to me. It was reassuring to know that he had a grip on his sense of humor.

"Kephart, we have—or did have—a Catch-22 situation here that I will attempt to explain. You certainly deserve to know all that is safe to divulge. But first, to make a point, let me offer an allegorical situation of sorts.

"Picture a man who has absolutely no experience at piloting a small plane. Now—as a passenger in one—he finds himself sitting beside a pilot suddenly stricken with a heart attack. Since the pilot has lost consciousness, the single passenger is abruptly thrust into a life-or-death situation. The plane has dual controls, of course, but the pilot is slumped against his own control yoke. His body is nosing the craft downward into a power dive. Now, if you were the passenger, what would you do?"

(I caught myself just in time to keep from thinking *you're kidding.*)

"I guess the first thing would be to try to push the pilot to the side, get him off his controls. It wouldn't do to try pulling him back if we were in a dive. After that I'd try handling my own controls to see what they did. I'd for sure look for a safe place to land. But then I'd need to know how to control the engine speed before trying to land. Then, if we were over water, I'd have to know how far it was to a coast line or a beach, and how far I could get on the fuel I had, and . . . I guess I'd try to radio for help. So I'd definitely need to figure out how to operate the radio . . . and . . ."

Shackleton was chuckling again.

"You are doing some rational thinking now, Kephart, and you do recognize that it would be well to seek information and coaching if possible. We all need to rely on others at times, especially when we are lacking in special knowledge or skills. Interdependence is both healthy and rewarding. But I have not given you the complete scenario. I will now give you a reason for having gotten yourself into this situation.

"Doubtless, you would be experiencing fear. But let's say you had chosen to take this flight because you wanted to overcome a fear of flying. This fear could be accompanied by a fear of having no control, of being placed in a helpless situation. If you were now experiencing panic, do you believe your thinking would be as rational as that which you just expressed?"

"Not really. No."

"Perhaps this flight had been taken as a foolish self-dare to prove yourself capable of conquering fear. This is a trait of yours, Kephart—to dare yourself and to set aside good sense. In the scenario I have just presented, can you see that some prevailing fear, a fear you wished to conquer, could impair your judgment at the very time you were challenged by a situation thrust upon you?

"If we are not careful, a suppressed fear can rule us. It can disable an otherwise-sound mind. And it can operate at a lower level of consciousness in an insidious and harmful way. There is nothing heroic in merely subduing fear as an enemy in itself. An act instigated by daring is not as praiseworthy or exalting as one produced by true courage. I am making a distinction here between daring and true courage, Kephart. The two are not synonymous in my view.

"Had the flight been essential, say, to visit a loved one having but a short time to live, your purpose may call forth a confidence more akin to courage. Fear is best mastered when we exercise true courage. We develop true courage when we battle fear with unwavering faith. Faith evokes the greatest power to vanquish fear.

"'For God hath not given us the spirit of fear; but of power, and of love, and of a sound mind.' Yes, Kephart, this is a scripture quote. But I offer it for you to ponder, because it can be faith promoting. Second Timothy, chapter one, verse seven. You may do well to memorize it."

How could Shackleton possibly know about my thoughts on faith? Why was he bringing this up now? Did he really know what I was thinking when I decided to enter the house through the bathroom window? How could he know that I considered fear to be my enemy then, or that I had acted impulsively? On the morning I first met him (I couldn't believe it had been just two days ago), I felt that he could see through me, that I was mentally exposed in some way. This was more than discernment. His powers were eerie.

"Now, I won't carry this any further at this time, Kephart, but be aware that you are soon going to be thrust into situations that will challenge your good judgment. There will be times when you cannot be given an entire picture because of this tendency of yours to both dare yourself and to satisfy your every curiosity. If you reflect upon your experience in the warehouse, I am sure you will see that, had you known what to expect beforehand, you would not have been able to deal with it as capably as you did. Anxiety—fear—would have adversely affected your performance. Indeed, you may have declined to take on the assignment except as a dare.

"It is because we each care about you that Laura and I must withhold certain pieces of the picture. Your safety is surely at stake. As you demonstrate developing traits of true courage, greater amounts of information may be disclosed to you. And that leads me to the Catch-22.

"Kephart, it would have been helpful for me to know more about the condition of the body of the deceased man. Laura reports that you didn't touch him. It is best that you did not, and it is perfectly understandable why you did not. Perhaps what I need to know can be derived just as well from your observations alone. I will now test your memory. Describe the body as best you can. Please."

"Well, you know about the eye. The face was twisted or contorted as though the man was in great pain when he died. It was an ugly sight.

"The body was stretched out face-up on a mattress on the floor. No bed. The legs were mostly on the floor. There was no sign of dried blood anywhere. Not on the face. Not on the body. I'm not really sure, but I think the body itself looked a bit bloated, but not as much as the bodies of the dogs. It smelled terrible."

"Do you recall the condition of the hands? Were the fingers curled upward? Did the skin appear to be leathery?"

"No. If anything, the hands might have been a bit puffy. The fingers weren't curled."

"Was there anything unusual or awkward about the positions of the legs or arms?"

"I don't think so. Not that I could notice. It appeared that the man had flopped onto the mattress in a natural way—or in the way a person would collapse."

"Thank you, Kephart. That will do for now. We may discuss it further yet.

"Why must I know the body condition? Because it can give me some idea of the number of days elapsed since the time of death. If the man's state of deterioration closely resembles that of the dogs, we may deduce nearly coinciding times of death, but allowances must be made for differing sizes, environs, and so forth. Temperature and humidity are important factors. They affect both the onset and cessation of bloating and rigor mortis in mammals. Prevailing ambient conditions can either accelerate or delay the processes. If you think about it, I have just explained how weather conditions relate to my continuing your investigation from the standpoint of safety, Kephart.

"If the man's death occurred before the arrival of the dwelling's living occupant, I can reasonably presume that you will be safe on entering the house, that you will not be confronting a killer—provided the unidentified person is the one we are seeking. I realize there is still the chance that there is more than one person alive in the house, as I am sure you will have already considered. However, I have reason to believe that there is just the one and that he is our missing man.

"I have ample proof that there is, or was, something in that house of inestimable value—an item that could well tempt some unscrupulous individual to commit murder to obtain it. This presents an additional problem. Not knowing the disposition—or desperation—of the vanishing husband, I cannot rule out his having killed. And if so—if he has killed—I cannot know but that his purpose for remaining inside is to search for the exotic item, had he gone there to obtain it in the first place. We don't as yet know the true cause of his disappearance.

"I must send you back into the house to learn many things, Kephart. Your having supplied the facts about the dead dogs helps me a great deal, but from a different standpoint and for a different purpose. Now, Kephart, the Catch-22 is this: In my attempt to calculate just how safe it may be for you to re-enter the house, I become stymied by the fact that I am compelled to first send you inside that very house to obtain a vital factor for my formula."

I couldn't help laughing. To me, it seemed so unlikely that Shackleton would have to deal with being frustrated. He seemed so immune to frustration. It was comforting to realize he had his human limitations and that he was not so superior a being as I tended to regard him.

"I'm grateful for your concern about my safety, Shackleton, but I can see there are unavoidable risks, no matter. I really don't like to be stopped by unhappy 'possibilities.' I mean, there's no end of unknowable things to threaten us—unpredictable things, things we'd be better off not knowing about. If we were aware of all of them, we might do nothing but spend our lives fearing some kind of a loss. And I don't call that living. So yes, I can see why faith is important . . . and hope. But there's more to lose than life.

"And I can see there are risks for you as well, from the standpoint of my being caught. You know I wouldn't associate myself with you publicly, but I can see how our association could come to light if you openly tried to defend my trespassing—if I should mess up. I've already messed up by not seeing the danger of bringing Jill along on my errand. But she did find the tracking dog for me, and she knew how to handle her, so she was a great help.

"It was an innocent mistake on my part, I guess, but it was a mistake just the same. It's caused me a lot of personal concern, as you must know. But if she hadn't been forced to leave me here, I probably wouldn't have gone into the house and learned what I did. Jill once told me she believes we'll ultimately see a good purpose behind everything that happens. I have trouble accepting that, especially when I see the unhappy things going on right now. It seems a bit Pollyannaish. And I still don't know about her personal safety, Shackleton. Laura said you'd taken some action to see to her safety. Can you tell me anything about that?"

"You will remember, Kephart, that I said I was under surveillance? It will be quite some time before I can disclose to you either the purpose or the means. The purpose I may never reveal in full. The means may be something you can learn for yourself. As you know, if you want to learn a complex thing, having someone 'show' you is unfailingly better than having someone 'tell' you. However, to 'involve' you in the matter is superior to both. You may at some time become involved in an experience that will disclose to you the means—should you apply your analytical powers adroitly. Even so, you may only touch the surface of understanding.

"As yet, Laura herself has no knowledge of my being observed. There is no real need for her to be privy to the fact. So you, Kephart, have now been placed in a position to keep something confidential yourself.

"But to answer your question, let me just say that Jillian is likewise under surveillance. However, our individual reasons for being observed are quite unalike.

"Kephart, we have innocently become involved in a complex and dangerous situation, one that I dare not fully disclose to you just yet. Trust me when I say that your having entered that peculiar house without permission has nothing to do with circumstances as they have evolved. Rest assured. Please.

"Oh, yes. About the matter of your trespassing—I will ask a simple question. Do you believe it likely that you would be accused of unlawful entry if you had found the house on fire and known there was someone inside to be rescued? Now, I am not attempting to rationalize or justify your act, Kephart, but I wish to point out that circumstances may at times put a different light on the interpretation and rigidity of a law. In this particular case, however, you were unaware of how closely your real situation may have resembled the example of the flaming house.

"And now that I am directing you to re-enter the house, I shall take full responsibility for any adverse consequences. Even so, I place full confidence in you and those strategies you might employ to preclude any chance of our being discovered. Still, I want you to know that my conscience is clear when it comes to the matter of trespass. I will never violate any civil laws or transgress correct principles to accomplish my purposes, Kephart. In this present situation, by taking advantage of discretionary knowledge, I can place my choice within the law.

"And now you must continue to receive direction and help from Laura. She should be arriving at any moment. If all goes well, there will soon be a time when we can have another chat in person. Until then, keep up the good work."

Our "chat" ended so abruptly that it left me speechless. (Or would that be "thoughtless"?) While we were exchanging thoughts, I saw a single car pass southbound along the highway. A few minutes later I saw two others traveling northward within minutes of each other at faster speeds. There wasn't anything unusual about the way the vehicles were being driven—nothing to invite attention. But now, as I recalled these events, I realized I wouldn't be able to identify Laura's car, because I hadn't been given a description of it. But then, I really didn't need to know what it looked like until it was parked where we could meet.

The main reason for my tolerating the discomfort of my perch was to keep watch for activities associated with the house, not to watch for her car. And now, as so often happened when my mind touched on her, Laura called.

"Hello, Kep. You should see me pass by any second now. There's no one ahead of me. I'm driving a red SUV. Are you still in the tree?"

"I'm still here, Laura, and I can't wait to get down. I know there are worse places to be, but these limbs are literally for the birds."

"I'll move slowly and warn you if I feel there's any reason I shouldn't park yet. If I had to try later, would you be able to hide on the other side of the dike until I returned?"

"Yes, but I couldn't watch the house or the road if I did. We'll make this work, Laura. I'm climbing down now."

"Then I'll sign off. Just please call me when you're ready to cross over the dike to my car."

"Right. Until then, silence means go. See you there."

CHAPTER 23

I reached Laura's SUV in good time and without incident. Laura appeared to be tired and stressed out but in good spirits. Her face brightened with a warm smile as I opened the door, and when I felt the comfort of the upholstered seat under me, I whistled a sigh of relief. I smiled back. It was good to be in Laura's company again.

She didn't waste any time handing over a small daypack filled with sandwiches, snack foods, and bottled water. Then she pointed to a thermos strapped to the pack.

"Hot ginger tea," she said. "You might find it to be just the right drink later on."

"Right. Thanks. I remember you saying it would perk me up, and it did. Did you put sugar in it?

"Yes, Kep. A heaping teaspoonful per cup—the same amount you used Friday night."

"It's hard to believe less than two days have passed since then, Laura. Doesn't it seem to have been a lot longer than that to you?"

"In some ways, yes, but there have been so many things crowded into these past two days that I've lost track of time. I know you've been through a lot, Kep. You appear to be holding up well in spite of the stressful things you've endured."

"I'm thinking I prefer stress to boredom," I said. "And it

looks like there won't be any letup of stresses very soon, so I suppose I should consider myself happy—being so well supplied. You must have had your share of pressures and demands, Laura. I know you're doing a lot more than I'm aware of. I just finished a ring talk with Shackleton before I came here. He called to say that I'm to get directions from you, so now I guess you can fill me in on what I'm to look for and maybe tell me how much longer you think this is going to take. I'm ready."

Laura sighed. Despite her obvious fatigue, she retained her poise and was polite in answering.

"Please feel free to eat while I talk, Kep. There isn't much I can tell you about what you're to look for—not just now. Time is pressing. We'll have to go our separate ways very soon so you can get back to your watch. You will be getting directions as you investigate. We'll use our rings to stay in touch with each other all the while. I will record everything you tell me, everything important that you see. And you can tell me if your situation changes—if you become unexpectedly threatened by some incident. Your safety will always be a first priority. As I told you, there are others watching this area. According to Shackleton, they aren't police or sheriff's deputies. That's all I can tell you. I'm sorry. Just avoid being seen—please.

"Kep, you won't be doing any looking around inside the house until you perform a task that calls for considerable risk—and . . . courage. You won't be able to conduct a search until you . . . accomplish the first part of your new assignment. I'll tell you what that is after I share some current information with you."

I caught the hints of hesitation in Laura's flow of words as they moved from 'risk' to 'current information.' I had a feeling she was stalling at disclosing the nature of the risk I was to take.

"Late Saturday afternoon I went to Letha Crotty's house, hoping to see if she could identify a hearing aid that had been found near the river by the first on-site searchers. Graham Walker had gotten wind of the discovery and asked us to follow up because Letha hadn't been very cooperative with the Skagit

County deputies. Graham thought Letha might prefer talking to *me* about it, since I had been the one to assure her the least amount of public exposure through private investigation. Normally, Shackleton doesn't deal with clients face to face. He leaves that to me after Graham does the preliminaries.

"The hearing aid was found in mud near a large blood-stained rock beside the river. The abandoned truck Letha's husband had been driving was towed away and later reclaimed by his employer, who owned it. The owner told Graham that Letha's husband—his name is Dan—usually worked alone installing insulation in older homes, completing short-term contracts that his employer didn't want to turn down. Many of these jobs went to Dan because he worked capably without supervision, but mainly he got them because of a hearing impairment that prevented his functioning well with co-workers. He'd been working for the insulation company for more than four years. His employer liked him and spoke well of him. But because Dan was totally deaf in one ear and often kept the hearing aid volume turned down in his other ear, he was left to himself. He wasn't a very congenial man, but he was reliable.

"Letha didn't answer the doorbell when I arrived with the hearing aid for her to identify. As I was going back to my car, a woman approached me from a mailbox across the street. She asked who I was and whether she could help me. I told her I was there to return something to Letha Crotty and that it was personal. She introduced herself as 'Ginger' and said that Letha had gone to visit a half sister in Port Townsend for a few days. Ginger had come to pick up Letha's mail as she had agreed to do while Letha was gone.

"This Ginger is a talker. Evidently, she's known Letha for several years. To keep this short, I'll just touch on the most significant things she gossiped to me.

"Letha works out of her house as a direct-sales manager for Captivation Cosmetics. She frequently holds sales meetings in her home. Ginger is one of her sales reps. She said Dan was always doing yard work and that Letha kept him out of the house most of the time tending to the landscaping. For some puzzling reason Letha considered him to be socially beneath her and an embarrassment to have around her visiting friends and associates. She called him 'Dreamer' and seemed to hold him in disdain. Ginger said Dan was quite good looking and that when Letha first met him, she called him 'Dream Boy.' But that didn't last longer than a year. She openly had other romantic 'interests' during the three years they had been together, and they'd lived together about a year before they were married.

"Letha grew up as the daughter of a woman divorced many times over. Besides that, her mother wasn't married to some of the men she'd lived with. She got Letha started on dance lessons at the age of three and began entering her in children's beauty pageants by the time she was six. She hoped this would eventually lead to some youthful employment for her daughter—possibly in advertising or TV commercials. Letha was strongly influenced by her mother's misplaced sense of values. Ginger was blunt in saying that Letha is a vain and very self-centered woman—even though she describes herself as being Letha's friend.

"It was no surprise to Ginger that Dan turned up missing. She held the opinion that he'd committed suicide. He'd distance himself if she happened to catch him working around the yard in recent weeks. She said he used to wave to reps as they arrived at meetings, but he'd become unresponsive to them—to all but one attractive brunette.

Laura paused and I gulped down some water.

"Thanks, Laura—for both the 'fill-up' and the 'fill-in.' I can see that a character assessment I made from a look through that notebook wasn't too far off. But I don't go along with the suicide angle. I don't think he's dead. I'm sure he had other plans. His scent has been traced from the river to the roadside mailbox. Why he came here is a mystery to me. And why would he come by way of the river?"

"I can't answer that, Kep, but I agree with you. I don't believe he's dead either, but he may not be the person you heard in the house. There's another possible explanation, and it's one that disturbs me deeply. I wish I could tell you more, but I'm not sure it would help you. Shackleton doesn't feel it would be wise to share that possibility with you—not yet. When he's ready, he'll have you listen to parts of a recent conversation with someone who came forward with news that changes everything about the way we must look at this case. Until then we can only take one step at a time. And that brings me to the first step of your new mission."

Earlier, while Laura was speaking, I had eaten a tuna-salad sandwich and washed it down with bottled water and a Coke. Now, as I unwrapped and began eating a peanut butter and jelly sandwich, she stopped talking a few seconds to watch my vanishing food act.

With a sparkle of amusement in her eyes, she said, "I hope you won't get indigestion from eating so fast, Kep, but it's good that you eat all you can *now,* because you have quite a lot ahead of you."

I nodded and tried to smile with my mouth full as I held up one hand and then the other with food and drink.

Laura opened her door and went to the back of her SUV. I turned to watch as she lifted the rear door and reached inside for a large backpack that she had placed out of sight. Next she pulled out a fishing pole complete with line and reel. She set the backpack and pole on the ground and closed the door. When she came forward and climbed into her seat, she wore an anxious expression as she looked up and down the highway beside us. She sighed and glanced my way.

To cover up my own anxious feelings, I said, "It looks like the first part of my new assignment is to catch fish and survive for a week while we wait for the guy to come out and show himself."

Laura smiled and said, "I wish it were so, Kep, but you're not far off when you say the man must show himself. We have to get whoever is alive in the house *out* before you can spend time inside doing what Shackleton wants you to do."

"Wow! That's a pretty big order. Then what's to keep him from getting away if there's no deputy on hand to catch him? He really could be a killer. How would Shackleton be able to deal with his conscience if it turned out that he'd helped a killer escape? And what's the point of finding him if we're just to let him get lost again?"

(Just then it dawned on me that I was doing the very thing Shackleton had asked me not to do.)

"I'm sorry, Laura. I guess I'm pushing you with questions you can't answer, and as usual they don't stop. I know you don't need any more frustrations, so I'll just keep my mouth shut and listen."

I bit into my sandwich.

"Kep, as I said, we'll take just one step at a time. For now, though, please finish eating and try to relax for the time. If something comes up, if I should suddenly have to ask you to leave, just don't forget to take your food pack. Go to the back of my car and pick up that backpack and fishing pole. Then go up over the dike toward the river. Just smile and wave good-bye to me as you leave. I'll pull away and call you later."

It was laughable to think I could take time to relax under the circumstances, and I wasn't about to wait for Laura to react to some situation that would force my departure. I sensed that she wasn't quite ready to tell me what I was to do next—that she would wait to call and give me directions. So I gave her a smile and a quick nod and stuffed my mouth with what was left of my sandwich. After taking a few gulps of water, I closed my food pack and reached for the door handle.

Then, seeing tears in Laura's eyes, I said, "It's okay, Laura. I should go now. I'll do just as Shackleton asks. I guess this is my big chance to use more faith. You practice using yours too, and everything will be okay. 'Ring' me when you're down the road."

Blinking away tears, Laura touched my arm and smiled without looking at me. I could see she'd do much better if I were out of sight. Her stress needle was pointed at the red line.

After shouldering the bulky backpack, I grabbed the fishing rod and my bag of food and headed up the bank of the levee. When I reached the maintenance road, I turned and waved. Laura backed down the access and swung around to head north past the house. She slowed and waved back to me through her open window before moving on. As I hiked back along the river side of the dike, I kept myself high enough up the bank to look over it and watch for other cars traveling the highway. There weren't any that I could spot. Laura wasn't being followed—not then, anyway.

Soon after Laura drove away, I became aware of where my own stress needle was pointing. Dealing with so many puzzlements had flipped it way over. I hadn't the foggiest notion of what was in the backpack or what to do with it. Obviously, the fishing pole could serve as a deception. It could neutralize the gaze of any curious eyes.

I began thinking about Dan Crotty as I stumbled along. Putting what I'd learned from Laura together with what I'd deduced from his notebook, it seemed most likely that this unhappy guy had abandoned his wife to take up with another woman. Quite possibly, he'd faked his death so they could escape to a different locality. Beginning a new life would require a new identity. That shouldn't be impossible to manage, but money had always been a problem. Now I remembered that his notes hinted this change could "be big" in its money offering.

One thing was certain: He couldn't walk away from the area without attracting notice at some point. Hitchhiking would put him at risk of being identified and reported. He'd need an accomplice to drive him. Who else but the woman? And she'd have to be trusted with secrets from this time on.

These thoughts led to a possible explanation for his scent being traced to the roadside mailbox. It was certainly possible that she had picked him up there during the night *after* the initial track-and-search was completed. In the meantime, he could have hid out in the car in the garage. That would account for the rear seat being damp if he'd gotten soaked by the river. When dealing with the river, either traveling upstream or coming ashore, getting wet might be expected. Being a big man, as Laura had described him, he might have moved the front bucket seat forward to give himself more room while hiding in the car.

How he'd managed to come up the river really puzzled me. Most of this stretch of the river was obviously very deep—too deep to wade. Although the current wasn't swift, it wasn't something one could swim against, especially someone who declared himself to be a poor swimmer, as Dan Crotty did in his notes.

The investigating team would have been most apt to begin their search activities along the terrain down-river from the point where the truck was parked. The probability of this would account for a plan to go up the river, even against the current, to avoid leaving any scent—a plan contrived to buy time while search activities were being completed.

Buy time to do what? To hide out and snatch a tempting thing of "inestimable value"? Wasn't that how Shackleton had described some exotic treasure in that house? He said he had reasonable proof that such a thing was there. If Dan Crotty knew about it, if this was the significant source of "big" money to be had, might he have gotten it and left already? Was some other "unscrupulous" person in there now searching for it, not knowing that Crotty had taken it? Could that be why others were watching the area—other accomplices who wouldn't know that Dan and his woman had already made off with it?

Could "her old man"—the "sick" one described in Crotty's notes—be both the father of this woman *and* the man I found dead? I suspected they were the same. Dan had noted that "he never did anything for her," so maybe no love had been lost between the two. I had thought him not to be sick because of all the devoured food, but could he have been suffering from some strange life-threatening disorder? Would Dan Crotty have been desperate enough to speed up the ailing man's fate? And then would this have been another secret for his girlfriend to be trusted with?

Still, my constructed mental movie of unfolding events didn't fully satisfy me. It was incomplete. I really didn't know why or how the man had died. There was no way I could account for obvious acts of violence or hateful drives—namely the poisoned dogs and the man's gouged-out eye (after his death). Did poisoned animals take some time to die? Maybe. The man surely didn't die from the loss of his eye. But the possibility that much of my deduced scenario was true brought me to a disturbing conclusion: Dan Crotty may very well not be the living occupant of that fetid house after all. This was just what Laura had said, so maybe she did have good reason to be "deeply" concerned.

When I reflected on Shackleton's disclosure that Laura genuinely cared about my personal safety, his choice of words suggested a caring that unsettled me a bit. I had never been sure about how I should take Laura's displays of affection, although I'd never found them to be inviting or engaging. I rather enjoyed the "lift" of her total acceptance of me. Then, too, I had felt her outpourings to stem from loneliness, from being trapped in an unfulfilling and frustrating female role. So in my view there was nothing between us that held any resemblance to that special connection that existed between Jill and me.

But maybe Laura's tears were more than womanly emotions spilling over from stress. Maybe I had to be more mindful of her as a woman in need. I obviously had a lot to learn about women—and about myself.

I had just returned to my stash under the fir tree when Laura "rang" my little finger.

"Hello, Kep. Are you where it's safe to stop and exchange

thoughts? I have something from Shackleton I can share with you now—something more than directions."

"Perfect timing, Laura. I'm ready."

"What I can tell you now is only part of the story, but Shackleton has agreed that it's something vital to share with you before you go back into that house. He'll tell you everything as it has developed, but for now the whole story will have to wait. We don't have much time.

"Not long ago an elderly man disappeared, along with a valuable specimen he'd been experimenting with. His employer desperately wanted to recover the missing item, and he needed help in locating the man, so he went to the local police and filed a missing person report. The man hadn't been employed for very long, and he'd just recently changed his address. The employer's name is Sheldon Hoyle. Graham Walker referred him to Shackleton for consultation. He's now a prime client.

"Since Shackleton has had to keep matters in confidence, he hasn't been able to share anything—not until this afternoon. It's now a certainty that the dead man you found is the one directly tied to the lost 'specimen,' as Mr. Hoyle calls it, so the two situations have run together. It may be that there is only one mystery to solve but, if so, it's complicated. Shackleton has to move quickly, so your mission will be vital in getting him what he needs in time. He must keep a step ahead of certain people in question.

"Really, Kep, no one but you can supply the needed pieces to the puzzle while keeping everything from going public—which would be a disaster. It would be a disaster because it would endanger lives in ways I can't explain to you yet.

"I have to tell you that Shackleton knows that the dead man was also wanted by government agents. I'm sorry to have to tell you that. It scares me to see that secret agents are taking an active interest in what I thought was a disappearance arising from a marital rift. We may be ahead, but things could fall apart in a hurry, especially if you are caught and questioned. And Shackleton can't put off reporting the dead man much longer.

"I'm to tell you that he's activated some unusual helps to assure your safety, but they'll be in place for just a short time. That's one of the reasons we're going to have to keep in constant communication with the rings."

My eyes swept over the things I had collected under the fir tree. Staring at the latest additions, I had to ask, "What am I to do with the backpack?"

"You're to take it into the house, Kep. But first be absolutely sure that you can get there without being seen. Maybe you'll want to climb the tree again to check for any parked cars along the highway."

"Right. What time is it, Laura?"

"About four fifteen."

"I'll take the time to scan the highway from the tree. If all is well, I'll go to the back porch to see if that door is unlocked. That way inside could save me time and trouble. I'll let you know when I get in the house. Until then I'm signing off."

I twisted the ring. Two things had become evident: I was crowded for time, and I wasn't going fishing—not in the river, anyway. There was no telling what kind of "fish" I might fetch in the house, though. My biggest concern was to avoid becoming someone else's catch of the day.

CHAPTER 24

So the food pack was mine, but the bulky backpack was for the mystery man—whoever he might be. Obviously (and thankfully) I wasn't going to be camping in the house. And I had serious doubts that I was hauling in provisions for the sneezer so as to make him more comfortable and lengthen his stay. But was I to cheerily meet him and deliver his present with a smile? For my peace and protection, I didn't dare let a rising flood of questions spill over the top of a just-built dam in my mind. I had to act.

After rolling up everything into my poncho and hiding it, I glanced at the backpack and quashed my curiosity. No time now to check out its contents. I had to get up into the tree and check for unwanted signs of curious "others." Besides, Shackleton's comment about my tendency to "satisfy my every curiosity" hadn't found a place to hide in my head yet.

This time the trip up and down the fir tree took much less time. I attributed that mostly to my having established a route—not to "heightened" expertise. There were no parked cars. The dike access lane was empty. But in the short time I spent doing my surveying, one dark sedan went past three times—first south, then north, then south again. Without question, it was the same car each time. The driver didn't park or return, so I felt less disturbed about the incident on climbing back down. Still, there was something about the car that made me feel uneasy. It looked somewhat out of place.

I have to admit that my heart was beating much faster than usual as I covertly made my way to the back porch of the house. I couldn't honestly ascribe the cause to physical exertion. My pulse rate went up as I turned the doorknob, and my jaw dropped as the door swung inward with little sound. It took a few seconds for me to realize that I had entered the house so easily. Compared to my earlier experience, this was a breeze. But, as before, my nose would have welcomed a breeze of a different sort.

The small enclosed porch contained very little: two mammoth-sized dog food sacks—one empty and the other nearly so—and some outdoor rainwear hanging from a wall peg. A pair of toppled rain boots lay on the floor. The floor was filthy.

The interior door was partly open. It led into a small kitchen. Beyond that I could see the dining room and a stairway. To the left of the stairway, I saw the short hallway I had previously entered from the bathroom—the one I had used to reach the dead man's bedroom at its end.

To make sure I had a quick escape route behind me, I turned around to check that both of the doors I had just come through were wide open. It was then I noticed that a sliding-bolt lock had been ripped away from the kitchen-door frame. It appeared to have been torn loose with great force. All I could think was that someone had forced his way in or left in a mad rush. Viciousness and angry impatience seemed obvious as well—plus exceptional physical strength. If the guy had entered by another way, it was most likely the same way I had first entered: through the bathroom window.

Again, the house was silent. No sneezes. No toilet flushing.

I twisted my ring and thought Laura's name.

Laura answered. "Are you inside the house, Kep? You're in the house already?"

"I am. I'm standing in the kitchen wondering what to do with the backpack. The house is dead quiet. I'm not sure there's anyone still in here, Laura. Before I do anything else, I want to check the lower house for more bodies—dead or alive. I haven't set foot anywhere new in this place, except for the porch and the kitchen. After the lower house comes the upper house. And after that, the attic—if you say so. My eagerness is inexpressible. But here comes that question again: Where do I put the backpack?"

"I think you already know, Kep. It's your choice as to where to leave it so it will be found as quickly as possible. Let's hope there's still someone there to take it. Once you've put it in place, you can leave. But then you must take every precaution to avoid being seen.

"You'll need to find the best place to watch all possible exits and see where the man goes. It seems that the tree would serve you best, Kep, and that means more discomfort for you. I really am sorry. Hopefully this shouldn't take very long. But that depends a lot on how soon the backpack is found. It would be a great help if you could learn whether there is someone still in there. Otherwise, we could be waiting a long time for nothing. If everything happens as Shackleton has planned, the man who leaves should go to that dike access-road where we last met."

"Do you really feel good about helping this guy escape, Laura? There's a good chance he's a killer, and there's a good chance, too, that he's not Dan Crotty—as you told me earlier. I'm having trouble accepting this."

"Whoever it is, he'll be heading to where justice will be served, Kep. Shackleton has arranged for that too. Please keep your ring turned on now. Stay connected with me, Kep."

"Okay, but I'm dropping the backpack at the foot of the stairs while I sneak around down here. No sense lugging it with me. I'll be quieter and quicker without it."

I moved ahead through an archway into the dining area. I could see that the short hallway was empty. So was the stairway on its right. To my right, through another archway, I saw part of the living room that extended across the front of the house. The card table and folding chairs I had seen through the front windows earlier still held the piles of just-moved household goods. Everything was the same. The stillness was creepy. It said I should be the same: both quiet and "creepy."

I slowly eased the backpack from my shoulders and carefully set it at the foot of the stairs. Then, as I moved through the wide archway into the living room and looked to my left, I found that just past the built-in bookcase, the room extended left around the staircase wall. Now I had to choose between that hidden area and a closed door on my right. The room behind this door had been empty earlier when I first looked through its front-porch window, but I didn't have any assurance that someone wasn't hiding in it now. Because it was nearest my escape route, I chose to investigate it first.

"The backpack is at the foot of the stairs, Laura. I'm in the living room now. I'm going to check out a closed-off room on its south wall. I'm turning the doorknob . . . "Totally empty. Nothing here."

"I'm with you, Kep."

"The lower house seems to be unused and lifeless, but I'm moving across the front of the house now to check an area where the living room extends around a stairway enclosure.

"There's a door here. It must access a storage room under the stairs. I'm opening it.

"Yep. It's an empty storage closet. No hidden bodies."

Just as I thought these words, I heard the stairs creak above my head."Someone's on the stairs above me, Laura! So you could say I'm trapped in this side section of the living room. There's a window here . . . and there's the front door out of my sight about twenty feet away. If he comes hunting this way, I can probably make an escape, but not without being seen, and I'll have to move fast.

"My best bet is to keep quiet and listen. I need to concentrate on what else my ears can tell me."

Now there were light shuffling noises reaching me from some point downstairs. Not wanting to look around the corner into the greater area of the living room, I held my breath and listened. (At this point I found it easy to procrastinate satisfying my curiosity.)

After a long wait I dropped to my knees to sneak a peek with my head nearly on the floor. The living room was clear.

"I don't know what to expect, Laura, but I'm going to move out of here. Don't talk yet. And please don't ask me to be careful."

After considering all options and precautions, I decided to do a race-and-dodge act to the back door and study the situation as it looked from there. This might be my only chance to run free. From the back door I might be able to see anyone leaving the yard—if I didn't encounter him on my way there. If I did, my best weapons of defense would be speed and surprise. From the yard I could spot any cars on the highway out front. Hidden spies were another matter, but that was a chance I had to take, since I had no choice now but to leave in a rush.

As I dashed through the dining room to head out through the kitchen, my eyes shot a glance at the stairway. The backpack was gone!

But which way did it go? Up the stairs or out the back door? I had to bet it liked the back door best. So if I was to keep track of whoever left the house with it, if I was to report the direction he took, I had to move fast.

The porch door was open. The fresh air smelled sweet. I took in all I could inhale of it while my eyes took in the immediate scene outside. Nothing on legs. No cars anywhere in sight.

Stepping cautiously outdoors, I stood statue-still and hoped for some movement to catch my attention. Only a few leaves and an occasional bird answered my expectant gaze as I saw them flutter on diminishing currents of air. The rainstorm had moved on, but had my mystery man moved on with it?

I had to get back up into the fir tree if I was to spy out anything significant. But if other watchful eyes were to catch me climbing it, I could be trapped for sure.

I remembered then that Laura was still tuned in to my verbal thoughts. So far my mind had been dealing mostly with visualized images and wonderings, so I didn't know what Laura knew at this point.

"Okay, Laura, I'm back with words. What have you picked up so far?"

(I was now crawling under the back fence as I worded my thoughts to her.)

"Oh, Kep. This is too much! Please explain what's going on."

"I'm on my way back to the tree, hoping not to be noticed. While I was listening for him, the man took the backpack, but I'm still not sure that he took it out of the house. I've got to gain some height before I can find out. I think he's cleared out, but I haven't seen anyone on the move outdoors yet. Believe me, my eyes have never done so much dancing. I'm watching for movements of any kind."

"I'm sorry that I was in a hurry to leave you as I did, Kep. I'm involved in other things that I can't talk about yet. I don't think I told you about the binoculars I put in your food pack. They're in the bottom under the bags of sandwiches. They should be a real help right now."

"Thanks, Laura! They'll be a great help for sure. I'm moving slow and low so I won't attract attention. I've got about twenty yards to go, so for now I'm just going to concentrate on getting there unseen."

"Kep, it's very important that you tell me the second you see the man with the backpack. That's just as important as telling me the direction he takes."

"Right. Just don't expect much from me until then."

(As far as I knew then, no one had spotted me. But I'd eventually learn that we tellurians never know how many eyes are on us.)

When I got to my stash, I found the binoculars under the bagged sandwiches, just where Laura said she'd put them. They were small but powerful. After adjusting them, I hung them from my neck and stuffed them inside my shirt so they wouldn't swing around when I climbed.

For no particular reason I grabbed up the cell phone and put it inside my shirt as well. Maybe I felt more secure having my shirt loaded with more "earthly" support. But then, maybe I was reacting to another premonition.

When I got about twenty feet up the tree, I was startled by the sight of a strange figure leaving the side door of the garage. He was a big man in coveralls—and he was carrying the backpack slung over one shoulder! His appearance was not anything I had previously imagined—not the sandy-haired Dan Crotty Laura had described. He wore a cap with a visor, and dark glasses covered his eyes. From beneath his cap, long strands of gray hair hung nearly to his shoulders. Quick, agile movements belied his apparent age.

"Okay, Laura! A man just left the garage with the backpack. He's big, but he doesn't—"

"Thank you, Kep! I'm leaving you for a minute while I report this. Please keep track of him. I'll get right back to you."

I yanked the binoculars from inside my shirt, hoping to get identifying features to describe to Laura, but the heavy lower tree branches began to obstruct my view of him. Then I realized it was more important that I climb higher to watch his movements, so I slipped the binoculars back inside my shirt and made my way higher while trying not to disturb the boughs that concealed me.

I saw him again when he pitched the backpack over the backyard fence. He dropped down, stretched out, and squirmed under the fence wires, then started off with the pack. But he didn't get far before he fell. He had some trouble getting up, and I got the impression that he wasn't well, or that he was in a weakened condition.

Laura came back into my head.

"Do you still have him in sight, Kep?"

"He's heading my way toward the dike, off to my right. He doesn't look at all like Dan Crotty, Laura—not as you described him to me. He's big, but he has gray hair. He seems to be pretty agile for an old guy, but something must be wrong with him. He fell once. He appears to be weak."

"What is he wearing, Kep?"

"Dark-brown coveralls, dark glasses, and a sort of baseball cap. He's carrying the backpack, so I guess he's our man regardless."

"That's the best news you could give, Kep! It is Dan Crotty, and he's following instructions. He's in disguise. Shackleton's plan is working! I left a typed note inside the top of the backpack—one Shackleton dictated for me. There was another possible intruder, but this rules him out. He wouldn't have been able to wear the outfit Dan is wearing. He's much smaller.

"He should be hiking that road along the top of the dike now, Kep, heading downriver. I'm going to leave you again for a few minutes. Just please ring me if anything goes wrong—if you're in danger. It looks like you'll have the time you need to make that search in the house now, but not until we get the word from Shackleton."

I was able to keep Crotty in sight now as he moved south, but he didn't stick to the maintenance road as Laura said he would.

Using the binoculars, I caught repeated glimpses of him moving along the river side of the dike embankment, just as I had done after Laura and I parted. When he reached the dike access lane, he must have been following directions, because he climbed over the dike and hunkered down near the gate.

Not one minute had passed before a dark green-and-blue sedan pulled into the access and stopped. Crotty opened the back door, tossed his pack inside, and climbed in. I had difficulty dealing with an unsteady view of the event at that distance through the binoculars, but that was nothing compared to the troubling of my mind when I steadied my hand and distinguished with certainty all the markings of a taxicab.

Crotty—a possible killer—was going via taxi to where "justice" would be served? No armed police escort? No one leaving the vehicle to place a hand on him? He seemed so ready and willing to be driven away. Where to? I couldn't imagine his being taken by taxi to a destination like the one where I was held and questioned—one to which I was driven in handcuffs.

Just as the taxi pulled onto the highway and turned to head south, a dark car came clipping along northward and passed it. Suddenly the car slowed and stalled. It came to a complete stop. I now recognized it as the sedan I had seen go past three times earlier while I was in the tree—the one that looked out of place.

The driver got out first, followed by two other men. All were dressed in suits. All appeared to be cursing as they slammed doors shut. With cell phones to their ears, the men began pacing beside the stalled sedan.

Within five minutes a gray car came from the north and stopped. Two of the stranded men got into it and were driven away, while the third stayed with the stalled vehicle.

Another ten minutes passed (at least), and I began to get anxious about no words from Laura. Didn't she say she'd be away for just a few minutes? I was about to reach for my cell phone to check the time when a tow truck with a long flatbed pulled up behind the dead sedan, passed it by, and then backed up to it. The driver of the car got out and showed great impatience in dealing with the tow-truck driver. He brought out some type of credential and handed it to the truck driver, who evidently had a form to fill out. Several more minutes passed before all exchanges were completed and the agitated driver signed the form. By the time the sedan was loaded onto the truck bed, I was feeling impatient and somewhat disabled myself, due to a disagreement between my body's limbs and the tree limbs. Still, I couldn't leave my "post." All I could do was watch and wait. It wouldn't do to call Laura unless I was in mortal danger.

When the tow truck moved away, I was surprised to see the driver of the sedan left standing on the shoulder of the road. He was gesturing with one hand while talking on his cell phone.

Very few minutes passed before another dark sedan arrived, much like the first one. The stranded man quickly got in it and slammed the door shut as the car began to move. The car rolled a short distance down the highway—then suddenly stopped dead. I was witnessing a bizarre repeat-stalling incident. At first I was astounded, but then I immediately became suspicious. This was more than a coincidence. The odds were incomprehensible that these stalling events were not controlled in some way. I could only guess at the initial reactions of the car's occupants. But then those minds must have quickly filled with emerging suspicions as well.

This time all four doors flew open and the hood was raised. While two men were inspecting the engine, three others had their heads swiveling with eyes intent on scanning their surroundings. Although they were about a tenth of a mile away, I felt as though I shouldn't take a breath for fear of being spotted. But was I really in danger? I guessed not. Not unless some of those men began walking toward the house.

At first I was relieved when I saw their cell phones going to their ears. But then maybe they were asking for backup, and who could guess at the numbers to be called forth? The number of men had already risen from three to five. I felt certain that those involved in the performance were government agents. If so, this really was a big deal.

If someone or something in the area below me was remotely causing the stalling incidents, might the house now become flagged for inspection? And then if the house *was* to be entered, how short a time might it be before the police or deputies arrived to deal with the ugly scene inside? There was enough commotion down there already. I didn't need more activity moving any closer. So how safe was I, really? Should I take this opportunity to gather up my things and clear out while I had a chance?

But then if I did succeed in getting away unnoticed, my mission must certainly be terminated. To succeed on the one hand would mean to fail on the other. Laura had said it would be disastrous for this situation to go public. I couldn't imagine why or how, but I wasn't in a position to question it. I only knew that my own performance was critical and a lot depended on my success.

As my anxiety sharply peaked, Shackleton's words about "true courage" jumped out from my memory bank. But where was I to find faith at a time like this? I could see now that its seed must be planted in a nurturing season. It needed time to sprout and gain strength so that storms could only test it—not sweep it away. For now I could only rely on the working faith of others and hope for happy endings. Of course, these thoughts led to Jill. I dared not let my mind rest on her at a time like this, but it did. Then, as usual, where my mind went, my life went. Soon she would move back onto the stage of my experiences—though not in a way that made me happy.

CHAPTER 25

FROM my perch, as I watched the activities below with mounting apprehension, I grasped at a possible explanation for the dying vehicle events. I couldn't attach the cause of the episodes to Earthlings as easily as I could to extraterrestrials. There were suggestions here of programmed interference that I couldn't ascribe to some earthly power. I supposed there was always some type of subversive organization intent on sabotaging or countering covert governmental activities, but were these opponents empowered with exclusive technologies? I didn't think so. At least I hoped not.

I felt certain I was witnessing secret agents engaged in a prospective interception and that this interference had disrupted their surveillance. Their actions defined watchfulness limited to this section of the river road. They were obviously looking for a known person to pass by—or to arrive. But why derail the watchers at *this* place—near this particular house? Would they have been watching for Dan Crotty? I seriously doubted it. If so, they just missed him.

At this point I began to wonder if I was witnessing Shackleton's "unusual help" being put into service for my benefit. But if this strange type of "aid" was coming from the Abiding Ones, I didn't see how it could be justified. And I wasn't sure how much Laura knew about the AO's limited involvements, so I couldn't include them in any upcoming dialogue with her. Shackleton had said that the AOs faithfully abided by a cosmic rule of non-interference except in certain justifiable situations.

Now I recalled him saying something about extraterrestrial artifacts—that they must not fall into our hands if their designed properties could be analyzed so as to give us scientific advances we weren't ready to be entrusted with. The AOs might judge well because they had accurate insights regarding Earth-man's collective spiritual evolution. Shackleton had said that inhabitants of other galaxies could be affected by our thoughts and behaviors, that we had no concept of the reach of our influence throughout the universe. This amazed and baffled me. But a significant number of our scientific creations already had the potential to be destructive within our own solar system. Examples of destructive use on our planet had been all too evident in my lifetime—and the thought of political misuses was scary.

As these thoughts flashed through my mind, I became sharply aware of a marvel that we tellurians weren't ready to play with for sure: the ring technology. I began to feel overwhelmed with a heightened realization that I was one of only three unique Earthlings entrusted with its use.

I was still pondering this when Laura called—at last.

"Kep. You're going to have to move fast. Are you there?"

"I'm up in my balcony watching a road show. There's been a lot of interesting activity down the highway from here. Two different cars have stalled. Five men have been stranded. Would Shackleton know anything about it?"

"I can't tell you anything about that, Kep. Just take advantage of the distraction if it looks safe enough to move. Does it look like you can get back into the house?"

"I'm on my way down the tree."

"Please, please don't be seen, Kep. If you're caught . . . you have no idea . . ."

"It's okay, Laura. I can do this. I'm watching, believe me."

"You don't have much going for you now except the diversion you see and the short time it can give you—and a prayer, as always, Kep."

"Thanks, Laura."

Laura's response confirmed one thing for me: The Abiding Ones were behind the stalling incidents. I couldn't imagine how. I could see nothing unusual in the surrounding trees or in the skies above. But there was definitely an invisible force operating in my behalf—maybe more than one. How long could this last, though?

It was a relief to drop from the tree and touch the earth. I'd had enough ups and downs for one day, in more ways than one.

As I made my way to the house, the garage and trees stood between me and the watchers on the highway, until I reached the back porch. As I neared its door, I came to a point where I could see the stalled car through the poplars and undergrowth along the south fence. I caught glimpses of men pacing beside the car, but I couldn't tell if all five were still there. Taking a chance on the house being empty, I shot through the door and into the kitchen.

"I'm inside the kitchen, Laura. Where do I start?"

"With the dead man—in that room, Kep. Sorry, but that's where you'll probably spend most of your time. Just tell me what you see that gets your attention."

I darted through the dining room and down the short hall. When I opened the bedroom door, I released a trapped stench that clutched me by the throat, choking me. Reeling, I covered my nose and mouth with my hand. With blinking eyes, I took in the revolting scene.

"It's a chaotic mess in here, Laura, except for some scientific equipment placed on the floor against a wall. The only spot that appears to have some order is a card table with a laptop computer on it—plus a box of Cheerios. The table gets my visual attention because it looks like some productive time was spent there.

"The thing that grabs my attention most is the stench. It's sickening. I can't help but mention that, Laura. I can only spend so much time in here before I'll have to get some air. Since Shackleton asked about it, I'm looking at the body again. It really doesn't look bloated so much as it looks puffy—especially the face and hands."

"Tell me more about the computer, Kep."

"I have to step over the corpse and around litter to get to it. I'm moving toward it.

"It's closed. There are three tiny lights lit up at the front—two green ones and a blinking yellow. I've never had experience with a laptop, Laura, so don't ask me much about it. I don't have my gloves on either."

"I don't think it will matter, Kep. The computer is probably in 'standby mode,' and I can lead you through some steps after you open it."

When I raised the lid, I found the screen blank. Nothing showing.

"It's open, Laura, but the screen is dark."

"Look around the keyboard. You should see a button that turns the laptop on. It should be obvious."

"Okay . . . I think I've spotted it. Here goes . . . the screen's alive now.

"What I'm seeing is a puzzle. It's strange. This is all a confusion, but I guess there's sense to be made of it. I guess it's a letter—part of one, anyway. The beginning doesn't show."

"I'm recording everything, Kep. This could be very important. We need to know who he was writing to. Look at the keyboard for 'page up' and 'page down' keys. Do you see them?"

"Uh . . . yes."

"Be very careful not to touch any other keys, Kep. Press the 'page up' once."

"Right . . . I'm looking at the top of this puzzle now.

"He wrote the letters 'm-o-n' at the top, followed by the number 8, so that must be the date. Next under that comes 'ally,' obviously the person he was writing to. Sounds like a friend or colleague. The rest of this looks like alphabet soup. A lot of words are connected or have reversed letters. No capitals, except for the single letter 'I' in places. There are lengthy spaces and no punctuation. Misspellings are everywhere. Letters are repeated several times within some words, but mostly at word end—"

"That could mean that the man was unable to lift his fingers from the keys at times, Kep. Maybe he wasn't able to because he was weak or ill. The computer could correct a single letter 'I' if it stood alone between spaces. Do these stand alone?"

"Yes. At first glance I thought it might be a tough message to decode, but maybe it's not. I guess it's readable—mostly. I think I can decipher it, Laura. Just bear with me while I try to unscramble it."

"Just interpret it as best you can, Kep."

"Okay. I'll read it as I see it."

It was a challenge to form individual words from the stumbling muddle before me, especially since I was nauseous and feeling the pressure of time, but Laura was patient. Eventually I was able to come up with the following:

"'no word from you. thought you come for prize by now. mailed letter from blue box long time ago. you must not got it. told about killer dogs got fenced backyard protect me. very sick long time now. if don't die from sickness I be caught. gov men find me soon now so dead man either way. they kill me later. make look like suicide. have their ways. know too much about specimen. talked too much letters sent to connection dayton. losing control of everything in body. can't think. pain in head drive me crazy. gaston cleaning man office came by. I thought was you knock at door like I told you do. don't know how found me. he threaten blackmail me. say where I hiding. very much angry words between us. got him out. want you have prize. worth treasure. must deal with man gave you name and address in letter. can't think it now. sorry. I just remember name col w bradford intelligence wright patterson. he tell you how to trade for deposit special bank account you switzerland. must be careful. dangerous talk any else. prize no good to me. not long die. sorry my life not good. sorry many things. take new cheer if come find me dead. glad if you do. take and go fast. look inside later. look for house on right side river bends away. only house this side. don't want use mail. can't walk drive. hope have your email address transfer this.'"

As I read the message to Laura, I became increasingly nauseated. Being confined in the miasmic stench was getting to be too much for me to handle. I had to get to fresh air.

"I'm going to have to get some air, Laura. Give me time for that, and I'll come back to continue."

"What you've found so far is worth all the risk, Kep! Please take the time you need. Let me know when you're back. Just don't take any chances."

I teetered over and around things and then headed for the back door. But by the time I reached the bathroom door, I knew I wasn't going to make it to the back porch before I'd throw up. I managed to get to the toilet just in time. While in the bathroom, I decided to open the window for fresh air and leave it open just in case.

When I got back to the laptop, Laura didn't answer me.

I twisted my ring a notch and tried again. No answer.

On the fourth try she came back.

"Kep, I'm so sorry, but I had to transfer what you gave me to Shackleton so he could move on with implementing his strategy.

He's quite impressed and extremely grateful for your find! He sends his thanks. I asked if we could go three-way on the rings, but he prefers not to because he's involved with other aspects of this case and he feels we should stick this out together—unless you become endangered.

"Try using the 'page up' and 'page down' keys to see if there's anything else you can find."

I punched the keys, but they brought up just blank spaces at the beginning and ending of the document.

"Nothing, Laura."

"Then please leave the letter showing as it is and close the lid. No need to worry about your fingerprints if you haven't any prints on record. Are you certain you don't?"

"I'm sure, Laura. But if I'm caught, I could be in jeopardy, couldn't I? I'll bet this place is going to be dusted for prints, what do you think?"

"Let's not think about it, Kep. Is there anything else that catches your attention, anything unusual?"

"There isn't anything 'usual' about this place, Laura. The only thing unusual compared to everything else is the top of the card table. It's clean. There are scientific instruments that I'd have no reason to examine, plus scattered stacks of file folders and CDs that I can't take time to go through. This cramped little room is littered with garbage. And there's the dead body lying half off the mattress. I'll bet this man lived mostly on cold cereal, canned fish, and junk food. There are empty cereal boxes and opened fish cans everywhere. The only unopened thing around is a box of cereal on the card table.

"Laura, I'm needing fresh air again. I left the bathroom window open. Give me another couple of minutes."

"I'll check in with Shackleton and call you right back, Kep."

Back inside the bathroom, I spent a minute at the window sucking in fresh air. As I turned to leave, I nearly dropped over when my eyes landed on a strange item at the back of the little countertop. I was suddenly staring at what appeared to be a false eye! I'd never seen one before. The front and back parts were different shapes. The front portion had a natural, life-like iris on a specially shaped sclera/cornea. It was attached to a ball for the empty eye socket.

The possibility that the man had a false eye never entered my mind. This had to be his missing eye! Evidently, I had been so anxious about making an illegal entry that this eye didn't catch my own eye when I first glanced at all the stuff strewn over the counter. Shackleton was right: Fear clouds your mind and impairs your ability to think and act effectively.

I didn't wait for Laura to call me. She responded within seconds.

"Laura, a little item just caught my eye that might be of interest. There's a false eye on the bathroom counter. No—don't ask. I didn't touch it."

"Really?! Hold on, Kep, while I tell Shackleton."

It took just a few seconds for Shackleton's voice to join with Laura's. What a strange feeling it was to have two people in my head at the same time!

"So you've found a prosthetic eye, Kepart? How fortunate! Excellent! Now, give me a moment. Please.

"I'm going to give you some directions to follow. Tell me when you've completed each step, Kephart. Laura says you're in a bathroom with an open window."

"Yes."

"Does the wash basin have a stopper—will it hold water?"

"I'm looking . . . I'm pulling up the stopper handle. Now I'm running water into the basin, and it's filling up. Does it matter whether I run cold or hot water?"

"Cold water will do. Three or four inches should do it."

"Done. What's next?"

"Place the prosthesis in the water, Kephart, and observe whether it sinks or floats. Perhaps it will partially submerge. Tell me what you see."

"It's floating just below the surface."

"Indeed! Now you must follow directions carefully—for your own safety, Kephart.

"Is there sufficient room for you to step to one side of the window, leaving it clear?"

"Yes. I can work that."

"Do so now, and don't move until I confirm that you will be safe when you do."

"Okay. I'm at one side—straddling the toilet."

"Just remain there until I give you the next direction. Please."

My bewilderment and curiosity were mounting by the second as I waited for Shackleton's voice to return. At the same time, it was becoming increasingly hard to suppress my anxiety about those activities taking place out of my sight on the highway. Not to know what was actually happening both inside *and* outside the house gave me a feeling of being helplessly trapped.

The next thing to attract my attention wasn't a voice in my head. It was the feeling of my hair lifting from my scalp and arms. (Yes, my arms are hairy.) I had the feeling that some magnetic or static-electric force was tugging at my hair and skin. At the same time, I had an eerie sense of some presence in the little room—something unnatural. As soon as these sensations registered themselves on my consciousness, they abruptly subsided and departed. I hadn't seen or heard a thing. The effect of it all was a ghostly impression that set my adrenaline rushing.

The sound of Shackleton's voice startled me.

"Quickly now, Kephart. Take the eye from the washbowl and

place it on the table beside the laptop. Laura will give you instructions from this point on. Other urgent matters have suddenly engaged my attention. You have done very well indeed."

I fetched the false eye from the water and turned to the window to suck in a deep breath of air before heading back to the chamber of nausea. Suddenly, the sight of a wiry, dark-haired man stealthily approaching the house from the back fence set off an alarm in my gut. At that instant Laura's voice came to me.

"Kep! You're in danger! Run to the laptop with the eye. Leave it there, take the unopened box of cereal you saw, and leave the house with it. It's a vital item. Hide it from view as you go. Try not to lose it or let anyone take it from you. You may have to leave through the bathroom window.

"A man has been seen coming along the dike road from the north. Don't let him see you under any circumstances. He may come into the backyard. Watch out for him. He—"

"He's already in the yard, Laura. I just spotted him through the window. I can handle this. Just let—"

"Avoid confronting him at all costs, Kep. Please, please be careful!"

I dashed to the card table and made a quick exchange. Just as I got back inside the bathroom, I heard quick, noisy footsteps in the kitchen. Closing the bathroom door, I left it open a crack so I could peek through it. I had to know if this was the same man I had just seen entering the backyard. (Was I acting out of curiosity? Was I daring myself?) If this was someone else, I was in double trouble. My eyes went jerking back and forth between the window and my restricted view of the hallway.

When I heard the sounds of footsteps coming into the hallway, I poised myself for a speedy escape through the window. The man moved fast. He passed by the bathroom door, and I caught a glimpse of his back. I saw enough to recognize him as the same dark-haired man I had seen coming into the yard.

In two long strides, I went to the window and saw that my escape route was clear. At that moment I heard tires screeching on the highway in front of the house. I flew through the window, dropped to the ground, and shot straight toward the back fence on the run.

I kept to a route that prevented my being seen from the highway, a route I hadn't taken before. Finding no way to slip under the wire fence as I previously had done, I performed an athletic feat that I could only have managed with a high level of adrenalin pumping through me. Gripping a post, I vaulted over the top of the fence. Then, retrieving the cereal box I had tossed ahead of me, I sped through the trees to my stash.

Now there were shouts coming from the front of the house. Breathless, I stuffed the cereal box in my food pack, grabbed my rolled-up poncho and the fishing pole, and raced up over the dike.

CHAPTER 26

THERE was no way to learn whether I'd been seen. I wasn't about to stick my head up high enough to see if I was being chased. I could only keep low and keep moving—keep running.

Suddenly Laura's voice came to me.

"Kep. I can hear you running. Are you all right? Where are you?"

"I'm taking a little jog along the dike beside the river . . . heading downstream. But I can't go much farther before I'll have to move up higher onto the dike. I'm about to run out of beach. I don't think I was seen leaving. There's no one behind me—not yet."

"Were you able to get the cereal box? Do you have it?"

"It's in my daypack with the other food you brought me. But this doesn't seem like a convenient time to dip into it for a snack. Maybe later.

"Joking aside, Laura, I'm guessing someone will come to pick me up. Do I wait out of sight where we met before?"

"No, Kep. That's no longer a safe place—and you may have to wait quite a while. I'll let you know what Shackleton has in mind just as soon as I can. He's talking with Graham Walker at the minute. My understanding is that the county sheriff went into action right after Graham informed him about the dead man.

Deputies could be arriving at the house any time now."

"I heard tires squealing to a stop on the pavement just as I was getting away, Laura. There was some shouting, but I have no idea what was going on. Maybe it was the deputies arriving then. Maybe they were going after the man I saw in the backyard. But he was in the house by then, hurrying down the hall to the bedroom just before I got away through the bathroom window. I know for certain it was the same guy that I saw in the backyard—the one you warned me about.

"I don't get it, Laura. How did you learn that he was seen coming from the north along the dike maintenance road just then? That's different. Who saw him?"

"The highway has just recently come under surveillance by both the county sheriff and federal agents. Apparently they have different purposes and agendas. That's all I can tell you now. You'll have to wait for Shackleton to give you the details. You're safety has been his top priority, Kep. You've done an outstanding job."

"What's so precious about a box of cereal, Laura? This is crazy. Dan Crotty gets taken away by taxi, and I risk my life for a stupid box of cereal. Nothing is making any sense to me."

"It soon will, Kep. The box is a Cheerios box, isn't it? Isn't that the brand name on it?"

"Yes."

"And it hasn't been opened?"

"It looked new. The top looked sealed. I didn't have any reason to look it over—even if I had the time. All I could do is grab it and run."

"You couldn't have seen any reason to give it your attention then, I know, Kep. When I passed your deciphered message along to Shackleton, he intuitively picked up on a clue—one that you probably would have seen yourself if you hadn't been feeling so sick and rushed while you were working at the laptop."

"It doesn't matter, Laura. I can check the box out after I get to a place where I can hide and rest. Right now I just want to keep moving away from this place—far away."

"Whatever you do, don't open the box, Kep.

"I just thought of a perfect place for you to wait. There's a park by the river at Conway. I saw it when I drove through there to mark up the map I gave you. It should be safe, and it would offer all you need until someone comes for you. You should be able to get there by hiking the crest of the dike, but it's my wish that you stay out of sight every chance you get. Do you have the fishing pole with you?"

"I've got it. It's in my hand. I've got everything I've been given or collected on this adventure, Laura. I feel more like a pack rat than a fisherman—not that it matters."

"You should be able to reach the park in an hour or so. Call me when you get there. I'm trying to take care of another assignment right now, but you can always count on me to answer your calls, Kep. There's always the chance now that something unforeseen could delay my answering, but just please be patient with me if you must wait."

"I can be patient. No problem. My legs are happy to be moving now. It's a good way to use up the time. What time is it?"

"Five forty-eight."

"Thanks, Laura. I'll call when I reach the park."

* * *

Laura was right: The riverside park was a good place to wait things out—better than I had expected. As far as I could tell, no one had followed me. I'd used the dike maintenance road and kept up a good pace, dropping down near the river whenever possible, as Laura had "wished."

After using the public restroom, I found a picnic table located some distance away from people enjoying recreational activities and picnicking near the river. Their presence made me feel less noticeable than if I were totally alone.

Laura didn't answer my call, so I left a message to notify her that I'd reached the park.

Using the binoculars, I scanned what I could see of the little town of Conway. At a point along a frontage road beside the I-5 freeway, I spotted what looked to be the flatbed tow truck used to haul away the stalled sedan. It was empty. There were no dark cars visible in the company lot. The business was apparently closed for the day.

I pulled out my cell phone, turned it on, and checked the time: 6:55. Both the phone and my stomach said a sandwich and drink were overdue.

Two sandwiches, a small sack of crunchy corn chips, two bottles of water, and a half thermos of ginger tea later, I folded my arms on the picnic table and rested my head. I had just begun to doze off when I felt my hair raise from my scalp and heard strange noises coming from inside my daypack. Startled and confused, I jerked my head up.

The sounds were coming from the cereal box. My opened food pack was right in front of me on the picnic table, and I could see the box of cereal shaking as though some huge insect was frantically trying to get out. The shaking was intense.

I jumped away from the bench and stood back in alarm, remembering my very recent hair-raising experience when Shackleton had cautioned me to keep to the side of the bathroom window. As before, I sensed some eerie unseen presence.

There was no visible explanation for what I was witnessing. I could see nothing unusual above, around, or beneath the picnic table. Moving farther away, I stood transfixed as I struggled to accept the reality of the event.

The shaking abruptly ended in silence.

Now shaking a bit myself, I cautiously approached the table and stared at the cereal box. I was dealing with more than a bizarre experience—this was spooky. It took several minutes for me to decide what I should do next. At last I decided I should close up my daypack and get the box out of my sight—out of everyone's sight.

But then, as I began to zip the daypack shut, I felt strongly inclined to yield to curiosity. (Yes, I still struggled with restraining my curiosity.) Could I discover if the box had been opened and resealed? If I shook it, would I be able to detect anything about the nature of what it contained?

I knew I shouldn't open it—and I wouldn't. I would respect Laura's request (or warning). Surely this must be the secret hiding place for the prize—a prize incomparable to those placed in cereal boxes to amuse young kids. An extreme amount of importance was placed on my getting it away from the house and keeping it out of the "wrong" hands.

I turned my back to the riverside activities and slid the daypack from the table and into my lap. After assuring myself that no one was watching, I hunched over and pulled the box up high enough to examine its top. The original closure was secure. There was no evidence that someone had tampered with it.

I pulled the box out and turned it over. Nothing suspicious about its bottom either, but something had rattled inside as I flipped it over. I shook the box. Whatever was inside it had to be quite small, judging from the sounds it made.

When next I was struck with an urgent feeling that I should get the box out of sight, I stuffed it back down into my daypack, zipped it shut, and tied down the flap. No point in pressing my luck.

But then I began to consider another possible way for getting a small item into the unopened box. Couldn't it be pressed in under the lid from one side?

It wasn't long before I was untying the pack, zipping it open, and checking the sides of the box top. Sure enough, I discovered that by squeezing the lid, I could slide the tip of my mechanical pencil into the box from one side but not the other—not without using a force that would break through the seal.

Having gratified my curiosity on that point, I scanned the park to learn whether there was anything obvious to account for the unsettling feeling that prompted me to hide the box from public view. My back had been turned toward the river-front activities, but now as I looked around, I spotted a man leaning against a parked car. He wasn't involved with the other folks eating, playing football, or tossing a Frisbee. I immediately saw that I wasn't the only one there with a pair of binoculars. This guy was resting his elbows on the roof of his car while studying all that surrounded him with his own optics.

I tucked the cereal box in the daypack as before—only this time my curiosity got tucked in with it. There was no point in guessing at what the prize in the box might be, and I had a gut feeling that I had just been the prime focus of the viewer's attention. Why? I really didn't want to find out yet. I honestly hoped I *wouldn't* find out under the present circumstances.

I checked the time: 7:27.

A short time later my ring did its thing. Laura seemed to be preoccupied or distracted as she spoke.

"Kep, I can only talk a minute. Sorry . . . I'm busy with a vital task Shackleton assigned me. I believe Bones will be coming to pick you up, but he's waiting to chauffer Shackleton home from a private meeting place. I have no idea how much longer he'll be involved. Shackleton isn't answering my ring calls. You're still in the park, aren't you?"

"Yes. But I think I'm being watched. Will Bones be driving the Lincoln sedan?"

"I'm sure he will, Kep. But if you're being watched, that could present a problem. Shackleton will want to meet with you at his home. You mustn't be followed there."

"Why not have Bones drop me off in Old Fairhaven? Then I could climb the stairway to his studio when I'm sure—"

"That won't put you out of danger, Kep. Just a minute . . ."

I waited for Laura to collect her thoughts.

"Kep . . . I have an idea that might be safe. If you see any reason to suspect you're being followed, have Bones take you to The Simple Pleasure restaurant in Bellingham. That's where he is right now, waiting for Shackleton. Have Bones leave you at the entrance—they close at ten o'clock Sundays, so you should be there in time. Ask Bones to drive away for five minutes while you wait inside and watch for him to return. He will already have taken Shackleton home or he wouldn't be the one coming to get you. If Bones can't come, you might have to be picked up by taxi. Oh, Kep . . . just keep in touch with me, please!"

Laura's thoughts sounded tinged with emotion.

"If you still feel you're being watched, stay out of sight. Bones will understand and report to one of us by cell phone. He knows how to be discreet. In either case, whether you're left at the restaurant by Bones or by taxi, follow these directions . . ."

Again, Laura paused as if to regain her self-control.

"Listen carefully, Kep. Go to the receptionist and ask to be taken to the Three-Cornered Orange section in the back of the restaurant. It's a reserved area for business people to eat and meet with clients in closed rooms. Since you're not a member, you'll be asked for today's code name. Say you're waiting for Mr. Gray. Give the code name 'Oliver' and order whatever you want. Shackleton has an account there, so he'll take care of the bill. Bones will come for you in a different car later. One of us will get back in touch with you before you leave. You'll be going out an alley door into a reserved parking lot. That section of the restaurant stays open as long as a guest is occupying a private room."

"Sounds good, Laura."

"If you're certain you're not being followed, just have Bones or the taxi driver take you through the Charleston Street gate. Shackleton has an exclusive driver arrangement for this kind of situation—one where he's dealing with missing or endangered people. His name is Aaron Linksey. He goes by 'Link.' He sometimes pilots Shackleton's seaplane for him since he lost his sight. You can trust him. He drives a blue-and-green cab . . ."

Laura hesitated, which made me wonder if she'd said more than she should have. She knew I'd seen a cab of that description come for Dan Crotty. I kept my mind quiet and waited.

"Please listen to what Shackleton has for you, Kep. He has included parts of private talks he had with Sheldon Hoyle. Their latest meeting was held this afternoon. I'm bringing this up now so you can learn about the dead man's past and how it relates to our present case. That should keep you occupied while you're waiting for Bones. Just please keep calling me if you run into a bad situation. Please don't give up on me, Kep. Do you remember how to retrieve messages if you should get interrupted?"

"I think so, but if not, I'll call it a 'bad situation' and have you rescue me, okay?"

"Yes, Kep. Here's Shackleton's message":

"Hello, Kephart! For your part in all that is bringing us to a closure in the matter of Mr. Crotty's disappearance, I express my gratitude and offer my compliments! Had it not been for your personal risk-taking that provided timely critical information in the related mystery of the dead man, various sorts of injustice and human misery would be certain—both now and in the future. Explanations will be offered soon enough, but for the present, you certainly deserve to be informed about the dead man's past.

I'll begin by summarizing some of what has been disclosed by a Mr. Sheldon Hoyle, who was the man's employer.

"The dead man's name is Kroy Koziol. Mr. Koziol was a rather mysterious fellow. Little is really known about him. Although he was recently retired, he came to Mr. Hoyle's Bellingham branch of a national engineering and consulting firm and asked for employment. That was sometime in April.

"Upon being interviewed by Mr. Hoyle, Mr. Koziol offered convincing evidence that he had worked as a physicist on top-secret projects at Los Alamos National Laboratory and at 'Area 51'—the Nevada location. He told Mr. Hoyle that he was suffering from an incurable disorder as a result of his experimenting with what he called 'elusive energy' and that he was attempting to locate a daughter he'd not seen in more than twenty years. He felt certain she lived in Bellingham under a different name.

"Evidently, Mr. Koziol had been forced to retire due to the nature of his illness. He was bound by oath not to disclose any details of his former activities or associations. Obviously he had just stepped a bit out of bounds by revealing what he did to Mr. Hoyle. However, he did explain that there are extremely high levels of government security that one dare not breach. His wish was to find some purposeful employment to distract him from his afflictions and to lengthen his life until he could reunite with his daughter.

"Mr. Hoyle had not advertised an available position, but he was sufficiently impressed and so offered to have Mr. Koziol 'try out' at various short-term projects. There were times between projects when he was not gainfully occupied. At these times he directed his attention to an unusual specimen Mr. Hoyle kept in a glass case. Mr. Hoyle had not had the specimen for long and was rather curious about it himself. Mr. Koziol convinced him that there were certain tests and experiments that he could perform that would not risk damage to the article but might enable him to identify it. Mr. Hoyle agreed but made it understood that there could be no compensation paid for the time Mr. Koziol devoted to it.

"Over a period of several days and evenings, Mr. Koziol became so intensely preoccupied with his experiments on the item that he gave little attention to anything else. He spent evenings writing pages of notes on his findings; however, he increasingly failed to communicate the results to Mr. Hoyle. He became rather secretive regarding his tests and findings.

"One day he didn't show for work. A short time prior to that, he asked for a morning off to have some medical work done in Ballard. He also informed Mr. Hoyle that he was moving into a different residence and requested that Mr. Hoyle give him permission to have his personal mail forwarded to his place of work temporarily. Mr. Hoyle granted his request, but he wondered about Mr. Koziol's health and change in behavior.

"A few days ago Mr. Koziol vanished from the scene, along with the article in question. After filing a missing person report and statement of possible theft, Mr. Hoyle was directed to Detective Walker, who referred him to me. Excerpts from our ensuing discussions would best inform you at this point, Kephart.

"I arranged to meet privately with Mr. Hoyle away from my home. We met behind closed doors at an establishment of which I am a member. Of course, he was not aware of it, but I used my stellar ring to record our conversations. I have extracted salient parts of them for you as follows.

* * *

"Mr. Hoyle, I know you're most interested in locating this man, Koziol, but let's go back to the missing article. Please describe it in detail."

"Well, he told me it wasn't a crystal as I'd first thought. I brought it to work thinking I could find some time to look it over. It was very unusual. Nothing like I'd ever seen before. But I'm not much up on rocks and minerals, so I was okay with having Koziol study it, especially on his own time. As I said, after a while he got to be obsessed with it. And it wasn't really mine. It was my son, Josh, who found it. He's just seven years old and—"

"Mr. Hoyle, you are not answering my question. Please. Describe the item as best you can. What made it 'unusual' in your view?"

"Yeah . . . ah . . . well, for one thing, it glowed in the dark, even when it hadn't been exposed to any light for hours. And it gave off different colors in daylight. Blue, green, and red mostly, but sometimes others, depending on where it was placed. It went wild when Josh held it near the TV. He—"

"Describe its shape and size, Mr. Hoyle."

"It was an octahedron . . . it had eight faces, all perfectly formed and flat. No wrinkles or lines. All of its edges and peaks were sharp."

"And its size?"

"Oh, I'd say ten millimeters or less for length. Very tiny and easy to lose. That's why I kept it in the glass case where I could—"

"What else can you tell about it? Did Mr. Koziol give any particulars regarding his experiments, anything significant that he'd learned?"

"Well . . . yes. He did. But he advised me not to share a couple things, because he'd learned from someone he'd corresponded with—some military officer he knew—that it would be best for his findings to be kept from the public for now. News gets around that might attract attention, he said. He made it sound like the crystal—whatever—was a valuable prize. I don't get what that could have to do with the military, but Koziol started to get pretty secret about what he learned from then on."

"Mr. Hoyle, you must understand that for me to be most efficient in locating this fellow, Koziol, I need to have any and all facts you can provide that could point in the direction he may have taken. That would include possible interactions with military or governmental officials. After all, what you suggested about his having dealt with people at high security levels in the past could either limit or expand the scope of my scrutiny. I have my own connections to serve me. All that I do or learn is always held in strict confidence. That is why you were referred to me in the first place. Are you unwilling to entrust me with any further information at this point?"

"No . . . I uh . . . I guess it's okay to tell you what I got from Koziol—if you'll keep it just for your use in finding the specimen . . . or finding Koziol, I mean."

"Of course."

"Well, there were two strange things he learned.

"One is that the specific gravity of the specimen would change drastically when it was placed in different fields of RF energy. Koziol was really troubled over that one. He said that it was impossible and hard to accept. He was fascinated by it. But then . . . oh, yeah. He said it was composed of eight different elements, but he could only identify five.

"Oh, I forgot a third thing: There were times when it just kind of disappeared from his view in an electron microscope. He said there were too many unexplainable things about it. That's all I know, or all I got from him before he took off with it."

* * *

"You're telling me *now*, Mr. Hoyle, that you were approached by government agents in this matter and that you knew at the time of our previous discussion that this fellow, Vitori Gaston, could have led you to Mr. Koziol's new residence for a price? As I see it now, your true purpose in seeking my help was to avoid being subjected to extortion.

"You've withheld critical information far too long, Mr. Hoyle. You have endangered other lives in ways I can't disclose to you. Your selfishness is reprehensible. How can I be assured that this Gaston fellow is about to do as you say?"

"He called me on my cell phone. He said he knows a way to get to the house without being seen. He said he'll take whatever share he can get now."

"Share?"

"Share of what might be paid by the government for the specimen.

"How long has it been since he called?"

"Less than an hour. Look, Mr. Gray . . . I'm through with this. I can see it isn't worth it. If I can help—"

"You can help by being totally honest and open with me, Mr. Hoyle. What makes you certain that these men were federal agents?"

"Yeah . . . ah . . . well, I think it was two days before all this happened when a couple of men in suits came into my office and flashed credentials in my face and said they were investigating—doing a search for some missing government property. I remember their names were Huffman and Burns. Agent Malcolm Burns did most of the talking. He said some correspondence between Kroy Koziol and a Col. Bradford at Wright-Patterson assured them we were doing tests on this missing item. How they could call it 'government property' or claim they owned it is a laugh. They had no idea that I knew what I did about where it was found. Nancy had told my boy, and he'd told me.

"These agents wanted me to turn it over to them—"

"Stop! Please. Mr. Hoyle, you must be coherent in your relating your story. Who is Nancy? Please."

"She's my boy's classmate. She was sharing her rock collection for show-and-tell. Well, this girl Nancy loaned it to Josh—my boy. She let him have it temporarily because he was always asking her to take it out of her book bag so he could look at it. I guess he got to be a pest about it. Then I got to looking it over myself when he brought it home, and I discovered that it was actually a polyhedron. It wasn't just some pretty rock."

"Go on."

"When I told them—I mean the agents—it had disappeared with Kroy and that I didn't know where he was, both men got testy with me. I told them they could search all they wanted to without a warrant but they wouldn't find it. I really didn't feel like cooperating with them one bit. They were too pushy—too high and mighty.

"This Agent Burns gave me his card and told me it would be in my best interests to call him if the specimen or Kroy or both showed up. I don't—"

"Do you have his card?"

"Not with me. It's in my desk. Do you want it?"

"No. You'll be the one to deal with him, Mr. Hoyle. I'm certain you have much more you can tell me if you will. It's vital that you do. Continue. Please. You say you know where the specimen was found?"

"Someplace in eastern Washington . . . over the mountains. Nancy's family was on a family trip. When she took their dog out in the brush to go potty, her dog sniffed at it."

"Then the polyhedron really belongs to this girl, Nancy? And you were intending to sell it and split your ill-gotten gain with this Gaston fellow? I'm appalled, Mr. Hoyle. I find your dissolute intentions extremely disgusting. However, your having confessed them begs me to desist from labeling you as a first-class reprobate."

"Well . . . I guess I should confess, too, that I'm afraid to tell the Tiptons—I mean Nancy and her parents—that the specimen has disappeared. I'd hoped to give them a good share of the money I got as an apology for its loss. But Gaston knows where I can find Kroy Koziol, so if I can find *him*, I'm sure I can get the specimen back some way. Can you help me without involving Gaston?"

"I can't assure you on any point, Mr. Hoyle. Especially when you're now dealing with federal agents—or that you are a focal point of their attention."

"I can just see the Tiptons asking me what I've been doing with Nancy's prize stone. Why did I let Josh keep it? Why did I let anyone experiment with it? How could I lose it? You know . . . those kinds of questions."

"In truth, those questions are entirely defensible, as you know, Mr. Hoyle. You'll deserve whatever censure you get. However, I'm certain you will find a proper way to compensate for any loss if you honestly pursue one."

"Well, I guess I'm worried a lot more about how far these government agents will go. If they insist on finding out where Nancy found the specimen, they might be badgering the Tiptons next. If they want to go that route, I don't have a chance of preventing it . . . do I? Any advice?"

"Not yet, Mr. Hoyle. And it may be too late to avert such an unfortunate circumstance. I hope you can see how vitally important it is that you cooperate with me in sharing everything you can. Timing is critical, as is a full disclosure of all that has transpired.

"I must learn more about this Vitori Gaston. Who is he, and how is it that he knows so much about the prize specimen? Where does he fit in?"

"Well, he works after hours at our office. I mean . . . he *cleans* all the offices in our building. He's employed by a cleaning and maintenance outfit. I've always gotten along with him okay, but he didn't like Kroy from the start. There was always some friction going on between them. I guess it's mostly because Kroy expected him to do things that weren't really his job to do, like shred the stuff he put in a basket on a corner of his desk. Emptying waste baskets is something Gaston always did, but he would have to take Koziol's papers out of our office to shred them, so he resented having to take the extra trouble to please him. Maybe he did it once a week, but with anger. I don't know.

"He has a hair-triggered temper, too . . . and he has the strength of a cougar. Once I saw him—"

"Do you have reason to suspect that he would have read any of the material that was placed in the basket for shredding?"

"That might be. That might be for sure. I mean, after I gave the okay for Kroy's personal mail to be forwarded to our office, he might have gotten snoopy. He's clever and sharp enough—I mean Gaston is. But he isn't very well educated. He has his drawbacks, mostly socially, but we can talk—"

"Before this Agent Burns informed you about it, did you know anything about Mr. Koziol's having corresponded with the officer at Wright-Patterson Air Force Base?"

"No. Well, not that I got any of it from Kroy himself. There was this letter that I found in Kroy's shred basket on his desk after he'd gone home early one day. It was supposed to have been shredded by Gaston, but he was late in getting around to his duties that evening. I'd worked late myself, and I was . . . well, you know, curious about what was going on with Kroy and the specimen, so I—"

"Snooped?"

* * *

"Mr. Hoyle. Please make every effort to stay on track with the information you're sharing this evening. Now, I do understand how Vitori Gaston got Mr. Koziol's secret address from the two twice-forwarded letters you described—the critical one being the statement from the firm in Ballard that modified his false eye. I ask that you make every effort to recover that statement from Gaston, even for a price if necessary. I will need it for evidence that may contribute much to justice in this matter, and I'm willing to negotiate a reasonable figure. Gaston will find the money available upon his release, when that time comes. From information that I have gathered on my own, I foresee that he will be held accountable for several criminal acts.

"When and how did Gaston inform you that he was sure he had the specimen in hand—that he was *certain* it was in this false eye he'd found but couldn't open? Quickly now! We've no time to waste."

"Well, he first called a couple of hours ago. He said he'd had the eye since Wednesday and was tired of hanging on to it. He admitted he didn't know how to deal with the government men anyway, so he'd hand it over to me for half of what I could get for it. I told him I had to haggle before I could give him a time and place to meet.

"So right then, I called Agent Burns, like you said to do the last time we talked—so he could follow the suggestion you gave me at first—to have Gaston secretly tracked to Kroy's place because it was possible there would be *two* false eyes there.

"I met Gaston in a share-the-ride parking lot. I don't know how they did it, but those agents had him tagged right from the time I gave him your twenty-five grand. I turned the false eye over to Agent Burns a few minutes after we—that's Gaston and I—split. But when they tested the eyeball, which they didn't waste any time doing, they discovered it was normal. There wasn't anything inside it, as you must have guessed.

"So, according to Burns, he called his trackers and had them pull Gaston over. They took back the money and told him there had to be another false eye. Burns told me people who wear them usually have a spare to wear when one is being cleaned. He said he was giving Gaston just twenty-four hours to find the other false eye with the specimen in it if he wanted the twenty-five grand back. That's as much as—"

"You will have to excuse me, Mr. Hoyle. I have an urgent matter to attend to, and I must act immediately. Thank you for your cooperation thus far. We'll be meeting again soon."

* * *

"This last extract I've shared with you is from a discussion held this evening, Kephart. I'm certain you will be able to trace today's events back to . . ."

Just then I became aware that someone was standing behind me. A tap on my shoulder made me shudder. I turned and faced the man who had been studying me with his binoculars.

He didn't look directly at me but smiled as he placed an index card on the picnic table in front of me. The name "OLIVER" was written on it in large capital letters. I had seen earlier that this man's car was a black sedan with tinted windows—not a green-and-blue taxi.

I shuddered again as I twisted my ring.

CHAPTER 27

I got a firm grip on my daypack and searched the stranger's face. Shackleton had made a point that I should study eyes, but this man's eyes never met mine. He just looked to one side and avoided making eye contact as he smiled at the table top. Next came "body language" as he turned away and motioned with his hand for me to follow. He didn't once look back as he moved toward his car. I sensed that he was totally confident that I would obey his signal—that I would comply without question.

No feeling of apprehension came with my compliance, and I wondered at its absence. This wasn't something I would normally do—follow a perfect stranger in response to a hand gesture. But I didn't feel any threat or premonition as I did so. I just felt detached and fairly calm as I picked up my stuff and trailed after him.

He opened the right rear door of his black sedan for me and then moved around to its front. Pausing there, he waved his hand toward a young girl sitting in a wheelchair beside a nearby picnic table. She hesitantly waved back at him, uncertainty written on her face. Obviously she didn't recognize him.

He then came back to my opened door and took the fishing rod from my hand as I was placing my folded poncho and packsack on the rear seat. Without looking at me, he walked to the girl and handed her the rod and reel. Her reaction was one of mingled surprise and delight. The girl had certainly been unable to participate in any of the family frolic. She could only be a spectator. She couldn't have been any happier than I was to see the donation made in her behalf.

At this point I felt confident that I was being "rescued" in a manner that Laura hadn't considered. Fatigue began to settle over me. But in the next minute my faculties awoke me to the realization that I was a "prisoner" of sorts.

Upon closing my door, I saw that there was a heavy glass partition separating the front and rear sections of the sedan. As this began to register in my brain, I heard the clicking of electric door locks. The well-insulated car interior was exceptionally silent.

Before I could react with any degree of alarm, a fragrant scent quickly began to permeate my plush sealed enclosure. It had a strangely powerful effect on me, and I succumbed to oblivion and insensibility.

* * *

I awoke feeling refreshed and alert, but I was no longer in the back of the Cadillac. I found myself now lying on a bench in a parking lot behind a tall building. Only a few parked cars occupied the lot. I saw no human life or activity. Startled, I sat up. Then I stood up to get some sense of my surroundings. Nothing looked familiar.

A panic swept over me as I futilely scanned the area for my daypack and poncho. Relief came when I discovered them pushed out of sight underneath the bench where the stranger had deposited me while I was in my unconscious state.

As I reached under the bench to pull my things toward me, I noticed a door with a metal sign that said "Exit Only." And in small orange letters below that were the words "Three-Cornered Orange."

So this had to be the lot behind The Simple Pleasure restaurant, where Laura said Bones would come fetch me after I got her ring call. I certainly hadn't spent any time in the restaurant, and Laura hadn't called. I tried to reach her but got no response, so I twisted my ring again and thought out the cue words for messages. There were none.

Remembering that Laura had asked more than once that I not give up on her, that she would always get back to me, I resigned myself to waiting.

As I sat on the bench with my stuff beside me, I felt conspicuously like a tramp. My morning "wash-up" had been brief. I hadn't shaved, and I'd scrambled through wet brush and squeezed under a wire fence a few times. I had worked up a sweat while running, and I'd climbed up and down a fir tree more than a few times. My clothes were dirty, and I probably didn't smell so great. I surely didn't feel like my best self.

This mental phrasing of "my best self" resulted in my recalling the verbal interplays Jill and I had shared. Now my mind began to dwell on her, and I once again felt concern for her safety. I wondered where she might be and what she was doing. If Shackleton had put her under "surveillance" for her protection, I couldn't imagine how that was to have been accomplished or how effective it might be.

She had written in her note that she missed me. A lot of time had passed since she brought me the cell phone box with that note inside. A lot could have happened to her. Much had happened to me—most of which I could happily have done without.

Thoughts of Jill brought me only frustration and anxiety. I managed to force my mind away from her and focus on the mystery at hand.

It was obvious that Dan Crotty hadn't found the rare prize of "inestimable value." Neither had he run off with his woman accomplice. But if Kroy Koziol *was* this woman's father as I continued to suspect, why had Crotty stayed on after his death? And what was the true cause of his death? Only an autopsy would tell.

I still thought it possible that Crotty could have had a hand in bringing the death about . . . or speeding it up. He was there for a reason—that was certain. And it had to have been linked to a plan. Otherwise, why would he have taken the personal risk and trouble to go *up*-river to that particular house?

Was it possible that a life insurance policy offered bigger, more easily obtained money than the artifact? Maybe I had misdirected my focus when I considered only the exotic tangible prize Shackleton's words had suggested. If Dan Crotty's girlfriend was designated to be the beneficiary of a large sum of life insurance, could she have used him and then abandoned him?

When I recalled what Laura had said about Crotty being increasingly unresponsive to the friendly gestures of the cosmetic reps—as his wife's friend Ginger had informed her—I also remembered mention of an attractive brunette being an exception. So I couldn't rule out this brunette as being Koziol's daughter—Dan's secret girlfriend. But I knew nothing about her, not even her name.

Then there was Gaston—a guy with a quick temper and a money motive for killing. I could imagine that he might definitely fit the description of a man who would poison dogs, rip out phone wires, and break sliding-bolt locks loose from door casings. He had taken risks to gain access to Koziol's house and gouge out the false eye. He was clever enough, and determined (or greedy) enough, to collect the information he needed to go after the prize specimen. He had threatened Koziol with blackmail (according to the laptop message), and he had no compunctions about double-dealing between Koziol and Hoyle for whatever amount he could get.

I felt that he would most likely have been caught by now, either inside the house or when leaving it with the hollow false eye I'd left on the card table. I couldn't see any possible chance for him to have escaped either the deputies or the agents. He didn't have enough time.

Maybe it was his plan to give himself up to the government agents for the twenty-five thousand dollars, thinking they would release him later. But since he would now have been unable to produce the specimen the agents were after, he had no chance at regaining the money they took from him. His release was definitely not imminent—that was certain. The county coroner's findings would determine what action would be taken if Koziol's death was shown to be the result of foul play. In that case Gaston would be a prime suspect as a killer.

Another thing was certain: The "specimen" was in my bag, and I must protect it for whatever purpose it might serve the Abiding Ones. There was no question in my mind about its being an alien artifact. If it weren't, the AOs would not have intervened in any activity connected with it. Besides, from what Kroy Koziol had learned, its properties were evidently beyond our present scientific understanding.

The artifact was definitely not a thing a child should have. I had a feeling that its proximity presented a serious endangerment to health. I derived this notion from Koziol's written message—the pains in his head and the accelerated loss of his mental capacity. It seems the more time he had spent with the artifact, the more rapidly his health had failed in general. Keeping it near his brain had probably contributed to the speed of his deterioration.

So maybe he wasn't murdered. Maybe he just died from multiple disorders. That would soon be learned. But in my view it was a good thing that the alien item was "lost" and taken from the grasp of Earth humans, no matter what their age.

As to what Shackleton told me, I believed it was true that our human society was not spiritually ready (collectively speaking) to deal with certain technologies. Undesirable human traits took a long time to curb—to overcome through self-mastery. My personal experiences with most people had shown them to be basically good and well meaning, but responsible behaviors were far from being the rule. Pride and power-seeking "ruled." In this particular moment of reflection, I couldn't see an all-inclusive victory—a total self-mastery—happening in any single tellurian's mortal span of life.

I supposed continuous steps could be taken to personally quash pride, but each step would require a persisting *desire* to change. Was such a desire possible to acquire? What kind of motivation would it take? What percentage of humanity would reach for it?

Unfortunately for me now, I began to think of my own condition. I had a lot of "growing" to do. It was scary. This very day, I had shown myself to be a law-breaker. Even though Shackleton had said he'd take responsibility for my trespassing, I knew I was personally accountable in the first instance. If I had been caught, I would now most likely be experiencing the legal consequences of my act. My life would have taken a different turn earlier in the day.

My fingerprints had been left in many places, but most incriminating were those on the false eye. I shuddered at the thought of what could still come of that if I were to be nabbed and fingerprinted later on. I still wasn't "safe."

The artifact was in my possession. So you could say, too, that I was transporting stolen property.

Knowing what she did, I could see now why Laura was so emotional when she stressed that I stay out of sight. I guessed that she didn't have to care that much, but she did. And she said she prayed for me. She didn't have to do that either. So I had two attractive young women praying for me. There must be a good reason for that, but I wasn't in a mood to deal with it. Still, I was thankful they did.

At this moment I had no doubt that my rescue was performed by an AO. For one thing, his car was specially equipped. More significantly, there were highly unusual aspects to his manner of dealing with me. He emanated a persuasive, controlling influence that was both non-threatening and undeniable. I had never interacted with anyone so kindly compelling—one who could lead me without a word.

Now I had to wonder how effective he may have been at evading any others who could have "found" me waiting to be rescued—others who had kept themselves hidden but who were in no hurry to pick me up. Learning my destination would be useful, especially to federal agents. From what Hoyle had said, they were exceptionally good at tracking Gaston while remaining unobserved.

I didn't know for certain that I wasn't followed from the house to the riverside park. And here I was, in a small secluded parking lot situated at the end of a dead-end alleyway. Thoughts on this made me feel trapped and vulnerable. My eyes were always glancing toward the narrow entrance to the lot.

So, lacking other distractions, I turned my thoughts back to the unknowns I had encountered during the day. First off, I really wanted to know who it was that Kroy Koziol was writing to in his tangled message. What kind of ally could he possibly have had? Was there some way for me to find this out? Would it help to know?

Shackleton had said, "What one looks for, he will surely find." (I know; he first mentioned "trouble"—if we look for it, we'll find it.) We evidently attract both what we fear and what we desire. I could see that if we kept our minds too much on what we hoped to *avoid*, our minds might very well attract that very thing or situation. So, yes, it would serve me best to check in on where my mind was taking me.

As I was pondering these things, I was startled to see a sheriff's patrol car bounce into the lot at a good clip. The deputy stopped right in front of me and studied my face as he left his car and walked to one parked close by. He put his foot on its rear bumper and scanned some papers on a clipboard. Then he stepped back to check the vehicle license plate. Next, he pulled a phone from his waist and began speaking into it while looking directly at me. I stopped breathing as my heart doubled its pace.

The deputy came toward me and asked, "How long have you been sitting here?"

I couldn't get my voice to work, so I just held out my hands and shrugged.

"Are you the one who parked this vehicle?"

I shook my head while clearing my throat to answer, "No, sir."

"Did you see the person who parked it? Can you describe him . . . or her?"

Again, I could only shake my head in answer as the deputy spoke into his phone again to say, "Confirmed. It's the stolen vehicle."

Very soon a tow truck approached from the narrow alleyway. On its door I read, "Big Tow Auto Wrecking." Bart was at the wheel. We each wore an expression of incredulous surprise as we looked at each other. *No way!* I thought.

CHAPTER 28

BART squeezed his lips out like the bill of a platypus. He squinched his eyes shut and shook his head twice before moving his truck to a point where he could line it up with the stolen car.

I turned my own eyes toward the access to the parking lot. My heart jumped when I spotted Laura's red SUV slowly approaching the dubious scene ahead of her. I leaped to my feet, grabbed my stuff, and ran to where she had stopped just short of entering the parking area. Apparently, she was unsure whether it would be safe to show recognition of me. When she saw that the deputy was involved only with Bart, she pointed to her front passenger door and motioned for me to get inside.

After pitching my daypack and poncho onto the back seat, I didn't hesitate to get the door shut and fasten my seatbelt. Laura shut her eyes and sighed in relief before backing out of the alley. She cautiously backed into the street and looked carefully for any suspicious signs of followers before moving on.

Although she appeared to be tired out, her smile was warm and her poise was intact. She reached over and gave my arm a squeeze. Neither one of us spoke. We both knew there wasn't much to say at this point. Each of us could easily guess at the price the other had paid for the day's ordeals.

"Happy birthday, Kep!" Laura said at last.

"What?"

"This is the fourteenth of May. Happy birthday!"

"It is? That's right. It *is* my birthday. But how did you—?"

"It's just one of a few personal things about you that Shackleton has shared with me. But he's shared them only for helpful reasons. There's nothing that you would object to my knowing about." Laura blinked at me and smiled.

"Okay. Thanks for reminding me to be happy, Laura. I don't have anything much to hide. So whatever you know about me can't be used against me. Right? Well, maybe my memory isn't serving me as well as I'd like to think.

"Anyway, you've shared quite a bit about yourself with *me*, Laura—maybe not all of it in *words*. I've come to appreciate you more for knowing what I do."

She nodded and smiled as she glanced in her rear-view mirror to check on the traffic behind her.

"There's so little I really know about Shackleton, though," I said. "One thing that makes him so different from most anyone I've known is his formal manner, especially in his speech. I've never felt like he's looking down on me. He seems to accept me for what I am. It's hard to put my finger on what makes him so different. But, except for my parents and their closest friends, I grew up around some pretty crude and rough people—good people, but not polished. It's easy to see that Shackleton has had a good education and rearing."

"He was raised in England, Kep. He *did* have the advantage of attending the best of schools there. As I told you before, his father was an airline pilot. He was away from home much of the time. Shackleton's mother looked out for her son's best interests. He was her only child. When his mother died, he inherited a large sum of insurance money and some real estate. She died when he was just twenty-three. He came to live in the United States not long after that."

"Do you know how old he is now?"

"Most everything I've learned about him I got from Rose. I think he's thirty-four. Isn't that funny? I know *your* birthday but not his. Let's see . . . he was six years older than Rose, and they were married five years ago when she was twenty-three. So I must have it right."

(My curiosity pushed me to take advantage of the mathematical moment.)

"You told me that you and Rose were like sisters. Who was born first?"

(I hadn't forgotten her saying they were born eight months apart.)

"Rose . . . oh! You're pretty clever, Kep! So now you've got my age figured out, too! I suppose there isn't much you can do with it, though, so I don't mind."

(I had guessed her to be about thirty when I first saw her, but it could be that she was now just twenty-seven.)

"That's good to hear, Laura. As I see it, chronological age doesn't matter so much as some might think. And some people grow up too fast, while it seems that others will *never* grow up . . . you know what I mean."

"I do, Kep."

"When it comes to education, I feel that my own was inferior," I said. "There were only thirteen of us in my graduating senior class. Our small-town high school wasn't what they called an 'accredited' school at that time. Maybe that's had some effect on my self-esteem—that and my limited social life. Shackleton told me I should think more favorably of myself. Comparing the two of us, I can't see why he chose me to be his assistant. Well, now that I think of it, this day hasn't demanded much from my formal education, has it?"

"Comparing yourself to others can be dangerous, Kep. You'll either put yourself down or feed your pride. You lose either way."

"I can see that you're right, Laura.

"One thing Shackleton mentioned about my education was that I spent a lot of time reading to my mother from a variety of good authors—from some classic books. That helped make up for some boring classes and a chronic lack of sleep. I've always liked to read. We never had TV. So I got a limited perspective of some human performances in the present-day world."

"You're no worse off for that."

"I guess in some ways I'm still naïve. But I like to learn. I'm thinking you won't laugh when I tell you that the dictionary is one of my favorite books."

She *did* laugh.

"Okay, Laura. Laugh. I probably have it coming. I don't remember prating so much about myself as I am right now. Maybe babbling and laughing are other ways to relieve stress—besides eating."

She smiled at me and said, "Laughing is good. We both could do more of it."

"It seems odd, but I don't feel like satisfying my curiosity or asking questions at the minute. I feel more like taking a break from all that's been on my mind. There's a part of me that's saying, 'Loosen up. Just be happy.'

"What one thing would help you most to be happy, Laura?"

She gave me a quick look and then turned her face away.

She was quiet for a time. Then, still looking away, she said, "I know that basically we *choose* to be happy or not, Kep. But it's hard to always be happy if our essential human needs are unmet or denied. Since you mentioned eating—a starving person can't claim happiness without relief from hunger. So I don't think . . . I don't want to answer your question right now."

She paused. Then with brighter eyes, she looked over at me and said, "But did you notice: You *did* ask a question! Even though you said you didn't feel like it. So what does that tell you?"

She laughed again. That was the second time she laughed since she retrieved me. It was good to see her laugh. And this time I could give myself a little credit for watering the "wilting flower." I couldn't help but laugh too.

I looked her over more closely as she drove. She appeared less fatigued and more alive, now that our being secretly shadowed wasn't so likely a threat.

Then, for the first time, I noticed what she was wearing: Above her waist was a frilled white blouse highlighted by a silver necklace and silver dangling earrings. Above her knees was a pleated blue skirt that highlighted shapely legs. Her shoes were high-heeled, white, and dressy. She looked especially pretty.

Pleasurably surprised, I found my mind moving along from wondering why to remembering that it was Sunday. I could bet that Laura's central happiness wasn't dependent on any one thing more than her religious faith. Yet, in a way, she had just admitted that her religion alone couldn't compensate for her unsatisfied emotional needs.

I didn't believe a religion could save anyone from tribulation or suffering. Not in *this* life—not in this world. Laura was living with the consequence of her choice to serve a man she loved with little hope of future fulfillment. How long could she endure that without giving up hope or giving in to temptation?

My guess was that she had dressed up to attend her church. It didn't seem possible that she could have fit in enough time for that during this day of incessant demands. So maybe the need to sustain her faith wasn't always satisfied either.

I felt sorry for her. But at the same time, I was troubled by my own feelings associated with her feminine attraction. I had to admit that she was sexually attractive. As I had done with Jill, I managed to check in on where my mind was taking me. Who *didn't* have unmet needs at some time or other—probably more often than not, I thought.

My mind took a quick step from there to thoughts of Jill. I was about to ask Laura if she had anything to report about Jill when I remembered what Shackleton had said about my asking her questions. I guessed if there was anything to tell me, she would have told it by now.

Five more minutes of driving took us uphill to Charleston Street. Laura parked a short distance back from Shackleton's property access and waited at the side of the street. After she felt assured that no one had followed her, she pulled up to the admittance box and entered the access code. She drove quickly along the forested drive as the heavy iron gates closed behind us to offer a greater sense of security. Sundown was approaching as we entered the circular driveway in front of the house.

Laura parked in front of the first garage door we came to and said, "Bones and Phoebe are away. Shackleton's giving them some free time to have dinner out while he finishes up late meetings with Graham Walker and other clients. He's spent a lot of time at the Three-Cornered Orange today. That's one of the reasons he assigned me instead of Bones to pick you up. The Judds will bring him home later."

Other questions jumped into my head when she said this. Did Laura know how I got from the riverside park to the restaurant? I had assumed that she knew something about the AO's involvements at this point. But did she? Did she think I was transported by the taxi driver, Link? How much did Shackleton tell her about his strategies and decisions?

Then I became troubled by other questions I dared not ask her, at least not at this time. How many of our thought exchanges got shared with the AOs? How deeply were they involved at this point? My rescuer had printed the name "OLIVER" on the card he showed me. That was a code name for this particular day only. How would he have gotten it, except from Laura or Shackleton? I presumed that he got it from Shackleton, but then why was I dropped off behind the restaurant without getting a ring call or instructions?

These questions abruptly dropped out of my mind as I saw Laura leave her seat and walk to the back of her SUV. She opened the tail door, pulled out two large, colorful shopping bags, and said, "I have something to show you, Kep. Take your things from the back seat and follow me."

She didn't head for the front porch, so my curiosity took over. She walked to the right side of the garage where—to my complete surprise—I noticed for the first time a thirty-four-foot tower that resembled a lighthouse. I had trouble accepting the fact that I had been so unobservant on my two previous visits to the porch. But then I excused myself as I recalled that I had been totally wiped out (when Bones first brought me) or extremely distracted (when dealing with Bart's delivery of the VW).

The tower was connected to the right side of the garage. Laura led me to the entry door, where she set down her two shopping bags and fumbled in her purse for a key. Without a word she unlocked the door, stepped inside, and flipped a light switch.

Beckoning me inside, she said, "This was one of Shackleton's favorite places to seclude himself before he lost his sight. He had it built before he married Rose but then had it remodeled shortly after her disappearance."

As Laura spoke, I stood looking at windowless conical walls that supported a circular stairway leading to an upper room through a narrow access.

"I don't know that he comes here at all, now that he's blind," Laura said. "Bones and Phoebe don't often know his whereabouts anymore, least of all me. When he disappears, he disappears without a word to anyone.

"I became familiar with the house and this tower when my mother and I came with my aunt to go through Rose's personal belongings. The finished upper attic rooms in the house have become storage places for the things Shackleton and Rose personally accumulated or acquired for the baby, including a crib. I don't see any reason for Shackleton to visit them if he can't see what's in them. Then, too, it would do him no good to stir up memories and prolong his sorrow.

"And I don't know what's in his secret room downstairs—the one behind the one I have access to in back of his little workshop. He had extensive remodeling done before he left for the San Juan Islands. Sometimes I wonder whether he might have *anticipated* his blindness, but I can't even guess how that could be."

Laura led me across the floor toward the spiraling stairs. The room was lit by lantern-like lamps mounted on the circular wall supporting the stairway.

"Shackleton calls this the Compass Tower," Laura said as we crossed the floor.

She pointed down, and I looked to see that a compass replica was inlaid in the entire eighteen-foot-diameter tiled floor. Apparently it was perfectly aligned with the true compass points of the Earth. It was an impressive work of art. Feeling that Shackleton was not a man disposed to extravagant showiness, I wondered what purpose, if any, this artistry served.

Laura began to carry her bags up the stairs and gestured for me to do the same with my stuff. A quarter of the way up the stairs, we came to a small landing where the tower wall adjoined the upper part of the garage. At this point she set her shopping bags down and said, "Just leave your things here, Kep. I want you to see the view above."

I did as she asked and followed her up the stairway. As she preceded me, I couldn't resist watching the enticing movements of her body or giving attention to the allurement of her attractive legs. She had never worn a skirt in my presence before. But now it seemed that she was presenting herself in such a way as to *invite* my attention. Was this an intentional act on her part? How could I know? I seemed to be more easily aroused, now that I had recently spent time alone with desirable young women.

The top steps passed through the floor of a furnished observation room. Here we had a panoramic view of Bellingham Bay and everything from the distant islands to Old Fairhaven's waterfront. At this time we were being treated to the closing moments of a superb sunset. The western skies were displaying an ever-changing mixture of red, gold, and purple before giving way to the first light of planets and stars.

We stood watching in silence, but I quickly became aware that Laura was experiencing awakened sensual feelings similar to my own. I looked her way and saw that she was breathing deeply and more rapidly. Although she made no other movements, I sensed her seductiveness and excitement intensifying. For me, both the time and the place were contributing to temptation as well. The moment's opportunity itself was enticing, and I knew we were both being affected by it. When she reached for my hand, I felt her fingers trembling.

From my depths something urged me to think the words "master the moment." I closed my eyes and managed to picture the innocence and trust that Jill's eyes had conveyed earlier in the day. With my eyes still closed, and for the first time I could remember ever doing so, I prayed a silent prayer for help to be strong.

Compelling thoughts and feelings surged within me. How could I possibly risk the loss of Jill's precious regard for me? Was I willing to exchange my potentially lasting bond with her for a brief time of gratifying lustful passion? Where could I go from there? I had to choose between submission and resistance, between weakness and strength.

Without giving conscious thought to it, I felt my hand reaching inside my shirt. In a detached state of mind, I tugged out the binoculars that Laura had put in my daypack. My movements seemed robotic as I pulled the lanyard over my head and pressed the binoculars into Laura's hand.

"I don't think there could be a better time to use these," I said in a husky voice.

Laura turned to me. She put her arms around my neck and pressed her head against it. I felt her tears on my neck as she nodded in agreement.

CHAPTER 29

WHEN Laura began to make an apology (in her typical way), I put my finger to her lips and shook my head.

"No need for that ever, Laura," I said. "If I ever find that you owe me an apology, I'll say so. And I expect that to go both ways, okay?"

My words brought a smile from her. I welcomed the calming, mutual respect that followed. And I expressed my thanks inwardly for my prayer being positively answered on the spot.

A silent understanding passed between us during the minutes that followed. We each came to feel our "place" and the boundaries of our relationship. There was no need for embarrassment or apology. We accepted ourselves, each other, and our natural human tendencies. In a distractive way, the binoculars did serve to draw our attention away from our "hunger" as we traded them back and forth to focus on all that the waterfront viewings had to offer at sunset.

Self-mastery gave me a feeling of exhilaration. I wasn't just reacting now. How could I know but that my choice would help Laura as well? No matter, I knew for sure that if I had chosen the opposite path, we would both eventually be experiencing unhappiness and disappointment in ourselves.

I didn't fully realize it at the time, but this was a turning point in my life. I had just made a significant choice that served to define my character. My memory flashed back to that time of self-discontent when I found Jill's penciled portrait of me. I remembered that as I studied my face in the mirror, I'd resolved to take a path that would shape me to become what I truly wanted to be—to have my eyes reflect what Jill saw in me. I wasn't ready to admit then that faith in a supernal power would be an important factor in this, but deep down I knew it would.

Maybe now I would be more willing to recognize that I could use some humility. It surprised me to think that my being humble could contribute to my being confident. What mattered was where I placed both my humility and my confidence.

Eventually Laura handed me the binoculars and turned to descend the stairs. I followed with a greater sense of self-direction, rather than a feeling of subservience to Laura's femininity. At the same time, I could more fully appreciate that wonderful, exclusive power of attraction bestowed upon women—a power that could either create or destroy lives.

I was beginning to realize now that a woman was empowered to make or to break a man, depending on the feelings she had for him—but only if he *allowed* this of her either way. He could resist, if he only knew it. A man ultimately had the power to choose for himself. But, aside from procreation, where would a man or a woman be without the other—without the one's influence on the other's self-creation? There was so much to learn and to ponder about human behavior and the gifts of gender.

When we reached the landing where we had parked our things, Laura pulled another key from her purse. She turned to smile at me before opening a door that would lead into a long hallway traversing the space above the ceiling of the triple-wide garage. But first, she held out the key she would use to unlock the door. I'd never seen one like it. It was in the form of a long, smooth cone. No teeth or grooves. Instead of these, the tapered shape had sections or bands of varying widths and colors.

"You won't find a key like this in any hardware store," Laura said. "And Shackleton isn't saying where this type of lock or key came from, but it's not hard to guess. So you know that at least some of the changes he made were influenced by aliens. That's all I can say."

Her comment fascinated me. I wondered if she was about to lead me to a secret part of the house—a place where I could learn more about Shackleton's link with the AOs. That wasn't about to happen. Not yet. But her showing me the key *did* provide me with a clue that I would find useful within the hour, after she had left me alone.

* * *

There were no windows in the hallway we entered, but there were lights at fifteen-foot intervals. The floor was carpeted, which contributed to a noiseless passage.

As we neared a door at the far end of the hall, Laura said, "We're over the breezeway between the garage and the house now. Shackleton had a doggy door built in the sitting-room wall below us so that Bogart can get outdoors. He goes through his little door to the covered area.

"There are stepping stones leading down a slope from there to a locked gate in the fence that surrounds the small courtyard I told you about. Bogart has a way into the courtyard. From there he can get through another doggy door into the workshop. Shackleton has a cushy bed for him in the shop and another one in his private study adjoining the piano studio.

"So that tells you something about Shackleton's love for his dog. Bones chose well when he picked Bogart as a companion and friend for him. He was definitely inspired in his search. You could say that he has done all he can to repay Shackleton for saving his life."

"Good words to hear, Laura," I said. "Thanks for sharing. The first time I saw Shackleton and Bogart together, I was impressed by the bond between them. But I can't help feeling that there's something supernatural about their relationship. There's an eerie kind of telepathic communication between them. It's strange, but it seems they were created or destined to share their lives together."

"That appears to be true for many relationships, Kep—if only for a brief time."

Laura sighed wistfully before moving to the door ahead. She used the cone key to unlock it. After we passed through the door, it closed automatically, just as the previous one had done.

When I again heard the click of the electrically controlled security system, I asked, "Couldn't you be trapped in that hallway during a power failure?"

"Shackleton has emergency power generators installed in a building in the woods beyond the house, Kep."

Laura's tone of voice gave me the impression that she didn't find the subject to be an important one. (Was this another gender thing?)

Still curious, I then wondered why the lights had gone out at the time he returned from the San Juan Islands. I didn't ask but could only guess that an alien craft could disrupt *all* power sources.

Beyond the door the hall turned sharply left. We came to two more doors, one facing us at the end of this hall and a wider one in its wall on our right. It was obviously intended that these hallways and doors be kept secret from visitors, and I was fascinated by this secrecy.

"The wider door on your right opens to a hidden elevator," Laura said. "I can't take you through that one, though. Sorry."

She pressed the electronic key into its receptacle beside the door facing us. The door silently opened inward. We now passed into a broad and spacious hallway with pictures mounted along its walls. We entered at its side through a section that had been demarcated by vertical strips of dark wood running from floor to ceiling. The entire hallway was separated into four-foot sections in this manner. I recognized this to be the very hall that Bones had led me through on the morning he took me upstairs to the guest bedroom I'd slept in.

At that time I thought we'd used the first door on the right to enter the bedroom, but it was actually the second one. The door Laura and I had just passed through was the first, but it was disguised. After she closed it, there was no way to distinguish it from the wall surrounding it.

She pointed to an obscure little hole beside the door's section encasement and then held out her palm with the conical key. I nodded and smiled my thanks for the non-verbal disclosure she offered. Now I was wondering what had prompted Laura to show me all she had to this point. Was it her own decision to reveal these things, or was she following Shackleton's instructions? Either way, what was I to gain by knowing these secrets?

Laura advanced down the hall to a bathroom at its end. After placing her shopping bags on a wide countertop inside the bathroom, she turned toward me.

"I can't say when Shackleton will return, Kep, but I'm sure you'll have time to clean up and rest. You'll find new clothes in these bags and everything else I could think of that you might need to be refreshed. Just consider whatever you find in these bags to be your birthday presents. You can deduce how I got your clothing sizes."

She gave me a warm smile and then looked to one side and blinked several times.

"I'm sure you can find your way downstairs to the den with the fireplace. There are countless books there to occupy your mind if you should want to read. Take your time. You can bathe or take a shower. You're welcome to spend the night after meeting with Shackleton—or Bones can drive you home, whichever you'd prefer."

I held out my hand toward her and said, "Thanks for the presents. Thanks for everything, Laura."

Blinking away tears, she took my hand and gave it a squeeze. Then she stepped closer and gave me a long hug before turning away. When she reached the hidden door, she opened it with her cone key and disappeared into the secret hall. It was the last time I would see her during this recorded adventure.

CHAPTER 30

I decided to shave and shower before eating. There were several sandwiches left in the daypack Laura had prepared. Food would be waiting.

When I pulled the binoculars over my head and laid them beside the shopping bags, I was struck with an awareness of all that Laura had done during the day. I could see that she had spent a considerable amount of time and effort in my behalf. Not only had she personally prepared and delivered my food pack, but she had apparently spent some hours in a shopping mall. Where else could she have acquired so much in so little time?

I guessed that while she was finding all that was needed to outfit Dan Crotty, she must have shopped for my birthday gifts as well. And Shackleton would certainly have assigned her many other vital tasks for the day. Knowing that all her errands and duties had been accomplished while maintaining thought exchanges between the three of us impressed me.

I peeked in the smallest of the shopping bags and found soap, shampoo, and a shaving kit full of supplies, including some stuff I'd never bought or used before—like aftershave. The other bag contained two shirts (one long-sleeved and one short-sleeved), a pair of brown corduroy pants (just my size), three pairs of socks, and a three-day supply of underwear. (Laura had picked boxer shorts).

When I pulled out the underwear, I found a sealed envelope. On its face Laura had written "21 years times ten." A bundle of ten-dollar bills was inside the envelope. I counted twenty-one in all. No words entered my head. I could only shake it in disbelief. I felt a bit overwhelmed with mixed, inexpressible feelings. There had never been such a roller-coaster birthday in my life, and this, my twenty-first, was a significant one. Yet here I was, at its end now—standing alone in an empty house. I was tempted to give Laura a ring call but thought better of it. "Thanks" had already been said.

Towels and washcloths were already laid out in the bathroom. I was slow to leave the hot shower.

My new clothes fit perfectly, but I felt a bit awkward in them—not at all like myself. Leaving one button hole of my shirt open, I tucked my cell phone inside the shirt where it was handy to grab. Then, while transferring things from my pants pockets, I came across Jill's silver button that I'd saved for her.

Memories of the day's events dashed through my head, leaving me spinning. After I'd regained a sense of purposeful direction, I found myself still dealing with lingering emotions—the prime one being a yearning for Jill. Was she safe? Was she home? What had her day been like since she left me? How soon would I see her? I should be getting answers soon. Shackleton should have them.

I rolled up my old duds, stuffed them in my poncho along with everything else, gathered up the shopping bags and daypack, and found my way to the den downstairs.

* * *

The den's former ambience was missing. No firelight. No reflections of glowing coals. Shackleton's absence added to the stark contrast I felt. In the dim light I found two lamps I'd switched on during my former visit. Their warm light brought some welcome cheeriness, and I moved to the high-backed chair I'd previously sat in.

I set my gathered stuff at its side, sat down, and dragged my daypack to my feet. The Cheerios box was the first thing I pulled from the pack. I shook it and it rattled as before. Only this time, the rattling seemed to sound a bit heavier than I remembered.

Not wanting to be exposed to the artifact's destructive, hazardous influences while eating, I left my chair to set the box on the floor below a narrow attached bookcase on the wall behind me. Just as I set the box down, I was surprised by the arrival of Bogart. He had quietly come down the carpeted stairs from the second floor. A couple of wet licks on my lowered hand and a briskly wagging tail expressed the warm welcome I'd missed. And his eyes were smiling. I rubbed his ears and thanked him for greeting me.

As I stood up, my eyes landed on several books associated with various religions of the world. Again, I was surprised to see evidence of Shackleton's interest in religion. But on the shelf above these books, there was something that reached out and grabbed my notice.

Here was a one-foot-wide sculptural depiction of those three proverbial monkeys posing with their messages of "hear no evil, see no evil, speak no evil." My curiosity was most sharply piqued by cone-shaped keys dangling from cords around the monkeys' necks. I knew each of the three cones had a place and a purpose. They were definitely not just decorative items for the primate rendering.

Intrigued, I immediately began searching for little holes in the wall. There weren't any to be found any place on the walls surrounding the bookcase. My frustration was sensed by Bogart, and he kept maneuvering himself around my legs as I scanned the adjacent walls. As I moved away from the bookcase and closer to the stairway, Bogart lay down, put his head on his front paws, and gave me a look of resignation.

"Okay, Bogart," I said. "I'm sure you know more about this than I do. Do you know where I can find a keyhole?"

He leaped to his feet and moved around to the left side of the bookcase. His eyes darted back and forth between me and a point on the side of the case at a level with the monkey trio. His tail spoke his excitement as he repeatedly jerked his nose upward while facing the side of the case. There was no mistaking his message. The dark wood was very effective at disguising the small hole I was trying to locate.

Dropping down to his level, I gave Bogart a hug and a brisk rub. How could anyone not believe that dogs understand human language—or read minds?

The second (middle) key matched the circumference and depth of the keyhole. When I pressed it into the hole, the entire bookcase moved inches away from the wall. Then it glided quietly aside to expose a walk-through elevator with foldable gates.

So this was the hidden elevator Laura had mentioned—the one she said she couldn't show me when we were in the hallway two floors up.

I opened the contractible gate and stepped inside the small elevator. Bogart followed close beside me. The keyhole in the opposite elevator door was easy to spot after I compressed that latticed gate. When this second door opened, the bookcase door behind us closed. Bogart moved ahead of me into the secret room. I tucked the key deep into my pocket and followed him.

He seemed to be familiar with the area we just entered. As I searched around, I became increasingly amazed with each discovery I made. At first look, I could easily see that several people might live comfortably within the windowless enclosure for weeks or months.

Every cubic foot of space was designed to provide for basic human needs. Two freezers and a huge refrigerator were stuffed with food. A six-burner gas cooking range stood next to these appliances. There was a big stainless steel double-sink with plenty of counter surface at each side.

Six separate bunk-bed sets were enclosed in cubicles behind heavy curtains. A narrow laundry compartment contained a stacked washing machine and drier. I opened two doors to find small, efficiently designed bathrooms with toilets, tubs, sinks, and showers. A third door opened into a large, versatile walk-in closet.

Every available wall surface was covered with cupboards or shelves. There was no space that wasn't utilized. I found two folding tables. Overhead, I was surprised to see a suspended legless table that could be lowered from the ceiling. The only space-taking luxury furnishings were two upholstered recliners. All other chairs were foldable.

Lighting came from wall-mounted lamps that were controlled both manually and automatically (the lights had come on when I opened the entry door).

Best of all, taking up more than half the total volume of space, there were massive provisions of food and household supplies stored in a separate, partitioned-off area. To me, the amount of food was staggering.

Amazed, I spent about twenty minutes searching through all the food. I estimated there was enough to keep six people alive for at least eight months—maybe a year. These provisions included canned, packaged, and freeze-dried foods, as well as durable staples. Every stored item was marked with an expiration date. Most canned or packaged things were racked in a manner that allowed for sequentially dated access.

I assumed that the water was supplied by a well. It didn't smell or taste of chlorine. But it could be that purifiers were installed someplace in case the water source should become contaminated.

This secret hideaway was equipped and stocked to deal with any type of disaster or emergency. But I felt confident that it had frequent use. For one thing, the refrigerator contained recently stocked perishables. Another indication was its cleanliness and the absence of dust. A third and most convincing sign was a damp dishrag draped over the center partition of the double-sink.

So now, considering all I had discovered, a few obvious questions came to mind. These were triggered by Laura's statement that neither Bones nor Phoebe had access to this part of the house. Certainly Shackleton could not involve himself in food preparation or in personally seeing to the comfort and needs of sheltered ones. I could only conclude that this was a place of refuge for temporarily displaced people. Or was it possibly a hidden harbor for visiting aliens? Maybe both?

Laura had to be deeply involved in the activities centered here. Who else? But why had she purposely given me clues that would enable me to discover her secret involvements? Was Shackleton in on this disclosure?

Again, what was to be gained by my knowing about this sanctuary? Was I being prepared to get involved personally with aliens—to interact with them? The very thought of this was unsettling, to say the least.

Now my stomach began to express its own unsettled state by giving me urgent reminders of the deprivation it had been suffering. After all, it must have been at least a half hour since I'd been derailed from my intended course (when I moved to relocate the Cheerios box), and I had since added insult to injury by nosing through a never-ending supply of stomach stuffing.

Time enough had been spent on this fascinating excursion. It was time to eat, for sure. What time was it? I wondered. I pulled the cell phone from my shirt and turned it on. 9:36. More than an hour had passed now since Laura left.

Just as I was about to turn the phone off, it rang. This was my first experience with its functioning as a phone (rather than a time piece), and the sound startled me. It took me a few seconds of fumbling before I managed to respond.

"Kep, lad!" It was Bick. "What's been keepin' you from callin', Chappy? Are you stayin' out of trouble? Old Bick is here for you, I are, I are. You shouldn't be . . . oh, sure, Luvvy. Here—"

"Kep?" Dozie had taken over command of the phone. "Where are you? Are you okay? Selma has been worried sick about you and Jill since you've both turned up missing. What's going on? Is Jill with you?"

"I'm okay, Dozie. Jill has been helping me with my new job. She's—"

"Is she driving you? Selma says the VW bus is parked in the drive and Jill's car is gone. She called us to get in touch with you after she got the first call from Jill's roommate to say that Jill didn't show up at church. Her roommate has called Selma twice now because she hasn't heard from her all day. That's so unlike Jill—to skip church and not get someone to take over her class."

"I can explain that, Dozie. It was *my* fault—not Jill's—that she didn't get to church."

"It's so good to learn that you're all right, Kep. I guess the thing that got Selma worrying the most is that Joel found the dog sleeping in your van, and she thought you needed it to do your job. Joel took the dog back to its owner late this evening after Selma got the second call from Emily . . . she's Jill's roommate.

"I hope you don't need the dog. Emily called quite late, so it didn't seem as if you would be using it any longer. It would be nice if Jill could get in touch with Emily, Kep. She and the other girls are quite concerned about her."

"When did Selma get the last call, Dozie? Do you know?"

"I don't know the exact time. Selma called me again just after that. It was getting dark then. I gave her your cell phone number, but I guess your phone's been turned off."

"Well, uh . . . Dozie . . . Jill can't be right where I am just now. I'm trying to finish up my day's assignments. If you can get me

Emily's phone number, I'll call her myself. It might be that Jill is already home. She should be. I have other transportation for myself. Jill may be on an errand of her own and doesn't have a way to make a call. I'll let you know what I can, but I'd rather not talk to Selma until I learn something to pass along to her—something to ease her mind."

(At this point I'd lost my appetite, and I had a gut feeling I wasn't going to learn anything that might be comforting to either Selma or me.)

"I don't have the number, Kep. I can get it for you by calling Selma, but I don't want to cause her any more distress."

"Try this, Dozie: Could you call Selma and tell her you just spoke with me and that we're okay? Tell her that Jill lost a heel from her shoe and that her skirt got damaged while she was helping me get the search dog. Explain that several unexpected things happened to us and that Jill and I are in separate places at this time. Tell her that Jill doesn't have a phone to use and I do, but its battery is losing its charge.

"Please ask her for Emily's phone number so I can catch Emily and her friends up on things quick. Get her to understand that because my phone's losing power, I need to act fast. Then get right back to me, please, Dozie. I'll fill you in the best I can . . . so long as my phone's working. My car charger isn't doing me any good here. Thanks, Dozie. My phone's on until I hear from you."

Bogart was at the elevator door ahead of me. I reached in my pocket for the cone key. As I was about to insert the key in its hole, my eyes fell on a silvery object at my feet. Curious, I reached down to pick it up. A close look at it brought both wonder and alarm. It appeared to be a silver button just like the one ripped from Jill's skirt!

I hurriedly reached into my pocket to see if I still had the one I'd tucked away earlier when I was making transfers between old and new pants. My fingers brought out an identical button.

Both had come from Jill's skirt—that was certain.

Now, as I struggled to deal with the impact of this discovery, my phone rang. It was Dozie.

"Do you have something to write with, Kep? I have the number for you."

"Just a second, Dozie."

I carefully set the phone down on the floor so I wouldn't risk dropping it. Squatting down, I groped inside my new shirt for my pencil and notepad. With the notepad on my knee, I felt more secure. I wasn't accustomed to writing while holding a little cell phone to one ear with my shoulder. Besides, I felt a bit dizzy.

"Okay. I'm ready."

I wrote the number she gave me and said, "I'll let you know what I learn, Dozie, but don't expect anything too soon. It might have to wait until morning. Thanks again."

I closed off the call and punched the numbers Dozie gave me. It took a minute for me to remember what I'd read about how to send a call. Being unfamiliar with using a cell phone added to my anxiety.

At last I heard a female voice.

"Hello?" (It wasn't Jill's voice.)

"This is Kep Stone. Who's speaking, please?"

"This is Emily Cook. Who are *you*?"

"I'm Kep. I'm a friend of Jill's. Is she home?"

"Oh. Hi, Kep. She's mentioned you. She's not feeling very well, though. Vanessa and I just helped her into the house from her car. I don't know how long she's been parked out there sitting in it. Not very long. She's lying down."

Hearing that Jill was home brought relief, but her discomfort and the timing of her return brought questions I didn't want to deal with at the moment.

"Would you please tell her I'm on my cell phone and that it's about to die? I really need to talk to her."

"Just a minute."

Emily was taking a long minute, and my phone was making beeping sounds.

"Hello, Kep? She says she isn't sure about you. She seems confused. She—"

My phone died.

I stood up and shoved both of Jill's buttons deep into my pocket.

Bogart's tail said he was eager to get back into the den. I wondered if it might be that he'd sensed Shackleton's return, but when the bookcase door slid open, I found both the den and the adjoining piano studio empty.

After the bookcase had returned to its position of deception, I gave the cone necklace back to "See No Evil." The mysteries of the two remaining keys would have to wait.

Bogart looked at me expectantly.

"You're probably in better shape to make a decision than I am," I said to him.

He moved slowly into the piano studio and sat down beside a small end table near the west window. Nearby was the recliner that Shackleton had sat in while I was dealing with the leather cash box on our first meeting. It looked inviting, even in the dim light entering from the den, and I felt disposed to just rest and think. (Food was no longer a priority thought.) Besides, Bogart deserved to have his ears rubbed.

I decided to give Laura a ring call. I wanted to ask if she knew anything about Shackleton's handling of Jill's surveillance and safety. I would say nothing about my discoveries—nothing about finding the secret area or about Jill's late return. And I didn't think it would spoil Laura's day if I was to thank her again for the specific gifts she'd left for me.

Laura didn't respond.

I supposed I'd just have to wait for Shackleton's own words of explanation, but I felt disturbed and distressed. Waiting was a trial.

As I sat there massaging Bogart's ears, I put my head back and closed my eyes. When I opened them, I noticed there was a telephone on the side table. Without giving the act any forethought, I decided to call Emily back and learn anything else I could about Jill's condition.

I left the recliner and turned on a light so I could see the number I'd written in my notepad. Bogart seemed happy with my decision to use the phone. (Could it be that I was acting on his suggestion?)

Once again, Emily answered my call.

"Sorry about cutting you off, Emily," I said. "My cell phone died. You were saying that Jill seemed confused. How do you mean that?"

"She can't remember where she's been or how she got home. And she was having trouble remembering who you are when I told her she had a call from you. It's scary to see her like this. She's always had a fantastic memory."

"I know, Emily. Does she have any marks or bumps on her head that you can see?"

"I've been rubbing her head and neck. I haven't noticed anything. She hasn't complained. She's been very thirsty. She's been drinking a lot of water."

"Is she improving, do you think?"

"I think being home again with us is helping already. Vanessa and Rachel are sitting on her bed with her right now."

"Is there a phone near her? Do you think she'd talk to me,

Emily?"

"I'm on a cordless phone, Kep. I'll ask her."

A muffled conversation followed. It went on for a couple of minutes before Emily got back to me.

Her voice was bright when she said, "Now she remembers everything up to the time her car stalled. She remembers a man and woman getting into her car, but nothing after that. She says she remembers you, but she doesn't want to talk to you now. I think she needs to rest, Kep. Maybe tomorrow, okay?"

"Thanks, Emily. I'll notify her mom that she's back with you. I don't think it would be a good idea to tell her anything more than that for now. How soon can I call you in the morning for an update?"

"We're all up by six thirty. Any time after that is okay."

"Thanks. It's been good to meet you on the phone, Emily. We'll talk in the morning, then."

After hanging up, I thought of calling Dozie with some news for Selma, but a red flag waved in my head. Was there any chance that Shackleton's home phone was being monitored? He'd said I should never use a phone to call *him*. Did that rule apply two ways?

I didn't know what being "under surveillance" amounted to for him personally. I'd already messed up early on in the day by inviting Jill along on my assignment. Maybe I'd just now made a big mistake by calling her home from his.

My stress needle was touching its limit peg again. And my brain was going into "overload" with new questions.

Laura's gift thermos of ginger tea came to mind. I needed to renew and refocus. Maybe the tea would help.

As I approached the high-backed chair in the den, I passed by the Cheerios box. It had fallen over and was lying on the floor. There must be a better place for it, I thought—someplace where it would get Shackleton's attention. But how could it get "noticed" if he couldn't see it? (I must have sensed at this point that I wouldn't be waiting out his return.)

For some reason I thought of his personal study. Bones or Phoebe had said he ate his meals there. A study should have a desk in it, a surface on which to work and be productive. Even if he used the desk only for eating, it should serve as a perfect place to drop off the "prize" I'd taken risks to get for him.

Bogart wasn't in sight. I went back into the piano studio and made a left turn to the study entry. The door was closed. When I opened it, I flipped the light switch and found Bogart lying on his bed. His bed was right beside Shackleton's desk—a huge desk at that. Bogart had entered through his doggy door. He didn't get up to meet me but apologetically thumped his tail against his bed cushion instead.

"No apology needed," I said to him. "You've been a great help already—and a wonderful friend."

Shackleton's desk top was uncluttered. I wasn't inclined to snoop or get curious about it. I just wanted to do my delivery errand and leave. By now I was having thoughts of leaving the house and coming back the next day loaded with questions.

I didn't feel that it would be wise to interrupt Shackleton's meetings by attempting a ring call. Strangely, I didn't feel like talking to *anyone* now. I had things to work out in my mind. The day's stresses had taken their toll.

I moved around the desk and placed the cereal box squarely front and center. Laying it on its side, I saw that the top was creased. A close-up look at it showed that the seal was partly broken at the point where I had slipped my pencil inside to test it. Where the insertion and removal of my mechanical pencil hadn't left a trace of entry, now there was an obvious gap under the box top. I had no trouble poking my forefinger into it. Alarmed and dismayed, my heart began to pound as I grabbed up the box and held it upside down to shake it. Feeling with my finger inside the box, I vigorously shook the object toward the opening under the lid. Eventually it came to rest against my fingertip so I could roll it and sense its shape and texture. What I felt was a small round stone—nothing like the octahedron Hoyle had described to Shackleton.

I had no doubt that this tiny rock was a deceptive substitute for the artifact that had been inserted by Kroy Koziol. The true prize had been taken *after* I left the picnic table in the park.

Now I began to have serious doubts about my rescuer. Maybe he wasn't an AO after all. Maybe I'd assumed too much because of his disarming manner and the means by which he'd relocated me. Now that I thought about it, I could see unlikely aspects about the way I was transported. Why should I have been made unconscious and left alone on a bench? Why wasn't I given a ring call as Laura had said?

And now I remembered that she had been concerned when I mentioned that I thought I was being watched. She had said that this could present a problem. It was then that she gave me directions for getting accepted at the Three-Cornered Orange. Laura hadn't mentioned a rescue being performed by anyone except Bones or the taxi driver, Link. She had also given specific instructions about how to escape notice and avoid being followed.

How could I have been so stupid as to be led by a total stranger? But then, how could the stranger have come up with the code name "Oliver"? Why had it been so easy to trust him?

To add to my confusion, there was the question of why a little rock had been used to substitute for the artifact. Once the prize was taken, why replace it with anything at all—except to deceive me in case I should shake the box as I did? So it may be that the substitution was made to falsely reassure anyone having knowledge of what I was secretly transporting. Other than myself, I could think of no one to attempt to fool except Laura or Shackleton. But then, weren't they the only ones who could have informed the deceiver of what was in the box? So why would they want to tell anyone else about the secret in the first place?

At the moment, I was too tired to give any further thought to the matter. I felt distressed and depleted. Although I needed food, I'd lost my appetite. I just wanted to get away to rest, reflect, and renew. Shackleton's home was not the place for that.

I made a decision. Leaving the cereal box on Shackleton's desk, I rubbed Bogart's floppy ear a few times and said "good-bye" to him. (He clearly understood my intentions.) Next, I gathered up my stuff from the den, switched off the lights, and left the house through the piano studio door.

CHAPTER 31

AFTER descending the stairs from Evening Star Lane, I went to the convenience store in Old Fairhaven where I'd parked the VW bus Saturday night. I remembered there was a payphone near the entry. When I found the phone-book hanger empty, I lugged my stuff into the store and asked the clerk if he had a directory I could use. He pulled one out from under the counter.

"You'll have to keep it inside the store," he said. "Do you need something to write on?"

He handed me a slip of paper and a ballpoint pen before I could answer.

I thanked him and moved down the counter away from the cash register. After searching the yellow pages and writing a few numbers down, I felt in my pockets for change and came up with twenty-two cents. Not enough. My wallet was empty of bills.

The clerk was staring at me and smiling.

"I remember you," he said. "You were in here last night asking about parking in the alley."

"Oh, yeah. Right. I remember you too. Thanks for the tip. Everything worked out great."

"No problem."

It bothered me to think that it was little more than twenty-six hours since I'd left the bus to climb the stairs and meet with

Shackleton. (The store clock showed 10:38.) How could so much happen in so little time?

It bothered me, too, to be coming up short of the change I needed to make my calls. I had intended to use some of the bills Laura had given me to finance my plan. I dug down into the big red shopping bag to search through my new underwear. As I pulled out the money envelope, I looked at the clerk to see if he had been watching my rummaging act. Thankfully, he was occupied and not watching where I did my banking.

Once again I felt thankful for all Laura had done for me throughout the day and evening. And once again I felt sorry for her—having learned all she had verbally shared or silently revealed about herself over the past forty-eight hours. With mixed feelings, I wished I could thank her again personally.

The clerk gave me change for a ten, and I left him a couple of ones as a tip for his kindness. (College students can always use more money.)

Having bills in my wallet, I pursued my plan. Having enough change, I made two calls: the first to a motel and the second to a city taxi service.

* * *

I paid the taxi driver and went to the motel desk to register. These were first-time experiences for me. I had never before hired a taxi or checked in at a motel. It felt good to be "grown up" now. It was my time to celebrate "coming of age."

The phone beside the bed grabbed my attention as I dropped my bags and poncho to the floor. It was too late to be calling anyone, but I read the instructions for dialing out. Feeling confident that my body would awaken naturally, I ignored both the wake-up-call service and the checkout time (11:00 a.m.).

I woke up at 9:25.

After paying my respects to the bathroom porcelain, I picked up the room phone and rang Jill's house. No one had answered after six rings, and I was about to hang up when a breathless voice reached my ear.

"Hi! Sorry . . . I was washing my hair." The voice didn't belong to either Jill or Emily.

"Hi, this is Kep. Who is this?"

"Vanessa. Oh! Sorry . . . I was expecting a call from someone else."

"That's okay. Is Jill there, Vanessa?"

"Everyone's gone, Kep. I haven't seen Jill. I think she left before the others. Can I leave a message?"

"I guess not. I called mostly to find out how she's doing—if her memory is back. Do you know?"

"Just a minute . . ." (She was back in thirty seconds.) "Her car's gone, Kep. I don't think anyone has seen her or talked to her this morning. She must be better, or she wouldn't have driven to class. Actually, I think she had an early meeting at the school where she's been doing student teaching. She must be okay, since she got away early. At least she remembered her Monday schedule."

"Thanks, Vanessa. I'll try again later, after my cell phone's charged. Have a happy *hair* day."

"You too . . . I mean . . ." We both laughed as we hung up.

It was good to begin the day with a laugh. Laura was right when she said we could use more laughter. But the prospects of my maintaining a lighter spirit weren't so great. I dreaded having to learn what Shackleton would have to say about the missing artifact. Nothing I could think would make sense or reduce my anxiety. Although I felt sure he could give some plausible explanation for its disappearance, I couldn't dodge all the questions rushing at me. And I hadn't had breakfast yet (or yesterday's supper, for that matter).

I decided to call Selma myself. Dozie was probably busy enough at this time of day without involving herself in my personal affairs.

Selma sounded rushed when she answered.

"Hello, Selma. Good morning! This is Kep."

"Kep! Wherever are you, dear? I be losin' sleep over you not bein' home and no calls from you."

"I'm sorry if I caused you to worry, Mom. So much has been happening with my new job that I couldn't begin to tell you all the reasons for not keeping in touch. Didn't Dozie tell you Jill and I were okay when she called to get the phone number last night?"

"Oh, she said you both be in different places, and your cell phone be a dyin', but that didn't give me much comfort, dear."

"Well, you should have some peace of mind now. Evidently Jill's at a school meeting and—"

"Oh? Listen, dear. I be in a rush. The men are out gettin' tractor parts, and I be leavin' with Inez to do my middle-of-the-month shoppin'. She be here waitin' out front to fetch me away. You please take care now."

"Right. I will. Bye for now."

I hung up feeling thankful for the good people in my life—people who genuinely cared. My short conversation with Selma made me realize that I *did* belong to a family. But then I felt troubled at this family's being naively unaware of the extent of the "human family" as it exists beyond the surface of our planet. And our collective Earth-bound family of billions was just a speck in the universe! This was mind-boggling to me.

Since I could no longer ignore or deny the existence of human aliens, I was now beginning to fully accept the reality of other-world beings. It was challenging to contemplate the scope and meaning of this. Much assimilation was going on at a lower level of my consciousness—more than I could deal with head-on.

I wondered if I could personally amount to anything significant—anything of value in the magnitude of this universal setting. But then, I could see that the only thing that truly mattered—the only thing that made life meaningful—was the give-and-take of love among humans. There could always be *someone* to care for. The better we could master loving unselfishly, the richer our lives would be. Pondering this, it became obvious to me that the only *real* love was that which came with no expectations attached.

Oddly, Bogart came to mind. He had to be a tremendous blessing for Shackleton. As with most domesticated dogs, he exemplified devoted, unselfish love. Humans could learn a lot from dogs about unconditional love, I thought. And dogs had a lot to teach us about forgiveness and patience as well.

By now my stomach was nudging me incessantly to say that it had no patience left. I remembered there was an offer of a free continental breakfast posted in the motel lobby.

I did a quick wash-up, slipped into my new birthday duds, and made a final call—for a taxicab. I guessed I'd have ten minutes to down a pastry and some orange juice before my taxi arrived.

It came for me two sweet rolls and a juice drink later.

Since the drive time would amount to twenty or twenty-five minutes, I asked the taxi driver if I could plug my phone charger in the cigarette lighter of his cab. He smiled, gave me a nod, and pointed his finger toward the lighter under the dashboard.

Before literally falling into bed the previous night, I had pulled the cell-phone box and charger from my poncho. The unhappy-looking sandwiches in my daypack didn't have much appeal by then, so I had discarded them to make room for my wadded-up poncho and other trappings, charger included.

Thankfully, the driver was a man of few words. Part of my plan for the morning was to review Sunday's events and notate the questions that begged for answers. I knew I could accomplish all of this with my ring in its recording mode. This time I was determined to be prepared for my meeting time with Shackleton, whenever that might be.

After giving the driver my destination, I slid down into my seat, put my head back, and closed my eyes. Thus I assumed a "do not disturb" posture. I knew I could ignore a ring call, but I knew I wouldn't. My curiosity would overrule any intention to disregard one. Besides, I needed to know when Shackleton would see me.

My first questions centered on Dan Crotty—the "missing man." I had located him, but then I'd helped him escape. Where was he now? Why had he faked his death? Why had he stayed so long in that stinking house? If he had done nothing wrong, why hadn't he reported Koziol's body? What was he after, if not the artifact? Who was to have been his accomplice—the "prettier" woman mentioned in his notepad? Where was she? The questions about him went on and on.

Kroy Koziol's missing eye had deeply troubled me at the outset of my adventure, but the thing that mystified me now was the *cause* of his death. More than that, I wanted to learn who his ally was, and *where* he was.

How much did *he* know about the artifact and its value? Could he have deduced enough from Koziol's first (mailed) communication to identify the deceptive package? Could he have just been waiting for someone to leave with it so he could follow unseen? Might he have been the one who substituted the little stone for the prize after I'd been dumped off at the Three-Cornered Orange? Or was he possibly the guy with the binoculars who took me away from the park? I knew absolutely nothing about him.

And then there was the artifact itself. How could anything so small create a commotion so big? What was there about it that would cause the Abiding Ones to give it their high degree of attention? True, I didn't know much about the scientific facts that Koziol had discovered regarding it (not that it mattered), but he evidently had transmitted enough to Air Force Intelligence to arouse a hullabaloo. And how far would the federal agents go to obtain another like it or to learn where it was found? Would the Tiptons—Nancy and her parents—ever have any peace or relief from the agents' relentless, oppressive tactics?

Was Gaston a killer? I presumed he was in custody. He may certainly have poisoned the attack dogs, but did he have any part in Koziol's demise? I felt impatient to learn what an autopsy would reveal. How long might that take?

And last but not least were those questions stemming from my finding another of Jill's buttons in the secret room. These last questions had shot to the top of my list.

No ring call came during my taxi ride.

The Whipple farm looked home-like and inviting, but I was still so immersed in troubling thoughts and questions when I arrived that I was unresponsive to its appeal. Finding no one home was a relief. I wasn't in a communicative mood.

Smooch and I exchanged our usual demonstrations of affection. He seemed unusually excited to welcome me home.

After taking my stuff to my room, I snatched up my cell phone and then headed back downstairs and out to the VW bus. I found Bessie Mae's recipe box on the front floor and Pokey's water pan on the back floor. The money box was in the cupboard under the sink, and the keys were in the ignition.

I climbed in behind the steering wheel and was just closing the door when I recalled my thoughts about devoted, unconditional love. It struck me that Smooch was so often alone—and so *much* alone.

I left the bus and went to the back porch.

Sitting down beside Smooch, I put my arm around his neck

and held him close. He felt so stiff and looked so old. I'm not ashamed to say I shed some tears. We shared a good ten minutes together silently arriving at understandings. It didn't bother me in the least to have his slobbery licks wash my face clean. I gave him hugs and ear rubs (but I didn't lick his face).

CHAPTER 32

I drove to the end of Whipple Farm Lane and parked. My midday hike up Singing Tree Hill in the warm sunshine was invigorating. Strangely, I wasn't hungry or thirsty—bodily speaking.

It was calming to sit on the flat stone under the Singing Tree and feel the cool breeze on my face. The atmosphere was tinged with mixed scents of sea air and awakened spring. Only the songs of birds and whispering young leaves broke the silence.

Nature's sounds and smells brought healing. They restored peace and sanity. I had come to partake of an afternoon of these renewing influences and to gain a fresh perspective.

Suddenly a metallic clatter broke my reverie. I spun around to locate the source of the noise close behind me. Dropping to my knees, I discovered a colorful Bond Street tobacco tin in the tall grass a few feet from the tree trunk. A shiny long-bladed pocket knife lay nearby. At the same instant that I dropped down into the grass, an exclamation came from a point high up in the tree.

A female voice cried out, "Oh! I'm sorry! Are you okay? Kep! Are you all right?"

I stood, shaded my eyes with my hands, and looked up into the tree. There was no doubting it was Jill's voice.

"Jill!" I shouted. "If you're taking up pipe smoking, I think you're using excessive measures to hide it."

Her immediate laughter brought more renewal to my spirit than I could have derived from an entire afternoon on Singing Tree Hill.

"Don't look!" she said.

She was carefully climbing down through a profusion of bright green leaves fluttering amid slender white branches. I *did* look and saw that she was wearing a loose-fitting denim skirt on this tree-climbing excursion. (I didn't question her choice.) As she got closer, I could see that she held a folded piece of white paper between her thumb and forefinger. The folded paper couldn't compete with her legs for getting my attention, so to be proper and respectful, I covered my eyes as she made it down the last six feet. This was the most difficult stretch of her descent (for me).

We didn't hesitate to embrace each other. There was no point in trying to hide or deny our feelings. This was the best kind of happiness. Our relationship far exceeded the bonds of physical attraction. We were truly connected in a spiritual way.

How thankful I was that I had been able to resist the recent temptations of my time alone with Laura—for *her* sake as well as for my own. My priceless bond with Jill was worth preserving at any cost. My only concern was that I couldn't share her religious convictions. But I didn't know much about them yet, if anything at all. Yet I knew she held them in the highest degree of priority. So the permanence of our bond might be a thing in question.

For now, I had to set that aside and live in the moment.

Jill clasped my hand and pulled me to the stone seat. It was obvious that she had just endured some significant experiences and that she too had many questions. But I was the first to ask a profound "opener."

"Okay, what's with the tobacco can and the killer knife?" I said.

"All through my teens there were times when I climbed this

tree, Kep, but I never climbed as high as I did today. I suppose that's because I've never had so much to think about before—so many new things to accept. I found this can wedged against a limb with the knife. The knife and the can look new, but this paper tells me they're not. I'll show you more about that in a minute.

"I just want you to know this is a place where I'd come to think and pray in complete solitude, especially when I was weighed down with a problem. I left the house early this morning to come here for that. But first I went to see if Pokey got back okay. After I visited with Bessie Mae, I decided to leave my car at her farm where no one would see it. I thought the walk would clear my head—and it did . . . but . . ."

"You're all right, then? Your memory's back?"

"I'm much better, but I'm confused by questions I can't answer yet, Kep."

I laughed and said, "That makes two of us. But we have a day to talk things out and learn what we can from each other. At least I hope you have a chunk of free time to spend with me. Do you?""

"I'm going to *make* the time, Kep. It's important to me."

"Great!"

Jill unfolded the paper she was carrying and stretched it out on her lap.

She brightened with excitement and said, "Just look at this paper I found stored in the tobacco can! The condition it's in tells some things about the Singing Tree that I've always thought to be true. I believe you've been suspecting the same things I have, Kep."

"Test me."

"Don't you think there's something supernatural about it?"

"Like?"

"Like it makes you *feel* it has some kind of intelligence. Don't you feel as though it heals your body and your spirit when you've been near it for a while? I always go away from it feeling healthier and uplifted."

"Yes," I said. "Don't laugh, but I've even felt as though it *listens* to me when I talk to it—which I confess I've done."

She didn't laugh.

I stood up and pulled out my mechanical pencil.

"Before I look at what's on that paper, I want to show *you* something, Jill."

I laid my pencil on the rock, and we watched together as it rolled uphill. Jill shook her head in disbelief and retrieved my pencil from the grass. When she placed it on the stone, she got the same results.

"You do see that it's rolling *up* the incline, Jill. Right?"

She nodded thoughtfully and said, "I've had pencils fall off this stone before, but I've never realized they were falling *up* instead of *down*, Kep. Why I've never noticed that before amazes me. It's hard to believe."

She repeated the act twice and then turned and stared at the tree.

Reaching for my hand, she pulled me down beside her. She handed me the paper. It appeared to be a short journal with just a few dated notations.

"Read the dates, Kep."

The first entry was dated December 25, 1937—Christmas Day. It was printed in pencil. The last was done in cursive with a pen. The date was April 6, 1947.

I read the first entry:

"Real early this morning I saw an orange light shining up on your hill. I climbed up to see if somebody had lit a fire. Everything looked ok. I know you knew I came to check up on you. There was a man I never saw before who came and talked to me. He said he knew how you got planted and that you were there for some purpose. He was kind of strange but nice. He said he knew I talked to you and he knew my folks didn't think I was crazy like some people think if I tell them. He said if I wrote to you like I am now besides just talk, he would come again sometime and tell me more things about you but I shouldn't tell anyone what he says. He asked me to save what I write high up in your branches. He said I would get the knife I wanted for Christmas, and he was right; I did get it. How could he know that? Jonathan."

After reading the Christmas Day entry, I looked over at Jill and shook my head in wonder.

"Wow! It's amazing to think this has been up there so many years. I wonder if this Jonathan's still alive. Do you know who he might be—or who he was?" I asked.

"It had to have been Jonathan Willoughby. He was the only son of Jon and Belle Willoughby, who used to live down below on the west side of this hill. Oat's father bought their land. They're both dead now, and their farmhouse is falling apart.

"There's a trail that goes around this hill to their old place. It follows partway up Trillium creek—the one that flows down and crosses under Whipple Farm Lane in a culvert. Another trail goes down from this hill and joins it. I hiked up here using those routes last Saturday. That was the day I left the portrait of you."

"Right! I couldn't figure out why your car was parked where it was. I can see you parked as close as you could get to the creek—right across from the Pottses' mailbox. I thought you might have gone to visit the Pottses, but I was hoping to find you up here."

Jill shook her head and smiled at me.

"Read some more, Kep."

"January 27, 1938: It's my birthday. I'm fifteen. I came to see you. The man didn't come. I haven't seen him since Christmas."

Several notes followed between January 1938 and November 1940. Evidently Jonathan was visited by the "nice stranger" four times over those years. Three of those meetings were on April 6. But the visitor had asked that Jonathan not write down anything he had learned from him yet. He said the dates were important to record. Jonathan had begun keeping his paper in the pipe tobacco can on April 6, 1938. Evidently the appearance of an orange light in the sky above Singing Tree Hill confirmed a telepathic message that the visitor wanted Jonathan to meet with him at the Tree.

Then on December 17, 1941 he made a significant notation:

"I'm going to war. I don't know when I'll be able to see you or write to you again, if ever. You've been a good friend for me. There's never been a friend like you to talk to, except for my dog Shakey, and I don't know if I'll ever see him again either. It doesn't bother me what people might think if I mention the light. My folks have seen the orange light too, and they believe me. I've kept my promise to the man and haven't told anyone about your beginning or the secrets he told me about you. He said a young woman would find these notes sometime in the distant future. He said this woman would know who she could share this paper with but that she should keep it where she found it. It beats me how he could predict this. I don't know anything about the woman he was talking about. He said I should write that you were brought here from another planet but that's all. That's a puzzler, but it doesn't surprise me. I really hope I'll see you again. You never know about war. It's hard leaving my folks and my dog. Jonathan."

"Obviously he got through the war alive," I said.

"Yes, but no one else seemed to know that, Kep. In 1943 he was reported missing in action after his military squad had been besieged in a nighttime combat. Every soldier's body was accounted for except his. It was the last thing Oat's father had heard about Jonathan before the Willoughbys left their farm. I remember the year 1943 because it's the year Oat was born, and the Willoughbys had come to see Oat's parents and their new baby boy. Oat said he remembers his father telling him when he was older that the Whipples had bought the Willoughby's place so they could leave. They were having a hard time dealing with the loss of their only child—at least they had assumed he'd been killed in the war. They wanted to get away and start a new life where they didn't have so many memories."

"Then it's a real mystery where he might have been located all those years until 1947. Maybe he was a POW," I said.

"Read his last note, Kep."

I folded back the paper and read:

"April 6, 1947: You know that Noaak's people are from a planet in the Pleiades. They were the ones who rescued me during a nighttime battle while we were surrounded. Everyone in my unit was killed. Noaak said I was spared for a reason. He said God sometimes allows his people and others to do certain things on this Earth, but they aren't called by Him to do anything on this Earth. He said the young woman who finds this paper would know what he means. I've learned so much from them. Things I can't write about or even describe. They taught me that everything that exists has intelligence and everything in our universe is connected. These years with them have gone by in a flash. Their spaceships can move faster than light, and time doesn't mean a thing while we are in them. Some of Noaak's people are over a thousand years old in our time.

"They brought me back and took me to where my parents live in Oregon. My dog has a gray muzzle and looks old, but he still remembers me. My mother thought she was seeing a ghost and almost fainted when she came to the door. My dad had to sit down, and they both cried. The folks look a lot older, but the time we spent together sparked new life in them. I spent a month with them before I came here to see you and write this. You look the same. I'm going back to be with my folks. They need me. I might not visit you again while my folks are alive.

Maybe never. But I can't ever forget you or what you've meant to me. I know what I'm to do with my life now. I believe you know, too. Maybe we will meet at the time when many of Earth's mortals will be gathered from the heavens. Noaak's people must die just as we do, but they live much longer. His people know this Earth's destiny. They said of all the worlds created, our world is home to some of the best of humans and to the most wicked of all. I can't write any more than this, but the young woman who will find this knows why and what it has to do with the purpose of this Earth's creation. Noaak said I should write that the woman who finds this should keep it safe in your top branches. She has the gift of remembering. Until we touch again. Jonathan."

I raised my head and saw that Jill's head was tilted to one side as she searched my face. She wore a sober, questioning expression.

"This is a wonderful, incredible discovery!" I said as I handed back the paper. "I can see those notes are very revealing and prophetic, Jill. You must know a lot that you haven't shared with me yet."

"I believe the same must be true for you, Kep."

I nodded and looked out toward the blue waters of Samish Bay in the distance. We clasped hands. Neither one of us spoke for a minute. Then I remembered I had something that spoke a question without words. I stood up and reached deep into my pocket.

I held out the two silver buttons in my palm. Jill's lips parted as she stared at them. When I could see that the question had obviously formed in her mind, I said, "Did you know you lost another one of your buttons?"

"Yes. But I don't know where I lost it, Kep. I mean, it was in a place I'd never been before."

Jill's eyes were wide with wonder and perplexity.

She said, "I know I've got my memory back, because I recall pulling the button off my skirt automatically, without thinking, and dropping it to the floor. It didn't make sense. I felt that some influence *made* me do it. Where in the world did you find it, Kep?"

"In a secret place—a place I can't tell you about yet. I wish I could tell you about it, Jill, but I can't yet. I discovered the place for the first time last night. It's funny . . . *you* knew about it before I did. Can you remember how you got there or who took you there?"

"A man and a woman I'd never seen before. They came up behind me. My car had suddenly quit running, and they got it started again. They were a little strange, but pleasant. The woman offered to drive my car while the man followed in theirs in case I had another problem. She was wearing a strong perfume that made me sleepy. I thought it would be best then that she *did* drive me. I felt okay with that.

"The next thing I remember is waking up in a recliner with this woman sitting in one beside me. I was very thirsty, and she brought me a drink. Not long after that, a young woman came to stay with me while the first one left for a few minutes. When I asked the younger one where I was, she said I had been put in danger and that I was being protected until it would be safe for me to return to my car. That's all she could say. I'm sure I've seen this woman before—maybe in a church meeting, but I can't place her. It's frustrating that I can't place her, Kep."

"She didn't tell you her name? Can you describe her, Jill? Maybe what she was wearing or . . ."

"Her hair was blond. She was wearing a white blouse and a blue skirt. She seemed distressed. I felt like she was studying me, but she was nice to me. She asked if I would like something to eat, but I wasn't hungry. She wasn't with me very long.

"Then she left, and the first woman came back wearing that overpowering perfume. This woman told me her name was

Alleri. She said the man's name was Azram. She even spelled their names for me because they were unusual. She spoke with a strange accent. Kep, I know there must have been something about her perfume that put me to sleep, because we had hardly begun a conversation when I drifted off again.

"The next thing I remember is waking up behind the steering wheel of my car in front of my house. I'm sure I didn't drive myself home. I couldn't have. It's all very strange and confusing. I don't know how, but one of those two women, or Azram, had to have gone to some trouble to learn where I live. My car registration gives the Whipple Farm address because Oat has my car in his name for insurance reasons. It's the address shown on my driver license, too. So . . . I don't know . . ."

"That's all right, Jill. Don't strain your brain about it. It's not really important."

(I didn't dare tell her that I knew who the young blond was. No good could come from her knowing.)

"Kep . . . I know I've seen the blond before. I just . . ."

"It's okay, Jill. It probably doesn't matter now. What really matters is that you were treated well and that you were kept safe. I didn't know it when I invited you to come with me yesterday, but I discovered that there was an unknown danger in my doing what I was assigned to do. I'm sorry you had to go through what you did. But you were a great help to me—more than you'll probably ever know."

"Are you always going to be in dangerous situations, Kep?" Jill's face was clouded with concern.

"I don't know, Jill. But I know your prayers for me are paying off," I said with a smile. "It might surprise you to learn that I pr—"

"Kep! I just remembered! At least I remember *one* place where I've seen the blond before!"

I kept silent and waited (not without some anxiety).

"It was in a church bookstore—a bookstore *associated* with my church. The church itself doesn't own or operate it, but it's managed by church members.

"This blond had come up behind me when I was waiting to pay for a picture I liked. She saw what I put on the counter and mentioned that she had the same picture on the wall beside her front door in her apartment. I told her that was just the place in my house where I planned to hang the one I was buying—a place where I'd often see it and be reminded of the most important choice I'd ever made. It's a framed picture of Jesus that I'd always wanted. It has a statement about *choice* alongside it that I especially like. That was about a year ago, Kep. So my memory's not so bad after all, is it?"

"That's impressive, Jill. What you said to me Friday about choice and purpose in everything has got me thinking new kinds of questions. I'm more thoughtful now of where choices could take me—even small ones. What does the statement beside your picture of Christ say?"

Her response didn't surprise me.

"It says, 'If, in the end, you have not chosen Jesus Christ, it will not matter what you have chosen.' And I believe that's true, Kep. But I want you to make your *own* choices."

"I guess I'm not getting what you're saying. So far you haven't decided anything *for* me, have you? I've never felt like you're trying to control me, Jill."

"Thanks," she said, eyes smiling and blinking. "What I want you to understand is that I don't want your feelings for me to cause you to choose my way—my religion—just to win me over or to gain my favor. I want you to express your *true* spiritual self. We can't have a lasting relationship if you make me your life's focus. I want you to come to know Christ yourself, not just know *about* him. And I want you to be led by him, not by me. I've learned to be cautious and see how things play out through individual choices. That's why I answered you the way I did at first—right after we met—when you asked if we could plan to meet again. It was to prove something about you."

"I'm happy now that you answered as you did, Jill. And I understand your reasons. What I don't know yet is how you came to be cautious."

Jill closed her eyes and sighed heavily. She paused, as if weighing whether or not to tell me. Then she pursed her lips and sighed again.

When she opened her eyes, she looked directly into mine and said, "I think I brushed lightly over my reasons for caution when you asked me whether I had anyone special I was seeing, as you put it. My faith isn't a 'Sunday only' kind of religion, Kep. It's based on eternal principles that we try to observe constantly. It's one that encourages dating and marrying people of the same faith. So I've always dated guys who are members of my church. But that hasn't proven to get me close to anyone in a complete sort of way. I mean, I've never found someone I've been emotionally or physically attracted to. Not until you."

She tilted her head and gave me a radiant loving smile.

I took Jonathan's paper from her hand, and we held each other close, side by side. There were no words to express my happiness or my own feeling of completeness.

"Kep, I have to tell you that there are some people of my faith who don't live the standards they claim to be committed to. It isn't that they're hypocrites exactly. Some are just shallow or spiritually immature. They lack depth of understanding. Some don't care enough to ponder deeply about things very often, especially spiritual matters. Two or three guys I dated had weaknesses that would have been a turn-off for me if I had been attracted to them in the first place. So I've become cautious about who I want to spend time with and get to know.

"Now I'm in a flip-flop kind of trial because I don't want to give you up. At least not very *soon*," she added teasingly.

I hugged her closer to my side.

"So now that I've confessed that I'm attracted to you, I want you to see that I need you to be spiritually strong. Right after we met, I sensed that you have depth and sensitivity. I don't want to make you uncomfortable, Kep, but this does set you apart from a lot of males I've known. You're a thinker. You *do* ponder things. Not all women need that in a man, but I do. That part of you appeals to me a lot.

"Two things are certain, Kephart Stone: The first is that we have something special—something people might call 'love at first sight,' but I believe it goes deeper and farther *back* than that. The second thing is that I won't break my covenants or put my religion beneath you in priority. And I don't believe it's fair for you not to know that."

"But I *have* known that—or sensed it—since day one," I said. "And that part of you appeals to me. I haven't known any girls growing up around me that came anywhere near being like you, Jill. As I said before, I like what you radiate."

She smiled and nodded in a pensive way as she gazed at the shining bay in the distance.

"I know—I'm young yet," she said. "I have time to learn and to wait. The last thing I want to do is pressure you to give your heart over to the God that I know. That's unworkable. It's not the Savior's way or example—to force us or to drive us. He always led with loving patience. I'm so thankful you are self-disciplined enough to live the standards that you have accepted for yourself, Kep. But either one of us could be tempted and fall in a weak moment. We're both human. And Satan is real, just as God is real.

"I know you can't relate to God until you have special experiences or take certain steps that will lead you to truly know him. But you should know that the first step must be a prayer of faith—*acting* on a belief that God exists and that your prayer will be heard. It's like planting a seed. And your prayer must come from your heart, or it's not a prayer. To quote a poet, 'A prayer not from the heart shall ne'er from Earth depart.'"

"What do people do if they don't believe that God exists?" I asked.

"Well, Kep, I've read about a man who had that very problem. He prayed something like this: 'God, if you *do* exist, please show me somehow that it is so, and I will forever serve you and obey your commands.' God granted his prayer because it was sincere and the man's commitment was genuine. Heavenly Father knows our true intent. He won't withhold spiritual truths from us. He knows and loves each of us. God gave this man an undeniable sign, but it was given *after* he had demonstrated his little faith. Faith always comes first. It can't ever come as a *result* of a sign, but it can be *rewarded* by one."

I nodded my understanding as I reflected on the results of my own prayer during my time with Laura the previous evening.

"True prayers must spring from the heart. A prayer might express true sorrow for some wrongdoing or an appeal for forgiveness. If we ask for a particular thing, God's response may come in the form of a 'yes' or a 'no' or a 'not yet,' depending on what would serve our best interest in the end. I'm sure he always considers how his granting our request might affect others in time as well. It isn't unusual to find that we must wait for the desired answer or result. And a prayer of thanks is always in order."

Jill's countenance was bright with warmth and excitement. I had never seen this aspect of her character before—this fervor and enthusiasm for something she loved. Her eagerness to openly share her working knowledge of her religion touched me.

"The Lord's Prayer teaches us to pray to our Father in Heaven, as Jesus prayed in Gethsemane. He didn't pray to himself. He and Heavenly Father are separate beings, but they're one in purpose and in spirit. The Holy Ghost is one with them, and he's the third separate member of the trinity or Godhead.

Does what I'm saying make sense to you?"

"Definitely. I don't have any trouble accepting what you've said so far. But you've brought up the word 'purpose' twice now. You said Friday that you believe there's choice and *purpose* in everything, and you just defined the Godhead as being 'one in *purpose* and in spirit.'

"I feel like you're circling just above my problem of understanding how a loving God can find a good purpose in allowing heartbreaking events or situations to happen. Bessie Mae's daughter Gracie is just one recent example out of many that have troubled me. I see her as an innocent victim of something that could have been prevented if God hadn't been neglectful—if he'd really cared about her. How could her kind of losses serve her best interest? Maybe you're circling to land on an answer for me. I hope so."

"We're getting close to my giving you the big picture," Jill said. "Did my example of Pinocchio's being free to choose his own acts help explain why God doesn't often intervene when people injure others or ruin and destroy lives?"

"Yes, it helps. But it doesn't fit situations where *people* aren't the cause behind tragedy or suffering."

I was surprised to see that my words brought a smile from her.

"We'll get to the big picture yet today, Kep . . . unless God has other plans for our day together. I like the sense of peace I get when I'm willing to yield to his will. And I know *opposition* describes Satan's way, so that's a good reason for me not to push my own agenda. So far I've always been happier with God's will in the end."

"Which reminds me, Jill . . . there's something I want to share with you, too. It should make you happy to learn that I prayed a quick silent prayer last evening. It was my first, and it had to do with values and our relationship. I prayed in a difficult moment for me. It's private, but I can say that it was definitely sincere and from my heart, as you said a prayer must be. And it was answered immediately. So I guess you could say that I've already taken my first step."

Jill put her head on my shoulder and then turned and held me close. When I put my arms around her, she pressed her forehead at my throat. Seconds later I was startled to feel her shaking. Then I felt her tears on my neck.

CHAPTER 33

JILL'S tears confirmed both the strength of her religious convictions and the depth of her feelings for me. They made me more fully appreciate what she meant by enduring a "flip-flop" kind of trial. She was torn between fully complying with the accepted precepts of her faith and satisfying her emotional needs. I supposed patience and endurance were key virtues being tested—but not all. I felt that Laura's and Jill's wellsprings of tears both had similar aspects. But I knew that I was just beginning to "get wet" with insights into the complexities of womankind.

When Jill had regained her composure, and while resting her head on my shoulder, she said, "I know there are certain things you must keep secret, so I don't want to press you with some questions I have—mostly questions about your job."

She pointed to Jonathan's paper.

"Jonathan wrote that he was told I would know who I could share this paper with. You're the only one I know who would fulfill that prophecy. And he said that the Singing Tree came from another planet. Is there anything you can say that would answer some questions you might guess that I have because of what he wrote? I mean is there anything you can say that wouldn't break your pledge of secrecy?"

Jill's delicate approach to the question of aliens impressed and amazed me. It was a manifestation of the depths of her intelligence—a revelation of her discretion and wisdom. Over the past several days I could never have hoped to share my newly gained knowledge of other-world beings. I had felt painfully isolated from those close to me because of this. Now the one to whom I felt closest of all was opening a door to invite the telling of my experiences.

It was my turn to get emotional, but I quashed disclosing my feelings in order to present a manly image. (This had become an acquired habit resulting from my years of laboring alongside the kind of men who regarded tears as "sissy" stuff.) I had to pause and clear my throat before answering her.

"I have to start with a question of my own," I said. "Does your religion shut out any possibility that other inhabited worlds exist? I have to ask because I don't want to say anything that might fracture the foundation of your accepted belief system."

It surprised me to hear her laugh. But it was that kind of laugh that comes with relief and an easing of tension.

"Truth is truth, Kep. We believe that God has created worlds without end, and we have a firm conviction that by him, other worlds continually come into and pass out of existence somewhere in space and time. We have scriptures that declare this to be so."

I was shocked to hear this. Although I'd read scriptures to my mother for hours, I had never come across any that had revealed such a thing. But then, I'd always stuck mostly to the Biblical books and verses that consoled my mother and bolstered her faith—the ones she had become most familiar with as she grew up.

"It's apparent that you belong to a different church than the one that Oat and Selma attend. How is that so?"

"I want to skip the answer to that for now, Kep. All I want to say at this time is that my faith allows everyone the privilege to worship how, where, or what they may. Christ will never deny those who believe in him according to whatever limited knowledge they have acquired of him. But anyone who doesn't have a *fullness* of his Gospel—as my faith affirms it has—is being short-changed with respect to all the blessings the Gospel offers. God's love is unconditional. We never have to earn it. But we do have to earn most of his blessings by observing certain principles and obeying his laws. God's final judgments will be based on individual accountability.

"Let's get back to my first question, Kep."

"Okay. Can you accept the notion that our planet has been visited by humans from other worlds?"

"Yes. Without a doubt. But I have to add that my church has nothing directly to do with them, because none of them are messengers from Heavenly Father. Only angels can fill that role. And there are different kinds of angels, including ministering angels and destroying angels. Incidentally, angels don't have wings as they have been depicted as having, Kep. Except for their glory, they look just like us. I suppose other-world humans could be *watchers*. I would think they must have the freedom to travel wherever their technologies can take them."

"Did your experiences with Alleri and Azram give you a feeling that they might be human aliens?"

"That's one of the things that I'm confused about. They seemed to be humans of a different sort. Different in ways you'd link to an unidentifiable race."

"Jill, I know I can trust you to keep to yourself what I'm going to share with you. The most important thing that I must keep absolutely secret is my employer's identity and how I might personally associate with him. So I'm confident that it's okay if I tell you that during the past week, I have dealt with other-world humans. And so have you. By the way, you'll probably find comfort in knowing that my employer is *not* from another world."

Jill nodded her approval and gave me a smile.

"That *is* a comfort to know," she said.

"I should tell you that human aliens are observing us and have been living among us from time to time for countless centuries. They have their reasons, but, except in rare cases, they abide by a strict code of non-interference in our affairs. Lately—over the past several decades—they've seen that we may be getting too close to being a threat to extraterrestrial societies by gaining technologies we aren't spiritually ready to deal with. I've learned that what we do here somehow affects other distant galaxies. But if we should become bent on destroying *ourselves*, they are bound not to interfere.

"As Jonathan's friend Noaak says, other-world societies are aware of the destiny and purpose of this Earth. Most visitors are here to observe us and to fill missions known only to themselves. So your idea of their being 'watchers' may describe them very well. But I've been told there are human aliens that have fallen from their higher state of spiritual evolution. And as you might possibly know, there are many other kinds of *non*-human aliens that visit our world as well. Many don't keep hands off. I've just recently learned that I was a victim of some alien practices when I was five years old. One thing is certain: We're not alone."

"In some ways, we have *never* been alone," Jill said. "But now you're making me wonder about how you could have learned all these things in so little time."

All I can say is that what I thought was going to be a simple task proved to be much more than that. It quickly evolved into an assignment relating to the solving of a complex mystery, Jill. It's still not totally solved. It involves an unbelievably tiny object that has drawn our government's attention. So I guess I shouldn't tell you anything more about it for now, but I'll tell you what I can when I can."

She fell silent—absorbed in thought. I supposed she was reflecting on the events of the past few days. We still had much to share about our individual experiences and how we might interpret them.

Thoughts about the similarities of some of our experiences came to me.

"Jill, you didn't know it, but yesterday I spent a lot of time up in a tree myself. I was hiding and making observations. I witnessed cars stalling as yours did. And like you, I was telepathically influenced to do something I would never have normally done. I was also exposed to an overpowering scent that made me lose consciousness. I was transported in an unconscious state to a place I'd never been before. We both spent separate times in that secret place where you left your button. We were both put in danger for different reasons. It's weird, too, that we've both suffered temporary memory losses, even if at different times and for different reasons. And we've both decided separately to come here to the Singing Tree to meditate—to renew our minds and spirits."

"Wow! Considering all that, you'd think we have enough in common going for us to assure an enduring relationship," she said.

We laughed together. But her comment made my mind flash back to an unspoken question I had brushed aside earlier.

"Jill, you mentioned a while ago that you felt our relationship was deep and that you believed it went *back* farther than a typical 'love at first sight' sort of thing. Were you thinking that we had known each other *before* this present time—maybe in a different time dimension? What did you mean?"

"Now you're touching on the 'big picture,' Kep," she said.

"I'm ready."

"I've thought a lot about how much I want to give you at first. The picture has depth and detail that can only be shown a little at a time. For now I've decided to stick to a silhouette for you to ponder—something to attract your curiosity."

"You'll learn soon enough that I'm overly curious, Jill. So if you get me started on questioning and probing, you might regret it."

She shook her head and said, "Maybe you'll think I'm being selfish by withholding answers, but you'll soon see that my reasons make sense. I'd really love to give you the whole day—just to share and explain things to your satisfaction. The problem is we can't fully appreciate or get a lasting hold on anything that comes without personal effort. This definitely applies to gaining a deeply rooted knowledge of what we call 'truth.' Truth has its price."

I recalled that Shackleton had pointed out this same thing to me. It amazed and pleased me to hear Jill come up with the same observation.

"I'll be happy to have you help me paint in details a little at a time," I said. "But it will give me all the more desire to spend time with you, if that's possible."

"Kep, I don't want to disappoint you. But I'd rather you searched and delved into gathering the details yourself by first doing some detective work. I want you to learn on your own what church I belong to. I'll confirm your correct discovery. That should be a fun start—and I'm sure it won't take you very long. Then you can get the answers to your questions from those who are prepared to provide them. My church has no paid ministry, and our missionaries earn and pay their own way for the services they perform. It won't cost you anything more than some time and effort to find them. So now I've given you a clue or two, but I want this to be your own adventure."

Jill must have read my disappointment, even though I tried to hide it.

"Kep, I guess I *am* being selfish in a way. But as I explained before, I want you to come to know Christ yourself without my influencing you. And that's because I don't want to lose you—ever. And you know I'll always be praying for you to be guided. Just you pray too, please.

"Another thing I can do is testify whether your findings agree with what I know to be true according to what the Holy Spirit has confirmed for me, Kep. If you're getting the answers I've gotten, we're sure to stay on a path that draws us closer than we are now."

Jill's face was now shining with the confidence and radiance that had attracted me to her when we first met.

"Agreed," I said. And as I spoke, I felt a spark of enthusiasm to accept Jill's challenge and make my quest an adventure. Deep down I knew this was going to take me on the personal journey I needed to take if I was to become my 'best self'—to have my eyes reflect what Jill had sketched in them in her portrait of me.

"Don't expect a trouble-free investigation, Kep. You're going to meet with opposition, both within yourself and from those who are prejudiced against the church. I don't think there's ever been a church that has been so maligned and misjudged, or that's met with so much opposition. The more you embrace its precepts, the more you'll become one of Satan's favorite targets. The reason should become obvious when you ponder it.

"But before I outline the profile or silhouette for you, I want to share my favorite puzzle that I know you'll like, Kep. It's a kind of parable. Ready?"

"Always," I said.

"Three men checked in to a hotel where they had been frequent guests. The manager was at the desk. The price of the shared room was thirty dollars. As the men took an elevator up to their room, the manager decided he'd give them a discount for being loyal customers. He called the bellhop over and gave him five one-dollar bills to return to the men when he took their luggage up to their room.

"While riding the elevator up alone with the luggage, the bellhop decided he'd keep two of the five ones. After all, the five dollars couldn't be divided equally among the three men. Besides, they should be happy with getting *any* discount, and they wouldn't know the difference.

"So he gave each of the men a dollar back. Now each of the men had spent nine dollars instead of ten. Three times nine is twenty-seven. Right?"

"Right."

"And if you add the bellhop's two dollars to the twenty-seven, you get twenty-nine dollars. What happened to the other dollar?"

I blinked and shook my head.

"Wait a minute," I said. "I don't think we're looking at this from the right perspective."

"You're right, Kep. But what's wrong with the perspective?"

"You can't look at the problem from the point of view of the three guests. If you do, you leave out the information the bellhop could offer. Sure, they might *think* they each spent nine dollars, but if the truth were known, they'd see that they each spent twenty-five divided by three, or . . . uh . . . eight dollars and thirty-three cents—plus a penny split three ways. To be accurate, you need to have the whole picture."

"The 'big picture,' right, Kep?"

"Right," I said. I smiled my approval of Jill's example of a limited perspective that could twist falsity into a believable truth.

"That's great, Jill. I won't forget that one."

"What I especially like about this story is that it serves as a sort of parable," Jill said. "If we liken the bellhop to Satan, we see that he does as Satan does: He offers us only a part of what's true, and he makes us feel happy to have less than what we are rightfully entitled to. He cheats us out of all that God would give us if we only knew. By withholding the full truth, he distorts the true picture and misleads us.

"As you'll see, Kep, if we don't have the fully restored Gospel of Christ, we struggle with part-truths that can defeat us in this life. And the fully restored gospel is what my faith is all about.

So you can bet that you'll meet up with Satan in all of his cunning ways while you're on your personal quest. I'll be praying that you'll discuss things with the *Manager*," She assured me.

"I'm in the dark about what you mean when you say '*restored* gospel,' Jill."

"That will be an easy puzzle piece for you to find—that and the one called the 'great apostasy,'" she said. "Write them down, along with any other labels for pieces that you'll see you need. Just be patient. You'll have them all eventually—if you're in the right puzzle box. As I said, this should be a fun experience and a rewarding adventure for you. Besides, it will be a great way to find relief from all those pressing worldly activities and questions that your new job must bring up. Your life could use some balance, Kep."

"That's for sure," I said.

"Remember when I asked you how many seeds there were in an apple?"

"Yes. It really threw me off. Sorry, but I haven't had time to deal with it since. I have to admit that I couldn't see how it related to our discussion at the time."

"Well, Kep, if you think about it now, you'll come to see that there is no end to the number of seeds. Not so long as there's any fertile soil for at least one of the apple's seeds to germinate in. The tree that grows from any single seed produces infinitely more seeds in its apples. So there's no end to the seeds contained in an apple."

"Thanks. And I remember that you asked something about beginnings. What was it?"

"I asked, 'If something has no ending, can it have a beginning?' But then I gave you a clue from the words of a song. Do you remember how it went?"

"Yeah. That stuck with me. It made sense. You said, 'Nothing comes from nothing. Nothing ever could.'"

"So, you believe that's true?"

"Sure," I said.

"I was giving you clues to prepare you to receive the big picture, Kep. If you can accept what you have so far, I think you're ready."

"I feel *more* than ready, Jill."

CHAPTER 34

"THE big picture amounts to an eternal perspective of life," Jill said. "To deal with it, you have to accept the truth that we will live forever—that we will never have an ending. And along with that, you must see that we truly never had a beginning. My faith teaches that we have *always* existed as self-aware intelligences.

"We understand from the scriptures that when God formed us as his spirit children, we knew him and lived with him in a premortal state of being. We were perfectly defined spirits then living in a spirit world, but we were incomplete without physical bodies.

"We learn that when we arrived in this life, we became mortals with our spirits residing in bodies composed of earthly elements. But these elements—"

"Wait a second, Jill. Sorry to interrupt, but I have to share something with you—a personal experience that supports what you're saying.

"When Joel came to my rescue right after my accident, I had an out-of-body experience. I was actually looking down on him as he bent over me to check my vital signs. To him I appeared to be unconscious, but I was definitely outside of my body watching him as he examined me. So I *know* it's true that I'm a spirit first and a mortal being second. I can't deny that. I know what you just said is true, Jill."

She closed her eyes, put her head on my shoulder, and held me close. A simple truth had become verified for her. It was evident that she felt indescribable happiness.

"I guess that hard knock on my head was worth it," I said with a laugh. "I just hope I won't have to learn all truths in such traumatic ways."

Jill smiled and shook her head.

"Truth has its price, Kep, but it shouldn't be *that* costly—not unless you're a guy who has to learn everything the hard way."

She laughed her cheery laugh.

"The price is mostly a matter of devoting time to studying and pondering with a sincere desire to learn," she said. Just *reading* the words of scripture won't do. Humble prayer is always a part of the cost. You need to pray as you read so you can experience the confirmation that the Spirit brings to those who are honestly seeking truth. You'll know it when you receive it, Kep."

"But I don't have any scriptures, Jill. And I wouldn't know where to begin if I did."

"When you find the right church—Christ's *restored* church—you'll have an opportunity to get all you need of scriptures and guidance, Kep.

"Now . . . if you're ready, I'll continue from where I was before you told about your rare experience. You shared something I'll never forget, so I'm grateful for the interruption. It was worth it. You have a priceless testimony of what's real."

"I'm ready," I said. "But I'd like to talk with you more about reality another day."

"Where was I? Oh. I was talking about the elements that make up our bodies. Earthly elements are just various forms of organized energy. Would it make sense to say that everything physical is just programmed energy operating in a different sphere than the one we existed in before?"

"Sounds good to me," I said. "I like that.

"You'll like knowing that in the *next* sphere, we'll inherit perfected bodies. Mortality is just a blink in eternity. But our choices here decide our future real life story.

"In this world the energies that make up our bodies undergo constant change, and we are subjected to death.

"When we arrived here, all of our premortal experiences were hidden from us. We may catch flashing glimpses of our former life at times, especially while in childhood, but mostly all is forgotten. In this life we sometimes recognize others we knew in our premortal life. I believe that's where our relationship really started, Kep. We were closely connected there."

"Now that you've explained it that way, I have a strong feeling that what you're saying is true. I've always felt comfortable and complete when I'm with you. We must have shared a lot of that first life together, don't you think?"

"I feel certain of it, Kep.

"Well, Kephart Stone, I've explained where we came from, but I haven't said anything about *why* we're here, and I haven't touched on life after death yet. Do you think you're ready to go on, or do you already have your head filled with a list of questions to get us side-tracked?"

I laughed. "What makes you so sure I make lists of questions in my head?" I asked.

"Your face tells all, Kep. Your eyes move around a lot, and you blink when you're listening and questioning at the same time. You're easy to read. When you're just listening, you look right into my eyes. Your face is an open book. It's a book I have fun reading."

"Okay, Jill. Let me hear about why we're here. I'll keep my eyes right on you. No questions. No interruptions. I like watching your face for other reasons, though."

My comment brought the smile I wanted to see.

"Our bodies are one reason we're here. We're here to become complete beings with physical bodies. Along with that, we're here to learn how to master the natural appetites and passions that come with mortal bodies. And we're here to learn how to be good stewards over the bodies we've received—to take good care of them and to make good use of them. I know you'll have questions about that—one of them concerning Gracie. But I think you'll be able to accept what I have to offer later."

"That's okay, Jill. I can wait." "You know, I hadn't thought much about it before, but it's true that we spend a lot of this lifetime taking care of bodily needs—everything from growing and preparing foods to getting shelter. And then there's sleeping—a third of our lives, more or less, for that. I know, most of us don't grow our own food or make our own clothing, but we spend long hours working to *pay* for our basic physical needs.

"And now that I think about it, I see that we're the lucky ones. I'm thankful that I'm not found among the masses of people who are deprived and suffering and starving in the world. So I can't keep from asking what the big picture can possibly hold for them. What happiness are they supposed to get out of living in mortality?"

Jill's face revealed sympathetic understanding and compassion, while her words brought correction and hope.

"Kep, you've already lost the eternal perspective, or you wouldn't be asking those questions—the questions you said you weren't going to ask. But I intend to shine a light for you yet today and brighten your gloomy view.

"We're here to learn how to develop faith and to put it to practice. This involves learning where to place our faith and how to act on that faith. 'Faith without works is dead.' That's a scriptural verse. Maybe you've read it before, Kep. It's an important one to understand. Belief alone won't bring results or change lives.

"You can watch someone ride a bicycle all day. You *believe* you can ride one, too. But until you get on a bike and take your spills, you can never honestly say that you *know* how to ride a bike. Acting on your belief is practicing faith. Faith is a doing word.

"Once we really understand it, faith can eventually inspire us. It gives us spiritual growth and brings us success and comfort. In this world—this life—we have lots of trials to bring us in touch with a need for faith, as I'm sure you know."

"Well, I can see that it takes practice using faith if we're to become strong in it. I know it takes faith to be good at basketball. Making a clean shot takes concentration and faith. I couldn't participate much in the game while growing up, but I enjoyed shooting baskets on my own."

"Good, Kep. And we have to move on after each failure, or we'll fail our *test* of faith—which is another reason God designed for our being here. We're to be tested—to prove ourselves. Now, who do you think we're here to prove ourselves *to*, Kep?"

"To God? To ourselves?" I asked.

"Both, Kep. God already knows each of us and where our choices are going to lead us. He sees each mortal life from beginning to end. But don't make the mistake of thinking you have an inescapable destiny. Our destinies are the results of our choices. Christ died so that we could *choose* to live a plan of happiness that was known before we came here. If we couldn't choose to change, Jesus died for nothing. Repentance isn't just refraining from sin. It's a change of heart and mind attained by acting on faith in our Savior.

"I suppose I'm sounding preachy, Kep, but if you're to see the big picture, you have to understand that we each knew our weaknesses before we came here. And we each accepted the challenges we knew we'd have to face, even before we inherited this mortal sphere of our endless life. We all came here with imperfections of some sort.

"Being spiritually perfected is an eternal quest. It's a humbling process. Some people could see that it would be well for them to be tested here by physical handicaps—many of them very painful or discouraging. Others of us knew that we would best be challenged by difficult relationships. For some, there were self-serving or life-limiting inclinations to overcome. There's no end to the perfecting types of painful conditions or situations we saw that we might have to endure in mortality, but we knew that experiencing them would be worth it—for good reasons.

"Each of us must rediscover our *own* good reasons. Our discoveries will ultimately bring us joy. One thing is certain: We can't make our discoveries without relying on Christ's gift of guidance. That's why I especially like the statement shown beside that picture of Christ I told you about.

"Every choice has its consequence. But at mortality's end, each of us will be judged by the sum of our choices—by what we have become. And we'll wind up inheriting the mansion we built for ourselves while we were here in mortality."

"Why should we be judged later if God already knows where our choices have led us?" I asked.

"Good question, Kep! There's another aspect of mortality that you must see: Time. It's something we're all locked into while we're here. I don't want to go there just yet, but I'll give you some food for thought: In reality there's only 'now,' and we have to see around and beyond time. If you want to test my memory, Kep—as well as your own, because I'm not stopping for you to write this down—look up Ecclesiastes one, verse nine; and then three, verse fifteen. These are scriptures to ponder about time. Read and ponder them several times.

"Our actions here justify the judgments of God. We're here to prove ourselves to *ourselves*. We'll find that God's judgment is fair and just."

"Okay," I said. "What about the big differences in lengths of time people have to live? That can range from near zero to well over a hundred years. So what's to be fair about basing judgment on choices made when some have *no* time to make choices, while others get time to make millions of them?"

Jill was smiling her patient smile again. Her head was slightly tilted in her typical manner of regarding me. I loved what I read in her eyes.

"That's where *accountability* comes in, Kep. Heavenly Father only holds us accountable for what we have come to understand. So things like time here and mental capacity and chances for exposure to Gospel principles are just a few of the countless factors that enter into individual judgments. Besides that, final judgments aren't to come until after the millennium. Keep in mind that God knows and loves each of us and that he knows our inherent intents and desires. I know that sounds incomprehensible, but it's true."

She became silent. Glancing her way, I became aware of the reason. I caught my eyes blinking. Our instantly shared laughter put them to rest.

"Go back to the big picture, Kep. Before we were born, each of us was aware of our personal limitations and spiritual imperfections. We were given a vision of what this earthly visit would entail. We knew every purpose for our coming here. For some, getting a physical body was enough.

"Oh, Kep! I get so frustrated over not being able to share with you all that I'd like to. I want so much to answer your questions and to prepare you with the scriptures that keep popping into my mind to support what I'm telling you. But there just isn't time. I couldn't give you what I want to in days. Not in months. So right now my patience is being tested—that and my faith that you'll find all the answers you want. But I guess by now you know that every answer you get just invites another question . . . or more than a few questions. I'm certain you'll find great satisfaction in your quest, though. It's the perfect adventure for you."

I believed her. She had me motivated.

"I need to get my hands on a set of scriptures, Jill. I'll have to buy a Bible. Could you at least write down a few scriptures for me to study while I'm starting out on this mission?"

"I guess I can do that, Kep—without influencing your efforts in my personal favor. But one thing you'll want to make certain of is that you buy only a King James Version of the Bible. I'll tell you why if you can't see why when you compare it with other modern versions or interpretations."

Her urging me to stick to the King James Version of the Bible caused me to reflect on Shackleton's own choice of reference. I was surprised and struck with wonder. Was there more than coincidence in this? I was impressed by the similarities between Shackleton's and Jill's concepts of truths as well—both physical and spiritual views.

Jill had given me plenty to think about. I could see she was right: This was a never-ending project. Filling in the big-picture profile was something that could take more time than I had imagined. For me, there would be no end of questions. It was my nature to always come up with another question.

Something else had become evident for me as Jill was explaining the big-picture profile—the "eternal perspective," as she called it.

"Jill, I think you might have already answered my big question about Gracie's misfortune—that as well as my mother's tragedy and countless other events. But I'm going to have to give it some thought. I guess I've got enough of the big picture for a start."

I looked and found her studying my face.

"That's good, Kep. You've got all you need to get you going. I can see that the more I tell you, the more you'll be influenced by me personally, and I want to avoid that. Everyone has to walk their own road—to find their own reasons for being here and to get close to God in their own way. Not trying to do that is a great mistake that can lead to tragedy, or to a wasted life.

"Just remember that there is only one true God and one fully restored Gospel. Don't be deceived. Pray to be led by the Holy Spirit, and you'll be okay. It's the only way to go. God won't deny you the truth when you're sincere and faithful."

I hadn't forgotten what Shackleton had said about the Abiding Ones—that they had learned to enjoy their journey and not make their personal happiness dependent on achieving an objective. But now I began to wonder when I might qualify as being spiritually acceptable in Jill's eyes, if ever. What would it take to prove myself to *her*?

She stood up.

"I'll put Jonathan's paper back where I found it now," she said. "I can see that you're pondering things already. I'm sure I'll have some questions of my own for you to answer when you can, Kep."

I turned and reached for the tobacco can and knife.

As I handed them to Jill, I said, "I guess we can remember enough of what's on Jonathan's paper to discuss it if we need to."

Smiling wryly, she said, "I'm glad you said 'we,' Kep. Fortunately, I can remember *all* of it, but that doesn't mean you won't have something vital to contribute by filling in messages and meanings hidden between the lines. I need your questions and your insights. Sharing individual strengths and gifts brings a happy balance."

"But for the most part, I'm only able to see what *you* have to offer, Jill," I said. "I have trouble seeing that I have anything much to offer in our relationship except my love and my labor."

Jill let the knife and tobacco tin drop to the ground. She faced me, put her arms around me, and pulled me close.

"Has anyone ever told you that your self-esteem could use a boost, Kep?" she whispered.

I recalled that Shackleton had mentioned that I should regard myself more highly. My head nodded a "yes," but I kept silent.

"Kep . . . you don't really know who you are yet, do you? Before we can advance in self-mastery, we each have to be aware of our characteristic personal traits—both the desirable and undesirable. I know . . . this isn't an easy thing to do. A lot of people don't want to go there. They make excuses. It takes honest introspection without comparing ourselves to others. We have to accept ourselves as we presently are without being *content* with that. I believe too many people tend to beat themselves up—to judge and condemn themselves. The prideful ones condemn themselves, too, without knowing it at the time. Either way, self-condemners can't move on—they can't grow."

In a way, Jill was saying the same thing that Laura had said as she drove me to Shackleton's tower: When we compare ourselves to others, we always lose.

"Kep, I love you *now*, just as you are now," Jill said. There's no way you have to change before I'll accept you. I just want us to be on the same path."

Jill's words brought comfort and relief. Once again I was impressed by the power of words. In a flash I could see how quickly I'd strayed away from enjoying my journey. Without being aware of it, I had foolishly misjudged Jill's present acceptance of me. As a result, I had needlessly placed my happiness in a future that already existed.

Although I realized that I must accept the possibility that we might not continue to stay on the same path, Jill's words caused me to feel confident that we would. I was enjoying my journey again—partly because of my newly gained little bit of faith.

Jill's face was bright with enthusiasm as she said, "If we get on the right path *here*, we'll always be growing *there*. There is no static state of arrival. How boring would that be? God created us to have joy, Kep, and joy doesn't come if we just stand still in one place for very long. Life is movement involving every aspect of our being."

Face to face, we hugged each other more closely, but it soon became obvious that we were both headed onto a path of temptation that must be avoided if we were to stay within the bounds of our accepted standards. Jill was the first to pull away from our embrace, although I could sense that she inwardly struggled to let go.

Her breathing was rapid, and she looked away from me as she said, "I'd better make my climb back up—in more ways than one."

I was silent as I reached down once again for Jonathan's shiny can and knife.As Jill took them from me, we both smiled silently and shared another brief hug. Our lips came close, but we dared not kiss—not yet. Somehow we each sensed the limits of our self-control.

* * *

Jill reached for a low branch of the Singing Tree and began her ascent.

For a time, as I stood alone, my thoughts remained centered on her impelling and inspiring faith. Then my roving eyes fell upon the white picket fence that enclosed Jesse's grave. I was drawn to it. Once there, I began to wonder what Jesse was possibly experiencing, as well as what might be in store for me in my own post-mortal life. It didn't take long to see that for me this was a pointless and futile mental excursion—to imagine and speculate about any individual's life after death.

Maybe Jill could fill me in on the potential realities of our next sphere of life in general, but I wasn't ready to go there yet. For the present, the best I could do was live in the present and experience all that it had to offer—which was plenty. And obviously *now* would always be *now*.

Presently my stellar ring insisted that I feel its presence. Good timing. In a few seconds my head was cleared of everything but Shackleton's distinctive voice.

"Hello, Kephart! I feel quite confident that your mind would benefit from a clarifying conversation—one that is long overdue. Would you be disposed at this time to accept an invitation to meet with me at my home this evening at nine o'clock? Refreshments are in order, of course. Not that you need such enticements, but I find them to be rather pacifying and conducive to harmonious communications. There is much that needs to be explained, and you need to be informed about all that remains of our partly solved mystery. What say?"

I dreaded the thought of having to account for the missing alien artifact—which I couldn't do with any certainty. But maybe I didn't have all the pieces of the puzzle. Maybe Shackleton could shed some light on the matter himself. Relief was just a meeting away.

"Nothing could keep me away! I welcome the chance to get answers to all the questions that are plaguing me, Shackleton. Well . . . at least to some of them."

"Splendid! I'm certain that you won't mind sharing our time together with a third party, Kephart. Tell me in all honesty if it isn't so. Please."

Apprehension swept over me.

"Who would that be?" I asked. "Laura? Graham Walker? Can you prepare me by telling me who it is?"

Shackleton chuckled as he said, "A mutual friend, Kephart. His name is Bogart."

At that moment Jill came up behind me and put her hand on my shoulder. She was apparently troubled on finding me laughing as I stood looking at Jesse's grave site. At first I was at a loss to explain my behavior. But her questioning look deserved *some* answer.

I turned and took her hand in mine as I said, "Jill, you told me that God created us to have joy. You might be surprised and pleased to know that I was living in a happy 'now.' And from what I've learned from you today, I can't see that graves must always be visited in sorrow. Isn't it possible that Jesse is experiencing happiness where he lives now? Isn't joy to be had in our next sphere of everlasting life?"

In answer, Jill wrapped her arms around my neck and kissed me on the cheek.

CHAPTER 35

JILL took my hand and led me downhill along the trail we had each climbed up earlier. Evidently, she wanted to leave the Singing Tree behind now and accomplish an errand she had in mind. I didn't question her act or voice any curiosity. I felt like walking and talking myself. I felt certain that Jill had no doubt that her abduction and detainment were a result of my association with Shackleton and that he was linked with human aliens. I knew she accepted Laura's explanation that she was being kept out of sight for her personal safety.

Wanting to dispel any doubts she might have about my secretive involvements with Shackleton, I said, "There are some things I can tell you about my employer, Jill, and this seems to be a good time to share them with you.

"I may have told you some of this before, but I want you to understand that he's dedicated to redirecting the minds and motives of those who have become—or who are about to become—victims of their misguided thoughts or attracted evils. At first I thought him to be manipulative, but I'm learning this isn't so. It's not his true nature.

"Because he's clairvoyant, he hopes to prevent certain unhappy events he envisions from occurring. He's returned missing people to their families when attempts by others have failed. His mission in life is to influence happy futures without taking away a person's freedom to choose. You could say that he works from the inside out. Just like you, he wants people to make choices that will get them on a path that leads away from unhappiness—or even from tragedy. I'm just now finding this to be a very challenging thing to be involved in. Any thoughts?"

Jill was silent for a time. Then she said, "One of the best ways to experience joy is to *give* joy, Kep. Your boss must be a happy man. Is he?"

"I think he hides great sorrow while maintaining a sense of humor and a positive outlook," I said. "He's suffered a tragedy that I can't truly say he brought on himself. He might have attracted it in some way. It might have something to do with his paranormal gifts, but I have no way to rightly judge the cause. To me, he's a mystery in himself. One person closely associated with him finds him to be unknowable and unpredictable—but absolutely worthy of trust and respect. He's already led me to see some flawed notions and practices I've had that have put my future happiness at risk. And he's taught me in kind ways. He made a point of telling me that I need to regard myself more highly."

Jill looked my way and asked, "Can you think of anything that would have caused you to have a low opinion of yourself, Kep? Now that you have a memory of your past, can you share what you've been doing since your mother died? Have you been a bad boy?"

I laughed. Jill's smile and twinkling eyes made me feel at ease. I decided to spill out my recent history for her.

"Well, my mother died not long after I graduated from high school. I was working in an ore-processing mill below town at the time. Part of our income source had been my mother's disability check each month. With my mother's passing, that was lost.

"For several years we had lived in an apartment behind a clothing store, but I couldn't afford to stay there on just my wages alone. The woman who owned the store was kind and had looked in on my mother often while I was away working. But I knew very few people in my hometown that I could call 'friends,' and most of them were much older. Truthfully, the only thing that appealed to me about my hometown was its beautiful mountainous setting.

"I had wanted to attend college using a one-year scholarship I got when I graduated from high school, but that would mean moving sixty-five miles away. While my mother was alive, that was out of the question. Her death brought newly found freedom, but I had debts to pay off before I could begin college. So I changed jobs and began working underground at a major gold-mining operation higher up in the mountains.

"My new home then was a bunkhouse where I lived with a variety of drifters from all places imaginable. Most of the men spent their weekends drinking and hooking up with easy women in town—especially after paydays. I learned to like most of the guys. They all had their good points. Most of them were lonely men in their thirties, forties, and fifties with no family ties. I was the youngest of the bunch.

"I had no reason to go to town very often. The mine had a shuttle bus. Every two weeks, I'd cash my paycheck and exchange books at the library. While growing up, I had seen so much drunkenness and immorality that I shunned it. So I didn't stick with the guys I rode to town with. Besides, I was earning my highest wage ever, and I was determined to wipe out my debts and save all I could.

"The bunkhouse was my home for about fourteen months. I lived and ate at the mine. I read a lot and kept mostly to myself. For entertainment, I enjoyed playing pool with some of the miners. I guess I've always been comfortable being a loner, but I've never been unsociable. I've always liked people and enjoyed studying them and listening to them. For some strange reason, folks just open up and spill out their life stories to me—even total strangers. So my mind has been mainly directed away from myself. Could that have anything to do with how I regard myself, do you think?"

"Maybe, Kep. Maybe you've been measuring yourself unfavorably without knowing it. Keep going. Tell me more."

Along with her words, Jill's eyes were encouraging me. It felt good to have my memory back—to accept her invitation and retrace my past a bit.

"I didn't have a car, so, after wiping out my debts, I was able to save most of my earnings. That was a good thing then. But not ever having had a car and always being in debt might have put my self-esteem account in the red while I was in my late teens. I'd taken a Driver's Ed course in high school. The school had owned an old four-door sedan that was available for student drivers to get practical experience. I got a Colorado driver license using a borrowed vehicle for my test. Later on, the license made it possible for me to drive a mine-owned truck for a time. Maybe my being poor affected my self- image, but it shouldn't have.

"Maybe I *had* thought of myself as a loser. I don't know. I do know that my former female classmates were mostly attracted to the rebel-type guys who lived on the edge and had a car to drive.

"In August of last year I took a bus to Grand Junction, Colorado, where I found two part-time jobs—one in a fast-food place and the other in a book shop. My college life began there as a probationary student, because I'd graduated from an unaccredited high school with some subject deficiencies.

"I settled into an upstairs bedroom of a young preacher's house. He was newly married and had a non-denominational congregation. I spotted his rental notice on the bulletin board in the student union building just after he'd put it up. It was a lucky find because I could afford to rent the room on my two minimum-wage incomes. Then, too, my first college term began with a full credit load, so that put a limit on my availability for work."

"Did you have a career goal in mind early-on then, Kep?"

"Not really. All I knew was that I didn't want to be a laborer all my life. Communications and journalism appealed to me. Maybe philosophy. I've always had a broad range of interests and a hunger for learning. My parents were both well educated. I always sensed that they had expectations of me. But then, I didn't graduate from high school until a month after I turned nineteen. I started grade school later than most kids.

"Right after Christmas vacation, I started having a lot of pain in my abdomen. Then I got a head cold, and when I took some cold medicine, I got very sick and began vomiting a lot. Shortly after, while I was walking down a hallway between classes, I passed out and collapsed. I woke up in a hospital and was told I needed emergency surgery for a ruptured appendix.

"I had no medical insurance. The preacher's congregation took up a collection and paid my medical expenses. I paid what I could spare from my savings, but I considered myself to be indebted to the church members. Anyway, by the time I had recovered, I had no choice but to withdraw from college. When I learned how weak I was and how slim my chances were for finding a good job in Grand Junction, I decided to take a bus to the big city of Seattle. I needed to find a way to pay off my debt and start all over again. By then I guess I *was* thinking of myself as a loser."

"It's easy to see why, Kep. But you know that none of what happened was really in your control. It's obvious that most people would have been quite discouraged under those circumstances. You can't point a finger at yourself and put yourself down because of adversities like that."

"Didn't you say that our experiences are a result of our choices, Jill?"

"Mostly, yes. But don't forget that before we came here, we *chose* to go through many experiences that would work best to help us grow and reach our highest potential here in mortality—spiritually speaking. So in the eternal perspective of our endless lives, Heavenly Father gave each of us certain visions, and we made some critical choices *before* we arrived on the mortal scene."

"I'll have to think about that, Jill. It's not easy to adjust to the big picture right off, is it?"

Jill nodded as she studied my face. "Keep going, Kep," she said.

"There isn't much more to tell. Seattle is a wonderful city. I love it. But for me, with my background, it was a bit overwhelming to throw myself into finding both a job and a place to live there in a short time, especially without a car. Don't ask me why, but I took a bus to Mount Vernon to look into the possibility of attending a community college there, once I could establish a reliable income. I found two jobs fairly fast. One was stocking shelves at night in a Safeway store, and the other was working in a bicycle shop. Even though I got shorted on sleep, I enjoyed my jobs and got along well with my employers and co-workers. And I built my own bike for cheap transportation."

"Where did you live?" Jill asked.

I shook my head. Since the day my memory had returned, the Whipple farmhouse still dominated any thought associated with "home." It had never occurred to me that I still had a key to my former short-term residence in Mount Vernon. I suddenly remembered a few personal belongings there—and some unpaid rent.

"Thanks for reminding me, Jill. I owe some rent on a one-room cabin in back of a landscaper's home. I know how to find it, and I need to follow up on that. The only place I presently think of as home is the Whipple place—*your* place with *your* parents.

"Tell me more about your own parents," Jill said. "What were they like?"

At first I hesitated to describe my parents, and the realization of this surprised me. However, I couldn't think of any reason not to, so I dropped back into the family life of my single-digit years as a youth. I'd crowded this phase of my life out of my mind. It had both happy and unhappy aspects to it. However, it was a happier life while my older sister was living at home. She married and left us when she was just twenty.

"My father was a mining engineer and an expert mineralogist who could identify all kinds of minerals. The one thing I got from my dad was a love of nature. He taught me how to identify all kinds of birds, and he had me learn the names of most wild flowers and trees found in the Rockies. He knew a lot about the habits and habitats of wild creatures.

"Sometimes his treasure hunting kept him away from home for a week or more. He always packed a loaded pistol when he was away from civilization to do his prospecting. When I was just six years old, he taught me how to shoot his forty-four revolver. Once, I came within an inch of blowing a hole in my foot.

"When I was younger, before I could actually work at mining, he always had me tag along behind him to tote sample bags and tools for prospecting. Sometimes I felt more like his pack mule than his son. Because he saw much of the natural world as being unpredictable, he wasn't overly protective. He took things as they came.

"He seldom openly demonstrated affection, but I knew he cared about me. He definitely had no interest in religion. It seemed his god was nature itself. Ironically, he was killed by a rock avalanche. I was almost fourteen at the time."

"And your mother?"

"She was a registered nurse, but I think of her more often as a gifted violinist. My dad had her care for injured miners when we lived far from town. That was before I started grade school.

"There were times when we lived in a tent-house and packed our water in pails and cooked on wood fires. We ate a lot of canned foods then, and we considered fish or wild game to be a treat. So my mother adapted to all kinds of deprivations and hardships. I can see now that there was nothing secure for her to hold on to, except her faith in God. "I'd describe her as being a romantic who loved good music and the fine arts, but except for playing her violin, I don't remember her having a chance to fulfill her interests in these things. She read romantic novels. Once I heard her say that she felt like a 'ragpicker.' I'm sure that whatever dreams she had never materialized.

"I don't remember my dad ever taking her away to a town of any size for a nice dinner—just to be alone together for a time. I know she loved to go on a drive when that was possible, which wasn't often, because we'd have to drive my grandfather's car. And then I was always with them. So what does that tell you?

"I mostly visualize her doing housework like cleaning, doing laundry, ironing clothes, and cooking. I had always worked at before- and after-school jobs, but I helped out when I could by doing dishes, cutting kindling, and doing other chores. My dad didn't involve himself in those things."

"You said that you felt your parents had expectations of you, Kep. What kinds of expectations do you mean?"

"Well, to put it simply, I always felt that my mother believed I could succeed at anything worthwhile or significant—that I had it in me to become whatever I aspired to be. But she never defined any particular role or position that she might have hoped for me to attain. I guess she left that part up to me.

"My dad always made it pretty much clear to me that I should be self-reliant—and not just by knowing how to survive in the wilderness. Even at a young age I sensed that success and financial wealth were synonymous with him. I knew that he expected me to be a 'success,' as he interpreted the meaning of that word.

"He and my grandfather and my uncle were all treasure-seekers in a sense. They wanted to get rich quick. I suppose that's why gold mining appealed so much to all three of them. They enjoyed some successes, but more often, they met with serious losses.

"Now that you've got me thinking about it, Jill, I believe one of my greatest frustrations has been that no matter how hard I've worked, I've always come up short when it came to providing material things, especially for my mother as I saw and felt her needs. Maybe that's why I told you what I did about being able to contribute only my labor and my love in our relationship. That's the way it's always been for me in the past."

"So do you think you can reshape your self-concept, now that you realize how the unfavorable one was formed? You know that you've been led to a whole new world of possibilities, Kep. And I personally feel this is so because of the traits that your mother saw in you. I can see many of these traits, but I don't want to give you an inflated view of yourself . . . so I'm not going to name them."

Jill gave me a teasing glance and a playful smile.

"Kep, I love you the way you are. Besides, more humility always adds to a person's good looks. Who knows? I might even see you at your 'best self' someday."

Our shared laughter brought us to a welcome bend in our shared inner road.

CHAPTER 36

WHEN we reached the VW bus, I said, "What's up? I see you must have some place you want to go—something you need to do."

"So much has happened in the last twenty-four hours, Kep. I forgot that I'm to deliver a personality profile to one of my clients today. The analysis is done. I just need to get it delivered before four thirty. So I need to pick up my car at Bessie Mae's place. After that, we'll have more time together. I'll feel better having my mind free of that obligation."

"Can we do lunch first?" I asked. "I have a place in mind. Have you ever been to The Simple Pleasure restaurant?"

"I know where it is, but I've never eaten there. I've heard it's very nice, but it's a pricey place, Kep. Are you sure you want to spend the kind of money it must cost to go there?"

"You just said I've been led to a new world of possibilities, and that's true. But all I want to say about my new world right now is that it's opened up financial doors for me that I'd never imagined seeing open in my lifetime. Trust me. I can and *want* to spend the money, Jill."

"Then could you take me to my place to get the analysis papers? You might have to wait a little while for me to go over the profile with my client, but if we could get that over with before having lunch, I'd enjoy it all the more."

"Consider it done. I'm sure I can convince my stomach that the wait will be well worth the sacrifice."

When I unlocked and opened the door to the VW bus, I noticed Bessie Mae's little box of diary poems on the front floor. Jill saw it too. She handed it to me as she got seated.

"Please help me remember to give this to Bessie Mae when we go there for my car," she said.

"That will be easier to do if we read a few limericks as we travel," I said. "That box is irreplaceable, Jill. I'll feel better when it's back in her hands. But we owe it to her to read more of her poems before we return it to her, don't you think?"

Jill smiled and nodded her agreement.

After we sneaked quietly past the Whipple farm entrance, Jill began to pull out cards and read them to me. As she read, we began to see an invisible part of Bessie Mae—a vital part of her that no one could readily see if they were to read only her bodily form and features. Her words reflected intelligence and humor, but they also revealed a depth that wasn't visibly evident. I could see how foolish I'd often been to judge people quickly on the basis of observed manners or appearance. It was obviously one of my weaknesses. I inwardly resolved to work hard at correcting that tendency. I'd be much happier if I whipped it.

Jill read one limerick that stuck with me. It pointed out a need that I could easily satisfy for Bessie Mae this very day. And it would make us both happy if I fulfilled it.

I loves my telephone.
It helps me be alone.
I sits me up,
Sips from my cup,
And listens to the tone.

I said, "You know, Jill, there's little chance that we can spend meaningful time with Bessie Mae in person on a regular basis, but we could *phone* her often enough to make a difference in her lonely life. All it would take is keeping her phone alive. Don't you think Selma would give her a call once in a while as well?"

"I'm sure she would—especially if she were aware of just how terribly lonely Bessie Mae is."

"Well, today for sure, 'I finds the cure,'" I said.

* * *

While Jill was going over things with her client, I found a phone directory and looked up both Bessie's phone number and the address of the local telephone company. I had no trouble getting the phone company to accept the money needed to pay the Pottses' bills up to a year in advance. I stuck the receipt in the little red-and-brown recipe box.

There was one more errand I wanted to perform, but it would have to wait. I didn't want to find Jill waiting for me, so I hurried back for her. Regardless, I found her waiting just the same. She came up to my door as I rolled down the van window.

"Don't look so apologetic, Kep. I haven't been out here more than a couple of minutes. My client is interviewing another prospective employee and getting more handwriting samples to discuss with me. If anyone needs to apologize, it's me. I might need another half hour here before we can eat. Is there anything else you might find to do but sit out here and wait?"

"That there is, Jill. I'm never without something to do. And the timing for my next errand should match perfectly with yours."

We gave each other a parting smile and a hand squeeze.

My next destination was a cell-phone kiosk in the mall, where I bought a phone for Jill just like the one Bick gave me, chargers and all. By the time I had the phone activated and her account set up in my name, I found myself rushing back to prevent my finding her waiting again. I was thankful to find her still inside her client's office. I was also thankful that *I* would be the one to take the patience test, not her. So I occupied myself with resisting impatience—and quashing curiosity.

I did okay with "patience," but not with "curiosity." My mind went back and forth over the various unknowns connected with the mystery in which Shackleton had involved me. I found myself increasingly dwelling on the identities of Koziol's ally and Dan Crotty's girlfriend. How could I learn who they were? How could Crotty have learned about the alien artifact in the first place—except through his friend? How could she have learned about it?

Frustrated by these dead-end mental excursions, I began reflecting on the eternal perspective Jill had shared with me and the spiritual "adventure" she had so enthusiastically challenged me to go on. Suddenly my mind put two pieces of her conversation together with a recent personal observation: Jill had recalled previously meeting Laura in a church-member bookstore. Apparently, they each now owned pictures of Christ with the statement about "choice" that I had seen on Laura's apartment wall. There just might be a chance they belonged to the same church—maybe attending at different times. If so, Laura could identify the church. Jill would certainly be surprised if I were to have completed that first piece of detective work during the past thirty-five minutes.

I gave my ring a twist and thought Laura's name. No response.

After a second futile attempt, I gave up without leaving a message. I knew Laura needed a rest, so I decided not to press her with more of my incessant questioning.

* * *

By the time Jill finished her business and we got to The Simple Pleasure, our "lunch" proved to be dinner. The menu had changed at 4:00. Jill ordered baked wild salmon. I had steak and lobster. The cuisine was an *exquisite* pleasure, one well worth its price.

Our "date" was a *social* pleasure I had never known in my lifetime. Much of our conversation centered on a surprisingly fascinating topic: handwriting analysis. Jill explained many of its aspects as we ate. This was a welcome change of focus. It was good for my mental health to learn without excessive questioning while Jill reviewed all the procedures for analyzing.

We spent nearly two hours just interacting in fun—something I'd been deprived of for time out of mind. I had forgotten what it was like to have fun with a friend. I was becoming sharply aware of just how much I'd become a loner during the past six years of my life. But, for me, Jill was more than a friend. She was a gift of happiness.

I was just finishing a dessert of crème brûlée when my ring gave its fiery signal. Jill was slowly savoring her dish of chocolate mousse.

I stood up.

"I'll be back soon," I said.

Excusing myself, I left our table to search for a restroom.

Laura's voice came into my head.

"Do you have a few minutes just to listen, Kep? There are some things I need to tell you."

"Sure. Go ahead, Laura."

"I'm going away for a while. I have to work out some things that have been . . . troubling me. My times with you in person and on the ring have opened my eyes. I've become sorely aware of all that's missing in my life. But it isn't just that. I knew what was missing before . . . before I met you."

By the modulation stresses in Laura's worded thoughts, I could sense strong emotion.

"I've come to care for you more than I should, Kep. And I've led Shackleton to depend on me more than is good for . . . for me. To be truthful, I've always known that Shackleton really does need someone he can trust to be his confidante and to perform his many errands. I knew that when I made my choice to serve him. Now I can't decide whether I'm being foolish or selfish to have other thoughts on the matter. He needs both of us, Kep. And now I'm suffering the stress of serving someone I've loved hopelessly, while at the same time containing my feelings for someone who makes me more keenly aware of what I'm being denied. Maybe I'm just overly tired. This has all happened too fast.

"Because of my troubled states of mind and emotions, I've placed you in some dangers that might have been prevented. I feel terrible about this, Kep. So I don't know if I can trust my ability to perform as I should. At the time I met Ginger—Letha's friend—I saw something that could have steered Shackleton in a different direction. I just recalled this vital clue—just minutes ago. It came to me when I was using a special feature of my ring.

"Our rings have certain powers that I can't talk about, Kep. Not until Shackleton gives me permission to tell you. It might be that he'll want to tell you himself, or maybe not at all. But for now I have to keep quiet. What I do know is very limited compared to what Shackleton knows, but it could be a great help to you when you're documenting this case.

"My immediate problem is that I'm not able to communicate with Shackleton. He's very involved and not answering my ring calls. I can understand why. But I'm put in a position of having to ask you to take care of an assignment he gave me. It's an easy task, but it needs to be accomplished before six o'clock, and I'm too far away to take care of it by then."

"Spill it, Laura."

"The hearing aid is definitely Dan Crotty's, but it was either water damaged, or it needs a new battery. Graham Walker couldn't effectively communicate with Dan. And there's certainly not a chance that there could be any productive interaction between Dan, being deaf, and Shackleton, being sightless. Shackleton desperately needs to get some information from Dan before the day is over. Graham can't keep Dan's location a secret much longer. He's—"

"Then Dan Crotty isn't in custody yet?" I interrupted.

"Not officially. But he isn't going anywhere either. I can't tell you any more than that for now, Kep. I'm leaving that and more explaining up to Shackleton while I take time out.

"I left the hearing aid at a place called Sounds of Life to be restored and tested. It's on—"

"I know where it's located, Laura. Is the hearing aid working now? Is it ready to be picked up?"

"Yes."

"Where shall I deliver it?"

"To Graham and Shackleton at The Three-Cornered Orange. Ask for Mr. Gray."

"What's the code name for the day?"

"Arthur. Can you do this, Kep? I'm so sorry to have to ask—but . . ."

"Consider it done, Laura. But if I need to call you, please respond."

"You're the only person I'll be responding to, Kep. Thank you . . . thank you . . . so much."

"You have a 'thank you' coming from me, Laura. Your birthday gifts were more appreciated than you can guess. The money gift was a bit over the top. But it did come in handy when I least expected to need it. Most of it's still to think about . . . I mean what I might spend it on. I'm not used to shopping for myself. The clothes fit perfectly. I'm wearing them as I speak.

"How long do you expect to be gone, Laura? Were you preparing me to take over some of your assigned tasks when you gave me clues on how to get into the secret room? I found my way into it, Laura—with Bogart's help. I can't guess why you wanted me to find it. Does Shackleton know about what you did? Did he ask you to give me the clues about how to access the room? Are you going to—"

"Oh, Kep! You are a never-ending questionnaire! The answer to your first question is, 'I'm not sure,' and I'll just answer the others by saying that I had my personal selfish reasons for leading you to the Compass Room and for you learning what you did.

"I have to make some spiritual and emotional adjustments. I've been neglecting to nurture myself in spiritual ways by letting my emotional needs rule me. And I can't be what Shackleton needs me to be for him if I let go of commitments I've made to God. I need the strengths God offers. So I owe you my thanks, too, for being strong last evening. It helped me regain my perspective. You've even helped me see some things by just listening to me during this brief time together on the ring. You're more good for me than you are bad for me, Kep. So you can know I'll be back."

"Since you've mentioned your religious commitments, do you mind telling me what church you belong to? Do you and Jill attend the same church? Just curious, Laura."

"We belong to the same church, but we attend at different locations, Kep. So we haven't found occasion to associate with each other. Our church is the same throughout the entire world."

She gave me the name of the church, but Shackleton has asked that I not disclose it in my writings. He encourages all who read these chronicles to be prayerful and to keep an open mind and heart as they search out truths without being influenced by the world. That's all he'll let me say. As I record this episode, I know nothing about Shackleton's religious associations, if any. But his views align closely with Jill's.

"Thanks, Laura. I'd best get going on the hearing-aid thing now. We'll talk when you're ready."

I let her go.

Jill was patiently waiting for me.

As we left the restaurant, I said, "While I was away from you, I received a call and a brief assignment. It's something we can do together before I take you to your car. I hope you don't mind. I'll have to pick up a hearing aid a few blocks from here and deliver it to Mr. G. It's a strange coincidence, but he's right here with a county detective in a private area of The Simple Pleasure. This shouldn't take long."

"Why would I mind, Kep? We'll still have some time together on the road. I'm going to have to spend some time this evening working, though. So I hope *you* won't be disappointed."

"The only thing that would disappoint me is your not accepting a gift I bought you. And I have another gift of sorts for you—one that you'll accept without question. But I'll save them back until I make my delivery. I have just enough time to pick up that hearing aid during company business hours. I'm really going to have to scoot, Jill."

CHAPTER 37

AFTER being admitted to the Three-Cornered Orange, I knocked on the door to Shackleton's assigned private room. Graham Walker opened it. He gave me a warm smile, shook my hand, and took the hearing aid package from me with mingled expressions of approval and relief. I had finished my errand just in time. We would have all been extremely disappointed if I hadn't.

Shackleton remained seated as he turned my way to say, "Splendid, Kephart! Don't neglect to put the cost of restoring this item on your expense account. Please. And, of course, I shall have no problem remembering to give you an additional bonus for your excellent performances of the past two days. You have been most indispensable. We shall meet as agreed at nine o'clock this evening."

As Shackleton smiled and waved his good-bye, Graham shook my hand a second time and closed the door. But I left with a sinking feeling that I had in reality failed miserably and that I was undeserving of all the praise expressed by Shackleton. So far as I knew, I hadn't been successful at accomplishing the most vital task of all. I had nothing of worth to show for my effort. The alien artifact had been replaced with a stone. And I dreaded dealing with that portion of my meeting time with Shackleton.

I was now more sharply aware of how much Laura

contributed to Shackleton's success. And the true weight of my own responsibilities and performances settled heavily upon me. But such a small act as delivering a hearing aid in good time proved that great things can evolve from small performances (as you will see later).

* * *

Since there was no big rush to get to Bessie Mae's place, I drove to Boulevard Park to enjoy the view of the bay with Jill and to relax. I thought it would be a good place to give her the cell phone so she could practice using it. And I needed to familiarize myself with my own cell phone as well. It proved to be another fun time.

When I pulled up the box from the back floor of the bus, it appeared that I was going after my own box—the one in which Jill had delivered her note to me. But when I had her pull out the phone and turn it on, she was quite surprised to see her name appear on the little screen.

With raised eyebrows, she gave me a questioning look, followed by one of disbelief.

"You can't be telling me you bought this for *me* today. Are you? Are you giving me my own cell phone, or are you loaning this for me to use? Either way, it's too much, Kep. I know cell phones have monthly fees, so there's more expense involved than the purchase, if you bought it as a gift."

"It's yours, Jill. And the account is in my name. So just be happy that we can communicate and share times we'd otherwise be missing. If you refuse to accept it, I won't tell you about another surprise I have for you. And it didn't cost me a penny."

Jill tilted her head in her typical way and looked at me with blinking eyes.

"Then you're making this an 'all or nothing at all' thing. Is that right?" she said.

"Right."

"You said you could *tell* me about the other surprise. It isn't something you will try to put into my hands, then?"

"No. I can only put it into your head. It can bring you happy thoughts. So it shouldn't be too hard to accept."

Suddenly, Jill opened her door and ran over to a grassy area. Easing herself down onto the lawn, she looked over at me and held up her cell phone. Pointing to it and smiling, she spoke a voiceless "call me."

When her phone rang, Jill's face wrinkled with displeasure.

Flipping it open, she said, "I'm simply going to love having this phone, Kep, but am I stuck with the ringtone music? It's more than weird."

"You're not stuck with anything weird except me," I said. "No problem with changing the incoming-call music. You can play with the ring choices until you find something you like. Are you ready to accept your other surprise, then? I can only assume you'll be keeping the gift in your hand. Is your head ready?"

"Ready," she said.

She waved at me and smiled her happiness. I could only hope that Laura had been right about the church she named.

When I spoke the name of the church into my cell phone, Jill sprang to her feet and ran back to the bus. She nearly dropped her phone as she opened my door to hug my neck.

"It looks like I'm not so bad at detective work after all," I said as I pulled her close.

"How did you ever learn that? How could you have possibly learned that in so little time?" she asked.

"I'll give you just one clue," I said. "I had a picture of Christ in my mind."

"Please keep it there, Kep, so we can both be on the same path."

* * *

After we'd spent another twenty-five minutes learning all we could about the basic features of our cell phones and storing numbers in them, Jill sighed heavily.

"I guess we'd best get going to Bessie Mae's place, Kep," she said.

"I have a surprise for her too," I said. "You should be able to learn what that is soon enough. We can share some more of her diary cards as we go."

Once again Jill picked up Bessie Mae's box of limericks. When she opened it, she couldn't help but notice the receipt for Bessie's paid-in-advance phone billings. She shook her head as she scanned it.

"Oh, Kep! I see you're going to have a lot of joy coming to you in this life. Even when I consider giving service or time, I have to admit that you should be okay with giving just your 'labor and your love,' as you put it. If we're unselfish, that's all that any of us are really giving in one form or another, isn't it?"

I confess that my self-esteem climbed up a notch when Jill spoke those words. Once again, words had done their magic.

Just as I backed the VW bus out of our parking space, my cell phone rang. Seeing that Jill wasn't the one calling, I came to a stop before I flipped it open. When I answered, I was surprised to hear Selma's voice.

"Oh! Kep, dear. I be havin' to ask when you can come help. Bessie Mae's Wilbur be in the hospital. Oat and I be here for her while Wilbur gets checked over. Bessie walked all the way to our place to call the emergency line.

"Wilbur be havin' maybe seizures. Bessie be a cryin' and won't come into the hospital from our car. She wants that I be with her, so I be hopin' you could ask Anjill if she could come help console the poor dear. I believe Bessie be afraid that people see her for fear of bein' judged poor 'cause of her clothes and all. I don't—"

"We're on our way, Selma. Which hospital are you at?"

"Mount Vernon, dear. How long might you be?"

"Wait a minute while I tell Jill about this, Mom."

Jill's face was clouded with concern as she asked, "Who's in the hospital, Kep?"

"Wilbur. Evidently he's had some seizures. Selma says Bessie Mae won't go into the hospital because her appearance embarrasses her. Selma's asking if you'll help console her while Wilbur's being diagnosed."

I put the bus in gear and began rolling as Jill answered.

"Of course, Kep."

I handed my phone to her.

"Tell her we can be there in twenty-five minutes. Ask where they're parked at the hospital."

When Jill had finished her brief conversation with Selma, I asked her what time it was.

"It's seven twenty. Don't be concerned about getting me back in time to do my work. I can stay up late to finish it."

"My guess is that they will want to keep Wilbur overnight for observation," I said. "How late are most stores open at the mall?"

"Some might be open until ten—most until nine. Why?"

"I have a plan. Tell me what you think of this.

"I take you to the hospital so you can spend a few minutes calming Bessie Mae. Assure her and Selma that you'll be right back after I take you to get your car. I'll give you whatever amount of money you think it will take to buy Bessie some decent clothes—and shoes. Convince them that I was planning on having you take her shopping for clothes sometime soon and that this is as good a time as any.

"Since there isn't much anyone can do for Wilbur for several hours, it would be best to keep minds focused on positive acts. Shopping is supposed to be good for a woman's mental health. Right? I'm sure Oat won't object to this. He can be inside the hospital while Wilbur's being tested. And he can report outcomes to the three of you on your cell phone. He'll have his car if he needs to leave.

"If ever there was a good time for you to have a cell phone, this is it. I have a very important meeting with Mr. G scheduled for nine o'clock. I don't dare miss it. But we can use our phones to stay in touch. Does this sound like something you'd be willing and able to do?"

"I'd love to do this, Kep, if you're sure you can afford it. It's my turn to give in some way—even if it means spending *your* money!"

As I headed for the freeway, Jill began sharing more limericks. Some were outright funny. Many were humorous—even though it was obvious that they covered some hurt or sorrow. They were Bessie Mae's means of lifting her spirits and achieving victory over depressive trials. Jill read one that caused her to ask that I make a brief stop before entering the I-5 corridor.

My heart gets broke in two,
So prayin's what I do.
I gets it fixed
Them times betwixt
'Cause God gives me the glue.

I found a suitable place to pull over, and Jill took my hand.

She asked that I bow my head with her while she offered an audible prayer. Her prayer was fervent and sincere—a prayer that Wilbur's symptoms not be indicative of some serious underlying condition. She asked that he be healed in any case.

She prayed, too, that Bessie Mae be truly comforted and that she experience peace and happy thoughts. She asked that her prayer be granted only in accord with God's wisdom and His will. She closed in the name of Jesus Christ.

I had never heard anyone pray as she did. Her prayer was simple and to the point. But I was most impressed by her humility. She spoke softly, as though God were standing right before her—as though she were truly in the presence of her Heavenly Father.

We were both silent for some time after. There were no words to express what I was feeling.

* * *

Hugs of consolation and sympathy were shared with Bessie Mae at the hospital parking lot. Jill said nothing about her plan to take her shopping. The timing wasn't right for mentioning it. But we definitely noticed that Bessie Mae was more at peace and in control of her emotions than we expected.

After Jill had assured Bessie Mae and Selma that she would soon return with her car, we left in a rush. Bessie even smiled faintly and waved at us as we took off. Selma's face revealed her own relief and thankfulness that we had become involved as we had.

At the Pottses' farm, before Jill got into her car, I made sure that she had her cell phone and that she knew how to speed dial my number. I checked her gas gauge after finding that the VW bus was in need of a fill. Pulling my cash box out from its hiding place, I gave Jill five one-hundred-dollar bills.

"Will this be enough for a start?" I asked.

Jill rolled her head and her eyes as she said, "Oh, Kep! I can see that you've got a *lot* to learn about a lot of things."

She held two hundred-dollar bills out toward me, but I refused them.

"Just take it all, Jill. You might need that and more, and I can't meet up with you again tonight. Besides, I've heard that women's clothing costs a lot more than men's. If you run short, put some things on layaway. I can pick them up tomorrow."

She tilted her head. Her eyes began to blink as she regarded me with resignation. Then, lowering her head, she clasped all the bills together and turned to locate her purse inside her car.

I checked the time on my cell phone: 8:25. Just enough time to get gas and make my appointment. I had mixed feelings of regret (about leaving Jill) and anxiety (over facing Shackleton with a failed mission). Still, there were so many questions to be answered. How would I think of them all?

Jill held out her arms as she turned to face me. I sensed that she was dealing with mixed emotions as well. Our lingering embrace brought us both comfort and exhilarating renewal. We both hesitated to let go.

I became aware of another truth: Touches and hugs could say much more than words at times. They gratified certain human needs. Too many people of all ages were deprived of them for various reasons. (Laura came to mind as I reflected on this.)

Eating the dust from Jill's car, I let her lead the way out over Oat's fields. She was in as much a hurry as I was, and she fed her little Honda all the gas she dared. When we neared a gas station on the east side of the freeway, we honked horns and waved at each other as she sped on and I slowed to a stop.

I was just approaching Old Fairhaven when Laura gave me a ring call.

"Kep? I'm ready to share something with you. Are you free

to listen?"

"This is a good time, Laura. As you probably know, I have a meeting with Shackleton coming up in ten minutes. What have you got?"

"I've thought about this long enough to be certain that I want to share my discovery with you, rather than directly with Shackleton. I know you'll find just the right moment to disclose what I have to offer. If you're discreet about your timing, it should bring Shackleton good feeling rather than disappointment.

"It makes me happy to think that you can be in a position to shine a light for Shackleton where he has great need of it right now. He will probably have no other immediate source for learning what you'll have to offer. Learning it too late might result in an innocent person's loss of freedom for some time."

"As always, I'm indebted to you, Laura. It's tough, but we both know our boundaries, and so I can only say 'thank you' in advance for what you have to share. My words of thanks will have to do. I'm listening."

What Laura told me was a shocker. Even though the information invited other questions, it put a vital puzzle piece in its place. Still, there were too many empty spaces that only Shackleton could fill. I was now looking forward to our meeting with more enthusiasm than dread.

When I expressed my reaction, I got no response. Laura had signed off.

I knew that she was refraining from any further conversation because of her emotional distress. It would do no good to attempt to reach her. And I was helpless to offer her my empathy. She was on her own to find solace in her religious faith.

I said a silent prayer in her behalf. It was all I could do, but maybe that was all that was needed.

CHAPTER 38

IT was two minutes past nine when I lifted the brass knocker on Shackleton's studio door and found the door slightly ajar. When I pushed it open, I was immediately greeted by Bogart. His eyes were exceptionally bright, and his tail was in constant motion as he led me to the den. Once again, a wood fire flickered in the fireplace. Adding to that, the scent of wood smoke was comforting.

My attention was inescapably drawn to the fireplace mantelshelf, where the all-too-familiar Cheerios box was placed in an obvious upright position. Apparently this was to be the first topic of discussion. The thought of this caused my spirit to droop as Shackleton arose from his winged leather chair. But then as he silently welcomed me with a smile and outstretched hands, my spirit rose to the occasion.

Evidently he had already signaled Bones to bring refreshments, because he arrived with them just as Shackleton and I sat down.

Bones's face beamed with pleasure as he faced me.

"Oh, Mr. Kep! You . . . you're a welcome sight to have . . . to have here again. Yes, sir!"

He set down his tray of various snack foods and packets of beverages.

"My Blossom, she . . . she wants you to know you . . . you're always welcome to come to visit us, Mr. Kep. That's for sure. So maybe you can . . . can be makin' a plan to do that. Maybe soon . . . if . . . that would be to your likin'. That would be real good. Real good, Mr. Kep."

As Bones spoke to me, he placed a blue-and-white checkered napkin on Shackleton's knee and began pouring hot water into our mugs.

I looked over at Shackleton and saw that both his facial expression and a quickly nodding head spoke encouragement that I accept Bones's invitation.

"I'm supposin' you'd like your . . . your hot chocolate best, Mr. Shackleton. Please tell me if it ain't so."

"Hot chocolate it is. Please. Thank you, Bones."

"That sounds good to me too," I said to Bones as he turned my way.

"Now, Kephart, I want you to be at ease," Shackleton said. "We most likely will not get through all that we'd hoped to discuss this evening. I'm waiting for more information. But we shall make good use of the time we have at our disposal."

Bones began his departure, smiling his crooked smile at me as he limped away.

"Give my best to Phoebe," I said to him and waved him on. "It's always good to see you too, Bones. We'll find some time to share for sure."

"Sorry to interrupt," I said to Shackleton.

I glanced up at the Cheerios box.

"I'm assuming that you'll want me to account for the missing artifact first off, sir. But I honestly can't account for its disappearance. It seems to have turned to stone."

I was elated by Shackleton's reply.

"Truthfully, Kephart, I could not be more pleased," he said, and he chuckled as he reached out to feel for a maple bar on the snack tray.

Speechless, I stared at him.

"Your report leads me to deduce that your curiosity is still intact. Or that it was yesterday afternoon," he added. "A stone indeed!"

His chuckle progressed to open-mouthed laughter.

"That little stone served to communicate to me that the artifact is now in the hands of the Abiding Ones, Kephart."

"What a relief," I said as I felt my tension diminish. "I've been dreading to learn that I'd failed to measure up—that I'd dropped the ball on my second assignment of the day. Or was it my third? So then, I couldn't be more pleased myself. Thanks for the lift."

"Kephart, there is nothing undesirable about curiosity. Don't get me wrong. It is a characteristic component of human intelligence and a desirable attribute when rightly motivated and properly managed. Without it, our useful learning would be quite limited. But it can be unhealthy when it becomes obsessive—if we let it *rule* us. Applying overall self-mastery is a vital aspect of learning to be truly happy."

"Over the past few days, I've had a hard time controlling my curiosity, Shackleton. Maybe it will be a lifelong challenge for me. I can see that self-mastery is needed for all kinds of things, though—like fear, frustration, impatience, and anger, to name a few. And I'm learning I've had a problem with prejudging people. I guess you could say I've become more aware of my weaknesses in the short time I've been your assistant."

"No harm in that, Kephart, if you will not just recognize them. You must work at overcoming them. Accurate introspection and self-monitoring can contribute much to good mental health when these practices are linked to a goal of self-improvement."

"Shackleton, can I safely presume that it was an AO who

delivered me to the place where I met Laura? You must have been the one who gave him the code name for the Three-Cornered Orange. I'm guessing Laura was too involved in her assigned tasks to have had time to convey the information or instructions he needed—unless she can use her ring to converse with AOs. Besides, she had given me different instructions and warnings without once mentioning this man. He never spoke one word to me. And he didn't ever look at me."

Shackleton's eyes were closed, and he was smiling as he said, "But she *has* given you his name, Kephart. Can you recall her having mentioned a taxi driver I call upon at times to secretly transport people in danger?"

"Well, yes . . . Aaron Linksey—or Link, as he's called. But this man didn't fetch me away in a taxi . . . like . . ."

(My mind was picturing the green-and-blue taxi that came for Dan Crotty.)

"Like the one you observed carrying Mr. Crotty away?"

"Right."

"Tell me, Kephart: Do all taxis look alike?"

"But this was a specially equipped luxury car. It was unmarked. Nothing like a car you'd expect to be for hire. And I was rendered unconscious by an overpowering scent and then dumped off while . . . I'm sorry, Shackleton. I shouldn't be trying to make excuses or justify my erroneous assumptions. It's just that things didn't go quite as Laura had led me to expect. Not that I begrudge that. She does an amazing job of conversing with us while performing various demanding tasks at the same time. I don't see how she does it all, really.

"But am I correct to infer, from what you've just said, that Link is an AO and that he communicates with you using a stellar ring? Are other AOs aware of my personal stellar code name? Can they tap in on my thoughts?"

Shackleton was silently chuckling again.

"To answer your first question, Kephart, yes. Your inference is correct.

"I will answer your second question by reminding you that your ring is a gift from the Abiding Ones. They have tested you and qualified you to be included in their society from a communicative standpoint, should your direct interaction be required. However, it is most unlikely that your direct involvement with them will occur, at least as things presently stand in my association with them.

"Question number three summons the rule of absolute privacy. There is no 'tapping in' where stellar rings are concerned, Kephart. You may rest assured that your ring is virtually in your control and yours alone. Your thoughts therefore remain exclusively your own if you so choose them to be. Remember, too, that removal of your ring renders it totally inactive, as does your death."

"Well, now that we're on the subject of the stellar ring, I have another question that you might be willing to answer," I said. "I've used my ring to retrieve stored conversations and messages, Shackleton. But Laura has mentioned something about our rings having the power to enhance memory recall. Can you tell me how? I would think that I could make good use of this power so as to maintain accuracy in documenting cases. And it should help sharpen my own personal memory of my past life, don't you think?"

"Indeed, Kephart. Yes. I believe you're ready now to utilize that power without letting it become a distraction. It does, however, bring into use another physical sense: your sense of sight. Memories are extremely visual by nature. If you wish to recall an event or situation, your memory will most aptly be visually stimulated. Sight stimulus using your ring requires that you take responsibility for focusing on more than worded thoughts—whether silent or audible. So you feel ready, do you?"

"I'm willing to prove myself. Does it take long to show me what I must learn in order to access this special feature of the ring?"

"Not at all, Kephart. It's a matter of familiarizing yourself with a simple access code and memorizing it. We'll get to that after—"

Shackleton was interrupted by my ringing cell phone.

"Sorry about that," I said to him as I reached inside my shirt to pull it out.

The call was from Jill.

"Hi, Jill. What's up?"

"I know I must be interrupting you, Kep. I apologize. But we just got a report from Oat. He said Wilbur is being discharged from the hospital. He wasn't having seizures after all. He was reacting to a restoration of his hearing! It's been *years* since he lost it!

"Evidently, Bessie Mae had put on an old phonograph record and had turned the volume up so she could hear it outdoors while she worked. It was a recording of banjo music. The music switched on some part of Wilbur's brain. Miraculously, his hearing is returning!

I'll tell you more later. I just want you to know that we won't be shopping for Bessie Mae after all. Not now. We're taking her back to be with Wilbur. Please call me when your meeting is over, no matter how late it gets to be."

"Wow! I sure will. Thanks for calling, Jill. It's okay. Take care."

"Obviously that was a call from Jill," I said. "She apologized for interrupting our meeting, Shackleton. But a neighbor friend of the Whipples was taken to the hospital for observation. What they thought to be seizures turned out to be his reaction to a miraculous restoration of his hearing.

"Jill knew I was to meet with you this evening. She only knows you as 'Mr. G.' That's *all* she knows about your identity."

"That's quite all right, Kephart. You haven't had your cell phones long then, have you?"

"No. Will that be a problem—my having a cell phone?"

"Certainly not, Kephart. I am confident that you will find it quite useful in your work. In fact, I believe it will serve to expedite much that will be required of you. I trust that you will be applying discretion in its use as well. And, of course, it will afford you opportunities to ensure a needed social balance in your private life—such as has been evident with Jillian just now. No, Kephart. There is nothing objectionable about your having a cell phone. I use one myself."

"Now that you've mentioned both Jill and my private life, Shackleton—and before we become involved in discussions centered on the mystery at hand—I'd like to have you explain why so much time was needed before Jill was returned to her home yesterday.

"I know that *you* know that Jill is aware of other-world beings because of what's developed in my assignment. That, coupled with her unavoidable awareness of my discrete association with you, has set her mind to work. She has been very good about not pressing me with questions. She's better about quashing her curiosity than I am in dealing with my own.

"And Jill is totally accepting of the truth that humans inhabit countless worlds throughout the universe. Apparently her religion supports this notion. I just—"

Shackleton raised his hand to stop my spiel.

He was smiling broadly as he interrupted me to say, "Allow me to provide the explanation you requested, Kephart. Please."

I zipped my lips shut. My silence spoke my compliance.

"I'm certain you will derive a satisfactory explanation from some limited disclosures that I can offer. My offerings might illuminate your perspective with regard to the manner in which the Abiding Ones justifiably work at times to protect us as individuals.

"Kephart, I have no access to any law-enforcement agency that offers protection to persons without eventually attracting unwanted attention. You were justifiably concerned for Jillian's safety, and you asked Laura to inform me of her need for protection. I have confidentially disclosed to you that I am personally under surveillance for unstated reasons. I therefore had Jillian placed under the same safe watch. It's obvious that I turned to the Abiding Ones to employ their own efficient methods of observation—and intervention if necessary.

"Incidentally, you will learn that the artifact you retrieved for them is directly linked to their secret means of observation."

"How could anything so tiny accomplish such a thing?" I asked.

Shackleton's hand went up again.

"One explanation at a time, Kephart. Please."

His words came with a warm smile—a welcome disclosure of his patience (and self-mastery).

Never pass up the chance to shut up, I thought to myself.

Shackleton continued. "Your association with Jillian has called for some preparatory measures to be taken, Kephart. We humans—whether earthly or alien—all share common social needs. It has never been my intention to introduce limitations in your social life as you become involved in serving me. Your moral standards are commendable, Kephart. But for your safety in upholding them, you have much to learn about the characteristic aspects of the female gender. Social neglect cannot serve your best interests in that regard.

"Now that the Abiding Ones have become aware of Jillian's interest in you, and because they have seen where she has contributed much to the success of your assignment, she has become an object of their attention. This focus on her has been for her benefit—not only for the present time, but for her *future* well-being, should your relationship develop into an enduring bond. I'm sure that you'll admit such a bond is possible, Kephart. Happily, the potential is there because she has proven to be a young woman of excellent traits and integrity. You are indeed fortunate that she has come into your life. It's a wonder that you've linked with each other in so short a time—and at such an opportune time.

"You might ask how I can make these positive statements about Jillian with such certainty, since I've never met her in person. The answer lies in the reason she was detained so long before being returned to her home. To put it simply, the Abiding Ones conducted extensive tests on Jillian without her knowledge of their doing so. Such tests were made on Laura—even before she chose to commit herself to my service in my personal quests. Laura has never been aware that these tests were conducted. Jillian, likewise, is not aware that she was subjected to these character assessments. The Abiding Ones conducted their integrity probes while these women were under a form of hypnotic sedation. There is nothing of value to be gained by their knowing about the AO's assessments.

"Should you be wondering if these assessments were made in order to qualify these women for any particular role, the answer is no. The Abiding Ones were determining the degree to which they must look after each woman's immunity to deception once she had been accepted into their society—a society dedicated to exceptionally high standards.

"You will eventually learn, Kephart, that the more you strive to obey irrefutable laws—eternal laws—that establish exalting principles, the greater will be the opposition confronting you. Such opposition can be overwhelming at times. You might say that the Fallen Ones yielded and gave up the fight. I'm sure Jillian can provide you with a way to avoid or escape such a dilemma. For Earthlings, there is no such thing as a point of no return during our mortal life *if* we don't stray too far off a path illuminated by our conscience.

"Kephart, I believe that you and Jillian can each learn and profit from your close association. Because of my paranormal gifts, I am happy to discern your individual contributions in advance."

"That's encouraging to hear, Shackleton. I've had some doubts about what I can contribute in our relationship, but I guess that remains to be seen. And I've wondered if Jill and I can continue to share the same path if I don't agree with all the precepts of her religion. Her religion takes priority over everything else in her life."

"And so it should, Kephart, if it is to provide a sustaining and governing faith. However, such a faith must be based on absolute truths derived from supernal revelation. We must approach and contemplate the sources of our faith with humble discernment if we are to avoid deception. Genuine sources of truth provide self-evident confirmation. Doubts flee and peace ensues when light is thrown on a valid source. But that will be for you to discover and verify on your own.

"Fanaticism will never be a characteristic feature of a workable faith in our true, living Creator. The AOs have confirmed that Jillian's personality harbors no such undesirable trait in the expression of her religious devotion, Kephart. You may rest assured on that point."

Shackleton's words sent my mind back to reflect on Jill's urging that I discover for myself what I must learn through prayerful study. No one could *tell* me what is true and have it take root. I had to acquire my personal testimony of what is true through my own efforts. No unshakable faith could come in any other way. But I could recognize or rediscover truths that came to me by the heartfelt, genuine testimonies of others who had "been there" and "done that," spiritually speaking.

I felt this to be so when I listened to what Jill revealed to me—from what she said she got from the Holy Spirit. I strongly sensed that I might get the same kinds of convincing feelings from others, since she had encouraged me to find and associate with those who had dedicated their lives to sharing their personal witness of what is true—the ones who could provide answers to my questions.

"Kephart, I am confident that your future discoveries will lead to whatever you need for your personal happiness. It has been gratifying to have you share your perceptions and feelings as they now stand.

"Now—permit me to answer your next question regarding the alien artifact and its application.

"As I understand it, the AO's artifact was one that worked in combination with thousands like it to provide weightless mobility and thrust to a small, remotely-controlled observation craft. This particular craft self-destructed when it sensed some threat of a collision—a built-in feature designed to obliterate any trace of the craft.

"Typically, thousands of these tiny octahedrons are arranged and encased together in such a manner that they respond variously to changing transmissions of ultra-high radio frequencies. They generate so-called gravitational forces independent of all others surrounding their geodesic enclosure. I say 'so-called' because it is my belief that gravity is a *consequence*, or result, of the presence of creative real energy—such as light—rather than a force in itself.

"The combined octahedrons also offer invisibility by bending light waves around the craft's enclosure, which is most often desirable.

"You must accept the fact that the AOs are humans, Kephart. As such, they are not immune to an occasional failure. In this case it was the remote, controlling operator who couldn't prevent the craft from getting too close as he or she attempted to avert a collision with a similar FO spy craft in the shape of a rod. The Fallen Ones and the AOs rarely get into each other's way as they go about their observations. Unfortunately, the FOs tend to be careless, so the Abiding Ones must always be on guard.

"The AO's observation units primarily transmit sights and sounds to remotely situated operators, but they are capable of sending all that our stellar rings can convey—except our thoughts, Kephart. So you can take comfort in knowing that only our rings can convey thoughts."

"There's something I've wondered about Shackleton. Don't our rings need to be recharged—like cell phones?"

"Our rings are called 'stellar' rings because they derive their power from 'star energy,' which is a discrete energy that differs from light. We tellurians aren't familiar with this force as yet, Kephart, but quantum physics will eventually disclose how to use it—when we are ready to deal with it."

"Well . . . from what you've just described about the artifact, I can see that it must be something the AOs wouldn't want us to be playing with or trying to replicate. And I see that it must have been a part of the kind of craft that was used to watch over Jill's movements without her knowing about it. It's kind of scary to think that we're being watched in this way, though—by both the AOs and the FOs. Are most all of us under surveillance at some time or other?"

"No, Kephart. Extremely few of us, really—at least as far as the AOs are concerned. There must be a valid need arising from our daily activities and involvements, innocent as they might be. You will recall that I said we can come prematurely too close to making and using discoveries that could eventually bring about harm to civilizations throughout the universe. This threat derives from our collective spiritual immaturity.

"However, the Fallen Ones are known to have searched out various Earthlings to physically analyze and interact with in order to serve their selfish motives. Having fallen, they recognize self-limiting departures from their former state of being. They pose sinister problems for us as they attempt to restore what they have justifiably lost.

"It is common for the Fallen Ones to attempt restoration

through biological means. FOs and other aliens might abduct some from among us for anything from cellular research to interbreeding. Unfortunately, it might alarm and disappoint you to learn that obscure agencies of our own government have been instrumental in arranging such abductions for the purpose of making exchanges through certain alien entities. Many thousands of abductions occur every year in this nation alone. We can only guess what percentage of these fall into the secret category of exchanges made to obtain partial insights into advanced alien technologies.

"Such dealings may not come within a privileged 'need to know' security classification or status—even where the executive branch of our government is concerned. I feel certain that newly elected presidents often experience their share of disappointing surprises relative to some discrete limitations of their power."

Shackleton had just dumped a lot of informative stuff on me—too much for me to contemplate at the time. My hope was to clear up as many questions as I could in the meeting time we had without straying off course.

"Okay," I said. "I'd like to clear up other questions I have before I get myself sidetracked. I guess the AOs must know where Nancy Tipton found her tiny treasure. Will they be looking for any other missed debris at the site of the craft's destruction?"

"Indeed, they already have, Kephart. They have made a second clean sweep of the site using highly sensitive detection devices. Nothing remains in the area."

"So how is Hoyle going to deal with Burns and the Tiptons, since there is no equivalent specimen available to the agents?"

Shackleton's facial expression reflected amusement mingled with satisfaction.

"You will be happy to learn that I have a scheme which was to be implemented early today," he said. "I feel quite certain it will gratify everyone concerned in the matter. As you must know, I've spent a considerable amount of time at the Three-Cornered Orange discussing various aspects of this case, in my attempt to bring it to a close. One person I've dealt with is Mr. Hoyle.

"The Abiding Ones wasted no time Friday in assuring themselves that there was nothing left to be found at the site of the artifact's discovery. I was immediately informed of this and so made arrangements to have Mr. Hoyle disclose to agents Burns and Huffman the precise longitude and latitude of the site. His handwritten statement was to be notarized with a copy made available to me. Mr. Hoyle had no need to know the source of my information, but I am prepared and willing to supply a convincing tale through an AO agent if need be.

"Mr. Hoyle was to deliver his letter in person. In exchange he was to receive a written affidavit stating that his disclosure would satisfy—"

Shackleton was interrupted by the call tones of his own cell phone. He quickly pulled it from his shirt pocket, flipped it open, and responded with, "Yes, Graham. I didn't expect your call so soon. . . . Of course. . . .

"Splendid! Ten thirty it is, then. Thank you."

Turning toward me and smiling, he said, "Kephart, I must bring our meeting to an early close, but I'm happy to share good news with you: Mr. Koziol's autopsy has been completed. Detective Walker has much more to reveal to me—critically needed information that we dare not wait to act on. Perhaps many of our questions can be answered without further delay."

"Great! Shall I wait for a ring call giving me a meeting time, then? I'll stand by and be available any time you say, Shackleton."

"Of course. Thank you for being flexible and cooperative, Kephart. I especially appreciate your being accessible on short notice, since Laura is giving herself a much-needed rest and is unavailable at present."

I was relieved by this comment. In a sense, Shackleton was saying that Laura had informed him that she was going to back away briefly from the never-ending demands placed upon her. So she didn't just slip away in a depressed state without giving notice. And I felt sure that Shackleton understood her need for a deserved break—a time to restore her peace and to refocus.

"Now, Kephart, you may choose to remain here and partake of all that Bones has delivered. He will drive me to the Three-Cornered Orange and pick me up when I call for him. Since it is doubtful that I will return before midnight, you are welcome to stay awhile and let yourself out through the studio door. Bogart will enjoy your companionship.

"Oh yes—Kephart! Should you want to freely gratify your curiosity without unnecessary guilt, you have my permission to again explore using the conical keys you found. However, you must remember that your discoveries are to be kept secret. Much of what you find will only lead to conjecture and additional questions—questions which I may never answer."

When Laura had subtly led me to use a cone key, should I find one, I felt she was encouraging me to explore. Shackleton's invitation now made me wonder if I'd been impulsive.

"But how . . . did . . ."

"I'll answer your unfinished question with a single statement that should carry a lesson for you, Kephart: Your unique body energy leaves its trace on everything you touch. This is so for every human being—for every living thing, really."

Smiling soberly, he placed his hand on my shoulder and gave it a squeeze.

"I'm sorry," I said. "I was just—"

"No need to apologize. I believe I have a fairly accurate insight into the means by which you were led to make use of the key. Another thing you should be aware of is that there are specific objects, such as these keys, that the Abiding Ones automatically monitor. Silent alarms alert them to unqualified touches. However, you are now identified as being a 'safe touch,' which excludes you from being subjected to their follow-up measures."

He proceeded to climb the stairs.

He hadn't gone far before he turned and said, "Kephart, because you have demonstrated a high degree of trustworthiness, it will please me to reward you. From now on you will find your name on the list of accepted members of the Three-Cornered Orange. All future meals you order anywhere within The Simple Pleasure should be billed to my account. That covers both yourself and your guests as well. The account is under the name H. S. Gray.

"It isn't common knowledge, but I am the restaurant's sole owner. I prefer that you not make this known to others.

"Polly McGreaham is the manager. She is one of a select few who know I am the owner. She can provide the daily code name if you call and identify yourself to request it for a guest. The permanent code name for all members is Harvard, which is secret."

I opened my mouth to thank him, but second thoughts stopped me. I knew Shackleton well enough at this point to understand that his clairvoyance or sagacity had detected my feelings. No need for spoken words.

CHAPTER 39

JILL had asked that I call her when the meeting was over. She answered her cell phone so quickly that I could only wonder whether she had it in her hand anticipating my call.

"Hi, Kep! Is your meeting over already?"

"Mr. G had to end it earlier than expected. He was called to another meeting in Bellingham. So here I am. How are things going with Wilbur by now?"

"He's a changing personality, Kep. He seems so different that I feel as though I've never known him. His ability to hear has restored former communications that leave Bessie Mae switching back and forth between crying and laughing.

"His speech is not always clear or understandable—kind of what you might expect from people who have impaired hearing. And he alternates between being self-conscious or shy and showing uninhibited, exuberant behavior. Being with him makes me appreciate my own ability to hear all the more. I see that we can take our gifts of senses for granted too much of the time. I'm counting my blessings."

"Just hearing what you've told me makes me thankful, Jill."

"Kep, I think Selma needs me here at their house to help her out. She's thinking about making arrangements to keep Bessie and Wilbur here overnight. I can't see that we should return them home just yet either. This is quite an unusual experience for all of us. So I can't say when I'll be able to meet up with you next.

"There's something Selma wanted me to ask you: Do you think you could sleep in the VW camper tonight? The only place she would have for Bessie Mae and Wilbur is your room. I can sleep on the living-room couch."

"That's fine, Jill. I've committed myself to be on-call for another meeting with Sha—with Mr. G tomorrow, so I can't give you any plan on my part either. I might stay in a motel like I've done before. I guess we'll just have to keep in touch by phone until we see what develops tomorrow. Something will work out."

"I feel sure of it, Kep. I'm so thankful for our having cell phones. Thanks again—for everything."

"Sure thing, Jill.

"Oh, yeah! I have a couple of questions I need to have you answer if you can. Do you have a minute or two right now?"

"Now is a good time, Kep."

"When you pulled your button off—when you were leaving the secret place—were you standing up, or were you being wheeled away?"

"I was standing up. I was being led into an elevator. But then I was put in a wheelchair after Alleri and I got out of the elevator. That's when I got another whiff of Alleri's perfume. The next thing I remember is waking up in my car in front of my rooming house."

"Okay . . . you said Alleri left you when the young blond came to offer you something to eat. Did they both use that elevator door . . . going and coming?"

"No. Now that you mention it, I remember Alleri left and returned through a door just to the left of the elevator door. Is your knowing that going to help you solve a problem?"

"I'm not sure it will help me solve a problem so much as it

will help me understand some things that I'm curious about. Thanks for the info, though.

"Are you going to be able to make up your missed class time if you stay away another day?"

"I'm going to be okay. My memory's still sharp."

"That's what I wanted to hear. We'll talk again soon. Take care."

"I'm missing you already, Kephart Stone."

"Same here. More than you might think . . . oh, Jill! Don't forget to charge your cell phone. You can let it charge all night."

"I'll remember, Kep. Bye for now."

My stomach helped *me* remember that I could use more snacks. I rolled up slices of meat and cheese from Bones's tray and shared all I could with Bogart while contemplating about how much time I should spend on Shackleton's invitation to explore. I decided that I ought to limit myself to a half hour to be safe.

I stuffed some club crackers in my mouth and downed a cold root beer from the tray before going to the three deceptive monkey ornaments. Bogart seemed exceptionally eager to explore with me. He watched every move I made and stayed close beside me as I lifted all three cone-key necklaces from the miniature primate sculptures. This time I noticed that the key sizes decreased in length as I withdrew them in order from left to right. Knowing this would help me get each key back to its rightful owner.

When we entered the former secret room, Bogart gazed up at me expectantly. I made a right turn and began to study the wall panel that adjoined the elevator wall. Once again Bogart began pointing with his nose, and it wasn't long before I discovered a well-disguised keyhole where the walls joined.

The first, or longest, cone key fit perfectly. So far, so good.

The door swung automatically inward as I pressed the key. But I was surprised and disappointed to find just stairs on the other side of the door. These were descending from above at my right side. I felt sure this must be the hidden stairway that Laura had mentioned in an earlier conversation, so it wouldn't surprise me to find that it led to the secret hallway two floors up.

Bogart and I were standing in an enclosure that housed the stairway landing. I saw no need to climb the stairs, and Bogart wasn't showing signs of leading me upstairs at this point. I began to realize that he had not proceeded beyond this point except, maybe, to climb the stairs. No fun in that.

So I guessed that the innermost secret room—the one that Laura had never entered—must lie behind the wall straight ahead of us.

Exploring the wall was a frustration. Bogart was unable to help me as I searched back and forth, up and down. The wall wasn't paneled. It was dark brown in color, but it had no lines of demarcation as the paneled walls had. The wall at my left separated this enclosure from the secret survival room. After some minutes of futilely feeling and scrutinizing, I stood back and mentally weighed the matter while hoping for inspiration.

Then it dawned on me: The keyhole I wanted could be hidden in the wall at my left. It didn't have to be located in the wall I was intent on passing through.

I stood back and looked the left-hand wall over; then I moved up close to examine a small area that showed faint signs of scuffing. No keyhole there, but the evident scuff-worn marks impelled me to press my fingers against them. When I pressed against them, a small rectangular section rotated outward to reveal two keyholes next to each other. Surprised by this unexpected result, I blinked in wonder.

Concerned about the amount of time it had taken me to get this far, I hurriedly pulled out the shortest of the conical keys and tried it for fit. It fit the right-hand hole, but nothing happened when I inserted it by itself. Then I went for the long number-one key, inserted it in the adjacent hole, and got immediate results by using both keys at once.

A section of the facing wall moved inward and slid silently to my right. I was now stepping into a tiny anteroom that contained a small empty table and two wheelchairs. This anteroom led into a very large room that contained strange furnishings. The immediate eye-catcher was a long oval table surrounded by unusually shaped, cushioned chairs—maybe fourteen or fifteen in all. They appeared to be adjustable.

The room itself was constructed of a slate-colored metallic material I couldn't identify. Every corner in the room was rounded. All of the walls curved where they met the floor and ceiling. There were no angular adjoining surfaces to be seen, nor were there any windows.

Despite the absence of windows, a refreshing, bracing air wafted toward me.

Bogart stood back in the stairway enclosure and sniffed at the invigorating atmosphere. He showed no desire to enter the unfamiliar room, but he appeared to be unconcerned or undaunted by it.

I didn't want the door to automatically close behind us as the others had, and I was hesitant to take out the two working keys and leave Bogart behind. So after giving it some thought, I decided to remove the long key and return to the secret survival room with Bogart. From there I would lead him back into the den. He had no problem accepting this choice, even as I led him back through the elevator.

When I returned and prepared to re-enter the innermost secret room, I removed the two companion keys to let the sliding door close behind me. There was a delay time of about one-half minute before I was shut in.

Once enclosed inside, I found the large room too dark to inspect. No sources of lighting were evident around the dark walls. Then, when I *thought* more light was needed in the room, it brightened. I found this to be an amazing thing, so I experimented. When I thought *dim*, it dimmed. When I thought *dark*, I could see only lighted places around the oval table. These lights emanated from built-in visual monitors. Their screens displayed no pictures or symbols. They just glowed in the dark.

I thought *bright* again and saw that each monitor station had two hand-shaped depressions in the table surface—one for each hand, right and left. There were no devices to move by touch—only spaces in which to rest both hands.

Moving toward the back of the room, I discovered a long enclosure where shiny garments were hung. There were three groups of differing lengths. They hung limply on pegs along the back wall. I pulled one toward me and was fascinated by its texture. It felt very light and soft, but it had a metallic feel as well. Thinking *very bright* (for lighting), I discovered that the garment's only opening was at its top. Evidently it could be easily spread and stretched to the point of accepting a human body feet-first. When I put my hand into a sleeve, the garment seemed to wrap itself around my arm and lightly cling to it.

On a shelf above the garments I spotted a few orderly piles of material similar to the fabric of the shimmering outerwear. I reached up and brought down what proved to be several headbands. These were made of a heavier, denser combination of materials. They too could be stretched to fit and cling.

My thoughts went back to the time of my being suspended in a beam of greenish light. The two aliens who approached me in the warehouse were unaffected by the column of light as they stood inside it to perform their tasks. They were wearing the same kind of shining garments and headbands that I just found. So, for me, this proved to be a fascinating and provocative discovery.

I went to the oval table and sat in a cushy adjustable chair. Pulling it up close to its monitor station, I placed my hands in their obvious resting places. The glowing screen before me immediately began to flash a rapid display of brilliant colors. Then it presented a stream of strange symbols—all of them foreign and undecipherable.

Knowing that I was unequipped mentally to proceed any further, I decided to quit my explorations of the evening. Just as I backed my chair away, my ring yanked my attention away from my intriguing surroundings. Shackleton's voice seemed to resound in my head.

"Hello, Kephart. I hope you're not far from Bellingham and that you are not pursuing some personal or social interest, because I could use your assistance. Would that be possible at this time? Be honest with me. Please."

"Actually, I was just about to leave, but I'm undecided about where I'll spend the night. I've given up my room to overnight guests of the Whipples."

"You are always welcome to be my overnight guest, Kephart. There's no problem in arranging that, even on short notice. Accept my invitation. Please."

"Thank you, sir. That sounds good tonight. What do you want me to do?"

"Meet with me at the Three-Cornered Orange. Detective Walker will let you in through the restaurant entry door and lead you to my room at the back. How soon might he expect you to arrive?"

"Within twenty minutes, depending on where I'll park. Any suggestions on where to park . . . safely? I don't want to find that the bus has been towed away when I leave."

"The street should be just fine, Kephart. There are no restrictions at this late hour."

"Then I can be there in twenty minutes for sure."

"Thank you, Kephart! We'll discuss things further in my room."

I began to wonder what kind of assistance I could offer Shackleton at the Three-Cornered Orange. It seemed so unlikely that I could offer anything more than Graham Walker might have. Shackleton had been filled in on everything I'd learned Sunday. Laura had passed along everything except the news she had confided in me personally, and that was for me to withhold until a time when I felt it would most benefit Shackleton.

Taking the conical keys, I closed all the disguised doors behind me and met up with Bogart in the den. We shared our mutual affection in silence as I returned the keys to their rightful primate stewards, and then I gave Bogart a brief ear rub and a hug before closing the piano-studio door behind me.

CHAPTER 40

GRAHAM Walker saw me arrive and opened the glass entrance door to The Simple Pleasure as I approached it. He placed his left hand on my shoulder and gave me a firm handshake before leading me to the back of the restaurant.

We descended several steps into a carpeted hallway, where Graham knocked on the third door at our right. He then opened it and admitted me into Shackleton's private dining room. Shackleton was alone.

"I'll be in the next room here," Graham said as he pointed to the fourth door. "There's someone there I must remain with for a while."

He smiled and waved as he left me.

The small dining room had a warm inviting ambiance derived, in part, from two wall-mounted lanterns. The lanterns emitted an amber glow that highlighted a white tablecloth spread over a circular table. There were no windows, but the back wall was decorated with a soft-white drapery.

As was typical of him, Shackleton silently arose with outstretched hands to greet me. He had been seated in an upholstered chair—the one nearest the door. With a wave of his hand, he indicated that I should sit in a fourth chair nearest the back wall. As I got seated, I noticed that both the hanging drapery and the tablecloth were covered with small subtle prints of orange-colored triangles. Their visual statement obviously related to the Three-Cornered Orange.

Shackleton quickly got to the point of my being summoned.

"I'm sure you are eager to learn what kind of assistance you might be able to offer at this late hour, Kephart. So I will first alleviate your burden of curiosity. I need you to be a witness.

"Due to both his particular performance and the scope of his involvement in this case, Graham Walker cannot serve as such. However, you will soon see that I have chosen you primarily because of your unique privilege of being a stellar-ring bearer. But first I must update you on the latest findings regarding Mr. Koziol."

"I hope the first thing you can tell me is what his autopsy revealed—how he died. Is the cause of his death known at this point?" I asked.

"Fortunately it has been determined that he was *not* murdered, Kephart. He died from multiple causes, the most extensive one being a complete failure of his endocrine system. His pituitary and pineal glands had become practically non-functional. They were severely damaged, as were the brain cells in his frontal cerebrum. Much of this condition may have been a result of his former elusive-energy research while employed by the government. However, hiding the octahedron in his prosthetic eye must certainly have intensified his disorders. Doing so was a poor choice indeed."

"I guess that leads me to the big questions: What was Crotty doing there? What led him to go *upriver* to Koziol's place? How could he have known about the artifact—if that was his purpose in going there? Who else was in on it? I don't—"

Shackleton was apparently amused by my emotional outflow of questions. He interrupted me with an upraised hand as he said, "Let's deal with one question at a time, Kephart. Detective Walker has done some private investigating that could help us obtain the answers to one or two of your questions. And your having provided Dan Crotty with his restored hearing aid contributed much to Graham's success.

"Incidentally, the question of *how* Dan Crotty managed to go upriver is no longer a question. It was inadvertently answered earlier today by Mr. Crotty himself during an interrogation session arranged by Graham Walker."

"How?"

"He wore waders and suspended himself in the saddle of a fisherman's flotation ring."

"But I doubt he could have touched the river bottom that way in some places," I said. "The river is narrow and deep there—right after it widens out with a beach behind the dike near Koziol's place. So how did he propel himself against the current?"

"He used two three-pronged grappling hooks, Kephart. Who would think of it? They were fastened to each end of a long rope—a contrivance he used whenever his installing insulation required that he climb about steep rooftops."

"I don't get it," I said. "What would he grapple onto in a river?"

"Bushes, trees, rocks—anything he could toss a grapnel to along the riverbank. When he reached a secured point ahead, he would pitch the other hook forward and pull himself the obtained distance."

I shook my head as I pictured Crotty's maneuverings.

"It's interesting to learn that Graham had just begun his interrogation session when the conversation got sidetracked by Dan's alluding to his innovative tactic for getting upstream," Shackleton said. "Obviously he wanted to impress Graham with his ability to solve problems and to work independently at overcoming obstacles. Then, too, I'm sure it was a ploy to delay or distract Graham's interrogation—all of which increases the necessity for questioning him further."

"I can see why his employer could depend on him to work

successfully alone without supervision," I said. "But his activities took some forethought and preparation, so he must have had a definite purpose and plan in mind—that and a strong motivation to get to Koziol's place undetected."

"Indeed, Kephart. However, Graham was unable to extract his purpose from him. Although I was not present during Graham's questioning, my clairvoyant gift convinces me that Dan Crotty is withholding his incentive in order to protect someone else. He is not aware of it yet, but he can no longer be held on suspicion of murder. However, he must undergo a preliminary judicial hearing relating to his entering and remaining in Koziol's house without reporting the man's suspicious death.

"Another thing I wish to convey to you, Kephart, is that I am confident that Dan Crotty had no intent to perpetrate a criminal act. He is most likely a victim of evil intent. We shall see soon enough."

I found Shackleton's statement to be disturbing. All of Crotty's plans and proposed secretive activities spoke of obtaining something illegally while involving himself in an immoral relationship. He had faked his suicide or accidental demise to purposely give the impression that he wouldn't be returning. According to both Ginger and his notebook, his marriage was not a happy one. There was much to support this. He had hopes for a "new life," most likely far from his present home and surroundings. I was puzzled, but at the same time, I was aware that Shackleton's paranormal gifts were reliable and that he had a reputation of being successful in applying them.

"You may not be aware of it, Kephart, but I have depended heavily on both Laura and Graham to provide me with vital information to protect you and to be efficient in making good use of the time we have had at our disposal over the past several days. Graham has contributed much at a personal cost of being absent from his family. So I would like to share with you some of what he has discovered.

"I'm sure you are aware of Laura's dealings with a Ginger

Wells at the time of her attempt to identify and confirm the hearing aid as being Dan Crotty's. Ginger gave Laura a business card at that time, which she, in turn, passed along to me.

"Graham and I both wanted to pursue answers to raised questions relating to an attractive brunette mentioned by the talkative Ginger. We wanted to identify and rule out all irrelevant associations or relationships so as to focus only on any that might have supplied Dan with knowledge of the prized artifact.

"Because Dan Crotty's personal associations were quite limited, Graham felt he could quickly identify who it was that Dan was obviously trying to protect. Although I felt strongly that this brunette would not prove to be a woman of interest, Graham took it upon himself to extract all he could from Ginger Wells and the brunette, whose name is Allison Brooks."

(You can bet that I was on the edge of my seat at this point in Shackleton's tale.) "You may want to record on your ring what I'm about to relate, Kephart."

Shackleton closed his eyes, lowered his head, and pressed his fingertips to his temples.

"Ready," I said.

"Graham derived the following from telephone conversations and in-person discussions with Ginger Wells and Allison Brooks.

"Letha Crotty is purportedly visiting a half sister in Port Townsend. She has temporarily turned her sales management responsibilities over to Ginger Wells while she increasingly deals with little hope of her husband or his body being found.

"At this point Graham is purposely keeping Crotty's name and whereabouts out of the media. We presently have no immediate way to inform Mrs. Crotty about Dan's reappearance or condition because, at her request, her mail is being forwarded to her at 'General Delivery,' Port Townsend. Her half sister's name and address are unknown—even to her friend Ginger. Evidently she wishes to be left alone for a time. She is not responding to Ginger's attempts to reach her by cell phone—all of which raises questions, some of them relating to marital fidelity.

"On the other hand, Graham learned a great deal about Allison Brooks. She had just returned from Denver after having attended her father's funeral there. She had been away for the past several days. Upon being informed about Dan's disappearance and possible suicide, she broke into tears. Graham thus sensed that her affection for Dan ran deeper than mere attraction.

"Allison was widowed ten months ago and came to live with her divorced mother in Lynden. Her maiden name was Ingersoll. Due to her father's apathetic nature, she and her father had never been close. But it is most intriguing to learn that her father died of physical disorders quite similar to those evidenced by Kroy Koziol.

"As a physicist, Mr. Ingersoll had, like Kroy Koziol, been employed doing top-secret research at Nevada's Area 51 and at Los Alamos National Laboratory. We might surmise from his fatal disorder that he too had been engaged in energy research.

"It's interesting but not surprising, Kephart, that Allison openly confessed that she had a selfish motive for attending her father's funeral. Her aloof father had few friends, so she expected that there would be few people there. However, she was hoping to find a former colleague and sometime friend of her father in attendance. This friend was about the same age as Mr. Ingersoll and had treated Allison as being his own child. When she was older, she came to realize that she had emotionally supplanted this man's true daughter—his own offspring—who had been kept out of his reach after his wife divorced him when his own daughter was about two years of age. Unfortunately, Allison was disappointed to find that he was not at the funeral."

"Wow! It really *is* a small world, isn't it, Shackleton? Unless you view the similarities of the lives of Koziol and Ingersoll as being more than coincidence. Do you? I mean, it is strange, too, that Ingersoll's daughter lives just north of here and that Koziol came to this area to search for his own daughter before his time to die."

"I seldom regard notable events in human lives as being coincidental or without reason, Kephart. I truly believe all things happen for a purpose. Our experiences lead us along paths that help us develop and realize our true potential in this life—*if* we maintain an awareness of where we are headed and are not caught up in our own self-will. Please realize that we are not *preconsigned* to a destiny—not so long as we can maintain any personal control of our choices."

(Because Jill had made similar statements about choice and purpose, I was more than impressed by Shackleton's remarks.)

"I truly believe that what you say is true," I said. "But I see now that I've caused you to digress from where you were headed in relating Graham's findings. Sorry about that."

"I believe we have covered enough of what is salient this evening, Kephart. No need to apologize. I must now prepare you with a description of how you are to serve as a witness, so that Graham can be free to go home as soon as possible.

"As you might have suspected, Graham and a deputy have Dan Crotty with them in the adjacent dining room. I will be questioning Dan here in your presence alone. Graham and the deputy must wait out the time we spend with him before they can return to the station with him in custody. So far Dan has been fairly cooperative in every respect—except for complying with requests that he disclose his associate's identity or that he tell his purpose for traveling in secret to Koziol's home.

"I rarely meet with clients or others being investigated in connection with them, Kephart. This case has been quite unusual in that respect. Either Laura or Graham has served to obtain answers to questions that I prepare for them. Most typically, it's been Laura's task, but you might be asked to fulfill her role to a greater extent in the future. I have never met Dan

Crotty personally. Neither one of us could, as yet, identify the other.

"You will not be introduced by name. Neither shall I. Our identities will remain unknown to Dan Crotty. You will not be asked to participate vocally. Your task will be to use your ring to record all that transpires between Dan and me, but since I will be doing the same with my own ring, your most valuable input will be to continually inform me of all that you read of Dan's body language. In other words, you will compensate for my loss of sight, and I shall do my best to prevent Dan from detecting it."

"This should prove interesting," I said. "I'll give it my best shot, Shackleton."

"Indeed, I have no doubt that you will, Kephart."

Shackleton reached for his cell phone. I was impressed by his sightless dexterity as his fingers flew lightly over the keypad to find the numbers he wanted.

"We are ready to receive Mr. Crotty now, Graham," he said. "Please. Just let him in and point to the seat at my left. I'll make this as short as possible. It may be that I'll have to continue in the early morning, but we'll make your deadline."

Graham gave two quick raps on the door before opening it to admit Dan Crotty. Dan had a scruffy growth of beard, and he looked worn and depleted. But despite this, it wasn't hard to distinguish his underlying youthful appearance and good looks. In all fairness I had made up my mind in advance not to make any prejudgments regarding his character but, instead, to let his words and actions speak for or against him.

He glanced back and forth at the two of us as he got seated. Shackleton remained silent and looked down at the table.

I gave my ring a twist, thought *Shackleton*, and waited. Shackleton raised his head and spoke in Dan's direction.

"Mr. Crotty, I want you to understand at the outset of our meeting that we are here to help you avoid a judicial hearing, if possible. However, I assure you that it will not be possible without your full cooperation. We are not officially associated with any law-enforcement agency. We will introduce ourselves only as being the ones responsible for supplying your disguise and means for escaping official arrest—and just at the very last moment, I might add.

"We have information that leads us to believe that you are innocent of any intent to do harm to the tenant of the home you occupied for several days. But you must understand that if you should be subjected to a judicial hearing regarding your having remained in that home for such duration of time without reporting the suspicious death of its legal tenant, you most certainly will regret the consequences.

"By noon tomorrow you may be placed in official custody without hope of release until a hearing has taken place. You have avoided any and all human contact possible. Circumstantial evidence surrounding your inaction and avoidance of communication in view of what may have been an apparent murder does not speak well for your innocent lack of involvement."

Shackleton became silent.

Since Dan had not attempted to interrupt or to respond to Shackleton vocally, at this point I thought it would be well to describe his body language.

"Dan has been shaking his head. He appears to be very distressed. Now he's looking toward the wall with a look of bitterness. Obviously his hearing aid is working."

"Detective Walker has done all in his power to relieve you of wrongful incrimination, but this is highly unusual for a man of his responsibilities—to step out of his official role in someone's behalf. He has done so at great personal risk, solely because of his trust in our reputation and the information we contributed.

"He originally became involved in your disappearance as it was reported by your wife. At this point your wife is not available. Supposedly she is visiting a half sister while she awaits further news, should any come forth. Your reappearance is being withheld from the media until she can be notified. When and if you are brought before a magistrate, your reappearance will become public knowledge. Is there any reason you would hope that this dissemination not occur?"

"He's pounding his forehead with his fist. Very agitated."

"You must respond to my questions if we are to continue, Mr. Crotty. Give me your answer. Please."

"Yes! Yes! I don't want to involve anyone else," Dan said heatedly.

"But it is obvious that someone else *is* already involved, Mr. Crotty. The fact that your scent has been tracked to the dead man's mailbox is an indication of your expecting some other person to meet you—perhaps to receive or exchange information, if not to assist you in escaping. You will be quest—"

"Dan's fists are clenched," I reported.

"I knew it was a mistake to toss the waders in the river with the float and other stuff!" he interrupted with expletives and vehemence. "I could've used the boot parts to cover up my scent. I've never had to hide myself before. I hate being secret. I hate having to—"

"I don't believe it is your nature to be secretive," Shackleton said. "Without disclosing the name of the person involved, can you tell us the purpose of your trek to the mailbox? We must get this discussion moving if we are to serve your best interests in the little time we have. Please, Mr. Crotty. You must treat us as your friends."

"He's heaving deep sighs. I think he's about to let go, Shackleton."

"She was . . . there was supposed to be a message for me at the mailbox. I went out there at night . . . several times. No message."

"He has his head down, covering his eyes with his palms."

"So you were trapped in the house. Is that it?" Shackleton asked. "You had no means of escaping without being seen eventually. Was this person to have driven you somewhere . . . eventually? Was there a plan made in advance, or was the message to have included a plan?"

"It was her . . . it was planned in advance."

"He's teary eyed," I thought.

"So why is it that you didn't phone the person? Wasn't there some other way to get in touch?"

"There wasn't any dial tone. I couldn't have heard anything more than that without my hearing aid, even if there was one."

"Isn't there a chance that the message could have been removed from the mailbox—perhaps by the postal delivery man or woman?"

"No. It was going to be taped underneath the box where no one could see it."

"Can you tell us what the content of the message might have been?"

"A time when I would get picked up by car—maybe at a different place."

"Mr. Crotty, we have every reason to believe that you were to have been given some item of great worth. This was not an item to be stolen, but was to have been *given* to you. Isn't that true?"

"He's shaking his head yes."

"Please. Tell me whether the watch dogs were alive or dead when you arrived at the home of the deceased."

"Dead."

"Didn't you question this—that there were three dead guard dogs in the yard?"

"Sure."

"How did you enter the house?"

"Through the back porch door. It was unlocked. I was told to go through the back door because the old man was sick."

"So it's true, Mr. Crotty, that you were informed by an accomplice. Were there more informants than the one you are protecting?"

"He's shaking his head no. Lips tight. Eyes shut now."

"Weren't you concerned about the guard dogs? Did you know in advance that you might have to deal with them?"

"No. I was glad to see they were dead."

"Did you expect that the man you were to see might be dead?"

"Maybe. Mostly just sick and about to die."

"What did you do when you found him dead amid all the disorder?"

"I went to the garage and got in his car to get away from the smell—to hide and get dry."

"Mr. Crotty, from what you have related thus far, your seeming avoidance of reporting the deceased is defensible—to *us*. However, to have remained so long in the house under any circumstance will easily arouse suspicion on the part of a magistrate.

"Your situation was a consequence of an attempt to remain unseen; therefore, your motive for that would most likely be interpreted as highly questionable. A preplanned purpose is evident. An accomplice is obvious. Your motive will be relentlessly pursued, as will the identity of your collaborator. And if the occupant's autopsy were to reveal murder as the cause of death, can't you imagine what the future days and weeks would hold—not just for you, but for your accomplice? Can't you see the futility of your attempt to protect your partner?"

"His head is on his folded arms on the table. He's obviously crying. I think his days of stresses with little or no food have tipped him over."

"Mr. Crotty, you have been under much stress for nearly a week with little or nothing to eat. I'm sure that this has taken its toll and has impaired your ability to think clearly or to make meaningful decisions. However, it shouldn't be difficult for you to see the obvious and *only* choice for you, if you are to have any hope of escaping public awareness and a miserable future. You must disclose the truth to us if you want to avoid being compelled to make it known to those engaged in law enforcement within the next twelve hours.

"Tell me, did you not find anything to eat during the time of your seclusion? Were you not aware that there was an unopened box of cereal next to a laptop computer on the table near the dead man?"

Dan turned his head to one side to answer.

"I didn't spend any time in that stinking room. It made me sick just to open the door to look inside. I found some stuff to eat in a box on the table in the dining room, but it didn't last more than a couple of days. After that, no food until my face was bandaged and I was fed by some woman in the place where I was taken by the cab driver, wherever that was. I was blindfolded someplace along the way. I've had food since then."

"So, I must presume that you spent no time searching for the gift item in the dead man's room."

"No. I was told he would hand it to me. Besides, I was having dizzy spells from the time I bashed up my cheek and head by the river. Sometimes I'd have to sit in a chair by the dining room table until I got my balance back. So I poked through all the bags and boxes of stuff stacked there. After that I got to hoping I'd be told in the message where to look if the old man didn't come to the door."

"Did you not see that the dead man was missing an eye?"

"No. As I said, I never went inside that room. He was missing an eye?"

"He's covering his eyes with his palms again, Shackleton."

"I can't believe she didn't leave any message for me," Dan said (mostly to himself). "Maybe she got scared off by cops patrolling the road."

"How well do you know Allison Brooks?" Shackleton asked.

"That question brought his head up fast, Shackleton. He's squinting as he looks back and forth at the two of us. He seems surprised. He's staring at you now . . . eyes wide and questioning."

"What about her? Why are you asking about *her*?"

"You unquestionably have already identified your accomplice as being a female, Mr. Crotty. From all that we have been able to learn about you, it is apparent that you are not known as being a very sociable man. Of course, your type of work as an installer of home insulation is quite isolating. And it has been reported that you spend a great amount of time at landscaping and maintaining your yard when you are not at work.

"In our attempts to gather information to help us determine whether you might be dead—or alive and missing—we found few people who could offer much about your personal life. Apparently, for some time, you were noticeably friendly with Allison Brooks whenever she came to sales meetings at your home. Naturally, from all that we could gather, she was about the only one we could list as a possible accomplice in your disappearance, should you have actually tried to fake suicide or abduction. We weren't able—"

"You'd better not try to implicate her in any way with what I've done!" Dan interrupted with vehemence. "Just leave her out of this!" he shouted.

"He's standing up with his fists clenched . . . a threatening stance."

"I told you I don't want to involve anyone, and I mean it! I'm not going to answer any more questions if you're going to bring up names!"

"Very well," Shackleton said. "No more names. But perhaps you will have a change of mind in the morning when your head is clear and you fully realize the pressure of time running out for you. You are bound to be placed in official custody at noon."

"He's getting back into his chair. Shaking his head. Breathing heavily. Palms on table."

"Without mentioning her name, let's get back to a simple question: How well do you know her? It may be that we already know what you could possibly tell us. We shall do all that we can to protect her as well, if necessary. Once again, I must try to convince you that we are your friends—that we are perhaps the only ones who can prevent you and any accomplice from having to endure unrelenting legal action.

"You have not as yet been given any information relating to the autopsy of the deceased. There is much for you to contemplate without yielding to anger, Mr. Crotty.

"His head is down. He's sighing heavily."

"All I know is she was the only one who ever showed me some understanding. We only met in my yard on days that she came to meetings. She said she's a widow. Her husband was a window installer. He had a heart attack and fell off some scaffolding—three stories down. She's been maybe my only friend, but I've only known her for maybe eight months. She lives with her divorced mother. That's all I can say now."

"His eyes are closed. Head down."Shackleton became silent. He was engrossed in thought, obviously. A full minute passed before he spoke.

"You will not be spending this night in the comfortable facility we have previously made available to you, Mr. Crotty. Detective Walker will no longer be able to release you to our private surveillance. As I have already stated, he has done so at great personal risk. He is now professionally obligated to retain you to ensure that you may be placed under official custody at noon. There are many questions that cannot go unanswered.

"All I can offer at this point is one last opportunity—one last meeting tomorrow morning—for you to come forth with answers that may equip us to prevent your being subjected to public scrutiny and drawn-out legal proceedings."

Without giving Crotty a chance to respond, Shackleton took up his cell phone, called Graham Walker in the adjacent room, and asked that he take Dan away.

"I request one more meeting in the morning," he said to Graham when he came through the door. "You may want to give me a time that is most workable for you—sometime after nine o'clock is preferable, but I'm always available, as you know."

Graham put his hand on Dan Crotty's upper arm as he answered.

"Early is best . . . no later than nine."

"Thank you, Graham. I will be expecting an early call from you in the morning, then."

Shackleton smiled, first in Graham's direction and then toward me.

After the door was closed and we were alone, I asked, "Why did you make a point of assuring Crotty that we are his friends? There seems to be so little to support that we *should* be. He's definitely hiding something more than the woman's identity. I feel like he's hiding his reason for protecting her. I feel that he's not being open for some other reason than to withhold her name. But why should we consider ourselves to be his friends when he clams up the minute you push for her identity, let alone their motive for meeting in secret? All that you've done has been for his benefit, but I don't see any sign of appreciation on his part. I don't get it, Shackleton."

"One thing you will find as you serve with me, Kephart, is that I don't expect or ask for appreciation. What might you expect as a sign of his appreciation?"

"Well, for one thing, I'd expect that he explain more about his secret reasons for being at Koziol's house. After all, he did everything possible to get there undetected."

"Did you not detect his sadness, Kephart?"

"Not as you must have. I mean, I could see him being unhappy about his situation. So maybe his sadness came from his plan being foiled. I guess I'm not being as sensitive as you are about things that cause people to hurt."

Shackleton smiled and said, "That will come, Kephart. But for now you will have to trust my reason for making a point of friendship. A strong part of my reason is derived from my intuitive insight—my clairvoyant gift, if you will.

"Now, I must notify Bones that his services are needed. It shouldn't be long before we'll be giving Bogart the joy of receiving us back home. I'm requesting that you stay as my guest tonight, Kephart. We may be having a short night's rest and little notice from Graham about a meeting time—that is, if you haven't made other plans for the morning. Have you?"

"I'm ready and available whenever you ask," I said. "Should I follow Bones? I don't feel good about leaving the VW bus on the street, or anywhere in Bellingham. It's an attention grabber, and it's had its share of tow-away times."

"I can see no reason why you shouldn't follow us at this late hour, Kephart. I will have Bones stop just ahead of your parked vehicle after he picks us up in back of the restaurant. You can follow from there. We'll see that the Charleston street gate remains open for you to enter behind us."

"Thank you, sir."

We both fell silently into other thoughts.

I was hoping to find a good time to tell Shackleton what I had learned from Laura, but so far a favorable opportunity hadn't come up, at least nothing that would give him relief in the way she had described. Just as I began to think about ways I might lead him to this piece of news, Shackleton brought up the conversation we were having at the time he got derailed by Graham's phone call requesting that we meet as we did.

"Kephart, I received the call from Graham just as I was explaining how Mr. Hoyle might deal with the missing artifact and how he might appease the government agents as well as the Tiptons in the matter. In the few minutes that we await Bones's arrival, I will explain the tactical approach I offered him.

"I knew that people who wear prosthetic eyes typically have a spare, so I felt certain that Mr. Koziol's modified eye was still somewhere in his house. I therefore gave Mr. Hoyle twenty-five thousand dollars to offer Agent Burns as a temporary loan that he could use as a negotiation incentive for Gaston to return to Koziol's house and locate the second false eye. It was indeed likely that Vitori Gaston was secretly afraid of being caught with Koziol's body there. At that time the body had yet been undiscovered by anyone except Gaston, Dan Crotty—and you, of course, Kephart. A significant incentive was vital if Gaston was to overcome his fear and be moved to action.

"I told Sheldon Hoyle to assure Burns and his agents that they could be confident in locating Koziol's house if they would secretly shadow Gaston. However, as it turned out, he sensed that he was being followed. He went over the dike unseen and upriver to hide.

"At this time *you* were in the house, Kephart. You will recall that Laura warned you when Gaston was approaching from the north. He had evidently yielded to his greed and had taken the chance to enter the house a second time to search for the modified false eye."

"That was one of the scariest moments of my adventure, Shackleton," I said.

"Mine too—for your sake, Kephart. Now I have arranged for an Abiding One—a long-enduring Earth visitor—to visit the Tiptons in official government disguise and inform them of both the extreme hazards of handling the fascinating octahedron and of Mr. Koziol's death. The AO will ask approximately where the artifact was found, even though he knows the precise location of the find. His asking will keep his inquiry and my reports honest. He will also inform them that a significant compensation for Nancy Tipton's loss is forthcoming.

"Mr. Hoyle is to write a hand-delivered letter to Agent Burns. His letter will disclose the exact longitude and latitude of the artifact's discovery site as it was (in all truth) derived from original information provided by the Tiptons. In exchange for the letter of disclosure, Hoyle is to receive a notarized written promise from Burns that the Tiptons will *never* be questioned about the site of the artifact finding, since he'd then have been given all that is known. Hoyle is also to retrieve the twenty-five thousand dollars, which Burns will have taken back from Gaston due to his failure to produce the artifact.

"Mr. Hoyle has agreed to give all of the twenty-five thousand to the Tiptons, along with whatever amount of his own money he can possibly afford to add to it. He must offer his sincere apology for his despicable conduct in the matter. This is my way of seeing that he takes responsibility for his evil intentions and to redirect his mind to beneficial pursuits. He is to look upon this as a lesson learned in true values and to consider the potential threat he had introduced, in that his own son might have been sought for abduction.

"The Tiptons will then have no reason to be critical of Hoyle. They will have no knowledge of all that went on, except that the specimen posed a very real threat to Nancy and others who might have spent time with it."

Shackleton's handling of the on-going potential challenges involving the government agents and the Tiptons was, to me, impressive. But that he would endeavor to lift Hoyle up from the pit of his inclination to be dishonest won me over fully to his cause. I felt truly honored to be his assistant.

My memory flashed back to my first meeting with Laura. She had expressed her respect for Shackleton in various ways and at different times throughout the evening. At this moment I realized how much I missed our ring conversations. These thoughts of her now led to the thought that this might be as good a time as any to share her surprising news that I was to deliver to Shackleton. Maybe he could benefit by some time to "sleep on it" before he met with Graham Walker in the morning.

"It's a comfort to know what you just shared, Shackleton," I said. "I've had unsettled feelings about this aspect of bringing this case to a closure. But now I have something to share with you that I just learned from Laura this evening. She thought it best that I pass this along to you at a meaningful time. I guess this is it.

"Today, when she was using her ring to bring up visual memories of her various involvements in this case, she was struck with a mental picture that had previously escaped her attention. It was recorded at the time of her meeting with Ginger Wells. I'm sure you'll find it useful in assessing what would best be discussed—or not—during the meeting with Crotty in the morning. I don't know what you can do with the information, but I'm sure it will influence your handling of all that you're confronted with.

"Ginger was holding Letha Crotty's mail that she had taken from the mailbox to mark up and forward to Letha. She had already marked the forwarding address as 'General Delivery' on the pieces of mail she was holding. The top letter was from an insurance company. It was addressed to 'Aletha Koziol.' Ginger had crossed out the name and corrected it to read 'Letha Crotty.' I know this changes the perspective of the case. You must know what can be done with it. But for me it just adds confusion."

Shackleton's facial expression abruptly changed to reflect a mixture of shock and pure joy.

"Great galloping gastropods, Kephart! You bear the best news I could hope for!" he exclaimed.

CHAPTER 41

MY cell-phone alarm woke me up at seven. I'd spent some time figuring out how to set the alarm before I went to bed shortly after midnight. Being waked up by a ring call from Shackleton didn't appeal to me. Neither did a rap on the guest-room door by Bones. I suppose my choice was an expression of my inclination to be independent.

I'd been offered two options for breakfast: I could meet Shackleton at The Simple Pleasure, or I could have an early breakfast with Bones and Phoebe at their table. I had inwardly chosen the latter—partly because I needed a break from being immersed in the complexities of Shackleton's case and partly because of my newly formed friendship with the Judds. Besides, I had agreed to follow up "soon" on Bones's invitation to visit with them. This was about as soon as it could get.

I took my time shaving and showering. My morning routine was typically one of rushing through it all and moving on. However, this morning I deliberately took a slow pace and relaxed. I especially enjoyed a long, hot shower.

Phoebe served orange juice, link sausages, steak fries, scrambled eggs, hot chocolate, and freshly baked biscuits with choices of honey or jams. From the way Bones and Phoebe and I interacted in our conversations, one would think we'd been friends for years. Although it was short, this occasion was a refreshing, cheerful event, and I left their place restored and thankful for their goodness and friendship.

It was nearly eight thirty when the iron gates closed behind me and I entered Charleston Street. I was headed for Bellingham when I got my first ring call of the day.

Shackleton's voice entered my head.

"Good morning, Kephart! There will be no hurry for you to get out of bed. Graham Walker has been quite busy already today. He has postponed our meeting time with Dan Crotty until ten thirty. I know this news will greatly arouse your curiosity, so I will explain briefly that I was the cause of the delay. I requested that a fourth person be present. Graham agreed to follow up on this arrangement, but doing so required that he take certain steps to make it possible."

"Wow! This must be something big, Shackleton," I said. "You told me that you rarely meet face to face with clients or their associates. I think Laura once told me the same thing. Anyway, I know this has been an unusual case from the start, so I can't look for anything typical to happen, can I?

Shackleton chuckled and said, "I suppose not, Kephart. There is little that is typical in my world.

"Will you want to have breakfast with me at the restaurant? That is where I will soon be located. I just now spoke with Bones and requested his services. You could ride with us if you wish."

I laughed. This change of plan was welcome.

"Actually, I've just finished having breakfast with the Judds, Shackleton. Thanks. I got up early myself. And this change of plan gives me time to perform an errand that is long overdue. I'm sure you'll understand."

"Certainly, Kephart. All is well. We'll meet at ten thirty, then."

We signed off. Shackleton was right: Curiosity had me in its clutches.

* * *

I changed my course and drove south toward Mount Vernon on I-5. Thankfully, my restored memory served me well, and within twenty-five minutes I found the VW heading up the beautiful approach to Eden's Gardens—a first-class landscaping business that spread out over many acres.

In the six weeks that I had been gone, Aaron Eden had obviously declined physically. He and his wife, Irene, had been trying to maintain the grounds and greenhouses with the help of college students (such as I had been), but they were now showing the stresses of their labors. Their advanced years were telling on them.

As I approached Aaron, he looked both pleased and surprised to see me. He held out a welcoming hand and asked where I'd been and what I'd been doing. His interest in my sudden disappearance was obviously derived from a genuine regard for me. He showed no sign of being offended by my failure to inform either him or Irene of any "upcoming absence." They were truly gracious and kind people.

"Aaron, I had an accident that left me with a concussion and a temporary loss of memory," I explained. "I'm sorry that I failed to report this to you sooner, but I've been adjusting to a completely different life. I'm here to pay my past-due rent and to make amends if possible."

Aaron shook his head and smiled.

"The cabin is still available if you want to come back," he said. "You owe us nothing. We're looking for someone to take over the business so that we can enjoy some years of retirement, Kep. It's time that we faced the reality of our limitations. We can arrange to finance the purchase price of the Gardens if you're interested. We still enjoy a high volume of business, maybe higher than ever. You're young. This could be a fine opportunity for you as an investment."

He looked hopeful. I hated to disappoint him. Aaron had had a younger business associate. When I asked about him, I was surprised to learn that he had recently gone into business for himself—as a photographer. He'd had a youthful strength and stamina that Aaron had increasingly depended upon, due to his advancing age (Aaron and Irene were now in their seventies).

"I appreciate your offer, Aaron. You and Irene are wonderful people. I respect you both. But I have recently found excellent employment. I'm totally engaged in a new life that is challenging and rewarding. I can't jump off my present track. One thing I can promise is that I'll make a definite effort to steer a trust—"

My cell phone rang. It was Jill.

"Excuse me, Aaron. I can't pass up this call," I said.

He shook his head yes and stood patiently waiting as we talked.

"Hi. What's up?" I said. "I was going to call you when I finished an errand I'm on. Any plans for your day?"

"I'm taking Bessie Mae and Wilbur to shop this morning, Kep. Oat and Selma are going along, too. Wilbur doesn't know it yet, but we're going to help him find some decent clothes, too. Thanks so much for your generous giving. My morning will be filled up—probably my afternoon as well. Do you think we could get together this evening after I take them home? I miss you."

"I'm missing you too, Jill. I'll call you later when I know what's up for me. How about a dinner date—probably after seven thirty?"

"We can make it happen, Kep. Call me, please, when you know your agenda."

"For sure. We should have some stuff to share by then—both ways. Is Wilbur's hearing still restored?"

"Yes! You can't imagine what a change has taken place in both Wilbur and Bessie Mae. I'll fill you in this evening, okay?" I love you, Kep.

"Love you too."

Aaron smiled as I slipped my phone back inside my shirt.

"I'd say your new life has a variety of absorbing interests, Kep. I hope all of your new challenges are positive and happy ones for you."

"I guess they are, Aaron. They're good for me, at least. I'm troubled by a new relationship, though. The phone call I just got was from the first girl I've ever dated in my life. It's troubling to me because I'm impatient and I've had to learn a lot about women in a short time."

Aaron tipped his head back, closed his eyes, and laughed a jovial laugh.

"You'll find out that's a never-ending course, Kep" he said. "Why so impatient? Impatient for what?"

"I know this must seem strange, Aaron. Maybe I'm being foolish, but I want to marry her already . . . and I'm sure she feels the same way toward me. But she puts her religion ahead of everything she might personally want for herself."

"That says a lot for her, Kep. Nothing wrong in that."

"But she wants me to have a religious testimony that I don't have yet, and if I don't have one, I'm sure I'll eventually lose her."

"Testimonies take time, Kep. There's no point in your being impatient. What church is she associated with?"

When I told him, he raised his eyebrows and pulled his head back in surprise.

"Kep, that's one of the reasons Irene and I want to retire. We want to go on a mission. That's *our* church. It's our church, and we want to serve on a mission while we're still physically able to perform effectively."

I was stunned to hear this. I blinked, shook my head, and laughed.

"As to marrying young, Kep, I must tell you that Irene and I got married before I was twenty. She was a year older. We knew each other just three weeks before we got married. Three weeks. Our fifty-second anniversary is coming up in August. But our attraction for each other was more than physical. Maybe you and your girlfriend feel the same way. I hope so. If it's just physical, it won't last. Marriage takes commitment on both parts. Here's the big question: Are you both willing to take on responsibility and commitment? Not so many young people seem to be willing to do that these days."

"I really think we are, Aaron. But we've only known each other less than a week. It seems like it's been much longer than that . . . but . . ."

Aaron was smiling with his eyes closed as he said, "I'll have to tell you about a friend of mine. He's passed on now, but you need to hear this.

"During the second World War my friend served in the Navy. He met his wife at a USO dance. They knew each other only three *days* before they got married. He was due to be shipped out, so they had just a little window of time to consider marriage and a total commitment to each other. His wife waited faithfully for his return at the end of the war. They raised five sons and one daughter. Their marriage lasted sixty-odd years. They had their trials and tribulations, of course. But they were basically a happy couple. He's gone now, and his wife lives in an assisted-living home."

I stood silently pondering all that Aaron had just shared with me. His words were comforting, but they didn't quell my impatience.

"I don't have a Bible, Aaron. Jill—my girlfriend—says I should have a King James Version. Do you know where I can get one—this morning if possible?"

My impatience was obviously influencing me more than my desire to hide it.

"If you're here to pick up some personal things you left in the cabin, why don't you go do that while I bring you just the thing you need," Aaron said.

He turned back toward his house as I headed for the cabin.

At first everything in the cabin appeared to be just as I had left it. My small book pack was on the bed. My suitcase was on the floor beside the bed. But when I began to take my few clothes from hangers, I noticed that they had been ironed. This was something I'd never done since I left home—iron clothes. I'd always folded them and stacked them in a box. Everything smelled fresh and clean.

I turned to the bed and discovered that the sheets were tight and smelled fresh, too.

When I opened the dresser drawer, I found that my underwear had been laundered and folded. My socks were paired and rolled together. I couldn't believe that the Edens had gone to this trouble for me, especially since they had no reason to expect my return after the first couple of weeks.

I was still puzzling over this when Aaron appeared in the open doorway.

"Why is it that you and Irene have gone to all the trouble to do my laundry—and to fold or hang up my clothes?" I asked. "I would think you'd never expect to see me again after a full month's disappearance. How could you do all this without hearing a word from me?"

"Faith, Kep. Faith that our prayers would be heard and answered. We felt nothing but peace when we prayed. We knew it wasn't like you to be irresponsible or to just walk away from your job and your few belongings. And we never got a feeling it was your time to go. We *did* sense that you had met with some temporary dilemma, but our overall feelings were to trust in God and to be at peace.

"We've undergone similar experiences with one or two of our children as they got older. The blessing of parenting brings responsibility that calls for personal revelation if you want to have any peace, Kep. So you pray a lot more as your children grow older. No, we don't consider you to be our child—but we've loved you just the same."

He held up a large book and turned its cover toward me. At first I was unable to read its cover because my eyes were filling with tears. I then became too emotional to hold my head up. I had never anticipated this kind of reunion with the Edens. I'd sensed their caring, but not to the degree that Aaron expressed.

He went to the bed, sat down, and motioned for me to sit beside him.

"This is a King James Version of the Bible, Kep. It's yours to keep. You'll also find translations of the writings of other prophets since the time of the Tower of Babel."

I took the Bible from him and shook his hand in silence.

"You'll find more of the restored gospel here as you look through the pages that follow. Irene and I have acquired unshakable testimonies of the truthfulness of these scriptures, Kep. We've put them to work in our lives and tested them for decades. We're eager to share them more fully now. As I told you, though, unfailing testimonies take time—and a lot of prayers, I might add."

Sitting beside this aging man as he openly shared his strong feelings reminded me of those moments when Jill expressed her own conviction—when she got carried away with her enthusiasm for the principles that guided her. But I could safely say that neither Jill nor Aaron exhibited anything close to blind fanaticism. What I felt coming from them was a sober, moving spiritual experience that passed into my being without words. It was enlightening and uplifting to be in their presence during their sharing.

Aaron stood up and asked, "Could you use some help getting your things to your car?"

"You won't accept anything for all you've done?" I asked. "Not for the scriptures? You won't accept my payment of past-due rent?"

"Would you expect that Christ would?"

"I guess not, Aaron," I said, shaking my head and sighing in resignation.

He went to the hangers and began folding my clothes over his arm with the hangers inside them. I picked up my little backpack and my suitcase.

As we walked toward the VW bus, Irene came out of the house to meet us. She had evidently been busy cleaning her kitchen. Her graying hair clung to the perspiration on her face and temples. She had a wet dishtowel thrown over her shoulder.

"I knew it. I just knew you'd come back, Kep!" she exclaimed. "But I see you're taking your things away with you. Will you be coming back later?"

"I sure will, Irene. I definitely will. But not to live or to work—just to let you practice your missionary work on me . . . as long as you're here for me. Aaron can fill you in."

She held out her arms and hugged me. Then she pushed me away and put her hands on my shoulders.

"Then I hope you'll have a lot of questions for us, Kep," she said, laughing softly.

"Oh, there'll be no *question* about that," I responded jokingly. "And I'll be sure to bring the key to the cabin next time I come. Could I get your phone number? I'll want to be calling you soon."

"Do you have anything to write on?" Aaron asked.

"I'll just punch it into my cell phone," I said as I pulled it out from my shirt.

Both Irene and Aaron looked amused as they saw where I kept my cell phone. When they saw me pause to check the time on it before entering their phone number, they became aware that I had to be moving on.

"I have an appointment to keep this morning," I explained. "I know you can appreciate my reason for having to leave. You can't know how much I appreciate your kind welcome and your labors in my behalf, though. This has been a happy reunion as well as an emotional one for me."

Aaron moved on toward the VW and opened the front passenger door. As he placed my clothes over the back of the seat, he looked at me and gave his head a shake.

"God moves in mysterious ways, Kep," he said. "Be sure to thank him."

CHAPTER 42

AARON was "right on" when he commented that God moves in mysterious ways. I could see that my perspective of life had changed drastically over the past several days. Even though I had been riding a roller coaster of daunting trials and uplifting victories (however small), I presently felt that there was a purpose in my experiencing them. And I definitely had found the greatest joys of my life as I dealt with the challenges. I felt that I had been led meaningfully along a hidden path of my own making. (Shackleton's "inner journey" comment came to mind.) But I was now aware of a supernal influence in my making choices. God truly did move in mysterious ways.

When I left Eden's Gardens, I headed back north toward Bellingham on I-5. I would have about thirty minutes of free time to reflect and ponder on the remaining issues of Shackleton's mystery before we'd meet. No time to visit the Singing Tree. But I was attracted to the inviting walkways of Boulevard Park and the waters of Bellingham Bay. This place, too, was conducive to my errand of thought-collecting.

As I drove northward, my mind became focused more on the relationship I had with Jill than on mystery solving. Along with that came a personal assessment of the change in my attitude toward God. Jill's "missing dollar" parable stood out as a classic example of our being misguided by part-truths. Sadly, a lack of the *full* truth was prevalent throughout our society. Did Laura and Jill and the Edens really have access to the guidance of a fully restored gospel?

* * *

It was midmorning, so there were few people and plenty of parking places in Boulevard Park. I locked the VW and began my relaxed pace along the walkway that traveled beside the bay toward Old Fairhaven.

As I walked, I decided to sort out the "knowns" from the "unknowns."

First off—things I felt I *knew*:

According to reports given to Shackleton, Koziol's autopsy had ruled out murder as a cause of his death. He had died of multiple disorders. The lengthy time he'd spent handling the alien artifact (above all, keeping it near his brain) had evidently intensified the life-threatening disorders he suffered. He was not a man of high standards, at least not in these last years of his life.

I knew that Dan Crotty had not yet been informed about the autopsy results. Evidently, Shackleton was withholding this information from him as leverage for obtaining the critical answers he was seeking, but he couldn't withhold the coroner's findings much longer.

Koziol's communications with Col. Bradford had brought on a variety of endangerments for himself, for Crotty, and for Gaston—to name a few. (I suppose I could include myself in the bunch.) But they had also initiated eventual life-saving consequences (such as for Hoyle and the Tiptons), insofar as they would prevent future hazardous contacts with the artifact. However, Sheldon Hoyle's selfish acts had, in the beginning, jeopardized the peace and lives of others as well. He too was not a man of high integrity, but hopefully he was of a disposition to change for the better.

Apparently Vitori Gaston was being held in custody for unlawful trespass, and for theft and transportation of stolen property. (Was I lucky or what?) He was probably (but not yet certainly) going to be held accountable for killing domestic animals, as well as destroying personal property.

For me, the three unknowns remaining were most troubling:

Who had been Koziol's ally?

Who was Dan Crotty trying to protect?

How did Crotty or his accomplice first learn about the alien specimen and its tremendous value?

I decided to first devote some thought to the third and last question.

Kroy Koziol was first to learn anything about the potential value of the prized article. Gaston and Hoyle were next in line (not to include Malcolm Burns or his associate agents). Obviously, none of them had ever been associated with Dan Crotty.

These facts led me to believe that Crotty could only have learned about the artifact from his accomplice. She would have to have been the one to devise a secret strategy to obtain it and thereby begin a new life with Crotty—most probably under assumed identities. Crotty's own declarations led Shackleton to believe this was the case. But according to Shackleton's interrogation tactics, the specimen was confirmed by Crotty to have been a gift, not something that he was going to steal. This puzzled me.

From what I witnessed of Dan Crotty's fiery emotional reaction to Shackleton's mentioning Allison Brooks by name, I couldn't help reflecting next on Graham Walker's input regarding her.

She had been in Denver (or was on her way) at the same time that Dan had disappeared. So if she was the one who was to have left a taped note for him under the mailbox, she obviously could not have performed as expected. Dan's disappearance occurred at the very time that she was away to attend her father's funeral. His reappearance was not yet made public and wouldn't be until his wife had first been notified. Letha still hadn't been available to be informed that he was alive.

This realization caused me to accept another "known": Neither Ginger nor Allison were yet aware of Dan's re-emergence. So Allison's strong emotional reaction to the news of his complete disappearance and possible suicide was to be expected—especially if she felt that this was due to her failure to uphold her part of their agreed-to plan.

As I gave further thought to Graham's findings, I came to suspect that Kroy Koziol might actually be the former colleague and friend of Mr. Ingersoll. Koziol's own death would account for his absence at the funeral.

At this point in my attempt to clarify my thoughts and rid my mind of confusion, I got another ring call from Shackleton.

"Good morning again, Kephart!" he said. "I must inform you that our ten thirty meeting has been canceled. However, your assistance is surely needed. How long might it be before I could expect you to be available?"

"If you want me to be at the Three-Cornered Orange, I can make it there in about fifteen minutes," I answered.

"Indeed! Splendid! Just give the receptionist your permanent membership code name and go directly to the room we occupied last evening. Do you remember the code name?"

"Harvard?"

"Correct! I shall expect you soon, then, Kephart. Thank you."

Shackleton's voice abruptly left my head.

As I walked briskly back to the VW bus, new questions began to step quickly into his vacated space.

How could the postponed meeting be canceled at such a critical time? It seemed there was so much to extract from Dan Crotty yet. Was there an earlier interrogation held without me this morning in which Crotty had yielded and spilled out answers—possibly those to my first two questions? Had Graham's early-morning tasks produced the identity of Crotty's ally? Could this ally possibly be the fourth person Shackleton had requested to be in attendance?

My unchecked curiosity was causing my accelerator foot to get heavier with each mile I traveled. I eased up on the gas. No sense in getting stopped for speeding. I scolded myself for letting my curiosity rule me.

When at last I entered the restaurant and was admitted to the Three-Cornered Orange, I got no response to my sharp knocks on Shackleton's door. After a second and third futile try, I discovered that the door was unlocked, so I let myself into the room and sat at the empty table.

I checked the time on my cell phone: 10:38. The "postponed" meeting time had already passed. Now I was being put to the test of mastering impatience.

Three or four minutes later the door was opened by Graham Walker. He smiled at me and shook his head as he led Shackleton into the room. Shackleton felt for his chair near the door, leaned his white cane against the table, and sat facing my way. Graham waved at me and gave me a loose salute before leaving the two of us. He appeared to be rather jovial.

Shackleton seemed to be in a buoyant mood himself.

"I apologize for causing you to suffer from impatience and curiosity, Kephart," he said assuredly. "However, I'm quite certain you will find your tests to be sufficiently rewarded."

"Oh, I needed the waiting time to practice self-mastery, as you must know," I said. (And I meant it, unfortunately.) "Are we to expect others to join us?"

"In time, Kephart. But this is a good time to discuss the many new developments of the morning. There are things you'll want to hear—things that may surprise you.

"But before I relate the morning's events, I would appreciate hearing your latest thoughts and views regarding all that has transpired over the past few days. From your perspective at this point, Kephart, how would you answer the remaining questions presented by the mystery as you've had to live it?"

"It's uncanny to me, Shackleton, how you're so often coming up with comments or questions that coincide with what's recently or presently been on my mind. I was trying to unravel the complexities of this case and clear my head of confusion when I got your ring call to come here.

"All I can say at this point is that I'm strongly inclined to believe that Allison Brooks devised the plan for Dan Crotty's disappearance and that her father's death prevented her from fully carrying out her part in it. I've come to believe that Kroy Koziol is the one she looked to as her father's only friend and that Koziol's death was the cause of his not attending the funeral—however inexcusable that might be."

Shackleton's facial expression had progressively been reflecting what I perceived to be approval as I spoke. My last comment brought laughter—a sign of his life-prolonging sense of humor. I was grateful for both.

"And while I was sitting here waiting for you, the thought entered my mind that Koziol's laptop message was meant for Allison," I said. "He could have called her Ally as she grew up—a shortening of Allison."

Shackleton sat shaking his head with eyes closed and eyebrows raised.

"Amazing! You have an amazing analytical talent, Kephart. I'm truly impressed with what you've derived thus far. It gives me great pleasure to have you as my capable assistant.

"However, for your sake, there are some points you may want to work on, as you will see shortly. I leave it to you to identify these aspects of your character and to work at correcting them over time. I'm aware that you are already cognizant of your particular weaknesses and that you are attempting to surmount them.

"As you may recall, at our very first meeting I made a point of stating that there is no mortal man or woman who is without weaknesses. Still, we must accept ourselves as we are at present—but we must never be *content* with what we are, Kephart. We must move on to realizing our higher potential as far as our allotted earthly time permits.

"With that said, I will update you on the events of the morning.

"Dan Crotty spent the night under county surveillance—to the relief and satisfaction of Graham Walker. Dan was not booked, because there was no valid reason to justify filing charges as yet—not as long as Graham withheld his knowledge of Dan's hidden location and seeming avoidance of reporting a possible murder. However, Dan's undesirable overnight accommodations profoundly impressed upon him the potential threat of Graham having to fulfill his professional responsibilities.

"Graham *could* report that Dan had been located in the presence of a deteriorating corpse. He had spent several days under these circumstances without reporting the obvious possibility of foul play. He had avoided being seen. He was reported to have been a missing person, and that's where Graham had first entered into the situation. He could not delay reporting Dan's re-emergence for long. Dan's wife must be notified.

"You were the source of disclosure of Dan's location as it was reported to Graham. Therefore, much responsibility devolved upon you as well, Kephart. Your revealed identity would make you a target for questioning. There could be many serious ramifications if this were to be made known and attract publicity. It should now be obvious why Laura and I were so greatly concerned for you. We had to assure that your involvement remain a secret."

"Thank you, Shackleton, for looking out for my safety and enabling me to avoid unhappy experiences. There were some close calls, though, weren't there?"

"Indeed. More than I would have supposed."

Shackleton continued. "The increasing stresses caused by his full realization of Graham's impending action led to Dan's breakdown. Very early this morning Graham found him extremely despondent and unresponsive to offerings of food. He had been crying and hiding his eyes in his arms. He was so deeply depressed that Graham became concerned, wondering whether he might need medical attention.

"Fortunately, Dan was wearing his hearing aid. Graham specifically asked him if he knew where Letha's half sister lived in Port Townsend. He explained that if he couldn't learn it from him, he would have to get a court order to have the Post Office release her sister's address there—the one relating to the General Delivery application. He told Dan that he was legally bound to inform Letha of his reappearance and condition, in response to her declaring him to be a missing person.

"When Dan was confronted with this, he flew into a rage, exhibiting uncontrolled anger. This emotional outburst was in stark contrast to his former despondency. It took quite a long time for him to calm down, but Graham stood patiently waiting for some verbal response.

"Eventually, Dan said he wanted to talk to *me* because he considered me to be a friend who could help him. He wanted my advice. Graham consented and got my agreement to meet with him. It was after nine o'clock when I met with him alone. I didn't feel I would need your assistance at the time, Kephart, because Dan had obviously requested verbal communication to get my advice."

"What kind of advice?" I asked.

"He wanted to know if I could find or suggest a place where he could live. He wanted to move out of his house before Letha returned. He wanted nothing more to do with her, and he didn't want her to know his new place of residence. It was no surprise to me when he informed me that Letha's half sister lived in California, not Washington. The only person she had ever associated with in Port Townsend was her former live-in boyfriend. They had been living together just before she and Dan met, after which *they* entered into the same type of physical relationship."

"People sure do bring a lot of troubles and misery on themselves—mostly through immorality," I commented. "Dan Crotty is another example of this."

"That's true, Kephart. Lustfulness is one thing, but please also consider the deprivation of true affection so many humans suffer before you judge them. I make no excuse or justification for sin. But my intuitive insight tells me that Dan Crotty was denied much natural love in his formative years. He presently suffers a severe lack of positive self-esteem for reasons we cannot take time to discover. Genuine love can heal many of the world's ills. Let's just hope that he will find it . . . and contribute to it.

"The consequences of sexual immorality are always painful—eventually more painful and far-reaching than the lack of affection suffered in the first place, if such was the case. As you work with me, you will find that great numbers of Earth's humans are struggling to cope with hidden disorders, whether emotional, mental, spiritual, or physical. It is most rewarding to take part in redirecting and assisting them, Kephart. But no individual must ever be denied the agency to choose for himself or herself."

My thoughts immediately went to Laura. Then to Jill.

"Your Jillian may have much to offer in the way of both the

prevention and cure of our worldly ills, Kephart. I suggest that you be mindful of her guiding principles, should she desire to share them."

"She already has—and is," I said.

Shackleton nodded, closed his eyes, and smiled his approval. He reached inside his shirt pocket and brought forth his cell phone. With eyes still closed, he let his fingers fly over the keypad.

"Yes, Graham. Have they finished their meal? . . . Oh, really? Then let's not delay you any longer. Bring them to the door and let them in, please."

"Perhaps it would be best if you were to sit in the chair at my right, Kephart," he said.

I had just moved when Graham rapped on the door to usher in Dan Crotty and a very pretty young woman. They were holding hands.

(Yes, she was a brunette.)

They moved their chairs closer together and sat at right angles to each other. The brunette could only have been Allison Brooks. I'd say she was in her late twenties, no more than thirty. She cupped Dan's left hand between both of hers and smiled, first at Shackleton and then at me.

I was surprised and impressed to see a consoling and caring expression on Allison's face when she looked at Dan. Her mien and mannerisms reflected self-control and adherence to high standards of conduct—nothing akin to what I'd envisioned of her before meeting her in person.

My ring finger tingled. I waited for the fiery itch to pass.

"I invite your participation in our ensuing discussion, Kephart. Please. Just leave your ring activated. You may speak to me either openly or in thought, using your ring."

I responded with, "The woman—Allison Brooks?—is looking

at you, waiting for you to speak, Shackleton."

He smiled warmly in the direction of Dan and Allison and lifted his white cane for them to see.

"It will soon become obvious to you both that I am blind, so with that in mind, we will conduct our conversation accordingly," he said.

He waved his uplifted palm in my direction.

"Because we are to be *secretly* engaged in locating missing persons, it is best that we not disclose our identities," Shackleton explained.

I could immediately see just how much Laura had contributed to Shackleton's quests. I felt certain he sorely missed her at a time like this.

"Dan, you are already acquainted with the two of us. I acknowledge that your companion here is Allison Brooks. I must apprise you both of Detective Walker's unofficial efforts in making this meeting possible. He not only arranged a time earlier this morning for Dan and me to meet privately, but he personally sought after you, Allison, to report that Dan had been found. This effort was made in consequence of Dan's declaration that he considered you to be his only *true* friend. So I encourage you both to express your personal appreciation for the detective's compassionate nature. He is a highly respected man who has been known to devote many extra hours to following up on missing person reports.

"Because it is his primary responsibility to inform the person who filed a missing person report (particularly a spouse) that the missing one has been found, Detective Walker went to great lengths to speedily obtain a court order and fax it to the postmaster at Port Townsend. The address alleged to be that of Mrs. Crotty's half sister proved to be that of a single male—a former live-in companion. A locally dispatched deputy there confirmed this to be so when he went to inform Mrs. Crotty of Dan's whereabouts. All of this was accomplished in little time, thanks to Detective Walker's efficient tactics and influence.

"Detective Walker's professional obligation to report Dan's discovery has thus been fulfilled. He sees no point in bringing this matter before a magistrate.

"There is another supporting justification for this decision, Dan. I'm happy to inform you that the dead man's autopsy has been completed. It reveals that he died of multiple disorders. You are therefore not to be held under suspicion of murder or of contributing in any manner to his demise.

"After all, did you not suffer a temporary disabling head injury? There are some things that might just as well be kept hidden or unspoken, in that there is nothing to be gained in the world by revealing them. Don't you agree, Dan?"

Tears welled up in Dan's eyes. He shook his head in agreement as Allison put her hand on his shoulder. She exhibited true compassion for him. I was mystified by the apparently innocent aspects of their relationship. Allison wasn't at all the female that I had prejudged her to be.

"I have something to offer that will interest you and Dan both," I thought to Shackleton.

"By all means, speak up, Kephart."

"I've learned that you will want another place to live, Dan," I said. "I don't know for sure how you feel about your present employment, but I can refer you to a fine old man who just this morning offered me employment working at his landscaping business. I used to work for him.

"He has a cabin that I once lived in behind his greenhouses. It's got everything you'd need for now. But he'd want you to work for him if you were to live there. He was paying me more than twice the current minimum wage, and the cabin rent was cheap. I'm sure he'd be happy to interview you. He and his wife want to retire, so he'll need someone to eventually take over the business and manage it. I have his phone number if this interests you."

Dan's face brightened with a look of hope. Allison gave his hand an obvious squeeze as she smiled at me. Shackleton was beaming with pleasure as he regarded me.

"God truly does move in mysterious ways," I thought.

All I had intended to do was retrieve my sparse belongings and to pay my past-due rent this morning. I couldn't believe my choice would have brought about all that I now saw before me. And the timing was incredible.

"Indeed he does, Kephart." Shackleton's voice in my head reminded me that we were still "connected."

"How many possessions were you hoping to move out of your home today and tomorrow, Dan?" Shackleton asked. "Will you need a moving van and a storage place?"

"I don't have much of anything at all that I could call mine," Dan said. "Mostly tools and clothes . . . and maybe some pictures. There's an old recliner that I maybe don't care about that much. Letha wouldn't want it, though.

"I don't have a car. I've always been able to use the company truck to get around in when I wasn't installing insulation."

"The landscaping business has vehicles that I got to use," I said. "How do you feel about working outdoors?"

"Fine! It's what I've been doing for nothing at my house for a long time . . . maybe two years now."

"If that's all you've got to move, my car will handle it, Dan," Allison said.

Shackleton looked in Allison's direction as she spoke for the first time. Her voice reminded me of Laura's. It was soft and pleasant, but it lacked the tone of being apologetic.

"As for you, Allison," Shackleton said, "how do you feel about working for Letha Crotty now that you know what you do about her conduct, especially her having betrayed Dan?"

"I don't really *have* to work," she said. "I've been doing cosmetic sales work to help me focus on people and activities in a distractive way—a way to keep my mind off of my husband's accidental death. His life-insurance proceeds will supply all I need for years to come, if I don't spend foolishly."

"I'm curious about something, Allison," I said. "There's no good reason for you to share this, but I'd like to know the name of your father's friend—the man who treated you as his own daughter. I'd like to know because he must have had some influence on your feelings and behaviors as you grew up. I'm impressed today by your evident understanding and compassion for Dan in his present situation. If I'm right about a suspicion I have, I might be able to explain this friend's absence at your father's funeral."

Allison's eyes spoke her own curiosity as she answered.

"His name is Kroy Koziol."

"Then I can say without a shadow of a doubt that he died just days prior to your father's passing, Allison. I'm truly sorry to learn of your personal losses over the past months, but I'm confident that there are brighter days in store for both you and Dan."

"Thank you. You seem so certain of this. I have to believe you. Thank you."

I looked over at Shackleton and saw that his eyes were closed as he sat smiling and nodding his approval of my little bit of contribution to the meeting.

CHAPTER 43

SINCE Dan Crotty was free to go after our midmorning meeting, Shackleton offered to provide him with transportation and a hotel room until he could get re-established. (Graham Walker had left to resume other duties.) But Allison Brooks expressed her desire that Dan allow *her* to drive him to his house.

"I'm free to help you gather all you want to take, Dan," she said. "I'm sure we can't take your recliner in my car—or on it—but from what you said, I suppose you won't greatly miss it . . . will you?"

Dan gave her a weak smile and slowly shook his head.

"I'll be glad to take you up on your offer," he said, and he put his arm around her and briefly drew her close.

I was pleased to see that there was no attempt on her part to be controlling or domineering. Dan surely didn't need those undesirable traits in a friend—or a wife, if their relationship ever developed to that point.

Before they left Shackleton's room, I got Allison's cell phone number from her, and I gave Dan the Eden's Gardens phone number. I now felt confident that Aaron would be interviewing Dan before the afternoon was over.

After the door was closed, I went back to the table and sat with my legs stretched out and my hands behind my head. Shackleton had remained seated. His eyes were closed, and his fingers were loosely interlocked across his chest. He wore a smile of peaceful satisfaction.

"You appear to be content with the outcome of this meeting," I commented, "but I'm still struggling with unanswered questions. I'm sure you must have answers that have escaped me. And I'm sure you can come up with the very questions that are disturbing me."

I knew that Shackleton could readily see that I was relying on him to relieve me of my puzzlement. But I had sensed lately that he wanted me to arrive at accurate conclusions on my own—to practice being more self-reliant and confident in my analyses. I had been right about some things I'd deduced, but totally wrong on others.

"I encourage you to let go of your perplexities for a time and see what inspiration you get on your own, Kephart. It is quite likely that your mind will arrive at the solutions you seek if you give it a rest—if you relieve it of the pressure you've been putting on it. Perhaps the answers have already arrived somewhere at a lower level of your consciousness. A common way of determining this is that you 'sleep on it,' as they say.

"Bones should still be waiting in the parking lot. Let's say we meet at my home tonight at nine. That should give you some time to divert your mind to other things and to do some research where '*re*-searching' is necessary."

(I took his emphasis to be a clue.)

"I'll be there," I said. "Will you let me assist you in finding the door to the parking lot?"

"Thank you, Kephart, but no. "I've got every step of the way memorized.

"It will be a pleasure to engage ourselves in a 'de-mystifying' conversation tonight. Let's look forward to that."

* * *

It was about noon when I opened the door to the VW bus. I decided to call Jill and learn how the shopping was going for Bessie Mae and Wilbur. Jill answered her phone with an exceptionally cheerful voice. (I'm now convinced that shopping puts most women in a happy frame of mind—if they've got money to spend.)

"Are you having any success in finding clothes that the Pottses are willing and happy to wear?" I asked.

"Yes. But the whole experience is a bit overwhelming, especially for Bessie Mae.

She's so money conscious that it restricts her ability to make decisions. I've had to insist that she is deserving of her best choices and that she doesn't need to look at the price tags. It's hard for her to accept that every item is a gift. This experience is beyond anything she's ever known. It's kind of sad, but rewarding at the same time, Kep. I wish you could be here to watch her."

"What about Wilbur? Does he make his own choices, or does Oat have to make them for him?"

"He's relying heavily on Oat's guidance, as you suspect. I wouldn't be surprised if we were to learn that he's been wearing the same raggedy overalls for five or six years. Oat says Wilbur told him he has nothing else to wear. Apparently his clothes are all clean, though. Wilbur must have just stayed in bed or covered himself up at least once a week while Bessie hand-washed and hung up everything to dry. I doubt they have a washing machine to use—certainly not a clothes dryer.

"I guess they're about finished with Wilbur's shopping tour, Kep. I think they're looking for shoes now, or boots. I don't remember ever seeing Wilbur smile or interact as he is now. It's amazing.

"Different kinds of shoes for Bessie are next. Then I'm taking her to a salon for her very first makeup and hair-styling experience. Is your meeting over now?"

"Yes, but I have some things to wrap up yet this afternoon. I'm looking forward to our dinner date. Maybe we could change the time to seven o'clock, if you're through with Bessie and Wilbur in time, as I'm thinking you'll be. What do you say?"

"I'm sure we'll be through early enough, Kep. I'll call you when we're through."

"Sounds good to me . . . oh! Do I have it right that Bessie Mae *walked* all the way to your folks' place to call for help when she thought Wilbur was having seizures?"

"Yes."

"Don't they have a truck or car that runs?"

"I guess not. And that reminds me of another one of Bessie Mae's limericks I ran across that we didn't get to share. I have it memorized.

Our pickup's gone to pot.
It smokes and shakes a lot.
It blows a breeze
Between my knees
'Cause floorboards it ain't got.

After we laughed together, I said, "That's another funny-but-sad one, Jill. Maybe I can help out there as well . . . without being extravagant.

"I have to tell you that I've been thinking if we're going to spend more time together—as we'd best be doing at *least* once a week—I would really prefer not to drive you around in the attention-grabbing VW bus. I'm happy to have it for my personal use, but I want to elevate my means of transportation to a higher standard of appearance for our shared road time—

something less conspicuous. Am I being too prideful, do you think?"

"That depends on what your true motive is and just how much higher your acceptable standard goes. Only *you* can assess those things, Kep. I'm perfectly content with riding in anything you can afford, if it will provide a way for us to spend more time together. We could use *my* car, you know. I'll even let you be the one to drive."

That brought a laugh, but I knew she meant what she said. For balance in my life, I could see that I would benefit by Jill's good sense and humility. Regardless, I wanted to do the "guy" thing and check out prices for decent, reliable used cars.

I drove around Bellingham and found three dealerships of interest, but I didn't stop to inquire about anything I saw on the lots. Something was holding me back from talking with sales people. The timing didn't feel good. Again, I felt as though I was being led for a reason.

Just as I had decided to abandon my search, I passed a used car lot with a shiny blue Chevy pickup parked along the street front. It was six years old. I parked the bus and walked over to inspect it. There was a shallow dent in the tailgate. The window sticker advertised low mileage and a limited warranty. A salesman approached me and told me it was a one-owner vehicle with a maintenance record I could look over. After test-driving it and inspecting its maintenance record, I wound up buying the pickup—cash on the spot.

No feelings of doubt came with my choice. But then I knew I hadn't bought it for myself.

I checked the time on my cell phone (1:10) and then drove south to the Whipple farm and parked the VW under the tall chestnut trees. Next, I called for a taxi and gave Smooch a chance to lick my hand and wash my face. After rubbing his ears and hugging him close, I went inside the house to clean up and make sure I was somewhat presentable.

During my taxi ride back to Bellingham, I concentrated on arriving at sensible answers to questions that still had me stumped.

I now felt certain that Allison Brooks had not influenced Dan Crotty to become secretly involved with her in any conspiracy. My brief observations of their respectful attitudes toward each other ruled out any chance of immoral plots or strategies either way. I read their relationship to be derived from compelling needs for empathy—both ways. Although each was now without a spouse—due to vastly differing causes—they were alone and confronted with all that loneliness could bring.

Kroy Koziol's unsent e-mail could have been intended for Letha, since her true name was *Al*etha. If she was about two years old when her mother and Kroy were divorced, "Ally" could just as well have been an affectionate shortening of her name as it might have been for Allison.

My memory of the laptop message told me that Koziol's first letter sent via the U.S. Postal Service offered "Ally" (Letha) an opportunity to take the alien specimen as a gift. She was then to communicate with Col. Bradford and arrange for an exchange settlement. I supposed the money would be secretly paid into a Swiss bank account under her name.

All of these newly perceived scenarios fit into the puzzle with a fair degree of plausibility. But from this point on, I wrestled with confusion.

If Letha Crotty *had* told Dan about the alien artifact message from her father, and if this was to be a gift they could share, why had Dan gone to the risk and taken the trouble to go upriver in secret to get it for her? He wouldn't have done this to avoid the possibility of being detected by government agents, because at this point the agents had no knowledge of where Kroy was hiding out.

Letha had reported Dan as a missing person. If he was on a mission to get the gift artifact from Kroy, what was the need for her doing so? And who was the accomplice—the one to have left a note under the mailbox?

These thoughts were getting me nowhere. How was I ever to gain enough peace of mind to "sleep on it" as Shackleton had suggested? Then, in my state of frustration, I recalled that I had taken Shackleton's remarks about "*re*-searching" as a clue. Maybe I was missing something in Dan's notebook or on Kroy's laptop message that would steer me onto a path I hadn't seen yet.

The laptop was now inaccessible to me. Dan's notebook was in the VW bus, along with other remnants of my adventure. Would it be possible to clarify my visual memory of the words in these sources using the power of the ring? Laura had used that power to come up with Letha's former name . . . the one she used before she and Dan were married. Shackleton was going to give me the cue words to access this special visual memory bank, but he'd become distracted or was interrupted.

I decided to give Laura a ring call—to see if she would respond to one yet.

Laura came through with an immediate reply.

"Kep! What a pleasant surprise! You must have a good reason for calling me, though. I'm sure this isn't just a social call . . . is it?"

"Just checking to see if you are still 'a thought away,' Laura. You have been greatly missed by both Shackleton and me. I feel certain that I can speak for Shackleton as well as myself because I wasn't able to replace you as I worked with him in a discussion with Dan Crotty today. Imagine that! I haven't been able to replace you, Laura.

"Actually, you are irreplaceable in every sense of the word. And I'm curious about how you're doing at reclaiming your emotional balance and strengthening your personal values. I feel good that you're taking time out for this, but I miss you just the same. We'll have a sharing time when you're ready. Right now I'm—"

"Oh, Kep!" (She was laughing.) "Let me get in a word here! I've already talked with Shackleton . . . early this afternoon. I called him to let him know that I don't need any more 'vacation' time. I'm already back and ready to become involved again. So I hope your curiosity is satisfied.

"What else were you calling me for? Just let me be the curious one for a change."

We were both laughing now. It felt good to laugh with Laura and to know that she had called Shackleton. The "wilting flower" sounded clearly refreshed and renewed.

"I need to know how to access the visual memories stored in my ring. I'm trying to recall details of the e-mail message Koziol had stored in his laptop. Shackleton said he would give me the coded access words, but he got sidetracked before he got started.

"I know—it means I must take on greater responsibility for what I visually access, but he felt I was ready. If you need to check with him first, I'll wait, Laura. It's okay."

"I'm sure you're ready, Kep"

She gave me three words I must think in a sequence. It was so simple it seemed childish. But the visual recall experience was strangely exhilarating.

"Wow! (I now saw a vivid picture of Kroy's message.) "I've got just what I wanted, Laura! Thanks much. Just to satisfy your curiosity, I'll tell you why I need this.

"You know that Koziol's laptop is no longer available, but Shackleton gave me a clue to help me clear up some confusion I have. I think he'd be happy to find that I can correctly deduce the final answers to the mystery we've been involved with. I'm sure he already has it all solved, but he doesn't want me to lean on him any more than necessary.

"He said it would help if I did some re-search. I'm guessing he's referring to this laptop message—either that or Dan Crotty's notebook. Maybe both. I'm to meet with him tonight, but I've got other things going this afternoon, so wish me luck."

"You know I always pray for you, Kep. There's no luck connected with prayer."

"Right, Laura. I know better. You might be happy to learn that I've got all the scriptures associated with the restored Gospel now and that I'm praying more often."

She was silent for some time. There was emotion in her response as she thought.

"Kep, I want you to know that we will seldom meet alone in person again—maybe there will be times when we have no other choice. But we can always keep in touch using our rings to share important events. Working conversations—those that relate to Shackleton's quests are okay anytime. I know our lives will remain intertwined for the duration of time we devote to supporting Shackleton."

"I'm glad you expressed that, Laura. And that's a good thing. I think we'll always be close. I've learned now that people can be attracted to others they haven't committed their lives and love to, but you and I both know that we have to live within the bounds that are acceptable to God. Anything other than that will bring heartache and painful consequences. I can see that God's commandments are kind and that they assure our happiness in the long run."

"You've come a long way in a short time, Kep. I guess we both have . . . thanks to your refusing to give in to strong feelings and temptations."

"I'm not taking any personal credit for resisting my natural desires and feelings for you, Laura. They were out of my control, really. I have to give credit to God for immediately answering a desperate, last-minute prayer—a prayer that each of us could be strong. I somehow knew that by 'giving in,' we would ultimately feel shame and regret and that we'd damage personal relationships all around.

"Just think of it: We can always be close and hold respect for each other now. We know we've been empowered to keep our relationship healthy and happy just by staying within the bounds God sanctions. I thank you too for your continuing prayers, Laura."

We signed off on a happy note—one of reinforcing our former understanding.

* * *

It was 2:23 when the taxi driver let me off at the used-car lot to claim the pickup. After driving around and spending the necessary time to complete paperwork for registering and insuring the vehicle under the names of Wilbur and Bessie Mae Potts, I drove back to the Whipple farm in the pickup to exchange it for the VW bus. Once again I repeated the greeting routine with Smooch, and by the time I returned to Bellingham, it was nearly 4:30.

My stomach insisted that I stop by The Simple Pleasure for a bowl of chicken noodle soup, plus half of a ham-and-cheese sandwich.

(I justified this as being "food for thought.")

As I forced myself to eat slowly and to dwell in depth on Koziol's laptop message, I found one incongruent thing that stood out: The first part of Koziol's message mentioned "killer dogs" fenced in the backyard. Then further on he said he thought Gaston's knock on the door was Letha doing as he had instructed her to do. The only door that would have been safe to knock on (because of the dogs) was the *front* door.

So, again, what would have been the point in Dan's traveling *up* the river to be met by the attack dogs before he could gain access to the back porch door? In our first meeting with him, he specifically said that he was told (by his accomplice) to go to the *back* door.

As I ate and mulled all of this over, I couldn't help but to wonder whether Kroy Koziol's mental capacity to recall or to think clearly was so seriously impaired prior to writing this letter that it was of little value to me. My perplexities had only increased so far. I had just begun to reexamine the laptop letter when Jill called.

"Hi! Are you and your parents finished with all you set out to do for Wilbur and Bessie Mae?" I asked.

"We are, Kep. It's after five, so I'll be able to have an earlier dinner date with you, as we had hoped. But I'm sure that Bessie and Wilbur and my folks could use something to eat before heading home."

(I began to have some feelings of guilt for having eaten in private already.)

"Then I suggest that you meet me at The Simple Pleasure, Jill. I have an open account for myself and my guests, courtesy of Mr. G. Would your folks and the Pottses be okay with eating together in our absence? The reason I ask is that I could use your help in another matter. They could all get home in your folks' car, couldn't they?"

"I can't see any reason why they couldn't, Kep."

"Then would you explain to Oat and Selma that I need your help for a time and that we have a dinner date coming up at seven? Please ask them how they feel about this arrangement. It would mean they'd have to get the Pottses back home, but their dinner's on me . . . my pleasure."

I waited for Jill to do as I'd asked. She was quick getting back with an answer.

"That's fine with them, Kep."

"Thanks, Jill. Just park on the street in front of the restaurant. You'll see the yellow bus there. I'll make arrangements for the bill to be paid. Meet me inside."

"We shouldn't be long. Thanks so much."

When I got my first look at Bessie Mae and Wilbur, I was shocked, to say the least. Bessie's new hairstyle and facial makeup made her unrecognizable. Her blouse and skirt reflected Jill's practical influence coupled with good taste—considering Bessie's age and deportment. She appeared to be a totally different woman. (But her smile told me she could use some money for a new set of dentures.)

She smiled and happily gestured with her hands continuously.

Wilbur's appearance reminded me of an old-west cowboy—one who had just hit town for a good time. He wore a cowboy hat and boots (no spurs). The most striking thing about him was his complete change of character. He smiled and laughed a lot. He moved with energy, and he purposely made humorous puppet-like gestures that spoke of a desire to entertain those around him. I could just picture him plucking on a banjo at a country grange dance.

Oat and Selma seemed to be happily enlivened for having contributed much to the joy of their "friends of occasion." I could believe that there would be happy get-together times for the foursome in the months ahead and that Bessie Mae would be relieved of much of her loneliness.

My thoughts went to Shackleton and his personal quests. Once again I felt privileged and honored to be his associate.

After everyone was led to a table and given a menu, I took Jill's hand. We said our "good-byes" and headed for the old VW bus. I made sure Jill's car wouldn't be ticketed. (I saw two signs that said there were no parking restrictions after six o'clock.) Then we got in the bus and headed south on I-5.

Jill looked over at me several times without saying a word. I read her curiosity as long as I could. Keeping silent was a trial for me, but I smiled at her often to hide it."Remember that you told me the best way to receive joy is to give it?" I asked at last.

She shook her head yes and raised her eyebrows in anticipation of what was to come from my mouth next.

"Well, I wanted you to play a part in my giving, so I'm sure you won't mind *driving* a gift from your folks' farm to the Pottses' place. Your participation will include printing a large gift card to put on the windshield. I'm hoping you might find the materials to do that. Besides, you're artistic talents far exceed mine."

"I would have thought that you already deserved all the happiness you could receive in one day, Kephart Stone."

"Who's to say where giving should end—or that it should be timed out?" I asked.

"What will you do when your money supply ends, Kep? I think I'm going to be much needed to watch out for your excessive material generosity. You know there has to be a reasonable limit . . . don't you? And I think you know that the best kind of giving is giving of your caring self and of your talents—not tangible things."

"You're right. But I've never been in a position to give materially before. And supplying basics for those who are in dire need can't be interpreted as being extravagant, can it? Besides, I want you to know that I haven't spent more than two-thirds total of all the bonus money Mr. G has given me. His gifts to me are what I've shared with others. I haven't touched my first month's salary. I haven't been as 'spendy' as you might believe from all outward appearances. Trust me.

"So I've had fun briefly indulging myself before I see a financial advisor in the next couple of days—someone who can tell me where the best places are to invest and to save and how to preserve all I can for our future. I have faith that we'll have a future together. And I know that my spiritual future would be much less meaningful without you. So you'll always be number one for bringing me happiness in giving—and in loving."

I was comforted by a changed expression on Jill's face. A peaceful smile with closed eyes was saying more than words.

"Incidentally, I have another gift I want to share with you today. I received it just this morning. It's for me *and* you, really—for me to ponder and for you to either keep in your head or to hold in your hand for as long as you'd like, or both. But I'm sure you'll enjoy it best if it's in *my* hand more often. I'll share it with you at dinner time.

* * *

Jill was definitely happy as she helped me move the shiny blue pickup to the Pottses' place. I had her drive it there. I wanted to get her opinion about its ease of driving by both Bessie Mae and Wilbur. It won her stamp of approval. (She pointed out that it had floorboards!)

Before we drove the VW and the pickup from the Whipple's house to the Pottses' farm, Jill hand-lettered and decorated a large colorful "gift card" using a page from an old sketch book she'd left at her folks' place. After I secured this behind the Chevy's windshield-wiper blade, we headed back to Bellingham in the VW and arrived at The Simple Pleasure just before seven o'clock. There weren't many customers, since the main dinner crowd had cleared out.

The foursome was no longer there. After I'd assured myself that the cost of their meals had been placed on my membership account, I requested a booth for Jill and me beside a window at the back of the restaurant. We were led to a corner one that was cozy, comfortable, and somewhat secluded.

Before we looked over our menus, I offered to give a prayer of thanks. I didn't forget to thank God for all the blessings of the day before asking a blessing on the meals we'd be eating. For some reason, I didn't feel self-conscious or inhibited as I prayed in public. My oral prayer was sincere. It was from my heart. I didn't really care what people thought if they happened to look at me.

When I opened my eyes and looked up, I saw that Jill's eyes were teary.

"It seems I've brought a lot of tears to your eyes since we've met, Jill. Has that been the case with your former boyfriends—those brief relationships you've had with your church members? Am I headed for the discard bin?" I teased.

Jill looked down at the table. She shook her head and placed one hand over her forehead as she smiled.

"You know they've just been happy tears," she said.

"So I'm guessing you'll always be crying when I make you happy?"

We were laughing together when the waitress came to take our orders.

"Sorry, but we're not quite ready to order yet," I told her.

I found, as I looked the menu over, that this had been another day of neglecting my stomach far too long. The colored photos of the plated choices made me slump.

"Everything looks so good. I can't decide soon enough," I said. "I'll just take whatever appeals to you. You choose and we'll double the order."

Jill tilted her head and laughed.

"If we become too much alike, neither one of us will find a need for the other," she said. "But since you're not at all concerned about *spending* today, and since I'm too hungry to think about choices myself, I'm going to order steak and lobster. Will that bring happy tears to *your* eyes, Kep?

I covered my eyes with my palms and nodded silently.

We both seldom spoke as we ate, which said a lot for the excellent cuisine and our enjoyment of the choice Jill made.

When we were nearly finished with our meal, I noticed that Dan Crotty and Allison Brooks were being led to a booth beside a window near the entrance. They sat side by side and occasionally held hands after receiving their menus. Their presence became a distraction for me as I studied their interacting behaviors.

Dan's face reflected emotions that alternated between sadness and pleasure. The pleasure was derived from the comforting and observable affection of his companion, Allison. My earlier opinion of their innocent relationship was sustained at this time.

Neither Dan nor Allison had noticed me in the corner. At first I felt like trying to keep out of their sight—which was impossible. Either one could easily see me by just looking my way. My distracted attention from Jill began to make me uncomfortable. After all, this was our dinner date, and I didn't want to have anything detract from its offering.

I reached over and gave Jill's hand a squeeze.

Then I stood up and said, "I see the restrooms are located to the side of the receptionist's stand. I'll be right back. Please order our dessert. Make it something we can linger over. I'm in no hurry to leave this time of *simple pleasure*. Are you?"

"No, Kep, but I'm not sure I can eat a whole dessert."

"Whatever you can't eat I'll finish off. Okay?"

She nodded a yes and then smiled and shook her head as I headed for the reception area.

As I passed near Dan and Allison, I pretended to notice them for the first time. I walked over to their booth and shook their hands. They regarded me with friendliness.

I looked at Dan and asked, "Were you able to arrange an interview with Aaron Eden today?"

With an approving smile, Allison looked over at Dan and nodded. She let Dan speak for himself.

"He's already hired me . . . and he gave me the cabin to move my stuff into."

He stood up and held his hand out for a second shake.

"Thanks to you . . . uh . . . I don't remember your name."

"I didn't give you my name, because I can't, Dan. The man I was with explained that we are to withhold giving out our names because our work of locating missing persons demands that we keep them secret. Sorry about that. But I accept your thanks just the same.

"We have our rewards, but we don't expect recognition of any sort. My best wishes to both of you. I foresee happier times ahead. You can both count on it."

Smiling, I gave them a parting nod and turned toward the restroom area.

There wasn't any way to avoid being spotted on my return approach to the booth Jill and I shared. I supposed it didn't matter. I felt much more comfortable for having exposed my presence in the restaurant to Dan and Allison, so I could now devote my full attention to Jill.

She was using her fork to cut into a slice of lemon meringue pie.

"Looks good to me," I said. "Take your time. Do you have a lot of work to complete tonight? Did I tell you that I have a nine o'clock appointment with Mr. G?"

"Some—and yes, Kep. I can catch up on some of my work tonight: lessons plans and papers to correct. The rest can wait until early morning. It doesn't look like we'll have much more time before you'll have to leave for your appointment, does it?"

I was digging into my slice of pie as Jill spoke.

"What time is it?" I asked.

"Eight twenty-five."

"I really haven't forgotten about the gifts," I said. "The one is in the bus. Excuse me while I go to the VW and get it. Be right back."

Jill had just finished her pie when I returned with the book containing the Bible and other scriptures (all in one volume). I held it behind my back as I sat down next to her. I had no thought of finishing my own slice of pie from that point on.

When I held out the large volume and handed it over to Jill, she broke into an uncontrollable flow of tears. She reached out for my hand and put her head on it.

"I must have got the right thing," I said, "judging from your outpouring of happy tears."

(I admit that a few tears of my own got invited to the occasion.)

"Kep . . . how did you *ever* find this today . . . and *when*?"

"All I can say is that God moves in mysterious ways," I answered. "I'll explain more about it later. If you're through with your meal, I'll take care of the bill and we'll go to your car. I have one more gift to give you—one you *can't* hold in your hand.

Jill patted her eyes with her napkin and followed.

When we reached her car, I said, "I guess we'll have to call this the *ending* of our date and the *beginning* of our endless time together."

She looked at me with an expression of curiosity mingled with anticipation.

I took the scriptures from her hand and spoke softly into her ear.

"I've found an elderly couple who will be going on a church mission as soon as they can retire. They'll be providing answers to all of the questions I come up with—the countless questions you can't answer personally right now. Anyway, just accept the fact that we'll be on the same path. I'm already walking beside you—for my *own* sake. I've been told that most testimonies take time and commitment. I'm willing to give both, Jill. This is my gift."

Jill reached up and put her arms around my neck. Then she

put her hands on my cheeks and pulled me close to her lips. We shared our first-ever kiss . . . and then the second. After that I lost count.

CHAPTER 44

I was surprised to hear the sounds of Shackleton's piano as I came near the top of the zigzag stairs and approached the Overlook at the end of Evening Star Lane. When I came to his studio door, I found it slightly ajar. As I pushed it open, Bogart sprang up from his resting place beside the piano bench and came to greet me apologetically.

"No need to apologize," I said to him as I reached out to rub his floppy ear. It was evident to me that he enjoyed Shackleton's piano time. Maybe he had missed it over the past several days.

Shackleton smiled and continued playing until he reached the end of the piece. As I sat listening attentively in the recliner near the window, I marveled that he was producing all that I heard of the classical number from memory. Watching his fingers and hands move over the keyboard, I wondered whether it was tactile or visual memory or both that served him.

When Shackleton finished and turned toward me, I said, "I really enjoyed that. What was it you were playing?"

"That was Chopin's Premiere Ballade in G Minor. I've become a bit maladroit at it, I'm afraid. But it's a pleasure to recall it as I feel my fingers re-teach me measure by measure. Many things slip away from us if we neglect spending sufficient time with them, Kephart. That applies to meaningful relationships as well."

He stood and stretched forth his hands. As I arose from the

recliner, he placed his left hand on my right shoulder and shook my right hand. (This may have been an acquired habit resulting from his loss of sight—one that enabled him to avoid fumbling if he should touch my *left* hand first.)

"Shackleton, you touch on a point about relationships that I've never considered before. I pray I'll never have to deal with something like it in my personal life, but I came to realize for the first time today that marriage relationships may not only promote attraction, but they can provoke *repulsion.* What's hard for me to understand is—"

"I'm quite eager to hear what you have to say, Kephart, but let's go into the den and get comfortable before you continue, eh? I believe Bones has already delivered refreshments. I've given him and Phoebe another evening off in appreciation of their devoted service."

After Shackleton was seated in his high-backed chair in the den, I described for him the variety of snacks and beverages Bones had placed on the service table. This time he didn't choose the same snack foods as those offered him by Bones in the past. Instead, he asked if I would please load his paper plate with slices of smoked turkey together with cheddar and pepper jack cheeses. Along with this, he requested club crackers and pimiento stuffed olives.

(I felt certain he'd want a maple bar later. Fortunately there were four of them on the tray.)

His choice of beverage was freshly squeezed orange juice.

I closely copied Shackleton's choices for my own plate (doubling the amount). My stomach was rightfully claiming that I had cheated it at The Simple Pleasure when I left part of my dinner and most of my dessert behind. Time with Jill had been a priority then. But now my stomach was happy as I turned to an evening of partaking of snacks and engaging in mystery-solving with Shackleton.

"Now then, Kephart, you were saying something about

marriage relationships when I asked that we move into the den here to be more comfortable and snack as we talked."

As he said this, he began feeling around on the service table for something.

"Did Bones leave any napkins for us, Kephart?" he asked.

There were some just out of his reach on the table (blue-and-white checkered, of course). I unfolded one and placed it in his hand and then grabbed one for myself.

"Thank you, Kephart. I've become increasingly dependent on my staff to look after my needs and to respond to my requests, it seems. I suppose there's nothing wrong with that—if I don't become demanding. To *request* is best. There is an element of humility in a polite request. I've learned that it can be beneficial to *ask* others for their help or service, because humans are happiest when they are truly needed."

As he said this, I thought of Laura. Her "vacation" time was much shorter than I anticipated.

"You may have just now brought some understanding to what I was disturbed about, Shackleton," I said. "There are evidently hidden lines that some people are unable to cross in relationships—lines I haven't had cause to deal with until now."

"I perceive that you are talking about such lines that existed between Dan and Letha Crotty—not any that may have recently developed between you and Jillian. Am I correct?"

"Yes. I can see you were right about Dan when you said he has an inferior view of himself and that this could probably be traced back to his formative years. Who knows? But his excessive need for natural affection obviously led to his being manipulated by Letha. Any demand of him might have been looked on as being her *need* for him, which she later came to resent because, in her view, it made him a submissive follower.

"Is this explanation too muddled, or do you get what I'm trying to say?"

"I understand perfectly well what you're saying, Kephart. Just continue. Please."

"I've been told that women in general don't want to find their men being subservient to them. I'm guessing that Dan interpreted her demands of him as stemming from her needs for him. Is that possible, do you think?"

"That's possibly so, Kephart. But I'm assuming now that you have used your ring's visual memory enhancement feature to look over Mr. Koziol's laptop message. So I must ask what was in it that caused you to question Dan and Letha's relationship."

"Let me clarify that. It wasn't Koziol's laptop message that first got me to analyzing. It was a combination of things—mostly Ginger Wells telling Laura about Letha's feelings and attitude toward Dan and how these changed after they were married.

"Letha eventually considered him to be beneath her and regarded him as an embarrassment to have around—especially when her sales reps came to meetings. She made sure he was out of the house and busy at yard work before and during sales meetings.

"Then, in Kroy Koziol's unsent laptop letter, he told Letha that he had previously mailed a note to her, asking that she come and take the treasured artifact as a gift to be exchanged for big money. But she didn't come for it. Since she hadn't responded in any way, he questioned whether she had received the letter.

"My thinking then went along these lines:

"Maybe Letha didn't want to get involved personally with the artifact. It might have been a scary thing for her to have to deal covertly with a government intelligence agency. But she saw this as a chance for Dan to prove himself as being more assertive—to be the man she wished him to be. She could challenge him to find a way to get the prize and to deal with it. She came up with a plan that included Dan's getting a share of the money. However, in her plan (but privately in her mind), he'd have to prove himself by overcoming some obstacles, not just go and knock on Koziol's front door and have the gift handed to him.

"Maybe, once he had possession of the prize, it would be a strong incentive for him to convert it into money that would fund an entirely new lifestyle for both of them. If Ginger Wells was right about Letha's background and vanity, Letha should have been able to put on her best face and work her bodily charms to her best advantage. She could use Dan's vulnerability to get him started. And the plan would benefit her the most."

"Well done, Kephart! Well done indeed. As far as you've gone in your analyses, most all the inferences agree with the computer-stored letter. Many of the mystery's puzzlements could be answered by your deductions. However, certain questions remain.

"Why would Letha report to the police that Dan was missing? Would this not be more apt to assure his defeat rather than serve as a challenge?

"And why would she have failed to leave a note taped under the mailbox as planned? Certainly Dan would have no other means of escape, other than that which was to have been offered in the note."

"You're right, Shackleton. I just can't come up with a place for every piece to fit into the picture. There's been no satisfaction for me yet in my attempts to clarify every aspect of this case through deduction. Maybe I'm just not mentally equipped to contribute as much as you'd hoped of me."

"Don't get me wrong, Kephart! Please! You have contributed far more than I would have believed possible in the short time you've been devoting your talents to the achievement of my quests. And my pursuits have been accomplished in full largely because of your dedication and risk-taking. Mission accomplished, Kephart!

"Consider this: The missing man has been found and given a chance for a new life under much more favorable circumstances, thanks to you. Thanks to *your* efforts, the dangerous alien artifact has been taken from Earth-man's grasp. You have thereby eliminated a very real threat to us tellurians by your taking part in its return to the rightful and responsible intergalactic human society. You must—"

"But you're giving me much more personal credit than I deserve, Shackleton. I couldn't have done anything you're pointing out without Laura's hidden sacrifices and dedication. I'm sure you know that. If you're going to praise, please don't leave her out—or Graham Walker for that matter."

Shackleton interlocked his fingers, put his thumbs to his lips, and lowered his head. He nodded and smiled with his eyes closed—a typical reaction of his when he approved of an act or statement I made.

"There is something I'll have to say about Laura in a short while, Kephart. In the meantime, let me continue relating some things that should alleviate your present frustration.

"Let us remember that thus far this evening, we have merely been discussing causes, motives, and explanations that do nothing more than gratify our curiosity when it comes to the scenarios we've dealt with in this mystery. Whatever we come up with at this point in time will have no effect on inevitable outcomes.

"I must enlighten you about a great disadvantage that you have suffered in your attempts to answer your predictable questions. The disadvantage is that you do not *look* for evil . . . and that is a wonderful and marvelous trait that keeps good people good. You most often assign the best of human traits to those you study and interact with.

"Although you have a problem with prejudging people, you do not typically look for any *evil* aspects of their character. Because there is no evil in you, Kephart, you do not understand or look for evil in others. You may acknowledge evil when you are confronted with it, but you do not anticipate it in others.

That is not to say that you can ignore repetitious patterns of selfish behaviors typical of some individuals. Selfishness is just one of many seeds that sprout into evil. But only evil can accept evil. Only evil can identify with evil. The true perspective of evil is that it is the absence of good.

"Now I must emphasize an advantage that I have over you, and it is a tremendous advantage—one that is rare and one that I must be held accountable for when it comes to its use and application. That is my gift of clairvoyance.

"I know you haven't been previously aware of this, Kephart, but I must tell you that on the morning that I sent Laura to purchase the delivery van for your personal use, I handled the bag that contained the scent items Letha was supplying. I also handled some of Dan's unlaundered socks. As I've explained to you before, every human touch leaves its unique energy signature. I not only used my paranormal gift to discern spiritual dispositions, but I used my stellar ring to identify the persons linked to them.

"Letha's most pronounced traits were found on the bag containing the scent items she had prepared for Laura. You will recall that I said Dan was most likely a *victim* of evil. I also expressed to Dan during our meeting that we had reason to believe he was not a perpetrator of any harm to Kroy Koziol. You wondered how it could be possible that we should consider ourselves to be his friends.

"My greatest handicap was my inability to prove Letha's true relationship to Kroy Koziol, although I suspected it to be as Laura verified later by using her ring's visual-recall enhancement. Along with that, I was mentally alerted to the fact that most all insurance companies will not honor suicidal death claims within the first two years of the effective date of a policy.

"Putting that together with Letha's maiden name appearing as the addressee on the insurance-company letter and the two-year span of her marriage to Dan, I surmised that Letha was most likely inclined to go for the more easily obtainable insurance-policy offering. Dan's youth at the time could have qualified him for quite an attractive face value at a very low monthly premium. It was evident that the policy was put in force during a time when Letha and Dan were unwed. That in itself makes a statement about Letha, Kephart."

Shackleton's disclosures had me shaking my head in wonder.

"From what you've just been saying, Shackleton, I'm to see that Letha was attempting to send Dan into various death traps, or serious life hazards. I'm thinking now of Dan's being unable to swim, and the possibility of getting caught with the alien artifact by government agents, with no means of escape. No note under the mailbox and reporting him missing left him trapped. I guess you could say that Gaston saved Dan's life by poisoning the vicious killer dogs just a day or so before Dan came on the scene. Wow!

"I can also see why Letha was reluctant to give the deputies the scent items before her diabolical plan was fully underway. Laura said Letha had everything packaged and ready to hand to her when she came for them the very next day. She also questioned Letha's impassive attitude about Dan's disappearance.

"So I suppose there isn't any way Letha could be legally charged with an attempted crime, since there's no way to prove her *intentions*, right?"

"I don't believe charges are ever made based on intentions, Kephart. One might be led to *confess* an intended act, but I doubt whether that in itself could lead to prosecution. I'm not a lawyer. I just don't know. However, I do know that without feelings of remorse and a change of heart, an evil person will never be comfortable in the presence of his or her Creator. Evil must eventually (and forever) live with self-condemnation.

"If you continue to pursue Jillian's sources of Truth, you will eventually run across a scriptural statement that reads, 'Wickedness never was happiness.'"

"How could you possibly know that I'm preparing to study

the restored Gospel, Shackleton? How could you *possibly* know that?"

"Quite simply, it's a matter of putting three bits of information together, Kephart.

"First, you informed me that Jillian puts her religion ahead of all that she would personally desire for herself.

"Second, Jillian and Laura belong to the same church.

"Third, Laura and I do, at times, discuss topics that are not work related. We both care about you, Kephart. We've recently discussed the obvious spiritual growth you've attained over the past several days. In a recent conversation, Laura told me that you had asked what church she attended. What else could I deduce from these facts, knowing, as I do, your curious nature and your feelings for Jillian?"

(Although Shackleton has always retained his mystique, I liked hearing these brief disclosures of his keen memory and how his mind works.)

"I'm glad to learn that you and Laura have times of entering into discussions aside from those centered on your quests," I said. "I'm sure you know she suffers a lot from her denying herself basic human needs."

"I do, Kephart . . . which again points out the need for unconstrained understandings in human relationships . . . which brings me to the perfect moment for informing you that I have arranged to meet with Laura here in little more than an hour. Bones and Phoebe will be returning in time to prepare another snack tray and to rekindle the fire.

"Laura and I have rarely met here in the den, as planned this evening. But I have decided this should change. And you will be gratified to know that I have some comforting thoughts to convey to her."

No words coming from Shackleton at this time could have impressed or pleased me more than these.

I thought there was little else we could discuss at the present. Other things could wait. I also decided that there would be time enough for me to enjoy a maple bar.

"I have to tell you that what you've just said is a great comfort to *me* already, Shackleton."

As we sat for a few minutes, consuming snack foods in silence, my mind digested our shared disclosures and thoughts.

"There are four maple bars on the tray," I said. "If you'd like one, I'll hand one to you."

"I would, Kephart. Thank you."

As I lifted the maple bars from the tray, I noticed a curled strip of paper placed beside them. The paper evidently wasn't something accidentally left there.

"I see there's a strip of curled paper here on the tray. It seems to have been put here for a purpose."

"Ah! Yes, Kephart. I had Bones prepare it for us to briefly discuss during our meeting this evening. What time is it?"

"Nine thirty-five."

"Time enough, Kephart. And there is time enough as well for you to enjoy your maple bar as I lead you through a demonstration.

"The curled strip is called a Möbius band. It is nothing more than a length of fourteen-inch by two-inch-wide paper that has opposite corners twisted one hundred and eighty degrees and taped together. The dimensions are not important—only the half twist and the taping.

"Now, to serve its purpose, you will have to disregard the ends having been taped together and treat the entire piece as though it has no beginning or ending. Do you happen to have a pen or a pencil on you?"

"Always," I said.

"What you are holding in your hand is my choice of a model

of our universe and relative time, Kephart. From what you are now observing, how many sides do you see?"

"Two."

"Now touch your pencil to the side facing you and mark a line as you continuously pull the strip through your fingers. Tell me what you find."

I carefully followed his instructions.

"I wind up touching the pencil line where it first started," I said.

"So how many sides does the model *truly* have, Kephart?"

"Only one," I replied, fascinated.

"Now, to make efficient use of our time, I will tell you that you'll find that the same thing holds true for the model's edges. It has only one edge.

"You can imagine that it's possible to draw a pencil line all over a hollow ball or a donut-shaped tube and guide the line back to its starting point. But either one of those objects has an interior, untouchable surface.

"It will be obvious to you that drawing the line over the length of the Möbius strip takes more time than it would take to draw it over and around the model's edge and then stop it on what appears to be the back surface at the exact point *behind* its start.

"I can see that," I said.

"Consider the pencil line to represent time," Kephart. "What would take even less time than going over and around the model's edge to reach the established halfway point behind?"

It didn't take me long to see the obvious answer.

"Punch a hole through the strip with the tip of the pencil," I said.

"Aha! Now think, Kephart, *think*! Have you not just traveled halfway from what we assigned to be the beginning of the universe to its resultant ending in essentially no time at all?"

"Fascinating!" I said. "But I'm happy with learning from this model of the universe and relative time when I consider what you've told me before about these things . . . no, maybe it was Jill who told me. Anyway, I do remember that she made a point by asking, 'If something has no ending, can it have a beginning?' Then she gave me a clue from a verse in a song: 'Nothing comes from nothing; nothing ever could.' I've thought a lot about this and the things you've shown me. I'm always impressed by how closely your separate views align with each other and how they both ring true."

"I'm certain your perceptions will be expanded when you have time and solitude in which to dwell on what you've come to see as *Truth*, Kephart. It is obvious to me that Jillian is an excellent mentor for you. Once again I must say that you are indeed fortunate to have found her. You will do well to strengthen the bond of your relationship."

"It hasn't taken any effort for that to happen in the little time we've had to share together, Shackleton. Neither one of us has ever been happier."

He smiled his gratification as he said, "Kephart, I'm sorry that we too have so little time to share this evening. Regardless, there is much for you to absorb and contemplate before we meet again.

"Now, there are two things you must remember and understand about this model I've shown you.

"First, if you disregard the taping of the joined ends, it is without beginning or ending.

"Second, the line that represents time travels through various *orders* of time as it passes through ever-changing energy frequencies. Time is not the same throughout the universe. Neither are all elemental energies. Perhaps Jillian can quote a scripture or two that will declare or suggest these things to be so.

"You can easily see that returning to your starting point requires nothing more than passing back through the punched hole. However, with respect to the universe (as we perceive it), all changes relating to your time spent traveling will have taken place as if you had traveled your personal life's length along the line—regardless of its being an infinitesimally short distance.

"In any case, you will have changed in bodily composition as you return to what you first considered to be a starting point—no matter what path you chose. Punching a hole through the model is much like passing through a veil—moving into or out of a parallel aspect of our universe.

"You will eventually read that some human bodies have become translated (as was the case with the Apostle John). Being translated is not to be construed as being resurrected. It means only that the physical body is temporarily changed in such a way that death and resurrection are postponed and that the body cannot experience sickness or pain in its translated state. After resurrection we may inherit body energies of a telestial, terrestrial, or celestial order.

"Do you have your ring activated?" he asked abruptly.

"Always, when we share these meeting times," I said.

"I'm sure you will find great inspiration and comfort in studying your new scriptures, Kephart. As you might have deduced, before I became blind, I searched through a variety of religions of the world as a seeker of Truth. No other source has fulfilled my curiosity or offered truths as much as the source that you are becoming acquainted with through Jillian—and Laura, of course. I testify that I need not look any further.

"Now, Kephart, I want you to realize that both science and *inspired* religion pursue common or similar goals. Do you have some notion of what their similar goals might be?"

As I was taking too much time to ponder and think of an answer, Shackleton jumped in and supplied his own.

"They are attempting to learn and to act on the truth of all things, either temporal or spiritual, in order that human life might be advanced and improved upon. Unfortunately, they do not follow a common path. Now, which do you suppose follows the most direct approach?"

"My guess would be inspired religion, as you put it, but I—"

"What I mean by inspired religion is that which is based upon valid revelations from both past and present-day prophets. Direct revelation for any era of time has come from God's chosen prophets—those who have been called and authorized by God.

"Do you have the conviction that God is unchanging, Kephart?"

"I'm not so sure of a conviction, as I am of a *belief* at present. Will that do?"

"Yes, Kephart. I have no doubt that you will retain your inquisitive nature and apply it toward a goal of pursuing Truth, among other things. You must know that change is, and ever has been, present among all of mortal man's experiences and that the natural man has always been at enmity with God.

"You will learn that God is and always has been unchanging. Being perfect, he has no need to change. And he has no less need to warn and guide mortals now than in centuries past. Man is sinful by nature. The only way that man can meet with God face to face is that he first be sanctified and transfigured, as was Moses. However, most all prophets received revelation for mankind by way of the Holy Spirit.

"I attest to you that God has appointed prophets to guide, warn, and instruct man in these latter times as in times of old. But be aware that false prophets exist now, as they did in ancient times. Satan is real, and he is cunning. There are ways to discern between false and true prophets, as you will eventually learn, Kephart.

"Now, you may be wondering why I have chosen this limited portion of our meeting time to acquaint you with the Möbius band as a model of the universe. I am compelled to do so, because I foresee that you will shortly be dwelling in an inner world with few distractions—a world in which you will be sorting through myriad thoughts and realizations as you attempt to interpret your recent experiences and their meanings.

"If you have not already seen time as it truly is, the Möbius strip will show you that the only time is *now*, but that will take some pondering. Time is nothing more than measuring experienced change, both inwardly and outwardly.

"There is a verse of scripture that you may come to appreciate the more you ponder it, Kephart. Please fetch my Bible from its place and look up Ecclesiastes, chapter three, verse fifteen. If you will—"

"That's a scripture verse that Jill asked me to study!" I exclaimed. "But I haven't had a Bible to refer to until today. That's amazing, Shackleton! I mean, it's got to be important, or I wouldn't have had it pointed out to me by each of you on separate occasions."

By the time I'd found it, Shackleton was quoting it word for word from memory. He was right on, without error in his quoting as I read.

"That which hath been is now; and that which is to be hath already been; and God requireth that which is past."

"Thank you, Kephart. You can readily see that this scripture supports the statement that the only time is *now*. Why do you suppose that God would require that which is past?"

I had to give this some thought, but Shackleton was patient.

"Would it be that he will base his judgments on our past lives, or on all of our lifetime acts? I guess I'm asking, would our past acts *justify* his judgments?"

Shackleton's face revealed his approval, even before he spoke.

"Excellent! I have no doubt that you will interpret your scriptures correctly if you will take time to ponder them, Kephart. But bear in mind that scriptures will carry deeper meanings for you as your lifetime experiences bring changes to your points of focus on them. And above all, please acknowledge and appreciate the need for our merciful Savior—the one who intercedes for us and is our advocate—the one who has paid the price for the sins we've committed throughout our lifetimes.

"Tell me, Kephart, are your scriptures all contained in one volume or two?"

"One," I said.

"Indeed! That is best. And since you have my single Bible to refer to in your hand, turn to Ezekiel, chapter thirty-seven. Please."

"Okay. I've got it," I said after hunting for a couple of minutes.

"Read verses fifteen through nineteen to yourself. It will help your understanding to know that a "stick" can be equated to a modern book. The stick, as such, in ancient times was used to wrap parchment or papyrus around. The resulting scroll thus served as a present-day book of pages.

"Verse nineteen is especially significant, as it prophetically points out that the sticks of Judah and Joseph shall be "one in your hand." It will be evident to you that the Bible contains a record of the Jews, while the volume of additional scriptures contains a record of the descendants of Joseph.

"I'm certain that you may have wondered what has motivated me to study religion, as evidenced by the assorted volumes occupying my library shelves, Kephart. I have for many years been captivated by what both science and religion have had to offer as disclosures of Truth. You might say that I have been obsessed with curiosity in my quest to learn what is undeniably true."

He softly chuckled, realizing that he had just openly confessed to me that he too had an insatiable curiosity, although it was one directed toward a meaningful goal.

"Intellectualizing has been a futile distraction for me, and philosophizing has eventually led me down paths of self-delusion. Scientists have too often found it necessary to alter or completely change the conclusions of their premises.

"Truth can best be found where it springs forth from its spiritual fountain—the fountain being undeniable and self-evident."

"But can't the scriptures—the words of the prophets—be interpreted differently by various readers?" I asked.

"Indeed they can, Kephart. And that is just one fact that substantiates the need for a modern-day prophet—one who is qualified to clarify and promote correct understandings of the revelations of both the past and the present.

"The words of true, appointed prophets must be studied and pondered *prayerfully*, Kephart. They were especially appropriate for the era in which they were delivered, but they also ring true and make sense for all successive generations of truth seekers. Every appointed prophet in every age has been placed by God to serve the entire world populace, not just members of his true, established Church. Because God unconditionally loves every human soul, his words are to be disseminated to every one of his mortal children. Bear in mind that God's unconditional love need not be *earned*; however, his blessings are granted to those who are living in accord with obedience to eternal principles and commandments."

Shackleton's last declarations had intensified my motivation to search and read through my scriptures. But he had another helpful suggestion for me.

"You will find topical guides in your joined volumes that will greatly assist you in locating specific scriptural answers to your never-ending questions, Kephart. I urge you to make frequent use of them early on. Additionally, you will find footnotes on many of the pages. These will provide interesting cross-references to pursue."

I could see that Shackleton must have spent hundreds of hours delving into all that had fascinated him about the mysteries of God, not just the mysteries of men. There was so much more to him than I had supposed. But now I wondered even more about his being a member of Laura and Jill's church. I wondered, too, whether his blindness might have curtailed or stopped his activities, although I couldn't see any reason that it should. Braille or recorded versions of the scriptures must exist for the sightless.

I was just at the point of asking him about his having personal affiliation with this church when he put me on another path of scriptural exploration.

"Now, Kephart, because you are using your ring to record all that I am able to convey to you in the little time we have, I want you to acquaint yourself with an epistle, or didactic letter, from the Apostle Paul to the Hebrews—particularly the verses one through six in chapter eleven. These few verses support some vital declarations I have made in the past few days. The topics are faith, multiple worlds, and translation.

"Faith cannot be overly emphasized, since its practice is basic to all of man's achievements and growth, let alone his religion. Faith is well defined here. Verse three supports Einstein's statement that what we perceive to be physical reality is an illusion, 'albeit a mighty persistent one.' You will acknowledge that the Apostle Paul knew this centuries before Albert Einstein was born. Incidentally, you must know that Einstein was *convinced* that God existed.

"The framing of multiple worlds is pointed out in verse three. This is one place in the Bible (the stick of Judah) where the multiplicity of worlds is addressed. However, there are subsequent referrals to "worlds without end" in the latter half of your combined volumes of scriptures, Kephart.

"Now you will see that it has been my good fortune and blessing to be connected with the Abiding Ones—alien humans from other worlds who are aware of the purpose of this Earth's creation. I must point out to you that the AOs are unique *humans,* not humanoids (those creatures having only human characteristics). There are also biological robots that serve certain non-human species by remotely exploring other worlds, including our own. Dealing with such varieties of technologically supported societies can invite deception. That's a primary reason for testing Laura and Jillian regarding their immunity from deception, as well as their adherence to the principles and covenants of their vital faith.

"It is best that you be prayerfully guided as you engage in any scripture studies. There well may be some pursuits that you are not ready to deal with or that may distract you from your most advantageous path of learning at this time."

"I'm already looking forward to being guided by an older couple who are preparing themselves to perform missionary work as soon as they retire in the near future, Shackleton. You will remember the man who offered Dan Crotty employment and a place to live? He and his wife have already offered me their help. They're the ones who gave me my set of scriptures."

"Splendid! That is a welcome comfort for me, Kephart."

Bogart's tail suddenly began to flap on the carpet. He put his chin on Shackleton's knee and looked at him expectantly.

"Thank you, Bogart," Shackleton said as he rubbed Bogart's head and ears.

"Looks like the Judds have come home," I said.

"Yes, that will be Bones and Phoebe. They were to precede Laura in time to prepare for her arrival. I'm truly sorry that we can't spend more time just now, Kephart. But I will be giving you a ring call tomorrow to arrange for a follow-up meeting. There will be more to discuss, including the possibility of your becoming engaged in a new case—a reported possible abduction.

We shall see.

"Perhaps we can take care of all that is presently necessary using our rings. I presume that you will be available?"

"Your requests are my priority," I said.

Bogart licked my hand and headed toward the studio door.

No need for you to see me out," I told Shackleton. "Bogart is performing very well at that; although, he does seem to regret my having to go."

Shackleton smiled and waved as I left him.

The evening sky still retained its twilight glow. Low clouds were shining beneath the light of a bright moon. I stopped at the Overlook long enough to fully appreciate all that the heavens had to offer. As I descended the stairway, I heard Shackleton's piano come to life again.

CHAPTER 45

I wasn't sure where to head next. An early bedtime was out of the question. For some reason I felt drawn to the moonlit waters of Bellingham Bay. I suspected that Boulevard Park was closed to traffic after sundown, but I knew I could park the VW bus in Old Fairhaven and walk the appealing trail that led along the scenic water's edge.

Shackleton was right about my soon dwelling in an "inner world" while I tried to sort out in my mind what values and perspectives I could gain from my recent experiences of the past several days. I hadn't walked far before my mind was immersed in my adventures and trials.

Predominating overall were those emotionally charged memories of my times spent with Jill and, of course, the worrisome, anxious hours of her absence. I couldn't exclude her influence from any part of my experiences. She had become an essential part of me.

I had come to realize how vital relationships are between God and man—between man and woman—between faith and meaningful achievements (whether among mortals or supernal beings).

For some reason families and ancestries stood out, probably because I could see that every individual I had dealt with was more than a physical product of his or her lineage, to some degree. I couldn't point a judgmental finger even at Letha Crotty, knowing the reported misguiding influences of her mother. And how far back must one go to find freedom from adverse parental influence? Was there ever an example (mortally speaking) of parental innocence?

On reflection, I had gotten a glimpse of the importance of a way to bring all mortals nearer to a likeness of our spiritual Father in every respect. Genuine, unconditional, selfless love was the key. That was my perception of God's love. It was Christ's love. It must be that the combined volumes of scriptures that Aaron Eden gave me could show me examples of how to acquire Christ-like love.

I felt deeply humbled when I considered all that I lacked in truth and learning. But now I had hope. I knew where to place my hope and my little faith. Jill's "big picture" had steered me onto a different path, one with a new perspective.

Before I met Jill, I had never been so keenly aware of how alone, or how *lonely*, I was. I yearned to have a family of my own, but not with anything less than the man/wife bond I could envision with Jill. Our individual backgrounds lent us a great potential advantage through enduring understandings.

From my early teens forward, I had acquired an increasing appreciation for sensibly fashioned, "good" poetry—poetry that accurately expressed the author's feelings and inspirations with clarity. During brief moods of emotionally driven thoughts, I had tried to capture and convey my feelings with words. Some I had written, but many of the unwritten were lost. Most of my feelings I expressed with rhyming words. Some I didn't. One of these surfaced with the recalling of my recent years of loneliness. (I must have had many former years of dealing with loneliness.) I wrote these words during the years of my mother's decline:

Loneliness—a thief of Love—
Dwells not in Solitude,
But thrives unseen amid crowds or couples,

Feasting on Exclusion, Indifference, and Neglect.

My concept of reality had been yanked along from interpretations of former mundane Earthly experiences to those of cosmic associations and spiritual offerings of the past and present. I had arrived at a conviction that each individual's perception of reality was one of his or her own making—until undeniable truths changed that view.

I could see that Truth was God's reality, and the more we practiced learning bits of Truth through faith, the more we embraced God and his real world. In the words of Christ (as I'd read them to my mother), "Ye shall know the truth and the truth shall make you free."

Shackleton and Jill had both taught me many things over the past few days. I could barely grasp all that now entered my mind. I truly was thankful for the advantages of having the stellar ring so I could store and retrieve conversations and events. And I appreciated all that had indirectly come my way via the Abiding Ones. There was vastly more to appreciate of God's creations, both on Earth and in the heavens, than I could ever have imagined.

My mind needed a rest. I slipped into a creative mood and began to relax more as I walked in the moonlight along the edge of Bellingham Bay. Lines of poems began to enter my head, so I twisted my ring on to "record" and sat on a bench that faced the bay. It took me more than a half hour to complete the shortest one. It was a synopsis of the observations I presently had regarding myself. I thought of sharing it with Shackleton if an appropriate opportunity should come.

What I am now,
What I was then—
While much the same—
Are different men.

Unceasing change is
All about
My world within,
My world without.

My every choice
From sleep to sleep
Is what to toss
And what to keep

Of thoughts and acts,
Of heart's desires,
While subject to
Refining fires.

The other poem that began forming in my mind was inspired by the moonlit clouds and the lights reflecting off the waters of the bay. Although I had spent relatively little time near the sea during the past months, I had shortly come to have a profound affinity for the Puget Sound region and its coastal beauties.

The more I dwelt on constructing the second poem of the evening, the more I felt that Jill was the one it was meant for—the one I was directing it to.

Dream with me—
Of moonlit clouds on summer nights,
Of dancing waves reflecting lights
That greet a shoreward sea . . .
Come dream with me.

Oh, dream with me—
Of shoreline walks 'neath misty skies,
Of driftwood talks amid seagull cries,

Of captivating sea winds
Exploring endlessly.

Then dream of bright and breezy autumn mornings
When the sea-spray fills the air;
Of cresting waves that crash their winter warnings,
Of those long nights to come that best we'd share.

Dream with me—
Of ebbing tide at sunset's glow,
Of harbor lights and lamps turned low . . .
Then dream your footsteps turning
Toward home to dream with me.

Midnight had passed before I gave serious thought to finding a place to sleep. The VW camper didn't appeal to me. I had no idea where I could find a good place to park it—certainly not in the alley behind the convenience store. Besides, I needed to stretch out and succumb to deep, relaxing sleep, if possible.

Shackleton would be calling for a meeting time, and I would definitely need a breakfast before I got involved in any new events or discussions.

I headed for the motel.

CHAPTER 46

MY cell-phone alarm woke me up at 9:30. I took great pleasure in a long, hot shower. After dressing, I went to the motel lobby to enjoy my free continental breakfast.

Relaxing in a leather chair, I made two cell-phone calls.

The first was to Bick and Dozie to let them know it was doubtful that I'd ever be able to retain my on-call status, since my new employment was demanding so much of my time. I told Bick that I'd come by and have him service the VW (when due), as he'd asked. I said I'd definitely not ignore him and Dozie as friends, and I asked that Dozie please inform me when their new child arrived. (I was hoping it would be a girl this time.)

My second call was to Selma. She was very relieved and happy to learn that all was well with me, but she asked that I keep her updated on my life at least twice a week. She said that Wilbur and Bessie Mae were behaving like kids just out of school for the summer. She had already made an appointment for Bessie to have some dental work done. I told her not to forget that I'd offered to pay for it. I said that I would be paying more rent money than in the past, and I asked that she pass along my love and appreciation to Joel. After all, he'd been my life saver. It felt good to know that I was part of such a fine family.

I intended to stay at their home until my future life with Jill began, but I didn't mention it. I would always help out with money if they needed it, but I knew they'd never ask. There was no question about Jill keeping watch on their circumstances.

So now I felt relieved that I could commit my life to assisting others and maintaining meaningful friendships. My new perspective had already greatly influenced my values. However, I wasn't so naïve as to think that Shackleton was immune to sudden catastrophic changes in his health or lifetime pursuits. It felt good to be committed to looking after the potential needs of others, but I was highly dependent on Shackleton to be able to support my new status. If I were going to become responsible for the well-being of Jill and our future family, I needed to plan ahead. I made a mental note that I must learn all I could in the next few days about how and where to invest money, so as to protect my future interests, as well as theirs.

Not long after I'd completed my cell-phone conversations, I got a ring call from Shackleton.

"Good morning, Kephart! I sincerely hope that you have had sufficient rest and that you are now ready to meet with me at my home. My plan is to meet at eleven o'clock, if that is acceptable with you. I am eager to inform you of some changes that are taking place—changes that you should welcome. If they are not to your liking, I encourage you early-on to be honest with me in every respect. Please."

"Perfect timing," I said. "I'll be there. And you know I'll always be honest about my feelings, Shackleton."

"Excellent! Thank you, Kephart!"

Our conversation ended abruptly. I was now a bit anxious to learn about Shackleton's proposed changes. Change was unrelenting as it brought ever-present unknowns to man's horizon. In the past I was never so much aware of how it constantly challenged faith.

* * *

Evening Star Lane was bright with May sunshine when once again I knocked on Shackleton's studio door. There was no response to my knock this time. The sounds of his piano brought good music to my ears. I didn't hesitate to open the door and let myself inside. Bogart was nowhere in sight. This was disturbing to me. There had never been a time before when he wasn't there to greet me. Well . . . on second thought, he wasn't there to greet me on that first morning—the morning when I first met Shackleton.

I sat in the comfortable recliner near the west window and listened attentively to the captivating classical piece Shackleton was playing. I truly enjoyed it and said so when he finished the number. Once again I asked what it was that he'd been playing.

"That was Brahms's Rhapsody Number Two in G Minor. I'm happy to hear that you enjoy it, Kephart. There are many classical works that go unappreciated these days, I regret to say."

At that moment a scratching sound came from Shackleton's workroom door. Obviously it was Bogart wanting inside to join us. Without a word, but with a smile and a nod from Shackleton, I went to the door to let Bogart in.

My reaction to what I encountered was nothing short of astonishment. This was followed by shock as Bogart gave my hand a brief lick and raced forward to Shackleton's side.

Jill was standing in the workroom doorway.

Her face was beaming with pleasure and love as she came forward to give me a long, squeezing hug.

Shackleton's voice seemed to come from a great distance.

"As I said, Kephart, changes are likely to be occurring—changes that you would most likely welcome."

I was speechless. My eyes were blinking. Jill began to laugh.

Her infectious laughter quickly spread, and soon we were all caught up in its welcome, refreshing influence.

"I encourage you to take Jillian to The Simple Pleasure to enjoy a midday meal together as she explains the reasons for her presence here, Kephart. I'm certain you should have no objections to that."

"Not one," I answered. "Anyway, I'm not capable of doing any thinking at present, so we're all better off—don't you think?"

Shackleton arose from his piano bench. As Jill and I approached him, he reached out to give us each a shoulder-high hug. Then he felt along his piano and pulled a large envelope from its top.

Beaming with pleasure, he placed the envelope in my hand and said, "You can wait until Jillian has finished with her explanations before opening this in her presence, Kephart. Then it will please me if you will both spend the rest of the day in pursuit of whatever pleases the two of you. I'm sure you will find many things to share and discuss."

Jill looked at me and tilted her head with an agreeing nod.

"I arranged with the school to have the day off," she said. "Next week will be my final week of student teaching. We'll have oral and written evaluations after that."

"How did you get here?" I asked.

"Laura Rutledge drove me here this morning."

"Then you now have the privilege of riding in the yellow VW bus once again," I said, laughing.

Shackleton seemed to be amused as he listened to the verbal interchange between us. Apparently, he anticipated a question I had before I could voice it.

"I'm in no need of food, Kephart. Phoebe prepared an excellent breakfast for me very early this morning. I will be happy just knowing that you and Jillian are enjoying time together to eat and to discuss the recent developments that she will be sharing."

Jill was the first to shake Shackleton's hand. When he shook my hand, I felt it to be firm and assuring as we turned to go.

Bogart moved close between Jill and me to escort us to the studio door. His eyes were bright as he looked back and forth at each of us. He was definitely smiling. He had obviously quickly bonded with Jill in the short time they'd been together. Jill's affection for animals (especially dogs) had evidently been sensed and understood.

* * *

The Simple Pleasure restaurant was nearly half-full when we entered. We were led to a booth with a table covered by a white cloth and a glass top that had just been cleared and cleaned. It was located near a window, which I appreciated, and I thanked the hostess for her having steered us to it.

Before the waitress came to take our orders, I took Jill's hand and bowed my head in prayer to express thanks and ask that the food be blessed. Inwardly, I felt no inhibitions about being observed. Why should I? I was sincerely humbled and filled with true appreciation for the blessings that Heavenly Father granted us—more blessings than I could be aware of at the moment. (Later, as I was eating, I felt gratified to see another couple holding hands before they ate as they publicly prayed together.)

This time Jill ordered baked lasagna. I asked for ravioli stuffed with Portobello mushrooms. We each had tomato basil soup for starts, and the restaurant supplied us with a large bowl of salad to be shared. Freshly baked breadsticks brushed with garlic butter couldn't be hidden for long under a white napkin.

Once again, Jill and I each ordered a slice of lemon meringue pie topped with whipped cream for dessert. Eating was pure pleasure—which got in the way of our involving ourselves in meaningful conversation at the time. Then I ate in silence and listened intently while Jill took her time informing me about her early-morning experiences.

"I stayed up late correcting test papers last night," she said. "Laura woke me up with a phone call just before six. So you can imagine how confused I was to be getting a call at that hour from someone I scarcely knew. She identified herself by recalling the time we were in that secret room when she offered me something to eat while Alleri left us alone briefly.

"Laura first asked me if I could be free to devote some of the morning to learning about an opportunity and making a commitment that would keep me closely involved with *you* in your assignments. She told me that you were both employed by the same man and that, as you worked together, she shared some of her stresses and personal problems with you. But she made a point of saying that there were a lot of things neither one of you knew about 'Mr. G,' as you call him. She called him a man of many secrets.

"She explained that he wanted both of you to call him by his middle name, partly because of his desire to preclude public notice of any kind. She told me that he relied heavily on the two of you now. Although she'd been deeply involved for several years in his personal quests, he needed a different kind of help as well. That's why you were chosen.

"I have to tell you that her informing me of this made me very proud of you, Kep," Jill said. "But I *did* begin to have some jealous feelings when I sensed how close you and Laura had become," she added, blinking her eyes and tilting her head.

Then she smiled at me as she said, "However, my jealousy soon fled when she gave me her reason for calling so early. (I'll tell you more about that in a minute.)

"I actually began to have sympathetic, friendly feelings for her when she explained that she'd been devoting several years of her life to serving Shackleton because she'd fallen in love with him—

even though she knew it was a futile and fruitless love in terms of her ever finding self-fulfillment. She just couldn't let him go."

Jill began to laugh as she caught me blinking with my mouth open.

Then she paused, wearing a curious look.

"Oh! Sorry, Kep. Yes! I know his middle name too now, so you don't have to hide it from me anymore."

"From what you've just been telling me, I can see there must be some major change in the way Shackleton will be using Laura," I said. "So what *was* her reason for calling you so early? Tell me if I'm wrong," I added, "but my guess is that it was to see if you might agree to be involved in Shackleton's pursuits in some way—maybe provide relief time for her. I know Shackleton arranged to have Laura meet with him last night to arrive at some understandings and to give her some overdue comforting.

"Some time must have been spent preparing you this morning if you've been in Shackleton's home these past several hours. Am I right?"

"It's been both a scary and an exciting day for me, Kep. Except for taking time to drive to the school to deliver corrected papers and arrange for a substitute so I could take the day off, I'm not sure *where* I've been.

"What's been frightening is that I *first* had to agree to be sedated and transported to a place where I could secretly undergo a procedure that would prepare me for performing my tasks. Laura explained that unless I could agree to that, she couldn't give me any other details about what I would be qualifying myself for. So that was a daunting unknown that called for a lot of faith on my part.

"I told her I wanted to pray about it first and asked if I could call her back. She understood and agreed to that. When I called her back, I said I would accept on one condition (which she agreed to), and that was if I didn't feel good about continuing to be involved in some aspect of the assigned work, my request to be released would be granted."

On hearing this, I quickly nodded and gave her my smile of approval.

"So here I am, Kephart Stone . . . ready to serve. But Laura said that I would need to have *you* complete the balance of my preparation."

"Did she say *how*?" I asked, perplexed.

Jill shrugged her shoulders and shook her head.

As she looked at me expectantly, I tried to think of something that I could supply her with, but I didn't have the foggiest notion of what she had already been given. I could see that the likely reason for her to be sedated was to hide from her the *place* of undergoing a preparation procedure—which I felt certain was Shackleton's secret inner room.

Then, when Jill spread her upturned hands out on the table in a gesture of resignation and frustration, I was struck with the answer: She wasn't wearing a stellar ring. And I knew that our rings couldn't be swapped or loaned.

Just as this realization registered with me, I remembered the large envelope that Shackleton had given me. He said that when Jill had finished with her explanations, I should open the envelope in her presence. That had to be it.

I laughed. Then I stood up and took Jill by the hand.

"Back to the bus," I said. "The answer is hidden in the good-old yellow VW."

Jill was shaking her head in bafflement as I yanked her along with me to settle for the price of our meals and head for our parking space.

I opened the sliding door of the bus and handed her the large envelope. We sat together on the back seat.

When she withdrew two life insurance policies from the envelope (one for each of us), my face must have revealed my disappointment. (There was no ring.) But Jill's face disclosed shock and disbelief. She couldn't comprehend my look of disappointment. She was staring at the face amounts on the policies: one million dollars each!

She turned them toward me to read.

I sat stunned and speechless.

CHAPTER 47

I glanced back and forth between the insurance policies and Jill. She was obviously struggling with accepting their tremendous offering.

My first thought was that Shackleton must have had no doubt about the permanence of the bond Jill and I shared. The identical policies with their equal values as gifts in case of his death spoke of his non-preferential affection for the two of us—a mature, charitable affection.

A second thought was that Jill must have made a significant impression on Shackleton. He must have felt (or known) that she'd be involved in his beneficence for a considerably long time. This possibility may have been influenced by his clairvoyant gift, which gave me cause to wonder.

Questions tumbled into my mind. Were the Abiding Ones withholding the ring for the present? Was I all wrong in assuming that Jill had been qualified to have her own ring? What other kind of grounding could she have been receiving?

Regardless, my immediate problem of completing Jill's instruction was going unanswered. I put my hand to my forehead and covered my eyes as I tried to concentrate on where else I might locate the stellar ring that I still felt certain Jill was to receive. Had I missed a clue? Would a ring call to either Laura or Shackleton relieve my puzzlement?

Suddenly I felt Jill's hand on my forehead as she brought my own hand away from my eyes. I looked up at her. Her face wore a questioning expression as her other hand lifted a very small green bag from her lap. It was closed with a drawstring of the same color. The shade of green nearly matched the color of her skirt.

"This must have fallen in my lap as I pulled the insurance policies out of the envelope," she said. "Is this what you brought me here to find?"

"That's it! What a relief," I said as I reached for the little bag. "Yes! Thank you, thank you, Jill."

When she handed me the bag, I felt for the ring I expected it would contain. The ring was definitely inside this soft, velvety wrap. I handed it back to Jill.

"Open it," I said softly and eagerly.

Jill's eyes searched back and forth between my eyes and the bag as she deftly untied the drawstring and spread the bag open.

Her dark-green eyes widened and her lips parted as she let the ring fall into her upturned palm.

"It's absolutely beautiful!" she exclaimed.

It *was* a beautiful ring of artistic and feminine design. I couldn't have been more pleased to see it go to Jill. It seemed to have been designed for her only.

"Try it on for fit," I said.

Because she had her religious reminder ring on the little finger of her right hand, she tried forcing it onto the ring finger of that hand, but the ring was too small, too tight to fit.

I reached over and pinched the little finger of her *left* hand.

"Do you have some doubts that it would look good beside a wedding-ring set?" I asked. "Or are you thinking of only gold with your diamonds?"

She tightened her grip on the stellar ring and hugged me close with her head against mine.

Feeling her happiness tears on my face once again, I said, "Consider my questions to amount to a marriage proposal, Jill. What better place could I find for proposing marriage than the back seat of a VW bus—and a bright yellow one at that?"

She pushed herself away just far enough to gaze into my eyes and convey the depth of her love. Then, smiling and teary-eyed, she let her head drop to my chest.

"You know there's no one I could ever want to marry more than I do *you*, my Kep," she said softly. "It's just a matter of timing. For now, I'd be thrilled to wear an engagement ring. The marriage covenant will come after your baptism and confirmation. I will wait for however long that takes, but I have full faith in its happening.

"This past week I've seen you change a lot already. I've felt remarkable spiritual growth in you . . . and you haven't yet had anything more than prayers and faith to take you where you are. I believe in you, my Kep."

"What do I have to do to qualify myself for baptism?" I asked.

"You may already *be* there. You've demonstrated faith in Christ (that's a vital step) and a sincere desire to give up or avoid Satan's influences. I suggest that you talk with the elderly couple who are anticipating missionary service. They should be able to lead you to those who have authority to interview you and make the necessary arrangements.

"Remember, there won't be anyone you deal with who takes money or gets paid for their services. Not that it really matters to you, I'm sure. But it *does* say something about the kinds of people who will be serving and leading you. And you will feel their personal testimonies, Kep. You should be comfortable and happy through the whole experience."

Picturing an engagement ring on Jill's finger led me to ask, "What's to keep us from looking at wedding rings this afternoon? It might take a while to find just the right thing—a set that goes well with this ring you just got from Shackleton."

"Am I supposed to wear this ring all the time?" Jill asked. "Don't get me wrong, Kep—I don't object to that. It *is* attractive and it deserves to be worn constantly, but I have a strong feeling that it has a purpose, since it's been a part of my preparation. If it isn't just a reminder ring, what purpose does it serve?"

Her question made me realize how much my eagerness to disclose our engagement had distracted me from my reason for bringing Jill to the VW bus in the first place.

"Sorry for dropping the ball, Jill. I just got carried away with my desire to get your consent to a valid engagement. I'll need a minute to think about how I can best explain the various ways the ring you're wearing can serve you. You're going to be surprised and pleased. Just be patient while I give it some thought."

I dropped my head, closed my eyes, and secretly twisted my own stellar ring. When I thought Laura's name, I was relieved and thankful that she unfailingly responded.

"Hi, Laura. I've completed my share of Jill's preparation now. She's wearing her ring, but she doesn't have any idea of what it's for. Could you please surprise her with a ring call? The timing will be perfect."

"Gladly, Kep. I've been waiting for this moment! When I finish with her indoctrination, I'd like to have a private ring talk with you, too. I'll call you then, if that's okay. I won't take long."

"Sure, Laura. Thanks."

I raised my head and put my hand to my mouth thoughtfully as if I were about to speak. Not more than ten seconds later, Jill suddenly reached for her stellar ring with surprise and alarm spreading over her face as she looked my way.

"It's okay, Jill. Don't touch your ring or try to take it off. That feeling only lasts a few seconds."

She had just begun to smile and nod at me when her mouth

suddenly dropped open. Her head and eyes darted around as she obviously searched for Laura. (How very well I remembered my own futile attempts to locate Laura when her voice first came into my head via my ring!) Although I had sympathetic feelings for Jill, I couldn't help laughing at the same time.

"Her voice is in your head, Jill," I said. "The ring transmits Laura's voice into your head. You can respond to her by just *thinking* your words. It will take some time to get used to, but just try it."

Jill put her hand up to quiet me as she listened to Laura. Her eyes were open wide and her eyebrows were raised as she listened intently.

Shaking her head slowly back and forth, she asked (aloud), "You're sure no one else is listening to us?"

Silence.

"This is truly amaz . . ."

Silence again.

I presumed that Jill had just switched to thinking her words now. Her face reflected total involvement as Laura was evidently making her aware of the ring's wondrous powers. Knowing I wouldn't be hearing anything from this point forward, I decided to call Shackleton. I had some questions that only he could answer.

He first responded by saying, "Aha, Kephart! I've been anticipating your call for some time now. I trust that you and Jillian have spent a pleasurable day together thus far. Obviously you have questions and comments, so I invite them at this time."

"Well, first off, I want to express how overwhelming your generous feelings have been for us, Shackleton. Jill has had a hard time accepting gifts of such magnitude. But the same goes for me. As you must know, the life insurance policies grant us a rare degree of security for our entire lives. I've been thinking quite a bit about how dependent I am on you as the unique employer that you are. And I sense that our duplicate insurance policies disclose your confidence that the bond Jill and I share is permanent—or that it will be. How many soon-to-be weds are ever so privileged?

"You'll be pleased to learn that Jill has accepted my marriage proposal! I asked her to marry me just within the last half hour. We're going to look at wedding-ring sets next. Things are moving pretty fast, Shackleton. But not fast enough for me. I've never been happier. And I can't thank you enough for all you've taught me and granted me.

"Jill is using her stellar ring to talk with Laura right now while she receives further indoctrination in its use. She doesn't know that I'm having this conversation with you.

"I believe Laura has some things to tell me personally yet. Maybe she'll be sharing some of what you led her through to comfort her last night. I'm expecting her to call me next—after she finishes up with Jill."

"That's quite all right, Kephart. I'd prefer that she reveals her new visions and feelings to you herself, rather than me attempting to do so."

"I have a question that you might not be willing to answer, Shackleton. But I'll ask it anyway.

"When Jill was being prepared to receive a stellar ring of her own, did she undergo the kind of treatment that I did in the warehouse? I guess I'm curious about whether the AOs were the ones who did the work."

"Yes, Kephart. But she had a considerably more extensive experience than that which you had. The reason is that you had been exposed to years of recorded surveillance and in-depth life monitoring while that tiny sphere was implanted in your forehead."

"Did her preparation take place in your secret inner room—the one with all of the monitors inset in the long oval table?"

"Yes. But those monitors aren't there for that purpose, Kephart. Those stations are used by the Abiding Ones for guiding, controlling, and recording all that takes place with various surveillance craft—remotely controlled craft such as the one that self-destructed, leaving that tiny octahedron that our government agents were after.

"There are other stations in that room that you evidently didn't observe or recognize during your brief time there—one of them being equipped for deciphering the contents of little spheres such as the one the Fallen Ones had implanted in your forehead for the better part of your life. Another was used for evaluating and processing Jillian.

"One thing you will be fascinated to learn is that intergalactic spaceships do not employ the same stellar energies that the remotely controlled surveillance crafts use. These ships can surpass the speed of light. Light speeds vary comparatively throughout the universe. Various time warps and kinds of energy are applied in alien spaceships, depending on their proximities to star systems and their associated planets. These ships can literally skip on light waves, resulting in what might appear to be instantaneous space travel.

"They can also be made immune to hazards presented by any and all obstructions, because they are capable of altering their vibratory composition. You might best visualize this feat by comparing it with a child jumping through a rapidly swinging skip rope.

"Have you ever been aware that there was a time when scientists did not believe it possible for any aircraft to exceed the speed of sound?

"Remember, Kephart, all of physical creation is not made of that which appears to be to man. Faith is a critical component of creation. The elements are eternal. But they are nothing more than word-programmed energies. The Apostle Paul was well informed by ministering angels or prophets—if not by personal revelation. You would do well to read and memorize Hebrews, chapter eleven, verse three. It can have a profound effect on your perception of cosmic reality and your being within it."

"What you just brought up leads me to ask you a personal question, Shackleton. I don't mean to intrude into your personal life, but I've been wondering whether you belong to the church that I'm preparing to join—the one that Jill and Laura belong to."

Shackleton became silent and remained so for what (to me) was an uncomfortable minute.

"That question will have to remain an unanswered one by me personally, Kephart. I find it a tremendous frustration not to answer your humble, sincere inquiry. But there will be a time in the future when you will receive personal revelation. You will receive what is called 'the gift of the Holy Ghost' after your baptism. Prepare yourself to be worthy of learning the answers to your questions after that. You will then be privileged to know the mysteries of God.

"In the meantime, there is one thing you might do well to ponder and dwell on as you progress spiritually: There are worlds without end, but there is only ONE Christ.

"Considering this to be true, what questions arrive in your mind? What might the differences be between the purpose of this Earth and the purposes of other innumerable worlds? Why is it that men of this Earth typically imagine other planets to be places of habitation for threatening beings or targets for conquest? The answers will eventually come if you continue to pursue them. But it is unlikely that you will find them in your scriptures. Those answers come through personal revelation and are not to be shared.

"Being endowed with a gift of clairvoyance (such as I have) may lead others to arrive at an incorrect notion that I possess an elevated spiritual stature. I implore you not to look upon me as being anything more than a natural mortal Earthling—for that is all that I am. And I must yet pass through all the phases of mortality and immorality that you will, Kephart. I must abide covenants of which you are not yet aware, but you will most assuredly become acquainted with these covenants if you continue on the path you have chosen."

I nodded my head in silence while holding back other questions that seemed inappropriate to put forth at this time. It seemed that Shackleton had greater in-depth knowledge and understanding of the teachings of Jill's church than *uninvolved* study alone would provide.

I wondered why he must be so secretive about his personal life. His secretive nature did a lot to cultivate his mystique, which hadn't diminished in the least during the short time I had been working as his assistant. If anything, I had found him to be increasingly inscrutable. But I had also felt him to be more congenial and comfortable to be with.

My stellar ring signaled that Laura was calling. I told Shackleton I'd have to sign off but that I'd get in touch with him later.

He held me back for one more minute as he said, "I must warn you, Kephart, that should Detective Walker see you driving, he will be legally compelled to pull you over and give you a long-overdue ticket." (I felt sure I heard him chuckling as he said this.)

"For what?" I asked.

"For driving without a valid driver license. Washington State law requires that you obtain a new license within ten days of your change of state residence. I'd say he's been quite lenient in your case, wouldn't you?"

"Yes, sir," I said. "Thanks, Shackleton."

CHAPTER 48

I twisted my ring and thought Laura's name. She came right back in response.

"Sorry, Laura. I was talking with Shackleton when you called me. Did you finish up with Jill yet?"

"I didn't call you, Kep. It must have been Jill. I'll wait until she has her time with you. Just let me know when you're free to listen, please."

I looked over at Jill sitting beside me. She had apparently been watching me when I rotated my ring, because she was quietly laughing at me as I looked her way. I was happy to find that she hadn't taken my seeming to ignore her as being rude.

When I pointed first to her ring and then at her, she complied with my signal.

Even though we were sitting side by side, the "first-time" ring talk between us was a pleasurable experience both ways.

"This is an incredible creation," Jill said as she held up the stellar ring that now decorated the little finger of her left hand. She was obviously delighted to have been chosen to be its possessor.

"You do know that you're just one of four Earthlings who are now qualified to wear and use one?" I asked.

She nodded a yes and smiled at me.

"It makes me happy to know that you are," I said. "Did Laura tell you that Shackleton is the responsible steward of all four rings?"

"Yes, Kep. And it humbles me just to know that. She also told me that I could use this ring to record conversations without anyone being aware of it, so I must be circumspect when I'm involved with interviewing and gathering information for Shackleton. There's a lot of responsibility that comes with the ring, even though no one else may be aware of what I'm collecting and providing for Shackleton. I know that, Kep."

"Did Laura say anything about how soon you might be involved in assisting her—or in what way?"

"Maybe within a week, depending on what develops in a possible case of abduction."

"Do you feel good about becoming involved in Shackleton's work, even though it might detract from your prospective plans to teach school?"

"I'm okay with it for now, Kep. We'll just have to see what develops of the experiences that come with any assignments I get."

"Do you know who the Abiding Ones are or that they rarely involve themselves in the affairs of us Earthlings unless we've given them reason to believe that we've become innocently or knowingly caught up in some potentially hazardous aspects of their investigative missions?"

"Laura explained a lot of these things in the time we've shared today, Kep. She's bright and easy to listen to. I like her, and I like talking with her. I do feel sorry for her having to endure what she does, but I feel good knowing that I might give her some relief and chances to change her life.

"I think she wants to explain some personal things to you, though. I won't resent her taking the time she needs to fill you in, so don't be concerned about it, Kep—or about communicating with her in any way. She really needs understanding and social sharing time. She knows the boundaries of our relationships."

"Thanks for putting me at ease regarding her, Jill. You truly are a blessing if you have the kind of charitable love and maturity to allow her that— especially at this time, when you need to expect my full commitment to you. Thanks for believing in me and trusting me to be totally devoted to our eternal relationship. That means more to me than I can say."

She shook her head and smiled at me.

"Sure, Kep. What we've got is a treasure I wish everyone could have.

"Kep . . . I'm going back into the restaurant to use the restroom. Why don't you give Laura a call now, while I'm gone? I'll just wait in the front seat when I return. Take the time you need. We'll have plenty of time to look at ring sets this afternoon."

We both signed off. Jill blew a kiss to me as she left the bus.

Laura was quick again to answer my signal.

"I'm free now to talk, Laura. Jill knows you have some personal things to share with me. She's away at the minute, but she's encouraging me to give you all the time you need, so here I am."

"Jill's special, Kep. I like her, and I'm thankful for her just the same as you are—but in a sisterly way."

She laughed. It was always good to hear Laura laugh. Maybe she could find more laughter in her life now.

"Shackleton told me you were going to meet with him in his den last night, Laura. Anything to share with me about how that went? Did he express some gratitude and show some recognition of your personal sacrifices over these past years? He said he wanted to give you some comforting words or thoughts. I hope he did."

"Very much so, Kep. We came to understandings that I didn't ever think possible—mostly because he opened up with me about his own problems and feelings. Not his secrets, though. I guess there are things he just can't share yet . . . maybe he never will."

"Just to hear that he opened up with you is something to talk about, Laura."

"Yes, Kep. But it was a relief that I could open up and pour out my feelings and frustrations, too. And I know he listened; although, I knew he was already aware of what I wanted to say. His paranormal abilities surely offset his blindness."

"I guess the first thing I want to share with you, Kep, is that I have been wrong in dedicating my life and love to a man who couldn't express some love and hope for me to build on. It has been contrary to Gospel teachings for me to do this. There's nothing wrong with self-sacrifice, but I've not had a good cause or goal to justify my choice. It's all been so hopeless. To choose to live a hopeless life is not what God would have us do.

"I suppose I've known this to be so all along, but I've suppressed it and kept it below a level of my awareness. Why? Did I want to give myself reasons for self-pity? What would be the point in that? Maybe it had to do with Shackleton's choosing Rose instead of me.

"Shackleton did disclose an astounding secret to me last night, Kep! He cast new light on something that has been troubling me constantly over the past several years.

"He said that he has proof of Rose's being alive yet! And their son as well! But that's all he could tell me. And he couldn't tell me how he knew this or where they were located.

"He could only say that he had lived on hope these past years and that both the hope and the proof had been provided by the Abiding Ones. There are many vital secrets tied to this one secret, and so he can't share it with my aunt and uncle—or any other family members yet. He said he knows you will keep this a secret as well, and so he's given me permission to share it with you, Kep. It's to stop with us and go no further.

"When he told me this, I felt a great burden lifted from me. And I had a new vision of how I should be living my life from this point on. I'm sure you can understand why. I don't see any need for what I'm telling you to go beyond the three of us, do you?"

"No, Laura. No need at all. You have my promise it won't ever leave me."

"Another thing that Shackleton told me—something that gave me great comfort—is that he cares deeply for me but that he could never rightfully express his affection for me. He wanted me to realize that most all humans have affectionate feelings at some time or another for someone other than their beloved spouse— the one they've committed their life and allegiance to. It's a natural human trait—one that needs to be managed. But what matters is how they act or don't act on those feelings. There's good love, and there's lust. There's selfish love, and there's unselfish love. Unselfish love allows all good things to endure. I think we both know a little about the truth of that, Kep."

"You've stated everything clearly, Laura. You and Shackleton have provided me with a lot of understandings that I didn't think I'd be privileged to have. I can see why Shackleton implied that he thought it best that these disclosures come from you rather than from him.

"It's probable that you will be communicating with him before I do. If you do, please pass along my thanks for all that he's said and done to arrive at healthy relationships all around.

"Anything else you want to say for now?" I asked. "You know I'll always be open to whatever you want to share with me. And Jill is encouraging you to have more open communications, plus some overdue social life. So please take whatever you can get."

"No. Nothing for now, Kep. I'll be taking you up on your offer at various times, I'm sure. Please give Jill my thanks for this time we've had to spend on our rings."

"Sure thing. She just returned to the VW bus a couple of minutes ago. Adiós for now."

"Ready to shop for a ring set?" I asked as I put my hand on Jill's shoulder and gave it a squeeze. She was sitting in the front passenger seat.

"I'm excited . . . more than excited. This is the best kind of shopping a woman could hope for, Kep. It doesn't happen often in a lifetime, that's for sure . . . at least it shouldn't."

I opened the sliding door and moved to the front passenger side of the bus. Then I opened the door beside Jill and gave her a long hug before going around the front to climb in behind the steering wheel.

* * *

We spent about two hours going through the few stores that sold jewelry in Bellingham. I wanted something for Jill that was just right for her, regardless of expense. She was always looking at the price as well as the appearance and appeal of each ring set. Weighing price against desirability was evidently a part of her shopping habit.

I soon became a believer in the oft-spoken differences between most men and women when it came to shopping. Shopping just wasn't my favorite way to spend time.

As it turned out, we wound up going back to the first store we stopped in to buy a ring set that was one of the first we looked at. It was a set that I had first considered to be perfect for Jill, one that went well with her personality. It also looked great alongside her stellar ring. It cost more than Jill wanted to see me paying, but I couldn't care less about the price, because it represented an eternal relationship. And who could put a price on that?

What was amazing to me is that the set was exactly the right size—no need for resizing. That fact alone made a statement about who the rings were made for. (At least I enjoyed thinking this to be so.)

I had Jill wait for the sales clerk to put the rings in a "just-right" box while I went out to the VW bus to pull the needed cash out of my leather box.

As I was counting out bills, I became uncomfortable. The bus was parked curbside, and because there were people walking past, I had to hunch over the box to hide my place of banking. Dumb.

Packing all that cash around in a box under the camper sink these past days now struck me as having been a foolish and careless thing to do. But on reflection, I had to ease up on berating myself, because I had had so little time during business hours to spend on personal matters.

Today was different. And this troublesome cash-box experience led to some thoughts concerning Jill.

I was no less vulnerable to an untimely death than Shackleton—maybe more so. I had no life insurance. So I determined that I would open a joint banking account with Jill as soon as we left the jewelry store. That way she'd have money she could draw out to ease her through her period of grieving and to reestablish herself if I died. It would be much like having an insurance policy. There should be no problem in changing her name and signature on the account after we married.

I knew that either one of us would go through an acute time of grieving if the other died, no matter how strong our faith was in sharing a joyful, endless life in the world to come.

Another thought centered on how much time we should be committing ourselves to when we *both* worked as assistants to

Shackleton. There had to be a balance maintained. We needed time to devote to each other (and to our future family, when it began to arrive). Priorities couldn't be overlooked in our present or future plans. (My thoughts jumped to Bick and Dozie and their successes all around.)

As I headed back to the store with the needed cash, I thought again on how life was constantly changing and how little control we had over many aspects of our lives—except for the control which we might derive from humbly practicing faith.

Ultimately, we had to trust in the goodness of our Heavenly Father and to relinquish our own will in acceptance of his. ("*Thy* will be done.") There was humility expressed in genuinely praying that God's will and his wisdom prevail over all. I could now see that we must be careful about *what* we prayed for and *how* we prayed. I suspected that I'd be learning more about that after I was baptized.

Jill once said that she was always happiest when she gave up her *own* will just by preparing to accept God's will after she prayed. But I always felt that she was humble and that her heart was in the right place. I felt sure that made a difference.

After paying for the ring set, I put the attractively wrapped little box in my pocket, together with a valuation certificate, and took Jill by the hand. Her eyes were shining.

"Don't worry," I said. "You'll get to see the engagement ring on your finger at the right time and in the right place yet this afternoon. First, I have an errand to accomplish—one that I'll need your help with. But it shouldn't take long, and I don't think you'll object to it."

Her eyes spoke her trust in my agenda.

"Do you have a bank that you like—one that you feel good about as a customer?" I asked.

"I have a checking account, Kep. I've found it to be necessary for cashing my clients' checks and to keep track of my various earnings each month . . . and how much I *spend.* Why? Do you need some more money?"

She laughed, knowing my favorable new circumstances.

"The people I deal with as tellers are always friendly and helpful," she added. "Yes. I like my bank."

"Steer me to it," I said. "I mean, point out where to go as I drive, please."

As I drove, I explained to Jill that much of my "think" time lately had been spent on our upcoming life together and how I wanted to safeguard it from the consequences of regrettable choices or oversights. Instead of dwelling so much on Shackleton's mysteries and my assignment-related problems (as I had done over the past several days), I had turned my mind over to truth-seeking and contemplating the mysteries of God.

"Much of this has been a result of Shackleton's sparking my mind with thought-provoking truths to contemplate," I told her. "He confessed that much of his lifetime has been spent trying to satisfy his curiosity as a seeker of truths—as pursued through both science and religion.

"Between the two approaches, he made it clear to me that he's concluded that *inspired* religion (religion established by God's authorized and appointed prophets) was the most direct and accurate means for acquiring any and all truths—including scientific truths.

"He attested that he now looks to no other source for undeniable truths, but he apparently gets a lot of information from the Abiding Ones about various types of energy and intergalactic space travel. I don't know how he confirms the truth of what he gets or if that's even possible.

"He places emphasis on another important source of truth as being personal revelation as it can come through the gift of the Holy Ghost, but he told me that personal revelations are not something to be shared openly. He says valid, inspired personal revelation can only come from the gift that comes after baptism when we are worthy. So that makes me wonder even more about his having been baptized in the restored church.

"Any thoughts?"

"Not really, except it's possible that he could have gotten much of what he's shared with you from some church members who are filled with in-depth understandings of the Gospel teachings. But where and when and how—I can't rightly guess any better than you."

"One very important thing I've come to understand over these past days of exhaustive experiences, Jill, is when we honestly focus on effectively seeking answers to vital questions about the cosmos and all it holds, the more we get pulled into spiritual questions. I can see how Shackleton has had need to extensively explore spiritual realms as he has progressed.

"Jill, I know that Truth is God's reality. And I know that faith is a vital component of all creation."

"I'm wanting to hear more of the words you're saying, Kep. Your words ring like a testimony of where you've arrived in a very short time."

Jill's sober attentive expression verified her statement as being genuine and from her heart. I felt encouraged to search and prayerfully think about the scriptures more diligently.

"Shackleton has urged me to ponder specific verses of scripture that have helped me see things I'm ready to receive, Jill. As I've meditated on Hebrews eleven, verses one through three, I feel certain that the Apostle Paul had a strong testimony of what he wrote, and his testimony has become one for me as well.

"The same thing goes for scriptural statements of other prophets. I'm beginning to think now that authentic testimonies can be contagious!"

"I don't know if you're ready to hear me say this, Kep, but I believe I'm beginning to see you 'at your best self.'"

She laughed. I laughed. Then, as we laughed together, I thought, Laughter can be contagious, too.

* * *

I felt a bit conspicuous carrying the leather cash box into the bank, although there wasn't anything about the box that should attract attention. But when I placed it in front of a young female teller and turned it upside down, my eyes went into "search mode." I leaned over the counter before flipping it over and exposing its contents.

Jill was at my side. The only one reacting to my behavior was the young teller. It was obvious that she had not dealt with this method of cash transference before. Thankfully, her subdued exclamation escaped her mouth without drawing attention from anyone nearby.

"I'm sorry, but I can't open a new account here," she said. "You'll have to see the woman at that desk over there. Her name is Brenda."

She pointed to another bank employee seated at a corner desk, talking to a man sitting opposite her as she looked intently at a computer monitor. They were engaged in conversation that didn't appear to be nearing an end very soon.

Four empty upholstered chairs were positioned around a small table nearby.

Jill tugged at my elbow and said, "I know Brenda, Kep. She's quick and sharp. Let's just sit in a comfortable chair and be patient. (She had detected my impatience and discomfort.)

"Sorry, Jill," I said. "I guess I'm more than eager to get to my next destination—the place where I can make the most meaningful deposit on our new life together."

The puzzled, clouded expression on Jill's face softened and

then brightened as the light of understanding entered her mind.

"And that place would be . . .?"

"The Singing Tree!" she exclaimed.

"Can you think of a more appropriate place where we can share that special moment in private—just the two of us?"

Jill tugged at my arm and turned to give me a hug. As she pulled me close, I inadvertently pulled the opened cash box over the edge of the teller counter. The entire contents dumped out onto the floor. I must say I was extremely thankful and relieved that no one offered to help us gather up the banded bundles of currency.

CHAPTER 49

THE drive to Whipple Farm Lane seemed to take forever.

As we approached the lane entrance near the old farmstead, I asked Jill, "Are you having the same feelings as I am about passing by our folks' place before we've had our time together under the Singing Tree? As always, I'm trusting you to be honest."

"And just what *are* your feelings, Kep?"

"I asked you first . . . and because you're a female, you have the advantage of *knowing* how I feel because of your intuitive gifts."

Jill covered her mouth and looked away, trying to hide a smile.

"Well, my Kep, I believe our feelings are the same," she said.

Before we could continue our banter, we were nearly at the entrance to the driveway. The first thing that caught our attention was the Pottses' new Chevy pickup parked under the chestnut trees. That settled the unspoken decision, since I didn't want to get involved in any discussions that would delay our getting to the Tree. Besides, I preferred that Jill would be wearing her engagement ring when we met with Oat and Selma to announce our engagement. I preferred to "show" rather than "tell."

The late afternoon sun was already hiding behind Singing Tree Hill when I parked the bus near the wooden trailhead gate.

We took advantage of every wide section of the trail to clasp hands as we climbed.

When at last we reached the white, flat stone under the Singing Tree, I reached into my pocket and pulled out the ring box. Without hesitation, Jill sat and gazed up into my eyes, her face beaming with anticipation and love.

Assuming the traditional posture, I dropped down and knelt on one knee before her. I handed her the little box. When she opened it, she shrugged and shook her shoulders in sheer delight before removing the engagement ring and handing it to me. We both were laughing as I asked for her hand in marriage.

"Oh, yes! Yes, yes!" she exclaimed. We both stood up and swayed back and forth hugging and laughing. After repeated kisses, I pressed the engagement ring onto her finger. The ceremony was complete.

We were both sharing the happiest moments of our lives as the sun lowered above scattered clouds on the western horizon.

There is no possible way for me to express our emotions at this time.

Jill breathed out two heavy sighs as she rolled the wedding ring between her fingers to study and admire it before handing the ring box back to me.

I ran my fingers through her silky dark hair and said, "Maybe time will go by faster if we spend it making plans and building dreams we can share. So far we've been too busy to dream together, Jill. Every couple needs to dream. Life without a dream doesn't have much appeal to me anymore. Do you feel the same?"

She was studying me pensively. "Oh, I know we should check in with Heavenly Father as we go," I added. "There could be no lasting happiness if we didn't."

"I'm happy that you realize the truth of that, Kep."

"We'll need to agree on a place where we'd like to start out and take our first steps away from our current homes."

"Now that you mention our moving away from our current homes, Kep, I recall your just describing my folks as being *our* folks. Has it ever occurred to you that once we're married, Oat and Selma will be *my* 'in-laws,' considering them now to be your mom and dad as you do? And my mom and dad will be *your* in-laws as well! Is that funny or what?"

"That *is* funny. But labeling them so to others could bring cause for wonder."

"You could say the same about how human *tears* can be misleading until you know their actual cause, Kep. An example might be to compare our time here with our first meeting last week. You were wiping away tears of sorrow then. Today you're dabbing at happy tears. To see only your face, what watcher could know the difference?"

"I might have told you this before, but I didn't shed a tear in the company of others before I met you, Jill. It just wasn't the thing to do in the society of men I worked with. I kept everything hidden and locked up inside. Hiding my feelings became a habit for me. Now I can let some of my deeper feelings show, thanks to you and your acceptance of me as I am.

"A scripture verse I especially liked when I came across it as I read to my mother was 'Jesus wept.' It said something I wanted to hear—something that described me in spirit but that I couldn't show in the male company I had to keep then.

"When I look back on the very short time we've known each other in this life, it's a wonder to consider how much change will be taking place in other ways besides family relationships. I see how my goals have shifted in the eternal perspective you've given me. I owe you so much already, it's scary to think how much I'll become indebted to you over the years to come," I said, with a grin.

"I could collect IOU slips from you and store them in a can," Jill said. "That would give me leverage for getting *my* way in some disputes we might have."

I couldn't help laughing.

"That's a good one. I love it that you're sense of humor is alive, Jill. I can see that humor must be vital for any enduring relationship. I suppose I owe you for leading me to make *that* comment too now."

"Speaking of storing things in cans," Jill said, "I wonder if there's a slim chance that Jonathan Willoughby has been here since I put his journal can back up in the Singing Tree. I suppose he's too old now to climb trees. But something's telling me . . ."

"He could have had help," I said. "His prophetic alien visitor could have met him here—or brought him. Now you've got *me* curious."

"It might be that climbing a tree is as good as a walk for cardiovascular exercise, Kep. I'm going up to see if there's been any change. I'll be quick. From what Laura told me, you've had more than enough tree-climbing this past week to keep you in shape."

"Okay. But don't ask me not to look," I said. (Her green skirt was above knee length.) "I won't be looking at any other woman climbing a tree in a skirt. That goes for now and forever."

Jill raised her eyebrows and tilted her head. But she gave me a smile just the same.

Four or five minutes later she called down to me.

"It's gone, Kep! The can and the knife are both gone!"

"Then he's probably had help—if he's still alive. Anyway, the prophecy has been fulfilled, for the most part. Are you sure you're looking in the right place?"

"The knife mark is still in the tree trunk."

After Jill dropped to the ground from the tree, we held each other in silence as our minds became engrossed in sorting through plausible explanations for this latest puzzling event.

"There must be a good reason for all of this experience—from Jonathan's first note forward," I said.

Jill seemed to be unusually disturbed. She slowly nodded her head up and down and then gripped my upper arm and pulled me away from the Singing Tree. She ambled toward Jessie's grave site, tugging at my arm as she went.

Her behavior seemed out of character. Because it was so untypical of her, it called forth my full attention and concern, but not in an alarming way. She appeared to be responding to some unseen influence.

Stopping next to the grave's enclosing picket fence, she put her head on my shoulder and pulled me close. Her eyes were closed.

"The answer is somewhere here, Kep," she said.

Just as these words left her mouth, my eyes caught sight of a six-inch white stone resting on top of a fence post. It was holding down a shiny object that I couldn't identify at that distance.

"*There's* something I've never seen before," I said as I pointed at it.

Taking my hand in hers and pulling at me, Jill ran around the fence and stopped at the post. The stone was holding down Jonathan's shiny tobacco can.

Jill tossed the stone to the ground and grasped the can. She flipped the lid open and pulled out several folded sheets of paper. As she spread them open and began to study their contents, she slowly shook her head, seemingly oblivious to my presence. Her total attention overruled my reacting to curiosity and challenged my patience . . . until I saw tears welling up in her eyes.

At last she turned to me, handed me the papers, and began sobbing as she pressed her head against my shoulder. When her crying subsided and she looked up at me, I couldn't identify what emotions had caused her tears.

I waited in silence until she pulled her head away and whispered, "These were delivered by Noaak. I don't know what to say, Kep. Please read them to yourself."

On a small cover paper, I began to read:

To a woman named Jillian—

My name is Preston Willoughby. My father, Jonathan, died in 1998 at age 75. He had 2 sons and 4 daughters. I am the oldest of his children.

My father had told us about some strange experiences he had as a youth. They involved an unusual friend he had by the name of Noaak. This strange man came to my door today and handed me a tobacco can and a knife that had belonged to my father while he was growing up in Washington State. They had been left in a tree since 1937. I find that hard to believe, but evidently it's true.

Noaak asked that I write some things that he would deliver to you in exchange for giving me the heirloom knife.

Noaak's message to Jillian as written by Preston Willoughby:

Noaak said that many of the predictions he related to my father had come about, but there were some other things you would want to know and act on. Your identity was known to some human aliens who were entrusted with a prophecy relating to your future. He said you were to have a part in disclosing secrets about a mysterious tree and its impact on human societies in the last days.

Jillian, as you probably know, your natural father and mother died eight months apart. Your mother died last. You were then with foster parents until your adoption at age 3. Your mother had become despondent and broken hearted when she learned too late that your father had been telling the truth about a matter that deeply disturbed her.

Not long before your father died in a tragic accident, she had filed for divorce because he had tried to excuse questionable absences by claiming that he had been away to probe into his natural ancestry. She claimed that she could not keep living with this incredible tale and the prospect of his continuing such strange absences. She felt that their marital relationship had been shattered because of his apparent mental derangement.

Your father explained that he had been adopted and couldn't account for his natural lineage. He wanted to trace his ancestry for your sake, as well as for any future children he might have.

Your mother's issue was one of his claiming he had learned that he had descended from one of the lost tribes of Israel and that the presently assembled tribe was no longer to be found on the surface of this Earth. He said his ancestors often visited the lands of Earth's surface sometime after the confusion of tongues associated with the Tower of Babel. He said his natural mother and father were now essentially aliens.

He had told your mother that it was impossible for him to introduce her to any of his forebears unless she travel with him to the Earth's interior. She felt this to be so fantastic that she came to doubt his sanity.

Not long after his death, your mother was made aware of reports written by Admiral Richard E. Byrd of the United States Navy. These documents were directed to the U.S. Congress in 1947. The documents testified that while exploring regions of the North Pole, he had been guided into Inner Earth by some of its inhabitants. The government kept these reports and the claims of other witnesses hidden from this nation's populace until they were released by the Freedom of Information Act of 1966.

Jillian, your mother suffered much over this discovery supporting a probability of your father's having been truthful. But there is good news for you and for your natural parents in the Spirit World (as Noaak calls it).

Noaak wants you to know that the divorce of your natural father and mother was not properly documented and that this renders it legally invalid. Their marriage is still intact. So your natural parents can receive the religious ordinances you will eventually be qualified to participate in. Noaak says you know what this means.

All of the above that has been related to me by Noaak is extremely fascinating, but perplexing as well. I wish you well and hope that this leads you to happy endings. Maybe we will meet in the future, God willing.

As I read Noaak's messages, I slowly shook my head just as Jill had. So much was to be implied and comprehended! The verifiable existence of an inner Earth, according to Admiral Byrd's testimony, was in itself hard to accept. (I would later find much convincing evidence to support his report to the U.S. Congress through documented experiences and a few scriptural references.)

I now knew that Jill's tears were the result of a mixture of emotions. I put my arm around her and held her close, waiting for her to make some verbal response.

She remained silent, and I could understand why. The invalidity of her parents' divorcement triggered many questions that I knew could not be dealt with at present. (Answers from both Jill and the Edens would bring me much satisfaction later.)

I felt for Jill's ring finger. She turned and faced me with a brightened expression as I gave the engagement ring a slight twist. When she handed me Jonathan's tobacco can, I put the message papers inside it and stuffed it inside my shirt for safe keeping

The late evening sun was giving way to signs of an approaching twilight as we began our slow descent down the trail. When we approached the Whipple homestead in the VW, we saw that the blue Chevy pickup was still parked under the chestnut trees. The Pottses were obviously enjoying their lengthy visit with Oat and Selma.

"Shall we show your engagement ring to Bessie Mae and Wilbur, as well as to our folks?" I asked Jill.

She smiled as she looked to me and shook her head yes in acceptance of the prevailing circumstances.

The choice proved to be in happy accord with God's will. Our engagement announcement drew us all closer and promoted a festive atmosphere.

When I drove Jill to her house, I could easily sense her excitement in anticipation of sharing our engagement with her good friends. She still took time to give me a lengthy hug and a kiss before heading for her front door. I felt a high degree of pleasurable anticipation myself as I focused on my own sharing time with Shackleton.

CHAPTER 50

THE following morning was bright with May sunshine when I first attempted to reach Shackleton, but he didn't respond to my ring call. It was after 9:30 before I had success. An appointment time hadn't been previously discussed, so I wasn't surprised to learn that he had been engaged in a "closure" meeting with Graham Walker. They had met at the Three-Cornered Orange for breakfast at 7:00.

Shackleton suggested that 10:00 would be an opportune time for us to meet in his den and share a "second breakfast" from the service table, courtesy of Bones and Phoebe.

As I approached Shackleton's studio door, I heard the silence that followed the final measures of his piano piece. I waited, but no other sounds came, so I used the brass knocker to tap my arrival. The door immediately opened wide, and I was surprised to be greeted by both Bogart and Shackleton together.

"Perfect timing, Kephart!" Shackleton exclaimed. "Our breakfast awaits us."

After Shackleton and I shook hands, Bogart led us into the den. I was surprised to find that our midday breakfast was indeed waiting for us. The little service table was completely covered with it. There was barely enough room for the silverware and Phoebe's folded blue-and-white napkins.

Shackleton wasn't surprised when I offered a prayer of thanks. He was obviously pleased that I did, which made for a preferable start.

We immediately began to indulge ourselves, but it wasn't long before Shackleton began to tell me things that were on his mind—things that he had obviously been dwelling on for quite some time.

"Kephart, I have much to enlighten you with, and I want you to be receptive to all I hope to disclose in the time we have. I invite you, and I *urge* you to interrupt, should any questions or troublesome thoughts arise as I speak. My desire is that there will be complete understanding on your part. That can only happen if you open your own mouth as well."

"You have my word, as you must know," I said.

"In the very short time you have been serving with me, Kephart, I believe you have come a tremendously long way in many respects.

"I perceive that you have been made aware of the fact that all humans are mysteries in themselves. All human beings throughout the universe are a mystery to all who observe them or who *think* they know them—this applies to spouses as well. We never truly know ourselves, Kephart. And that is one of the reasons we are living our mortal lives.

"Can you accept this as being so, Kephart?"

"Without question," I answered.

"I knew you would answer as you have, but I needed to seek your confirmation—for the record," he added, chuckling. "Yes, I'm recording all of our conversations on my ring, Kephart. But I am confident that shouldn't trouble you. Tell me if I'm wrong."

I shook my head.

"Now for the more *personal* disclosures and questions," he said.

When he emphasized "personal," I inferred that he was about

to give a partial account of himself. But I was both corrected and surprised by his next question.

"How well would you say you know your Jillian, Kephart?"

Being totally unprepared for this question, I hesitated. But I had no trouble responding.

"I can only answer by saying that we both feel with conviction that we closely shared our premortal life together in what Jill calls the 'spirit realm.' This shared life must have extended over an immeasurable length of time. We feel without doubt that we knew each other long before we arrived here in mortality. I sense that we are spiritually connected in remarkable ways—I'd guess in more ways than many married couples ever experience.

"But I have to say that, as a mortal being, I'm learning more about Jill every day. And that goes both ways. So the unknowns are always there, evidently."

"And the unknowns, which can be termed 'mysteries,' will always exist, Kephart."

I had become a bit uneasy over Shackleton's question concerning Jill.

"Why would you question my knowledge of her?" I asked. "I'm prepared to accept her eternally, no matter what else I may learn about her. She radiates a combination of rare and beautiful qualities that I'm certain I couldn't hope to find in any other woman."

"Quite so, Kephart! But aside from your foreknowledge of her, have you ever wondered why these desirable traits are uniquely hers?"

"Not really. I've never questioned why," I said.

"You *do* know that she was adopted by the Whipples when she was a three-year-old child. Has she ever shared any disclosures of her natural parents with you? Does she have some knowledge of her natural ancestry? Does it matter to either of you?"

I was both amazed and unsettled by Shackleton's sudden inquiries concerning Jill's natural parentage. I wondered why and how all of this should come up now— immediately after the very recent disclosures related by Noaak. Again, I found Shackleton's paranormal powers to be both eerie and scary.

"Yes, it matters to us both. But not so much so until yesterday, when we just learned together the story of her father and mother as it was shared in a mysterious letter. I can't begin to relate the means or the message without causing you to digress, so I want to wait until I hear what you have to say. That you have brought this up at this particular time is totally uncanny."

"I must back up to explain some things you have not as yet been informed of, Kephart. We'll get back to where we are. Bear with me. Please."

"I don't mind waiting for truths, no matter how long it takes," I said with a smile.

Shackleton chuckled at my comment and then went on to ask, "What does the term 'alien' imply to you? In other words, just what or who is an alien?"

I had to think before answering.

"I associate the word with a synonym like 'foreign' or a phrase like 'out of place.' I think of people belonging to another place, or coming from an unknown place. Why?"

"Kephart, I want you to know that not all human aliens come from what we perceive to be 'outer space.' There are other unknown habitations to consider."

Shackleton's statement about our perceptions of outer space caused my mind to jump to the opposite concept: *inner* space. Naturally, this led my thoughts to Inner *Earth*, and I was confronted with an obsessive wonderment about Jill's ancestry— a thing that had not fully registered with me before. Her father's reported identification with humans from another habitation

(Inner Earth) placed Jill as a descendent of aliens.

I had now become enlightened, as Shackleton had mentioned at the beginning of our meal. But this was a divergence from what I had anticipated. I withdrew into myself as I began contemplating all that this realization implied: Jill's unique traits stemmed in part (genetically) from her having descended from unique ancestors.

The longer I considered all that this suggested, the more accepting I became of the fact that her lineage offered no challenge to our relationship. My feelings for her remained unchanged. I felt a deeper appreciation for all that she is. And I became inspired as I pondered on how this might affect our future offspring.

Shackleton had been patient as I remained silently absorbed in thought.

"Sorry. I've been considering other habitations," I said. "Where might there be other places for human aliens to live besides the galactic systems of our universe?"

"There are none that I know of, Kephart. The particular habitat I refer to is within our cosmos; however, it is not located *above* the Earth's surface. There is an *inner* Earth, Kephart. Indeed, it is the original home of some of the Abiding Ones.

"Do you have trouble accepting this?" he asked. "If so, this is the time to express yourself, Kephart. I can offer convincing proof and scriptural support if you'd like."

"No need," I said. "I can't doubt that there's an inner Earth, Shackleton. It's strange and amazing to me, but just yesterday I read about reports transferred to the U.S. Congress by U.S. Navy Admiral Richard Byrd. He testified in 1947 that he had been guided into an *inner* Earth by some of its inhabitants while exploring regions of the North Pole. I guess there had been testimonies of others submitted as well. These documents were all kept hidden from us—from this nation's populace—by our government. I've learned that they were released many years later through the Freedom of Information Act. For this reason, I can more easily accept the existence of an inner Earth.

"Because of the way you led into this Inner Earth 'enlightenment,' you implied much about Jill's ancestry. So now I've reflected on Jill's possibly being a descendent of aliens of Inner Earth, and I'm not in the least disturbed by it. I'm excited about the prospect, really."

Shackleton's face reflected astonishment—something I'd never seen him display before. He quickly recovered and continued.

"All that you've just said is extremely good news to me, Kephart! It releases me from having to explain what you already know. Now we can move on to other subjects that you may appreciate for their potential influence on your future.

"The most important thing I desire to come from this meeting is that you go away with the complete assurance and understanding that I will not involve Jillian in serving my pursuits to the extreme point that I have taken Laura. For the present she will be restricted to assisting Laura and giving her some relief in whatever ways are prudent and possible. As you will agree, Laura has been overburdened and is deserving of some liberation. There could be no better person than Jillian to bring this transition about."

My impassioned reply came without restraint:

"I can't express how I appreciate your realizations regarding both Laura and Jill," I said. "Your words motivate me all the more to continue serving with you. For all you strive to achieve, I have to say I truly respect you. I feel my words are useless, knowing how you can read my feelings and thoughts, but they need to be said. Thanks."

"Thank *you,* Kephart! You have just obliterated any concern I may have held about your acquiring assurances from our meeting."

"I'm wondering how Laura can find time to indoctrinate Jill in handling the kinds of tasks she'll be involved with," I said. "Will Jill be working alongside her for the present time? Will she be meeting clients and case-related people along with Laura? I'd think that if that were the case, it would inhibit open and candid discussions, but maybe not."

"I'm confident that Laura will be able to arrange optimum situations and work-in times for Jillian to receive all of the instructing she'll need. The two will most likely be close companions during the next few weeks. Jillian expressed enthusiasm when the two of us discussed the matter.

"But you mustn't overlook the stellar rings when situations present a problem for two investigators or interviewers being present, Kephart. You will recall the time you assisted me in dealing with a recalcitrant Dan Crotty. Our rings were indispensable at that time. They enabled us to be successful in bringing about happy prospects for two deserving people."

"Thanks for the reminder, Shackleton. And I can see that Jill and Laura don't need to be positioned at the same location. Jill can pick up or retrieve all that's said. I tend to overlook what a great advantage the rings are! I may be slow, but I'm learning.

"Jill told me there's a report of an abduction that might present you with a new case. Is that true? Anything you can tell me about it?"

"If it's true—and I believe it is—it will have to be dealt with as soon as possible. Graham Walker hasn't personally discussed details of it with me yet, but it was by him that Laura was alerted, and she, in turn, brought the matter to my attention. Evidently, she has mentioned it to Jillian because the two of them might become involved in it. I will keep you immediately informed as things progress, Kephart. After all, you are my number one assistant.

"And you must prepare *yourself* by giving some thought to another possible situation—one in which two concurrent cases may require that I delegate leadership regarding one of them to you. In such a circumstance you would interact directly with Graham Walker and be conversant with Jillian or Laura as events unfold. Of course, you would find me available to advise you in a pinch."

"I find the prospects of such a situation to be both scary and exciting! But I was never one who could live with boredom, as you have come to learn. So it appears that I have found my place in this life . . . thanks to you again."

"Kephart, there is another subject that I had planned to discuss with you at this time and that is my present life mission. I know Laura told you some things about my motives and personal goals during the preparation meeting she held with you. You had no way of knowing it at the time, but Laura was recording nearly all that you discussed together."

"Well, that explains why she deliberately fiddled with her ring during our conversations, or why she occasionally pressed her right hand close to her head. There were times when she would look away and slowly shake her head. I supposed then that she was troubled by some distractive personal thoughts. I guess I wasn't very far off."

"I'm sure you can now see explanations for many things that may have puzzled you, Kephart. I'm referring particularly now to human pursuits and behaviors. As you must have given thought to it, you can see that realities are of our own making. Every earthly human being lives in his or her own private world. No two minds perceive or experience exactly alike. That is one reason true understandings are difficult to achieve.

"However, as I've stated before, there is but one *true* reality, and that is God's reality, which is placed in the sphere of *all* truth. The more truths we embrace, the freer we become. No man or woman can be forced to see things in a different light. We can only be led. As you know, our Savior never forced his principles or doctrine. He only held out his hand, spiritually speaking, and invited man to follow. In part, he died that we might be empowered to choose for ourselves.

"Perhaps you can better understand how I'm to accomplish my mission when you give some thought to what I've just said. All meaningful or permanent change must come from within. So you can see that it is impossible for me to redirect motives or minds by compulsion. I can only lead people into situations or experiences that influence changes from within.

"Now that is where you come in, Kephart. I cannot achieve my mission without your vital contributions. Only *you* can act inconspicuously in such ways as to bring about changes—changes in situations that will hopefully lead misguided individuals to brighter futures. No one else can provide me with on-the-scene first-hand reports that will enable me to plan strategies or engage others' involvements. You must act as an interpreter of what your physical senses present to you. My paranormal gifts have limitations.

"In the past I have been instrumental in locating missing or threatened persons by relying solely on my clairvoyant powers. But that is because I have not had to deal with the more complex issues I am now confronted with. Detective Walker has been expanding his sources of information. His involvements have thrust more upon me. You are a true gift to me, Kephart. I feel certain this will prove to be so with your Jillian."

"Thanks for sharing all you have with me," I said. "I do feel apprehensive about failing to perform as I'd hope to. I don't want to disappoint you."

"Don't give it a thought, Kephart. Please. Knowing you as I do, you will never disappoint me. That's because I'm placing a great responsibility on you—one that can't be taken on by anyone else now. There is purpose and direction in what has already transpired. Let's take the happy prospects to heart and keep them uppermost in our minds. I am confident that we will be proving ourselves to be successful. Our position is certainly unique. I'm certain we will be much sought after."

Shackleton smiled his confidence and determination. I sensed that my "ship of life" was already sailing on newly charted waters.

Bogart's eyes expressed confidence in us as they glanced back and forth between us. Then his eyes went to the service tray as Shackleton and I both reached at once for a maple bar. My hand changed course to satisfy Bogart's taste for meat and cheese.

While walking in the shadow of shackleton gray,

I was led to the light of truth.

ABOUT THE AUTHOR

W. Paul Dunn was born and raised in the Rocky Mountains. His higher education was at the University of Idaho and University of Washington. He taught public schools for twenty-three years, and served four years of wartime service in the United States Air Force.

He has published a children's book and holds an international award for poetry. The father of nine children, he and his wife call the Pacific Northwest their home. "In the Shadow of Shackleton Gray" is his first novel.